THE DRY WELL

A NOVEL

By
Quelia Quaresma-McHugh

ISBN 978-1-63784-245-4 (paperback)
ISBN 978-1-63784-246-1 (digital)

Hawes & Jenkins Publishing
16427 N Scottsdale Road Suite 410
Scottsdale, AZ 85254
www.hawesjenkins.com

Printed in the United States of America

‘Come! And let him who thirsts come.
Whoever desires, let him take the water of life freely.”
(Revelation 22:17)

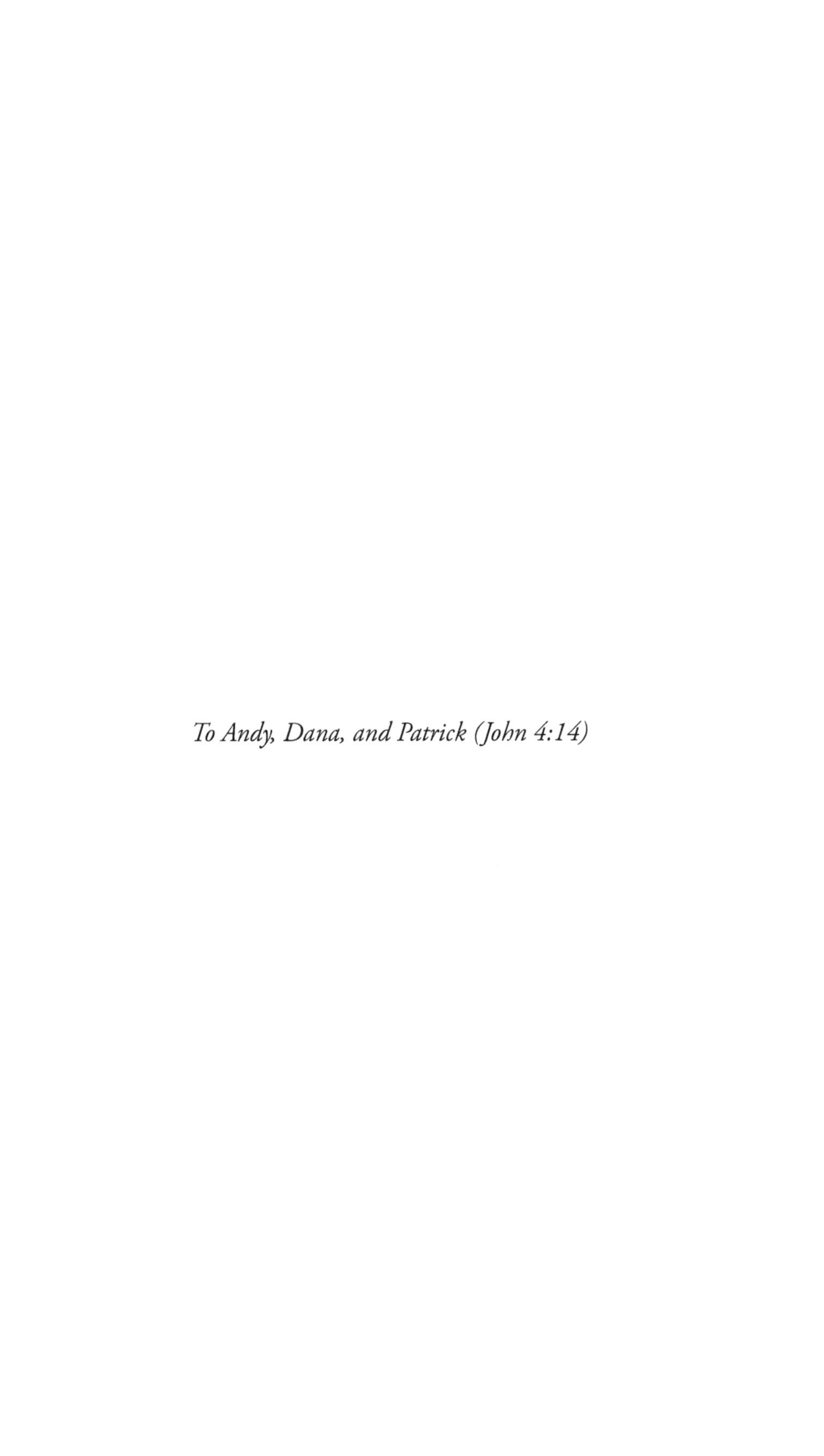

To Andy, Dana, and Patrick (John 4:14)

CONTENTS

PART I

THE BOY PROPHET

"If you came this way,
Taking the route you would be likely to take
From the place you would be likely to come from,
If you came this way in May time, you would find the hedges
White again, in May, with voluptuary sweetness.
It would be the same at the end of the journey,
If you came at night like a broken king,
If you came by day not knowing what you came for,
It would be the same, when you leave ***the rough road****"*

(T.S.Eliot, *Little Gidding, I)*

ONE

Under the late morning sun at a time when the sky hung cloudless and bluest a frail boy walked alone. The path he walked was uneven and brittle, embedded in millennial layers of beaten dust. On his naked shoulders two full pails of murky water lined straight across a wood pole. It was evident that the weight of the cargo made it difficult for young Daniel to walk upright. If looking from a distance one might mistake him for the cross-bound Christ fulfilling the fateful prophecy of Calvary.

To those living here, however, in the drought-stricken corner of Northeastern Brazil the skinny boy was just an ordinary fixture. One of many, hauling home the daily load of untreated water. The heavy pails arched Daniel's body slightly forward as he paced steadily onwards ever so careful not to spill the precious content. His was a strenuous balancing act—navigating the burning ground barefooted yet determined to win another round against the drought.

In the backlands of Brazil—a forsaken barren stretch of land away from the country's northeastern coast—rainfall consisted of unpredictable cycles. The 'big desert' or *sertão,* as the locals called it, was the cradle of droughts—*secas*—so relentless and stubborn that they ripped any sign of bounty from the ground even before it stood a chance to sprout. Immune to any type of prayer, hushed or clamorous, droughts answered to the call of misery only, and at Daniel's small town of Lajedo fresh water had been evaporating and pushing many dwellers out.

This year's *seca* spared no creeks, ponds, or streams but most alarmingly it sucked dry all of Lajedo's wells. Thankfully there was one reliable source not yet fully claimed and it was there where Daniel filled up his tin buckets of what was left. The loads consisted of a mix of muck and rainwater Lajedo residents had judiciously trapped during the wet season in anticipation of the next dry spell. The reservoir known as the *barreiro* harbored the villagers' hope, and for Daniel, fetching *barreiro* water everyday was a paramount duty. Despite the boy's tender age of eleven he understood the vital role he played in his family's survival. Without those painstaking trips thirst and despair might convince them all to give up and uproot as others had already done.

For months the sun's caustic heat had roughened the ground Daniel walked on. To dodge the scattered debris he had no choice but to tiptoe along the rocky surface, each step a calculated move. With great care Daniel trudged to prevent his feet from turning into one useless blister. Luckily, his cunning chestnut eyes and stable footing kept the two buckets impassively composed. Daniel was proud of his spill-free record so far. No stumbles to speak of, from the instant he left the embankment until the final stop at home, the daily execution was carried out flawlessly. As soon as the rod mounted across his bare shoulders Daniel's slim neck cocked slightly sideways and yielded a narrow dent to anchor the valuable burden.

Especially at midday when the buckets seemed even fuller under the burning sun Daniel prudently regulated his breathing and did his best to ignore the piercing pebbles around his wet toes. Every now and then, however, when Daniel's lean muscles inevitably cramped and his limbs stiffened he had to halt and adjust the weight with a gentle shrug. Sometimes he had to gingerly dismount the buckets to flex both arms before they went numb but not even then, Daniel was proud to admit, had a drop ever leaked out.

When Daniel paused and lifted his alert brown eyes at the surrounding landscape no details escaped him. Not too long ago on this exact spot, green leaves and plump stalks had blocked the view between the *barreiro* shore and Lajedo's outskirts. Today the withering branches pointed at distant barren groves instead. His favorite *Juazeiro* trees and their bright red flowers no longer bloomed. Branches that once stretched out robust in a chivalrous salute to the sky had turned into chalky skeletons someone neglected to bury. Nearly all the shrubs flanking the path followed the same fate and dwindled under the consuming heat. Worst yet was the dense silence filling the air. Lajedo's birds had fled in search of the elusive morning dew. They were the lucky ones—the ones who could escape whereas Daniel had to stay and watch the tragedy unfold.

Back on the path Daniel crept on while the sun stalled overhead. At this time of day his mouth felt as dry as cotton and that was when Daniel second-guessed his resilience. Would he ever make through another yard? He slowed down again to lick his chapped lips where specks of dust had landed. The temptation to splash water on his face mounted but Daniel bravely resisted. Out of despair he glanced at the opaque liquid floating inside the buckets. This batch of water had not been boiled and must not be touched as his mother had frequently admonished. A drop of it and his insides would turn out like the brush around him: wrenched and flushed. What he really longed for was a drink of cool, crispy water from the clay jug, not this nasty gunk.

"Keep moving" Daniel urged his sore feet and pressed the wood pole down the small of his neck. He was making good progress and to yank his mind away from the nagging thirst Daniel let his thoughts trail loose to more pleasant images of Lajedo. Not long ago, on March 19th the town had rallied in concert to honor its patron, Saint Joseph. As Daniel pressed forward exhilarating snippets from that day returned.

Many had woken up expectantly earlier that morning to greet the upcoming winter or the rainy season. The mild air stirred the top of the guava trees and inspired the *Asa Brancas* to a collective shrill. The traditional Catholic holiday marked the official beginning of the planting season all over the *sertão* and for the people of Lajedo it was a perfect excuse to put off work and party. Lajedo's plaza, where Saint Joseph church stood decked up with colorful flowers, paper flags, and food stalls was the envy of all neighboring towns.

On his way to Ms. Cabral's schoolhouse that morning Daniel had glimpsed at a group of women fussing over freshly cut stalks and bushels of yellow *azedinhas*, pink *cebolas-bravas,* and white *malvas* soon to be clipped and arranged into a fragrant arc around the church front door. Scores of men were already sawing and nailing planks of plywood together making them into vending booths for the evening fair. Hundreds of hungry guests were expected to attend the special Mass in honor of Saint Joseph right before sunset. They would pack the lit up church and bow before the large statue propped in front of the altar and eventually follow the priest and local dignitaries as the annual procession began. Every year the mayor, the sheriff, and many Lajedo landowners saved the special date to dispense handshakes and old promises while the parade skirted the plaza.

As usual, Daniel had watched the unfolding scene from a distance because his family belonged to the minority sect of Evangelical Protestants who condemned such idolatrous practices. *Seu* Benedito and *Dona* Dulce had strictly prohibited their children from even looking at the wooded sculpture of Saint Joseph let alone join the pagan procession. But while the Catholics queued behind the wreathed stretcher where Saint Joseph stood remarkably still, Daniel and his younger sisters, Dalva and Delfina could not help to steal quick looks at the splendid carving of the angelic man until it returned to its prominent spot on the altar.

Only then did Daniel's parents approach the decorated vending booths from where sparkling torches wavered. What Daniel remembered best about that evening was the profusion of lights, smells, and bustling clatter. When his parents paused before a tray of sweet *pamonhas* he and his sisters ran inside the church to peep at the garlands and burning candles cordoning the altar. Below Saint Joseph's pedestal a heap of wax body parts gathered. Hands, feet and heads of many sizes laid solemnly by his sandals, though strangely enough, beautiful blond and blue-eyed Saint Joseph did not seem as spooked as Daniel by the bizarre display. His gentle and noble countenance remained unchanged the whole time Daniel studied him.

When their eyes finally met, Daniel felt guilty and yelled at his sisters to stay away from the altar. Out at the plaza Daniel paid closer attention to his surroundings. All vending booths had been laced with paper flags in addition to the burning torches. Fused smells of confections, ripe fruits, and grilled meats made Daniel drowsy with hunger all over again. His tongue could now taste the sweetness of the pineapples and the irresistible chewiness of the coconut bars—*cocadas*. Out of the charcoal flames the scent of dry beef and grilled corn advanced towards him. For a merciful second he forgot the growling inside his stomach, closed his eyes and pretended to bite a mouthful off the cob.

Almost as delightful as the food was the music playing during the party. Musicians from a folk—*sertanejo*—band had climbed the church front steps and cranked up accordions and drums urging everyone to the middle of the square. Responding to the vibrant tunes the dancers began whipping the dirt off the ground like goats charging up a hill. Forwards and backwards the couples spun with such energy that for a moment Daniel thought that one person moved with four feet instead of two. The plaza quaked under the crowd's stomps and had it not been for the strict Protestant rules against dancing, Daniel would have joined the frenzy. "What must feel like to move for joy rather than toil?" he replayed the feast's grand finale. When the music stopped colorful paper lanterns were released up the sky. One after another they soared midair only to burst into bright sparkles of glitter that showered down on the cheering spectators.

The happy night of March 19th seemed so far behind. Back then the people of Lajedo still believed rain was coming. Daniel stopped again and glanced overhead at the bright blue dome. Months had already passed and the drought had already settled in. All his hope was now dissolved just like the burned paper lanterns.

"*Ai*", Daniel shrugged. The spot he loathed the most loomed closer. With the corner of his eyes he glanced at the dark dots gliding in circles knowing very well what they meant. Vultures were the only birds still flying around Lajedo, surviving at the expense of the dead.

Daniel knew they were after the rotted carcasses tainting the air with that overbearing, putrid stench. For as long as he could, he held his breath and mustering all the strength inside his tired body, he pushed on.

Past the church graveyard he finally exhaled, relieved that the worst part of his day was over. The same could not be said for the actual *seca*. Everywhere Daniel looked, signs of doom abounded. People no longer smiled and when they talked horrifying accounts of past droughts gushed out. Lajedo would soon turn into a ghost town. The insatiable thirst would drive people mad and the dirty water would make everyone sick. Those who boarded the *pau-de-arara* for the coast would never return.

Daniel had probed his father about the possibility of hopping on a *pau-de-arara* too. "Never" *Seu* Benedito grunted. No one in his family had ever deserted Lajedo. They had been predestined to survive the drought. "A real *sertão* dweller—a *sertanejo*—is above all strong, Daniel" he had grumbled. "Running away is defiance against God's will. Blasphemy!" Daniel could still hear the irascible tone. He wished to believe that too but was not convinced God willed this much misery. Was his father strong or just a fool?

"Faith in God?" Daniel mumbled defiantly with his back at Saint Joseph's church. The only faith he now had was in the *seca*. You could count on it coming in like an uninvited guest who left only after taking his fill.

"Bang!" the church bell threw Daniel's thoughts off track. The first of twelve deafening gongs reminded Daniel how much he hated this time of day. Right before lunch the buckets weighted over a ton. "*Meio-dia*" he swallowed the dry air. "Com' on" he murmured. "Never mind the blisters. Walk. Slow. No spills, *cabra*" *Dona* Dulce's husky nag echoed from afar. "One spilled drop is luxury we can't afford." Daniel's lips twitched. "Stay the course, *cabra,*" he whispered. "Straight. Don't you dare totter now. See the crooked gate, guarding nothing? There."

Relieved, Daniel kicked the gate aside and crossed into the deserted yard. Taking a deep breath he gently slipped the pole off his shoulders and placed the full pails on the ground. Feeling free again he let his arms drop and began rotating his shoulders until they loosened up. Next, he would bring the buckets to the cistern and then, yes, grab some fresh water from the clay jug.

As Daniel bent over however, a strong jolt bolted his skinny body upward again. It all happened so fast, as if it were a dream... Daniel's charred arms began to shake and break up in spiky goose bumps. Wide-eyed he watched his skin disappear under layers of glossy feathers that spread sideways into a pair of black wings that looked exactly like those of the vultures hovering the *barreiro* path. Slick and thick the feathers pressed against his collarbone and began to flap on their own. Surrendering to their forceful drive Daniel's feet left the ground and propelled into the Lajedo's suffocating air. His neck responded to the gush and craned upwards at the implacable noon sun. Legs split apart Daniel's toes hustled impulsively. He wanted to scream but his lips remained sealed.

"Am I flying?" he looked down at his pails and rod resting on the ground. "Am I leaving just like the birds did?" Daniel watched his belongings turn smaller by the second. Lajedo began to shrink in size with each of his wings thrust. The air grew cooler and shuffled Daniel's matted hair out of place while the entire *sertão* eventually vanished from view. Eyes shut Daniel surrendered and soared towards the sky wondering whether the drought was sucking up his mind. "Am I also turning into a dry well?"

TWO

"*DANIEL: CARA DE PAPEL*" the shrewd shout resounded from behind the cob wall.

"DANIEL: PAPER FACE" Daniel heard it again loud and clear identifying the instigators. He took a deep breath and stretched his neck blinking furiously at the spot. "Stupid girls" he wanted to retort but a strong scent of sautéed garlic, onions, and bay leaves stalled him. The soulful smell prompted his feet to clutch the ground and his body immediately realigned. Feeling his bare soles finally in place Daniel rubbed the ground for confirmation he was no longer airborne. A peek at the tilted gate was enough to assure of where he stood.

As swiftly and as mysteriously as it had come the frightening delusion vanished and Daniel sneaked to the corner where Dalva and Delfina were supposedly hiding. He moved quietly against the shaggy surface planning an ambush against the mischievous pair but when he peered over they had already darted out of sight. Only the cement cistern waited for him. It had to be refilled right away, so Daniel went back for the buckets.

For the next few minutes he forgot all about the numbing thirst and visceral hunger on which he blamed the surreal flight. After pouring the water into the cistern Daniel took a moment to wipe his forehead and breathe his mother's seasoning. All the familiar landmarks stood before him—the dry well in the middle of the yard with its round lid neatly settled over the rim looked so desolate. A short distance behind it, the outhouse door was pressed shut to block the rancid odor from reaching the kitchen where the black beans and white rice smelled mercifully ready. For now his morning ordeal approached its end and assuming the stance of a marathon runner about to cross the finish line, Daniel bent his head and charged inside the kitchen ready to collect lunch as if it were a much deserved gold medal.

Before the smoky stove he saw *Dona* Dulce watching the fire. She did no mind his arrival and continued to stirr the boiling pots in silence. Daniel shrugged at the expected indifference and headed to the table. For now the pleasant mist and a drink of fresh water would do as substitutes for maternal affection. Quickly reaching for the clay jug Daniel poured a good amount into a tin cup and repeated the motion a few times until his tongue resuscitated. From above the cup rim he continued to stare at the choreographed moves his mother executed in front of the fire. Her bony arms spun like batons in the hands of a virtuoso maestro. Without missing a beat she transformed a bowlful of boiled beans and rice into a feast.

Daniel always marveled at the strength concealed under *Dona* Dulce's frailty. Whenever she ferried the heavy ironware to the table using only a thin rag for protection against the scalding heat he felt like clapping though he knew that even if he did *Dona* Dulce would not take a bow or even lift her head from the plates, spoons, and cups she placed around the table.

By now everything looked ready for the main meal of the day and Daniel grew even more impatient when *Dona* Dulce temptingly removed the pot lids. His eyes swerved eagerly from the curling fumes to the front parlor from where in a moment's notice, his father would enter. No one was allowed to sit down before *Seu* Benedito did. If Daniel dared to object on the grounds of a growling stomach there would be serious consequences. Respectable Christian families in this vast land of Brazil had always exalted their male elders, no exceptions granted, not even when someone might have just returned from the heroic water-fetching chore, thank you very much.

The unfairness of the rule was obvious but Daniel still did not sit down without his father's consent. By now he knew too well his head would ultimately split in half under one of *Dona* Dulce's virtuoso whacks. One day though, Daniel would inherit the same respectable privilege and an insidious revenge plot against Dalva and Delfina began to brew in his mind. They were going to pay dearly for the dumb tease of minutes ago. Wait for the next hide-and-seek game, you two. As older brother he was going to declare victory even if he were the last one found. Who is paper face now, huh?

Seu Benedito's arrival should happen in a wink and with that in mind Daniel leaned against the doorway separating the kitchen from the scanty parlor in hopes to be the first one to capture the event. The mid-day sun gushed in revealing the long fissures on the decaying plaster and right on time when a bright gleam hit the doorway, *Seu* Benedito's straw hat appeared. His bronze, crinkled face was more sullen than earlier this morning. The drought was taking a toll on *Seu* Benedito too, forcing him to leave the house at dawn and ride the donkey miles away in search of ripe pineapples, guavas and *cajús* to sell at the market.

There he stayed until dusk breaking only for lunch and the mid-day *sesta,* leaving Daniel in charge as "man of the house" in the meantime urging him to take pride in the supposedly regal title. Before long, Daniel figured out the actual significance behind the promotion. Every time his father left and his mother yelled for him 'it's time!' he had to drop everything and rush to the *barreiro.*

"Man of the house means more work and less play" Daniel's stomach churned out loud. What *else* might he be expected to do as man of the house if the drought never ended? The supposition alone aggravated Daniel's grudge against *Seu* Benedito, *Dona* Dulce and this man of the house nonsense. He silently resumed the pacing around the table.

Daniel licked his lips in anticipation. "When can I eat?" he beckoned at the stool. "Well, not quite yet. The other rule, *ai...*" he moaned quietly. This other rule he disliked even more although his parents had proclaimed its importance over and over again. Daniel's family belonged to a small sect of Evangelical Protestants who, despite been seen as freaks by Lajedo's Roman Catholics, were the true Christians. Daniel had also been told that witnessing in front of non-believers was the most effective way to convert them all to the true faith. For that and many other reasons, which honestly Daniel could not keep up with, each Evangelical household in the village must deliver the message of salvation at all times.

Husbands, pastors of their homes, were therefore in charge of enforcing all evangelical rules including blessing of meals so the children would learn to be grateful and obedient. They also led devotionals, scripture reading and praise sessions on a daily basis, which

Benedito argued as collateral advantage of the man of the house rule. Daniel on the other hand abhorred each one of the rules and so far had managed to disguise his indignation with nods and smirks. Until he schemed a way out of Lajedo he had to put up with the embarrassment of witnessing in front of the many nosy neighbors in the alley.

The children somehow knew exactly when the Benedito comedy show started. At eight on the dot all the kids loitered by their front door for a fair share of hilarity. Everyone burst out in laughter at the off-key singing and absurdly encripted Scripture readings. So humiliating the affair was that Daniel often sat with his back to the door, downcast and blushed until it was all over. For the life of him he could not understand why his parents volunteered for such spectacle when the line up of nauseating, blood-shedding, flame-burning hymns usually enticed the audience's rude disapproval.

"There he is" Daniel captured *Seu* Benedito's solemn crouching under the doorway. Without sparing a glance around he advanced to the kitchen, pulled out the stool from under the table and sat down. Clasping his rough hands under his chin he waited for the rest of the family to follow suit. Daniel knew by heart what the rule of invocation meant: a short and desperate petition against deprivation. "Lord, bless this food you gave us to eat, bless our bodies in need of nourishment, bless the hands that prepared it, in the name of our savior Jesus Christ. Amen."

Immediately after, even before everyone's hands had seized a spoon *Dona* Dulce reached for *Seu* Benedito's plate first and began scooping the pots. Daniel was second in line according to the man of the house rule whereas *Dona* Dulce herself was the last to scrape the bottoms.

Under a veil of detached silence the family filled their mouths with black beans, rice, and resignation. Daniel listened to the cacophony of cheap utensils and rotten teeth colliding as the plates emptied. Every day they mushed on the same measured portion of destitution, apparently unaware this could be their last meal. Staring at his plate Daniel considered whether one day he would really fly away from there.

A deadly drought prowled at their doorstep but no one seemed to bother. Did they realize *he* was the one bringing in the water so *they* could eat? Without *his* full buckets *Dona* Dulce couldn't cook. Not even if *Seu* Benedito sold all the pineapples he fetched and with his money bought sacs of beans, rice, and flour, could *Dona* Dulce cook without the water *he* carried? Evidently not! They were all so mistaken. Jesus Christ was not their savior. What was the use of praying to *Him*?"

Eyes fixed on his muddy toenails Daniel let the sudden billow of narcissism crest. The drought might be draining his tolerance for conformity but dregs of pride were building up. The oppressive mid-day sun had added extra fuel to his craving for praise and flatter, something his parents had a very short supply of. At the end of each day of hard work Daniel returned home more defiant, more aware of his budding machismo. Had his father sensed the insolence in his stare? If not, why had he then abruptly interrupted his noisy grinding?

"Dulce, is the boy's birthday on the 16th or 17th this month?" *Seu* Benedito interrupted the tense silence.

"Not sure, Dito" Dulce replied still trying to swallow a spoonful of mush. "The paper is in there" she pointed her chin at the front parlor where the old bureau stood. "All I know he's gonna be twelve this year."

"1939!" *Seu* Benedito grunted keeping his spoon suspended in mid-air. "Sure remember" a spit of mush flew out of his mouth. "When Lajedo's first notary office opened" his eyes narrowed. "Bless President Vargas; that document got stamped without me having to chart a horse to Esperança" he swallowed the clump.

Seu Benedito's lips moved fast and the words had snapped in an incoherent jumble. Those were fragments of information Daniel had yearned to learn but had so far been denied. The revelation further aroused his appetite for self-awareness. A sense of urgency seized him as he pondered about aging. "Twelve?" Daniel looked down at his hands "how many years 'til I defeat the drought?" he surveyed the fingers in both hands. This must be his last year of helplessness. "Does it matter the day?" Daniel squeezed the spoon. "I'm becoming a man. Not just of the house but of my own. Must fight the drought" he chewed heartily.

He looked away from his plate and examined the walls in the parlor behind *Seu* Benedito. It was the first time he had paid close attention to how much plaster had crumbled off the walls. He sized them up barely rising halfway towards the cracked roof tiles. Down on the cement floor he followed the long crease linking the front door to the kitchen where it stopped to give room to the beaten dirt. From his stool Daniel could not see much more but he was quite sure the old bureau, the only piece of furniture in the front room, leaned directly across. It was there where his mother cluttered the family's meager possessions. "My stamped paper is in there" Daniel concluded.

"Beyond that door, a whole world" he now wobbled on the unsteady tripod considering whether to ask for another serving of beans and rice. Staying in the kitchen loathed him and after a moment of hesitation his voice broke through the renewed stillness.

"May I be excused, father?" Daniel's boldness surprised everyone. There he was breaking one of the rules, speaking out of turn without *Seu* Benedito's permission. For a split second no one breathed. All eyes turned to *Seu* Benedito as he weighed Daniel's insolence. "Was the boy really asking to leave the table before him?" *Seu* Bendito pondered while Daniel stood up.

Bracing for the inevitable he stepped aside but did not go too far. *Seu* Benedito's hands clenched and rose above the table. Eventually his fingers stretched and laced Daniel's skinny wrist. A burning squeeze followed. The quietness grew suspenseful and Daniel's knees buckled to endure the pressure. *Seu* Benedito looked straight at him and grunted: '*sim.*'

Had Daniel heard it right? In total confusion he dared not move. If so, he was to walk out the kitchen first. Proud of his first manly achievement Daniel held his head up high. He had earned a medal after all. The thick golden disc sparkled down his bony chest though no one else saw it.

THREE

Out of sight, at the front parlor, Daniel rubbed his arm. "At least it was not the ferule—*palmatória*" he inspected the red pinch. "It's nothing" he could still see Benedito's fingerprints branded on his skin. It would shortly disappear as the other bruises had and brushing the incident aside Daniel redirected full attention to the pair of rusty hooks hanging above the lone window in the front room. The low-cut sill offered a privileged spot for his hammock as it opened directly over the alley. Though the chance of catching a breeze was dismal this time of the day he decided it was worth a try. In any event, he must act quickly, before Dalva or Delfina started arguing over it.

While unfolding the spent bundle of cotton he used as a bed Daniel balanced on his toes to hurl the thick ropes around the hooks. The mismatched cuts of fabric of his hammock had presumably been stitched together by some weaver who before discarding them as trash agreed to barter it for a basket of Benedito's pineapples. The final product was an eyesore combination of forest-green stripes and screaming-orange plaids that inevitably drove Daniel's eyes to a twitch every time he held it against the sunlight. As he prepared to plop inside he felt lightheaded again and grabbed on to the tassels just in case another flying spell came on. With one certain jump he plunged in and disappeared at the bottom.

Struggling to find a comfortable position Daniel fluttered a bit before settling for his left shoulder facing the window. After pulling the hammock's border overhead he bent his knees against his chest, tucked both hands under his cheek and remained snug as a pupa. Through a tiny hole in the frayed fabric he blinked indolently at the deserted alley mapping its winding trajectory to the plaza. The morning dust had finally settled ushering another lazy Lajedo afternoon. By now the villagers had either retreated indoors or under a shade to take the mid-day rest—*sesta*. Like Daniel they all sought temporary deliverance from the sun's worst offensive of the day.

Except for the black mutt coiled against the neighbor's front steps there was no other living creature nearby. The rip on the fabric fit Daniel's half-shut eyes perfectly as he observed the wretched animal compulsive licking. The repetitive motion was hypnotic and Daniel's eyes quicly collapsed. His lips followed suit and his frail limbs sagged like a heavy lump. Not a speck of him could be seen from the outside of the wrap. Its rhythmic cadence ushered a delicious doze. From a distance the kitchen clatter finally vanished and Daniel's arm no longer ached.

Slowly the hammock waltzed him into the kind of stupor only infants at the end of a long suckle know. Out of his parted mouth a sluggish drool leaked imperceptibly and Daniel's breathing grew increasingly deep and loud. Meanwhile a timid breeze crawled in and delicately shivered the stagnant air in the parlor into motion. The hammock became an impenetrable cocoon of comfort.

Regular notions of time and space no longer applied as Daniel slowly disconnected from his earthly surroundings. Beyond a thin veil of light he slipped into oblivion. A dancing shaft moved in and out of focus before his shut eyes until the only trace left was a stream of luminous particles that soon expanded into a long thin arrow before the open window. Daniel then bolted out of the hammock, and leaped over the parapet.

He followed the demanding beam closely and advanced through the alley. No one saw him leave or tried to halt him. It appeared that his family, neighbors and the entire town for that matter had suddenly disappeared. Except for him and the floating beam not a living creature, not even the ugly stray dog from across the street, lurked through the ghostly streets. At the main plaza all vending stalls remained closed and vacant. Neither the wide doors at Saint Joseph's nor Ms. Cabral's schoolhouse windows opened. Breaking through the dimness the beam pointed to the edge of the square bending slightly left, past the church graveyard. Other town landmarks could not be quite distinguished from this shady angle but Daniel realized he was leaving the square.

Straight on he veered towards the beaten *barreiro* path and as promptly as it was mysterious Daniel's wood rod and tin buckets mounted straight over his bare shoulders. As if a natural extension of his body they cued Daniel to enact the daily routine.

Out of habit he carefully measured each step to avoid tripping over the gravel but within a few yards the turf underneath felt pleasantly different. Its expected parched and prickly texture had been inexplicably turned smooth and soft. Daniel could not put words together to explain where he might be walking but it somehow resembled a trek of sturdy polished wood. The surprise compelled him to stride confidently forward and forget about pebbles and thorns. Admitly, this new road worked much to his advantage. Instead of limping downcast as he normally would Daniel was now free to scan his surroundings without having to stop.

Morning now broke through Lajedo and outshone Daniel's floating guide. Its density was no match for the mighty Brazilian sun tearing across the backlands. The rising brilliance carried Daniel onward although here and there he lagged a little out of sheer curiosity. A peculiar scenery, something so foreign and unexpected emerged from the dusk. When Daniel looked again, intermittent clusters of lush gradually replaced the dreadful wasteland. Any time his head turned rows of ferns, bushes, and trees sprung straight up from the moist ground. Recent traces of the drought could not be found anywhere on the path's grassy hedges. Instead, a velvety carpet of green sprawled endlessly on either side providing a rich foundation for the rising roots, trunks, and branches that now blocked the distant fields from view. Daniel's nostrils widened eagerly to capture the sweet fragrance of what seemed to be ripe *umbuzeiros* and *juazeiros.* When he chinned up, a dome of leafy boughs swelled so high that for a moment it shielded the sun's regal rise.

Halfway through the wondrous road another pleasant surprise greeted Daniel. Cool air met him head on. A refreshing, soothing touch rattled his lungs out of apathy and he inhaled the energizing fuel wholeheartedly picking up a little more speed along the way. Tiny dots descended on his brazen skin and drizzled his cheeks like a refreshing ointment. Charged with unprecedented energy Daniel advanced expectantly towards the climbing sun at the end of the path.

The majestic orange disk delivered a breathtaking rendition of another daybreak in the *sertão.* Awestruck Daniel slowed down and briefly considered singing in honor of such beauty. The problem was all hymns he had memorized fell short of depicting such radiance. Unless he could make up his own lyrics Daniel was better off resorting to silence. How could this trip be turning out so pleasant? When was the last time lush and abundance gathered in one single spot? Even before the drought none of Lajedo's fields had yielded this much abundance. Was this for real or a figment of his imagination? The sweet fragrances, the loud chirps and the overall sense of plenty inspired him to the rush forward.

Indeed, Lajedo's wilderness had turned into a teeming forest. By the minute all signs of devastation disappeared as if a deluge had fallen after the feast of Saint Joseph. What could be awaiting Daniel at the end of the path? Could the *barreiro* have turned into a marsh, a pond or, who knows, a lake? Judging by what lay nearby anything was possible. Anything including the sudden switch in the air. Strong blows now whizzed by, looping the buckets out of place. No doubt the ground vibrated like a drum and although Daniel regretted having to put a larger distance between him and the speck of light ahead he had to make sure the surface remained steady.

On one foot he hopped then on the other, searching for potential cracks. After a few thumps a powerful gust hit him. It had stormed out of the forest and swept Daniel off his feet. The wind sent him paddling midair and engulfed the whole path in a wet porous cloud. As the blowing mass thickened it blew the faint beam out of course and rolled Daniel over like a tumbleweed. At the end of a few painful bounces he braced for a hard landing far into the woods. Fortunately, Daniel's belongings had followed him safely down and appeared to be in fair condition. To be sure he drew the buckets a little closer for confirmation.

Something had gone horribly wrong and Daniel could not believe his eyes. He had to wait a moment to process the situation for it looked like the wind had blown all the rust and dents off the tin and reshaped the pails into a pair of wood chests. Daniel blinked in disbelief when he recognized them as exact duplicates of the bureau in the front room of his home. Was the bright sun playing tricks on him? Why would he be hauling furniture to the *barreiro*?

Often *Seu* Benedito had admonished Daniel against magical tricks. Those were clearly evil and contrary to Biblical teachings but how else could he explain the occurrence? He patted the pails and there was no denying: they both had turned into wooded chests. Not only were they new and varnished but also stacked up with narrow drawers just begging to be opened. One sneaky tug at the shiny brass handles would surely reveal the contents inside, and Daniel could not resist the temptation to peep in even if there was a chance of being caught. Assuming he was still alone on the road he plucked the drawers open.

Scores of miniature toys moved cheerfully inside. In elliptical evolutions tiny train sets snaked on wood tracks whereas minute bears, lions, and elephants pirouetted alongside metal tops. Glossy marbles bumped against one another out of the way of chromed bicycles and fluttering kites enacting a fantastic choreography of grace and color.

Nearly breathless, Daniel quietly watched the festive display until he impulsively reached in to grab as many of the toys he could without realizing that with the slightest touch they treaded away. After repeated attempts to trap them Daniel resorted to a different strategy. He carefully cornered a few and clasped them inside his bony hands. Unfortunately, that only made matters worse because the toys startled and slipped off like running water.

Growing frustrated Daniel knelt down and threw both arms inside like an improvised fishing net. Still, the toys dodged out. In perfect formation the miniatures soared towards the bright sky. Afraid the chests would follow next Daniel threw his arms around them and pinned them down. In a fit of rage he hit and kicked them hard. He should have kept those drawers shut. "Now all the toys are gone" he whined.

A few steps ahead a sliver of the *barreiro* cove came into view. Behind it, leafy guava trees surrounded the still, shining water. Quickly, Daniel collected the chests and the pole, and rushed over. At the shore he dipped his toes in the lukewarm water and studied the effect of the sunrays pounding on the surface. The *barreiro* resembled the flat surface of a mirror and as Daniel stood at the edge clarity began to set in. "How am I supposed to carry water back home now?" The wood chests were absolutely useless and he would be in serious trouble showing up at home empty-handed.

Daniel needed his buckets back right away. He reached out for his rod and pointed at the chests. Eyes closed he circled the rod in the air pretending it to be a wand in clear defiance against another of *Seu* Benedito's rules. "Please, please, please" he begged the buckets to reappear "on the count of one, two, and…three" he shouted.

When Daniel opened his eyes a loud bang followed. It was then that a glare flashed and made him squint incredulously at the glassy water. Random pieces of tin clashed against one another making a loud dull noise and when Daniel waded closer hoping to retrieve the pails they both stacked up on top of each other. Up and away they rose into a colossal structure with four limbs cropping out, two on top and two at the bottom. For a head the scary creature carried a straw hat so large that it cast a wide shade across the cove. Daniel shrunk with fear because the tin giant looked very angry and mean. Out of its straw hat a thunderous menacing growl rippled: 'SIM, SIM!'

Dwarfed at its feet Daniel was easy prey for the monster and as he remained glued to the sinking sand unable to move he ended up frosted with mud from head to toe. Meanwhile the creature splashed *barreiro* water in all directions still grunting "SIM, SIM!"

Daniel decided he had to stop the monster even it was the last thing he did. Getting over the initial shock he courageously lifted up his rod and brandished it. "I'M GONNA KILL YOU", he tried to outshout his enemy but the ugly beast growled louder at the impertinence. Ready to strike, the monster bent over and stretched its metal arms in Daniel's direction. Its angry foaming and sloshing made it difficult for Daniel to aim so he resorted to more shouting as a distracting maneuver while waiting for the best moment to strike.

The tin giant did not like being yelled at and every time Daniel threatened 'I'M GONNA KILL YOU' its long arms thrashed wildly over the water and its long legs hurled like snapping whips. In between feisty sidesteps and sharp pinches Daniel drove the giant to the brink of madness, which was exactly his plan. Sooner or later the monster would stumble, and when that happened Daniel would sweep the rod in between its legs. At the right moment, he would strike the monster's ankles and watch its cumbersome frame waver. When it finally twisted and turned, Daniel did not hesitate and swept the rod under the monster's legs.

It was too late for a comeback and with one last roar the prodigious structure fell flat on its back and stuck down in the mud. Daniel waited a moment until the last ripple of resistance disappeared from the water. "I WIN" he whistled and danced in a way *Seu* Benedito would surely have condemned as pagan. Shortly after, the two buckets gingerly bobbed to the surface displaying their original rusty and warped shapes as if nothing had happen.

"Your punishment for challenging me is death by dunking" Daniel kicked and banged the pails so recklessly that in the process his feet slipped. He was carried under and holding his breath, assumed the unpleasant smell of the *barreiro* would suffocate him. Mouth and eyes shut Daniel dreaded his fate until he noticed another change. The water had been amazingly transformed into a flowing body of crisp freshness like the mighty Amazon River his schoolteacher, Ms. Cabral, had described in a geography lesson.

Though he had never seen anything like this before Daniel was sure this was a river, not a reservoir. Below the crystal surface it was safe to open his eyes and graze the fine grains resting in the bottom. Tiny crabs and turtles crawled fearlessly through a school of silver *lambaris* showing off their sparkling silver scales under the bright sun. Daniel spread his arms, flipped his legs and swam for the first time ever. Whirling through the current Daniel could not resist fingering the dancing blades of grass along the banks. At last his entire body abandoned to the pure ecstasy and meandered through the enchanted sanctuary of plentiful clean water. "Awesome!" he freely slithered down the stream. "The *seca* is gone. Goodbye buckets" Daniel's arms flapped up and down while his feet slapped hard against the forest-green and screaming-orange fabric of his hammock.

FOUR

"Daniel?" the call echoed from under a turbulent current.

"Son?" At the bottom of the Amazon River the water pressure is rather intense, so Daniel stirred his head towards the surface where a blurry disc hovered so close that it seemed the sun had fallen from the sky. It took him a while to recognize he was no longer under water and that *Dona* Dulce had been peering down on him all along.

She held his rubbery arms and whispered insistently "Daniel? Daniel?", trying to halt the restless flapping. "Wake up, *filho*!" she rustled until Daniel locked eyes with her.

He blinked at the intent glare realizing *Dona* Dulce was the one who had hurled the hammock's brim probably worried he would land on the cement floor. *Dona* Dulce's husky voice and firm grip dispensed composure since she knew Daniel's surreal escapades were no accident. Those were pre-scheduled appointments with the Almighty, which at first *Seu* Benedito rebuked as a heretic statement. From early in her pregnancy Daniel's erratic spasms and sudden leaps had kept *Dona* Dulce alert. So much restlessness was undoubtedly of divine origin.

When her due day arrived she finally confirmed the suspicion. Daniel's wide-opened eyes met hers with such scrutiny, and that dark dot stamped beside the baby's navel was surely the Lord's branding. Daniel had been born with oneiric powers just like his Biblical namesake. *Dona* Dulce insisted on naming him after the exiled prophet, the one who could decipher important messages from heaven. No other name would do. Daniel had been born to receive and deliver the Lord's messages and as far as Dulce was concerned there had been no prophet called Benedito, had it?

Finding no argument against *Dona* Dulce's evidence *Seu* Benedito agreed to hurry up and register the name at the new notary public's office the same day. After that, it did not take long for *Dona* Dulce's prediction to sink in with her husband as he watched Daniel's ability manifest. The boy had spent many restless nights tossing and turning under his parents' close watch. Whether the dreams foretold of fortitude or misery it did not matter. As long as Daniel received God's messages uninterruptedly *Seu* Benedito and *Dona* Dulce rested assured on the Lord's promises to His faithful servants.

In the course of Daniel's childhood *Dona* Dulce learned to deal with his condition. With a balanced dose of reverence and firmness she appeased the intermittent trances as they increased. Tentative and gentle strokes worked like a charm to ease Daniel out of the visionary dazes without running the risk of cutting the revelations short. Withdrawing from God's glory took some time and Daniel needed to stay down a little longer so he could slowly disconnect from Third Heaven and regain earthly restrain. As soon as Daniel showed signs that he could hear, see, and speak once more, *Dona* Dulce concluded the transmission had been completed and that she could quietly leave his bedside and focus on mundane duties.

"IT'S TIME, FILHO!" she would then herald from a safe distance to remind Daniel where he was. Time to carry on with worldly errands until God called again. "I NEED WATER" *Dona* Dulce yelled from the kitchen. "Laundry to do, your father left for the *feira,* you know?" she mumbled.

Daniel yawned indolently and sat up at the hammock's brim. "Slept too long" he looked around the deserted parlor. If *Seu* Benedito was already at the *feira* that meant he was definitely running behind schedule. Careful not to stumble down he lumbered off and hopped a foot at a time to make sure the ground was steady enough before trailing after his mother. In the kitchen both Dalva and Delfina were already noisily sweeping the floor and starting a fresh fire. Daniel knew what was expected of him though before gearing for the rod and pails he needed to answer a more urgent call.

On his way to the outhouse he threw a quick glimpse at the fuss with which his mother and sisters tackled the ashy heap. Squatted in front of it *Dona* Dulce looked like a sinner before the altar ready to drop on her knees and surrender to the higher forces of housekeeping. Daniel watched her hand the dustpan full of cinder over to the girls and though there was nothing remarkable about the affair today the image stuck stubbornly inside his fazed head. As he walked past the door he could not shake it off. The meaningless moment had locked in like the last piece in a jigsaw puzzle.

Once in place it disclosed the magnitude of *Dona* Dulce's hopelessness. Duty and resignation bent her knees to that dusty floor. She had repeated the same penitence all her forsaken life in the *sertão*. The uninterrupted toil had carved repulsive varicose prints on her emaciated legs. An ugly-looking crisscross of purple resembled the meandering courses traced by the tributaries of the great São Francisco he studied on Ms. Cabral's wall map. Except *Dona* Dulce's bruised legs displayed no traces of vigor. Chronic malnourishment, difficult pregnancies, and strenuous labor had drained her body's vitality. When she stooped down before the wood stove *Dona* Dulce looked more like a dry *Juazeiro* sprig ready to split.

The *seca* was wasting her youth away as she appeared much older than her presumed twenty-eight years. Bathing and grooming had turned into a splurge lately. Her once long silky hair was rarely washed now and hid unkemptly under a bun. Daniel witnessed the charm and grace of his mother fade everyday. Her voice also sounded raspier. Daniel suspected she avoided drinking water as if it were a superfluous whim. Granted she had never been much of a talker before, the drought was making *Dona* Dulce increasingly terse. Maybe her words were evaporating like the rest of Lajedo's springs and Daniel's thoughts. Only short sentences remained, and for Daniel in particular, she had resorted to two words: "*it's time.*"

If she expected another full load of water the two words conveyed uncommon rigor. Daniel could tell that was the case when he heard her from the kitchen just now. The words had not come across as a reminder such as 'it's time to eat, nap or go to church' when a touch of tenderness might linger. They spurted out like Saint Joseph's hollow bell proclaiming a calamity. "Less manioc roots to boil but more mouths to feed: "*it's time, it's time.*"

The words rang inside Daniel's head all the way to the privy where he hurriedly spread both legs across the hole on the ground. The scent inside the cubicle was awfully acrid and Daniel's snorted. He held his breath for as long as he could without fainting and hurried out. By now he was beyond late and had to dash. Ignoring *Dona*

Dulce's instructions to rinse his hands at the cistern Daniel scooped the rod and tin buckets and crossed the gate.

The dangling noise of metal aroused the sleepy mutt who shot both ears up in hopes of being invited along. Daniel disdained the idea of being followed by the wretched creature and skipped up the alley as fast as he could when two loud gongs droned out of Saint Joseph's tower. "It's time", Daniel broke in an anxious trot.

Between two o'clock and the Ave Maria hour vendors and shoppers had God's permission to reclaim their spots at the reopened town market. From the corner of Ms. Cabral's schoolhouse the first bargaining shouts reached Daniel's ears. He climbed on his toes and craned over to wave at *Seu* Benedito on the other side of the plaza to let him know he was finally on his way to the *barreiro.* But a gang of sluggish mules passed in front of him defying the herdsman's angry whips. "*Vai, vai pestes*!" the young man whipped the stubborn animals.

Anxious to catch *Seu* Benedito's attention Daniel sprinted on the sidewalk. Had his father already stacked up the fruits on the stall? If not, he would feel obligated to land a hand, something he was not looking forward to. The early afternoon sun tilted slightly to the right side and provided Daniel with a fleeting shade. He was tempted to drop the buckets and observe the swallowing traffic but the reek of fresh dung below urged him otherwise. When the last beast cleared away he quickly pushed through an animated ring of chit-chatters and hobbled on.

On the other side *Seu* Benedito's threadbare canopy loomed ready. His precious booth—baseboard, cover, and storage crates—were all set for the market's two o' clock reopening. A neat and clean presentation was another of *Seu* Benedito's strict rules to lure

Lajedo's stingy customers. From what Daniel could see his father was diligently wipping the fruits to a shine, arranging them in a pyramid-shaped display. The fat pineapples at the bottom formed an attractive foundation for the bright green guavas and yellow *cajús* to climb on in a triangular sequence all the way to the top in perfect symmetrical order. Daniel understood the reason behind his father's finicky act. This was shaping up to be a lucky week in quite some time. An unexpected find at a *sítio* past the *barreiro* had cost *Seu* Benedito only one trip this week. Of course credit went to God's mercy instead of the farmers who had been digging shallow trenches to carry the water over their groves.

Daniel had seen them at work the past weeks and came very close to pointing that piece of information out to *Seu* Benedito. But when he saw the heavy baskets hanging down the donkey's loin two days ago not to mention the flash of relief on his father's face, Daniel simply nodded and smiled. It was rare for him to witness *Seu* Benedito's brag about God's favor. "Look son" he had pointed at the bountiful load. "Praise the Lord, this right here should make a couple of days business" he almost smiled.

One day had already elapsed since the holy incident and there was still enough left to keep the booth open. Tomorrow? Daniel tried to count the half-empty cases tucked under the baseboard when the frame of a shopper obstructed his view. One quick glance at it was enough to identify the graceful outline before *Seu* Benedito's booth. No doubts the sleeveless white and yellow polka dot dress, the neatly coiffed blond hair, the curvy milky-white arms were the same that wiped the chalkboard five days a week.

Daniel's heart skipped a beat in anticipation of bumping into his absolute favorite person in the whole world. In the spurt of the moment he decided to stop over instead of just hailing from afar. Ever so expectantly he skirted around another ring of shoppers and yielded to the irresistible magnet pulling his feet in the wrong direction. A shy smile parted Daniel's lips. Delight or remorse? Perhaps a mix of both he had to admit. Ms. Cabral took a bite of the pineapple slice *Seu* Benedito had just offered as sample. Daniel's cheeks burned at the thought of having missed her morning lesson. For sure Ms. Cabral was going to call him on it and he immediately began juggling apologies in his evaporating mind. Should he lament the incident? "Huh…hello Miss, I…huh, had to fetch more water…huh…" Or pretend it had not happened? "Oh, hello Miss! *Boa tarde!* How nice to see you. How have you been?"

Ms. Cabral was one of Benedito's most loyal patrons but that was not how Daniel knew her. To him she meant much more than a source of steady income to the family. For as long as he could remember Ms. Cabral had been an ally, the only person who nurtured his endless curiosity. She made him feel at ease about questioning anything. Instead of blows she approached him with smiles or gentle taps on his shoulder that inevitably left Daniel with the impression he was the most important student in the class. "Well done—*muito bem,* Daniel" or "you got it right, my dear" her perfectly aligned teeth showed.

If it were not for Ms. Cabral's praise Daniel would have given up on school a long time ago. The crowded classroom, its desks, chairs, and sleepy pupils were all falling apart. Decades of neglect from the local authorities and parents had discouraged Lajedo's youth to pursue an education but Daniel could count on Ms. Cabral's flatteries like a well-off child expected a toy on his birthday. Daniel stored each compliment deep inside his neglected heart. Whenever he felt put down by *Seu* Benedito or *Dona* Dulce he recalled the smooth voice. There was another reason why Daniel idolized Ms. Cabral. No one else challenged Benedito's rules and got away with it. Though she could fool some with her delicate manners Ms. Cabral was never pushed around.

How many times had she reminded Daniel and the knuckleheads in his class that a good education was equivalent to a weapon? "The only one we can legally use in this country, children. Never forget that" she laughingly shook her index finger at the group pretending to it to be a pistol. "Read, read, read as many books as you can" she urged while handing out volumes from her personal library. So often had Daniel accepted Ms. Cabral's offer that he became known as the school bookworm. "Daniel *Minhoca*" they teased him but he could care less. The fact that *Seu* Benedito proclaimed Ms. Cabral's books sacrilegious was even a better excuse to devour them. The classic novels of Castro Alves, Machado de Assis, and José de Alencar had become favorites and under Ms. Cabral's guidance Daniel read them with a sense of urgency.

At nighttime after the family's dreadful devotionals Daniel looked forward to cuddling with a book. He read on until *Seu* Benedito stormed into the alcove to snatch both the kerosene lamp and 'the piece of trash' out of his hands. Fortunately, *Seu* Benedito's sour temper would never intimidate Ms. Cabral and the books kept on coming.

"*Boa tarde*, Ms. Cabral!" Daniel stood next to *Seu* Benedito.

"Good afternoon to you, Daniel" Ms. Cabral beamed while cradling three pineapples into her arms as if they were newborns.

"Where were you this morning?" the teacher probed Daniel's downcast face quite aware of the buckets hanging on his shoulders.

"I missed you today, and yesterday" she twitted while bending over her leather sac to stow the small bundles.

Buying time Daniel watched Ms. Cabral's gentle moves. He had drawn a blank and failed to retrieve one sensible excuse from the list he had drafted half a minute ago. Today's absence was his second in a row on the account of *Seu* Benedito's man of the house rule, not to mention God's recent blessing. Daniel shifted his gaze from Ms. Cabral to *Seu* Benedito who was prepared for vindication.

"Ms. Cabral" he began as if reciting Scripture. "Daniel is the other man of the house and I need him on call when I am away at work. *Senhorita*, times have been very hard lately. Very hard indeed… These pineapples you just bought are getting difficult to come by" *Seu* Benedito picked one out and ran his dirty nails up and down the rough peel. "This week the Good Lord miraculously provided, so I didn't have to go far" he pulled a handkerchief to dust the fruit's crown. "But when I have to, Daniel takes my place" *Seu* Benedito began to sound like a teacher himself.

"*Seu* Benedito, I beg your pardon" Ms. Cabral impatiently interrupted. "I *do know* what we are going through. This drought has been daunting indeed, the most severe in a long time. We are all suffering the consequences" Ms. Cabral's voice rose slightly. "However, sir, Daniel is *my* best student" she continued without disarming her grin. "I have told you many times how bright he is, how exceptional his reading and writing skills are for his age. Daniel must continue his education beyond the elementary level so he can secure a better future for himself. School is the only way…" she fired back and slung the leather strap back on her shoulders.

"Our future is what God chooses, Ms. Cabral" *Seu* Benedito cut her off pointing at the sky. "We don't get to make it, *Senhorita*.

The One above has already decided it for us" his eyes did not let go of hers while he turned to dusting the bright yellow *cajús*. "Besides," Benedito lifted the rag as if trying to wipe the whole plaza clean "there is nothing wrong with a future in an honest trade. Daniel does not need to read and write well to become a fruit vendor like me or my father before me" he theatrically folded the handkerchief in two.

Throughout the exchange Daniel studied the contours of his muddy toenails. Eyes on the ground he listened exasperatedly to his father's blab. It had been a while since he witnessed the same dispute unfold. Throughout it Ms. Cabral's sandals remained anchored on the same spot.

"She does not deserve to be talked to like that!" Daniel wanted to interject. "How dare you disagree with my teacher?" he pressed the wood pole hard on his shoulder blade and curbed the urge to spit. "If the teacher calls me best and exceptional it is because it's true. She knows me better. I hate this 'man of the house' rule. What future when wells are drying?" the unspoken words gagged inside his throat.

Ms. Cabral reached down for her wallet and the folded bills accomplished what he couldn't. *Seu* Benedito bowed politely and quieted down. In his shame Daniel wheeled around without saying goodbye. Within a few yards the shout came. "Daniel! Come right back after the *barreiro*, hear?"

Daniel heard it all right but refused to look back. Pounding his bare feet on the ground he waved. All over the plaza anxious merchants competed for costumers. Free samples, discounts and best deals ricocheted above Daniel's jammed head: "*Aquí: Senhor*—Here: Mister! The best mangoes and bananas in the whole *feira*! A bite, *Senhora*? Taste it for yourself: pure honey. And you, pretty *Senhorita*? Take a dozen onions and the string of garlic is free!" "Don't listen to him my Precious!" another one laughed. "Everything here is half off today! Right this way: let me show you."

Each exclamation Daniel heard he cursed under his breath. Pebbles and sticks along the way bore the brunt of his rage. "Who wants your rotten mangoes?" he kicked and stomped the ground all the way to the shore. "Fake deals, stupid chores!", Daniel yelled at the shallow water.

FIVE

"Why so much misery?" Daniel ruminated on his way back. He chose to take the lane behind the church cemetery to put enough distance from his father's stall. The mere thought of spending the afternoon with *Seu* Benedito made his stomach churn with repulsion. Those would be the longest hours ever.

"Is he to blame?" Daniel calculated each step forward as usual. *Seu* Benedito was the official enforcer of the ridiculous 'man of the house' rule after all. "Why wouldn't he question its merit for a change?" If only *Seu* Benedito knew about the education weapon, Daniel dragged his feet over the rocky ground. Like the buckets on his shoulder his mind was full of murk.

"How about me?" Daniel almost stumbled at the thought. He looked sideways and fortunately nothing had spilled. "I do question those rules but do nothing about changing them" Daniel challenged his own cowardice. If only he knew how to argue like Ms. Cabral. "Her arguments were always logical" Daniel informed the powdery gravel.

"If I could fly away never to come back" the reverie of a few hours ago returned. "Had he really turned into a vulture and soared toward the clouds?" the panoramic view of a shrunk Lajedo flashed back. "Was the vision from God? Is He telling me to leave?" Daniel let the possibility sink in. "Could God be the one to blame then?" and afraid someone might have overheard the blasphemy Daniel paused. "God has been good to you" *Dona* Dulce's husky whisper latched to his ears. "He has chosen you" she explained whenever he asked why so many dreams. "You are not to understand why son" she repeatedly told him. "Only believe" and *Dona* Dulce somberly shifted her gaze over to his navel. The dark birthmark first detected when he was born grew rounder and bigger each year.

"That" she had pointed out "is God's will" Daniel sulked. He had bent the corner of the alley and could spot the neighbor's filthy dog. "So far so good" he inspected the buckets with a sidelong glimpse. His precious cargo remained superbly inert as the crooked gate neared. Yet he was not quite done probing. "Aha!" he kicked the creaky wood. "The drought is to blame" he crossed over. It made perfect sense because before the drought settled he was allowed to enjoy a few simple pleasures. He played *futebol* using rolled-up socks as a ball, took trips to the fields where he and the boys raided bird nests and dug inside lizard holes. One time he had brought a slingshot along and returned home with a few dead mice—*calangos*—in his pockets to scare his sisters.

"When was the last time I had any fun?" Daniel licked his parched lips and thought of the Amazon River. Right after the Feast of Saint Joseph he had skipped a trip to the *barreiro* and paid no mind to *Seu* Benedito's announcement regarding their drying well. The boys had begged him to join as a goalkeeper and by the time he arrived home *Seu* Benedito's *palmatória* descended mercilessly on both his hands.

"This is for your own good." (BANG) "Playtime is the devil's snare." (BANG) "If you ever get tempted to overlook your duties again either pray or recite a Bible verse." (BANG) "Understood?" *Seu* Benedito had asked coolly as if he had simply finished wiping a pineapple from the stand. Then he grounded Daniel until further notice. "Might as well be grounded for life" Daniel shrugged and dumped the water into the cistern.

Inside the kitchen the clay jug seemed to be calling his name but it was *Dona* Dulce's voice Daniel heard first. "Just brewed it" she handed over a tin cup of hot, black, sweet coffee and directed Daniel to the stool across his sisters. Seldom greeted with pleasantries he gladly complied and sat down blowing the curling steam off. Tracking the rising smoke Daniel let the fragrant grip take over. He sat on the stool and rocked it back and forth with his feet. He could not wait to feel the coffee's sugary texture coat his throat. After each slurp he waited for the beverage to restore his resilience. *"Ai."* The thought of spending the rest of the day by *Seu* Benedito's side made his head hurt.

Done with his drink Daniel slithered his tongue inside the cup and licked the melted sugar at the bottom. Dalva found this habit of Daniel's particularly disgusting and cried out at once. "*Mainha:* Daniel is doing it again" her nose wrenched in condemnation.

"Daniel? *Arre…* No manners?" Dulce slapped the back of his neck while the girls giggled with delight.

Daniel knitted his brows and stuck his tongue menacingly at the girls. They both screamed at once: "*Mainha* look!" but to the girls' disappointment *Dona* Dulce was slow with the next whack and Daniel darted without looking back.

Out in the alley the nasty dog had nowhere else to go. Its disgusting bleeding sores shinned glossily under a coat of spit as the poor creature patiently rasped the ooze. When Daniel passed by, his bare feet pounded the dirt. Taking the cue as an invitation the mutt jumped up and chased joyously behind. "Back off you trash. Off, *lixo*" Daniel shouted angrily. "This should be your name, you know?" he panted. "*Lixo!* GET OUT! SHOO, LIXO, SHOO!" Daniel grew madder at the dog. Without slowing down he grabbed a few rocks off the ground and the pooch sat up in anticipation of a game of fetch having no idea Daniel was about to attack. At the first painful impact the dog recoiled and whimpered in the opposite direction. "Stupid dog" Daniel snarled.

Back at the plaza the raucous afternoon activities progressed in due course. Scraps of vegetables, cigarette buts, fruit peels, and dung drops scattered everywhere and clung to Daniel's bare soles as he ran over to *Seu* Benedito's booth. He did his best to scrape some of it all off before taking his post.

"Sweet, *Seu Dito*?" a patron demanded evidence.

"Of course, *Senhor* Moraes!" *Seu* Benedito acquiesced and handed over a juicy slice of guava. "Here: try for yourself" he also snapped two fingers. Knowing exactly what to do Daniel reached for the pile of newspaper sheets and quickly wrapped two pineapples and half-dozen guavas. While packing the order Daniel stretched forward to eavesdrop on the men's talk that sounded like tales he had caught wind of at the market.

"*Obrigado*, *Seu* Dito" continued *Senhor* Moraes. "Real good" he mouthed the guava and talked at the same time. "So, it was too late for the family to send for the doctor" he pulled a handkerchief and wiped his thick lips. "The poor girl's fever kept on rising like the flares in a bonfire" he turned to his gooey fingertips. "Too much heat for one little body and in a few hours, *Seu* Dito, she got delirious" *Senhor* Moraes crossed himself. "A blessing if you ask me" he took the bag from Daniel. "Had no idea what hit her" he shook his head.

After inspecting his order *Senhor* Moraes offered more details. "It ain't the first case neither, *Seu* Dito" he crossed himself again before lowering the tone. "This fever is spreading. Targeting the children" and he glanced at Daniel.

"May the precious blood of our Lord Jesus Christ cover us" *Seu* Benedito retorted gravely.

Daniel found it difficult to decipher his father's tone. For a second it seemed *Seu* Benedito had disarmed his frown and opened his mouth a litter wider. The grunt was not familiar, which meant that whatever *Senhor* Moraes disclosed was unexpected.

While dusting the pyramid display Daniel was all ears. "You're right, *Seu* Dito," *Senhor* Moraes went on pulling out a leather wallet from his back pocket "only the Lord Jesus can do something 'cause them doctors sure can't" he handed *Seu* Benedito a bill. "I tell you what. Them victims? I mean, them families?" he carefully counted Daniel's change "live out there by the *barreiro"* he tilted his head to the left. "It' s from there this fever is coming, *Seu* Dito. "Typhoid, they say. Kills like that" he flicked his fingers. "No medicine good enough. When one gets it?" *Senhor* Moraes stared past *Seu* Dito's shoulder "might as well dig up a grave, *Seu* Dito" his eyes landed on the cemetery gate.

"What causes it, *Senhor* Moraes? I mean, how does the fever spread?" *Seu* Benedito asked sternly.

"No one knows for sure, *Seu* Dito" *Senhor* Moraes shook his head. "Folks say it's the water: who knows?" he arched his hairy brows. "That *barreiro* is getting shallower by the day, don't you think?" *Senhor* Moraes now wiped the sweat off his eyebrows. "That water over there is dirty" he crossed himself again, kissed the tip of his fingers and put his wallet away. "How about you folks?" he asked politely. "*Dona* Dulce? The kids?" he lifted his straw hat implying the conversation was about over.

"All is well—*Tudo bem*—thanks be to God!" *Seu* Benedito bowed stone-faced and stretched his hand for *Senhor* Moraes to shake. "Thank you, sir, and come back soon. God bless" *Seu* Benedito lifted his straw hat.

An elderly lady had just rumbled right beside *Senhor* Moraes not bothering to wait for her turn and began squeezing the guavas. "These any good, *Seu* Dito? "she screeched. *Seu* Benedito and Daniel both scurried closer cajolingly. "A small sample *Dona* Guida*?* Special discount for you today; no spots on my guavas, see? Daniel, half a dozen" *Seu* Benedito secured another sale. As the afternoon dragged more costumers came by; some to get a free bite, others to bargain a discount. *Seu* Benedito raved about their blessed inventory, "dripping honey, all of it, Praise the Lord!", and for the next three tedious hours avoided commenting on *Senhor* Moraes' alarming report.

Daniel, on the other hand, could not let go of the enigmatic words: "fever, delirious, doctor." "What were they supposed to mean when put together?" he pondered. He would have to ask Ms. Cabral about it. For sure she would know what '*typhood*' meant.

At the end of the day foot traffic began to dwindle. Only a handful of women with small children in tow roved behind the closing booths begging for unsold scraps. The sun slowly lowered in the horizon and the sidewalks began to clear. After a heated day of haggling Lajedo's den of robbers was about to turn into a house of prayer.

In front of Saint Joseph's church *Seu* Benedito noticed the arrival of worshippers and with his index finger immediately pointed at the baseboard. "*It's time*," Daniel understood the sign. He had to pack up the crates with the unsold pineapples, guavas, and *cajús* before the six o' clock Mass. Still avoiding eye contact with his father Daniel slowly disassembled the booth.

It seemed *Seu* Benedito would have to scout for more fruit tomorrow, in which case, Daniel would be promoted to 'man of the house' again. Would he have to miss school then? Daniel sighed at the thought of disappointing Ms. Cabral and began folding the old newspaper sheets. At some point, large words jumped at him: "**FEVER, DELIRIOUS, DOCTOR".**

Seu Benedito in the meantime unfastened the donkey from the iron rail and interrupted Daniel's musing. "Go" he etched the familiar frown but this time Daniel deciphered a hint of secrecy behind it. None of what was heard from *Senhor* Moraes should be mentioned at home.

When *Seu* Benedito yanked the donkey away from the iron gate Saint Joseph's bells waged a loud blast. Five more would follow to usher the melodic *Ave Maria* carillon in honor of the Blessed Mother, holy patroness of Brazil. Under the blissful rendition Lajedo's day had officially ended and most villagers trusted that just about now the Virgin Mary spread her protective blue robe over the sky to light the villager's path home with its encrusted diamond studs. Daniel was obviously urged never to believe such fallacy but while staring at the sparkling twilight, he secretly admired its beauty.

SIX

Weeks after *Senhor* Moraes spoke the enigmatic words Daniel had not found a clear explanation for their meaning. Here and there he heard people repeat 'fever', "delirious", "doctor" in hushed tones as if suddenly the terms had been reduced to profanity. *Seu* Benedito refused to discuss any of it either at home or at the *feira* where the latest gossip inevitably revolved around another tragic case of the 'fever.'

In the meantime the drought tightened its grip. The days grew hotter, longer and exhausting. The villagers' morale sunk as low as the *barreiro* water and even the children in Daniel's class sat hunched over with empty stares on their faces. "The drought is here; the fever is here; death is here" everyone affirmed through blank glances. At Saint Joseph's church the priest added an extra daily Mass in case of emergency. A funeral or a precautionary christening was expected anytime and from *Seu* Benedito's booth location in front of the church cemetery Daniel observed the tides of change crash over Lajedo.

During the long month of July when school was in recess for half the time Daniel worked extra shifts at the *feira*. By the end of month a growing number of visitors to the graveyard had caught his attention. The distraught callers walked right past *Seu* Benedito's booth bearing somber countenances and gloomy outfits. To Daniel they looked like actors in a Catholic pageant, all dressed in black and morbidly bent like burned wicks. Leaning on each other they filed behind a wood box, weeping and praying all the way into the labyrinth of tombs.

After an hour they reappeared looking even more distressed though without the wood box. Beneath Saint Joseph's sorrowful gongs they lined up again, crestfallen and bent even lower, to kiss the priest's hand. Daniel assumed a dead body must be inside the wood box, but again, he could not ask *Seu* Benedito for confirmation. At this point 'fever' inquiries had been upgraded to another unquestionable rule. Death should not be explained, only accepted.

As the drought choked Lajedo out of purpose time dragged to an extraordinary crawl. To pass the time Daniel remained attentive to the *feira* gossip and eavesdropped on the costumers' tales at every opportunity. What he heard sounded hideous. People were getting sick and 'passing on' whatever that meant. *Seu* Benedito also listened but refused to comment. During his rare breaks Daniel also skimmed old newspapers used for the fruit wrapping in search of clues about who ended up inside those boxes. Unfortunately, another drought outbreak in the *sertão* was no relevant news. If he were to discover anything about the fever he had to keep snooping until classes resumed. He had yet to ask Ms. Cabral for an explanation.

On his last vacation day Daniel happened to be bored out of his mind at the *feira* when a small funeral party scurried behind *Seu* Benedito's booth. This time the wood box in question was different from all the others Daniel had seen. It had a bright white finish to it and it was light enough for one person to carry. Had he seen those people before? Could they be the neighbors at the end of the alley? If so, the box must belong to their only child who was not even old enough to walk. The realization hit Daniel hard as if a boulder had dropped down and crushed his lungs out of air. He forgot to breathe realizing the fever had claimed its littlest victim so far.

"Children are not supposed to die" Daniel turned nervously away from the iron gate and began dusting the fruits. *Seu* Benedito also noticed the muffled sobs coming from the young mother as she nearly fainted at the cemetery entrance. The heartbreaking scene drew attention and for a few seconds that corner of the plaza stood still. The discomfort was unbearable for *Seu* Benedito and not knowing what to do with himself he started shouting at no one in particular.

"*Aqui:* ladies and gentlemen, pineapples on sale" the announcement resonated rather like a threat. *Seu* Benedito waved his hands and paced in front of the booth trying to break the frightening spell. Daniel, and a few of the nearby merchants chimed in. "Here: fruit for sale" they yelled. *Seu* Benedito sliced and distributed pineapple chuncks with unprecedented zeal whereas Daniel turned anxious glances at the heartbreaking scene.

Aware of the fever's proximity he remembered the Virgin's robe fallacy. No longer limited to the town's outskirts as *Senhor* Moraes had suggested the fever had pierced through the presumably protective dome and now advanced beyond the plaza. "What if his house was next?" he could not wait for school on Monday. "How do we spell "typhood", *Senhorita*?" was going to be his first question for Ms. Cabral.

At least that was his plan when Monday morning came but when he sat at his desk, Daniel knew something was amiss. Ms. Cabral greeted the returning class with an impersonal nod and a jaded smile.

Daniel and the other students were not used to such indifference and immediately straightened up on their benches. Then they waited for the suspenseful silence to break. It took a while for them to hear Ms. Cabral's quivering whisper.

"Good morning, and welcome back, children" the words sounded awfully hesitant. "It is really good to see you here today" she admitted but her hands stayed clasped over her chest as if she had trouble breathing. Visibly agitated, Ms. Cabral was making an extraordinary effort to appear otherwise. "I am so very sorry to tell you children that Madalena and Josias are not here today be…be… because the they die died of the fe…fe…fever" she stuttered like a toddler and turned her back to grab a piece of chalk from the blackboard. Without offering anyone a chance to ask questions a math problem appeared on the dusty surface.

"Now, let us review some addition problems to begin with and when you are done bring your sheet over to my desk. No need to hurry" she held the chalk piece with unnecessary vigor.

No one dared to peep. The only sound heard in the stuffy room came from Ms. Cabral's grating scribble on the board. Daniel and his classmates diligently copied the assignment and avoided looking at each other. He could hear a storm of questions gathering. "When? How? Why?" Daniel could see the interjections enveloping him but like the rest of the class he remained quiet. Now was the moment to formulate the question. He had to ask whether this fever would indeed destroy Lajedo.

"Ms. Cabral, how do we spell typhood, please?" he murmured but his beloved teacher ignored him. Barricaded behind her desk she pretended to read. Daniel gave up and turned to the math problems on his pad. The uneasy silence in the room hijacked his thoughts and instead of numbers he saw the tin monster rising from the page. "If only I could use my rod against this fever and make it disappear" and with his pencil Daniel drew a long stick on the paper. Next to it he added a large picture of himself branding his rod. Sometime in July he had turned twelve and grown taller. This should be the last birthday he spent as a helpless little boy.

Thankfully, Ms. Cabral remained at her desk and did not walk around the room to check on the students' progress. When she dismissed the class to an early recess Daniel asked to stay behind and finished his picture. Surprisingly, she granted permission without asking for a reason and while the other students played hopscotch and hide-and-seek outside Daniel scribbled a plan to save Lajedo from the fever. When would he actually act?

Daniel put the pencil down and held the paper at arm's-length to scan the scene. He thought also about the rest of the day and the upcoming chores. He wished to go home now and take a *sesta* before going to the *feira*. During the school vacation *Seu* Benedito had gone overboard with the man of the house rule. Water-fetching, fruit dusting and selling, non-stop, *ai*! There had not been enough hours at night to recover from a full day of toil and if Daniel were to ever act as the hero on the sketch he needed a break. A day off, at least, might rid him of the cough, and aches. Walking to class this morning had been already exhausting. "Maybe I need more coffee" Daniel put his head down on the desk. "Stupid headache" he rubbed his forehead and closed his eyes. Lately, he had not been very hungry for his mother's beans and rice. Was it because *Dona* Dulce had run out of money to buy more onions? "That's it", Daniel blinked. His mom's cooking was getting too bland.

At dismissal time Daniel's body felt like it had endured a major blow from *Seu* Benedito's ferule. On the days that followed he dutifully tried his best to act normal like Ms. Cabral had at school, nodding and smiling whenever sent out for chores. No onc should know he had stopped dreaming, that his appetite vanished, and that he could no longer hold a book after the evening devotionals.

What Daniel did not predict, however, was that his lousy acting would drive both *Seu* Benedito and *Dona* Dulce mad. They began to yell at him for taking his sweet time fetching water and loafing away in the hammock when called for in the mornings. Daniel took the criticism in stride. True, his feet were slowing down at the *barreiro* trek, his shoulders, legs and head had stiffened like wood but should he worry too much about *Senhor* Moraes' words? "Fever", "delirious", "doctor."

Early in August, however, there was no more pretending left in Daniel's body. It would be a while until he heard *Dona* Dulce's full account of that fateful day when her gentle taps and calling failed to wake him up. He could not recall the smell of the burning candle or hearing the rooster crowing outside when *Dona* Dulce strolled in at the crack of dawn and lifted the fringes of his hammock. She told him about bending quietly over calling "*it's time.*" Apparently the rooster was the only one who reacted to her husky voice. "Daniel, you dreaming?" she whispered. "*It's time,*" she squeezed his hand.

Nothing moved in the room except for the candle flame. *Dona* Dulce hovered the light over Daniel's sealed eyes and colorless lips assuming he was indeed receiving a transmission like no other. She placed the candle on the floor and used both hands to shake the hammock a little harder. Still, Daniel did not budge. When *Dona* Dulce ran both hands about Daniel's head her heart jumped. His skin burned to the touch. *Dona* Dulce stepped back and instinctively covered her mouth. Giving in to her maternal instinct she noosed Daniel's neck in a steady embrace and pulled the boy's chest closer to her. It felt as light as a bird. "Daniel, son, you dreaming?" she searched for a trace of spunk.

Daniel's arms fought off her grip and never before did *Dona* Dulce think such insolence would cheer her up. Out in the yard the rooster crowed again; a long happy cry to praise the sun's imminent ambush over Lajedo. *Dona* Dulce felt encouraged. She could use more light to examine Daniel's long lashes perfectly clasped over his sunken eyes.

"Son—*filho*—can you get up?" she entreated.

How in the world was she going to carry the day's workload without him? *Seu* Benedito was soon to leave for the orchards and she needed water right away. Daniel could barely keep his head up but out of his chipped lips a sound finally came. "Stupid pain" he said. "Dizzy…" he added through a rasping cough.

The rising sunrays filtered through the window. When Dulce gently let go of Daniel. She took a deep breath. Something was terribly wrong. Dreadful thoughts stormed in. For a moment she could not act except for tucking an oily curl behind her ear. The candlestick melted by her feet when out the window the obstinate rooster released a final, overjoyed cry. The day had begun and *Dona* Dulce had much to do. Where to begin? Blowing the candle was enough for now.

She walked to the window next dismayed at the assumptions her anxious mind conjured. The neighbor's flowerless *mandacarú* cactus seemed so far away and over the horizon the sun froze. *Dona* Dulce prayed for courage, "Jesus, please raise my son from that hammock as you did Jairus' little daughter" she mumbled. "*Talitha koum—Little girl rise!*" she repeated the scripture verse while walking out.

Dona Dulce had to break the news to *Seu* Benedito who was already saddling the donkey. Her legs wobbled and her mouth dried up the moment she stalled by the kitchen door. "Dito: the boy is sick. I need water!" the words stormed out. At least it was to his back that *Dona* Dulce spoke. She didn't want her husband to see tears glossing her eyes. In nearly fourteen years of marriage *Dona* Dulce had never cried in front of *Seu* Benedito and today, she was determined, would not be the first.

Still concerned with the donkey *Seu* Benedito did not reply. When he turned around, the morning sun coated the tiled roof and cast a convenient shadow over *Dona* Dulce's alarmed stare.

"Dito" she repeated. "The boy is sick. I need water!

Seu Benedito took the information in motionlessly. His thoughts swung from suspicion to repudiation while glimpses of Daniel's recent behavior flashed before him. "Not to worry—*mulher*" he finally dismissed the announcement. "An indisposition—*mal estar*" he added matter of fact. "Let him rest more. I'll go to the *barreiro*" he walked by her without making eye contact.

"No, Dito. You don't understand" *Dona* Dulce grabbed his arm. "Fever, cough, body ache. Go for the doctor" she pleaded.

"*Calma*" *Seu* Benedito stepped back. "Children are fussy" he shook his arm free. "Sugary water, and in no time—*já, já*—he will get up" *Seu* Benedito grabbed the buckets. "Pray!" he yelled from atop the donkey before *Dona* Dulce had time to protest. Whether she spoke again *Seu* Benedito did not hear. The donkey hoofed over the gravel blatantly and thudded his ears shut.

SEVEN

As much as *Dona* Dulce prayed and wished *Seu* Benedito's diagnosis were true, Daniel's condition declined. Overnight his skinny body shook as the fever spiked, unresponsive to *Dona* Dulce's regimen of sugary water and soaked rags. The dry cough caused such a strain that beads of sweat clung to his pale lips. While night turned to dawn squatting over the pot chamber became impossible for Daniel and *Dona* Dulce resorted to wrapping towels around his waist to prevent more embarrassing accidents.

By mid-morning the wraps turned up increasingly soiled, forcing *Dona* Dulce to abandon the household chores altogether. She rushed from the alcove to the washtub outside with no time to stop at the kitchen. Left with no other choice she unveiled the secrets of the wood stove to Dalva and Delfina who worked all day pulling batches water from the cistern and boiling it to prepare Daniel's sugary drink. Fortunately, the girls were solicitous and stood by to spoon-feed their ailing brother, nursing him with the devotion saved for a baby doll they never had.

Still, Daniel remained aloof to the commotion around him. Not even when *Dona Dulce* propped him up on the hammock did he complain or object. His skin burned to the touch and his eyelids quit blinking now and then. His squashy limbs stalled except when shivers overtook him, comforting *Dona* Dulce that God's messages had not been interrupted. During those short intervals Dalva and Delfina were instructed to tap the soaked the rags on his forehead and ease the transmission.

As far as Daniel was concerned time had stagnated. He no longer discerned the difference between day and night though his mind was not completely gone yet. Hazy images dancing before his eyes led to spurts of alertness whereas his ears captured the humming of voices. The sugary mix pressed against his lips and the soft texture of cornmeal over his tongue convinced him an angel of the Lord had stood by pushing a spoon through his lips ever so gently until he swallowed the mush. He could also track the hammock thrusting him further up towards heaven.

By the end of the second day *Seu* Benedito began questioning his reasoning. This was no common indisposition. Daniel's symptoms had worsened after the prescribed regimen of rest, sugary water, and prayer. A frightening thought shook *Seu* Benedito's self-righteousness to the core. Daniel could well be suffering from the fever raging through Lajedo. Late into the night he stopped asking *Dona* Dulce how things were going as she walked out of the alcove to fetch another cup of sugary water.

Past midnight *Seu* Benedito peeked down Daniel's hammock. The boy's head looked frighteningly lopsided and his body morbidly frazzled. At her wit's end *Dona* Dulce had just changed another soiled towel and swore the fever was spiking again. The dark circles hanging under her eyes were hostile testimonies to her lack of sleep and confidence. *Seu* Benedito's heart rattled at the gloomy sight. There was no point in being so stubborn, let alone stingy. Might as well count their meager savings lost and run to Dr. Leal's clinic first thing in the morning. Until then he had to pray harder, loud even, if necessary. In and out of the small quarters he glided like an apparition, pleading with God for his boy's healing.

At dawn the rooster's timely crow interrupted *Seu* Benedito's vigil and out the door he darted to retrieve the tin buckets and saddle the donkey. Might as well do something useful before Dr. Leal's clinic opened. Going to the *barreiro* seemed the most reasonable task.

Shortly after refilling the cistern *Seu* Benedito left again for the plaza. The sun ascended high and mighty, guiding Lajedo's Catholics to Saint Joseph's. At the clinic's door he heard the bells six loud blows and stood at the closed door worried it was too early to knock. With an ear pressed on the wood *Seu* Benedito prayed his hardest yet for Dr. Leal to be there. He listened momentarily to the quietness on the other side before tapping.

No one answered his timid stroke, and asking for God's forgiveness, *Seu* Benedito swiftly twisted the knob. The door gave in and assured him of divine permission to trespass. Hesitantly he slipped into the dim vestibule and humbly removed the straw hat in case Dr. Leal showed up. Alone in the narrow waiting room he screened the walls unsure of how to proceed. Should he yell or wait for someone to meet him? He had never called at a doctor's clinic before but his growing despair demanded action.

From the corner of his eyes *Seu* Benedito spotted a doorway. Through its narrow gap a crackling sound escaped, and assuming Dr. Leal was somewhere in there, *Seu* Benedito praised the Lord for the favor. With a deep breath he hugged his hat tight praying the doctor did not take offense at such impertinence. Under his ambivalent push the door finally yielded, revealing a cone of light above doctor Leal's stout back. He was busy putting on a wrinkled white jacket when *Seu* Benedito whispered.

"*Dotô?*" he softly pleaded. "Sorry?—*desculpa?*—" his bronze round face leant on the doorpost.

"*Bom dia*" the doctor turned around and squinted. "Come in, please" he looked puzzled. "What can I do for you, mister?"

"Morning to you too, *Dotô*" *Seu* Benedito bowed and humbly accepted the invitation. "My boy, *Dotô* Leal" he barely made eye contact and poured his heart out about Daniel's deteriorating condition.

"For how long, *Seu…?*" the doctor inquired.

"Benedito, *Dotô*" he bowed lower still. "The fruit vendor, your servant, *seu criado, Dotô*."

"Of course, *Seu* Benedito" Dr. Leal exclaimed in recognition. "For how long has your boy been sick?" the doctor asked pulling a chair for *Seu* Benedito to sit down.

"No need to sit down, *Dotô*" *Seu* Benedito waved his hat. He was unworthy of such courtesy; he just a fruit vendor of no distinction, begging for help, and in a hurry too. "Two days, *Dotô*, high fever, the runs, not eating. Sugar water and a bit of cornmeal that's all. Not getting up neither" *Seu* Benedito expounded in one breath.

"I see…" Doctor Leal's brows contracted. "Take me back with you, *Seu* Benedito" he proceeded. "I must examine your boy right away" and squeezing out of his office jacket he retrieved a worn out leather valise and a pelt hat from his desk.

"We're off—*vamos*—" Dr. Leal commanded stomping his chubby legs out the room nearly trampling over the incoming nurse as they crossed the reception area. "*Bom dia*, Alzira. House call" he tipped the pelt hat. "Hold the first patient if necessary, please" and quickly shut the waiting room door.

Down the stone steps the two men quickly winged to the right and strode by Ms. Cabral's schoolhouse. *Seu* Benedito took the lead to steer Dr. Leal to the right again and only stopped skipping at the unhinged gate. From there *Seu* Benedito ushered the doctor straight to the children's alcove.

Dr. Leal saluted *Dona* Dulce and the two yawning girls with a quick "*bom día*" and unfastened his leather valise. Solicitously, Dulce offered the doctor a stool, which he promptly accepted as a safer option than the dirt floor. He then bent over Daniel's ugly hammock while four pairs of anxious eyes observed each of his strange maneuvers. *Seu* Benedito, *Dona* Dulce and the girls had gathered around to watch Doctor Leal's undecipherable facial expressions. He turned Daniel aside, pressed his wrists, stretched his eyelids, and finally stuck a slim glass stick under his armpit.

Holding a metal ring attached to a pair of rubber cords the doctor quizzically padded Daniel's chest. At that point the apprehension in the room fermented like yeast. No one dared to breathe or exchange looks until Dr. Leal finally removed the stick from under Daniel's armpit. He held it against the window and finally spoke up. "*Seu* Dito, your son has typhoid fever."

"*Dotô?" Seu* Benedito cocked his head. "Fever? You mean the, The Fever?" he stepped a little closer to the doctor. "The, the, the very one?" he leaned on the hammock for support. "Going round, *Dotô*?" *Seu* Benedito stuttered like Ms. Cabral had recently done at school.

“What fever, Dito?” *Dona* Dulce pitched in not sure she understood fever had names.

“*Senhora*?” Dr. Leal’s brows arched in surprise. “You have not heard what is happening in town?” he removed the stethoscope and stared at her. “An epidemic of typhoid fever is sweeping through Lajedo.”

“*Dotô*” *Seu* Benedito sheepishly interjected. “She, my wife, she don’t get out much…” and shooting a frown back he gritted: “let the doctor talk, Dulce.”

Dumbstruck, *Dona* Dulce shifted her eyes from *Seu* Benedito to Dr. Leal. No one had ever mentioned those big words before. Typhoid? Epidemic? And when she returned *Seu* Benedito’s frown she was tempted to challenge him with questions of her own. “How can I know anything happening in town? Do I talk to anybody anywhere?” her eyes accused. “You always hurry us back here right after church” she wanted to say but this was not the right time. The doctor said something was wrong with her son and that was more important.

“*Dona* Dulce” Dr. Leal kept an even tone “typhoid is a disease one catches from contaminated, I mean, dirty water” he explained. “Because of the severe drought the *barreiro* is drying up fast and the water there is getting very dirty with germs. Boiling the water is best but sometimes not good enough to kill all the germs. If a person handles or drinks dirty water the germs can get inside the body. When that happens, the person develops a fever and some other symptoms just like the ones your boy has” he crossed his arms over his potbelly and went on to urge her to keep Daniel hydrated at all times.

“Give him plenty of boiled sugary water mixed with a pinch of salt since he has not been eating much” he encouraged. “Fortunately” he continued, “there is a new medicine available for sale at the clinic.

It is called antibiotics, *Seu* Benedito" he shifted his gaze to the man of the house.

"Make sure your son takes a spoonful twice a day every day for the next week. I will come back to check on him unless there is a turn for the worse" the doctor neatly stowed his tools inside the valise. He politely touched the brim of his hat and headed out of the alcove with a sympathetic smile.

A long trail of silence followed Dr. Leal outside. *Dona* Dulce felt like the annoying rooster was suddenly crowing inside her head. Its loud screech shook her thoughts out of place so fast that she forgot to thank the doctor for coming. She should have also offered him a cup of fresh coffee but it was too late now. Dr. Leal was already out of the gate with *Seu* Benedito in tow.

Dona Dulce planted herself by the front door. She struggled to sort out all of Dr. Leal's instructions trying to decide which one was first. "*Tibiotic* or sweet and salty water mix?" Meanwhile, *Seu* Benedito had returned with the brown bottle and a devised plan. "God is going to cure him, Dulce" he handed her the bottle. For a moment it sounded as if *Seu* Benedito might be feverish too. He looked agitated and his pitch oscillated from high to low in the same sentence. "This medicine is no good without God's blessing" he tugged one of the bureau's drawer and whisked his Bible out.

"No time to waste, Dulce. Hear me?" he leafed the thin pages and paced like a caged beast. "Right now we begin the right treatment. Go give him the medicine first, Dulce" he pointed at the brown bottle. "Go Dulce! What you waiting for? A spoon!" *Seu* Benedito barked and pushed her to the kitchen. "You Dalva, and you Delfina go on" he raised his hand at the terrified girls. "Go stand next to your bother" he directed them to the alcove. "In, right now, inside" he tapped their shoulders as if talking at untamed dogs. "Dalva, near your mother. There" *Seu* Benedito formed a circle in the room. "Delfina: right here by me" and still hugging his Bible *Seu* Benedito approved of the arrangement.

While *Dona* Dulce dispensed the medicine *Seu* Benedito searched for the fifth chapter on the Book of Job. "Ready?" he looked at *Dona* Dulce and began reading as if to a multitude. "*Happy is the one whom God reproves! The Almighty's discipline does not reject. For he wounds, but he binds up; he strikes, but his hands give healing*" he declared.

Downcast, *Dona* Dulce and the girls listened to the recitation and repeated it as instructed. Daniel captured the distant buzzing assuming the angel was now talking to him. He had no idea *Seu* Benedito had at that moment launched a new household rule to get him cured. From that day on the family had to gather around Daniel's hammock to pray, recite scripture and sing praises when it was time for him to take the medicine.

The next day, convinced his plan would generate better results if more voices joined in, *Seu* Benedito called on the church members for support. Many accepted the invitation, and in the evenings they came with Bibles to read passages on Jesus' healings of the sick. The list of miracles was long—the blind man, the leper, the Roman official's young son, and of course, Lazarus. "This sickness will not end in death" was a favorite verse out of John's gospel. After reading and praying, singing followed:

> "*There is pow'r, pow'r, wonder-working pow'r*
> *In the blood of the Lamb;*
> *There is pow'r, pow'r, wonder-working pow'r*
> *In the precious blood of the Lamb…* "

The joyous voices broke through the alley's nighttime stillness. A miracle was in the making. "Daniel would soon be cured for the Lord's Glory" Lajedo's Evangelicals encouraged one another before leaving the boy's bedside.

Within a week, Dr. Leal returned to the house as promised and could not hide his optimism. The fever had rescinded and Daniel, although visibly weak, was reacting nicely to the medicine and *Dona* Dulce's sugary drink. Doctor Leal upgraded the patient's condition from critical to stable. Another round of antibiotics was in order in addition to "whatever else you have been doing" he winked amusingly at *Seu* Benedito.

Sure enough, on the following Sunday what Lajedo's Evangelicals expected happened. Daniel not only opened his eyes but asked for food. He appeared a bit disoriented at first when *Dona* Dulce walked in the alcove with the bottle and the spoon. "*Mãe*, I'm hungry" he declared after swallowing a spoonful without assistance. *Dona* Dulce had nearly spilled everything at the sound of Daniel's voice. "Praise the Lord Jesus Christ" she put the bottle down and shot her arms up.

Out of her trembling lips words tumbled with an unprecedented vigor. *Dona* Dulce thanked God for being the first to witness His miracle, "*Father I thank you that you have heard me. I knew that you always hear me…*" was the scripture verse she recited. She knew all along that Daniel, her boy prophet, had been cured to preach God's salvation to the *sertão*. Once his story spread, Lajedo's Catholics would convert to the true faith. That had been God's purpose all along.

"Praise Jesus!" Dulce repeated barely able to hoist up. She bent over Daniel as she had done only on the day he was born and kissed his forehead. Warm tears trickled down her cheekbones and hit Daniel's lips. The sour taste made him pout. "*Mãe,* I'm hungry" he pulled away in disgust.

"Of course, son, right away—*filho*" she looked at him apologetically, wiping the tears off. In her haste to reach the kitchen *Dona* Dulce shook the hammock hard. Taken by surprise, Daniel almost fell off. To the stove she darted, throwing logs in the fire, then running out to the cistern she scrubbed her hands with coconut soap. With clean hands she carefully opened a sack of cornmeal and threw the yellow flower into the boiling water. She thickened the mush with milk, sugar, cloves and cinnamon just the way Daniel liked. The delicious oblation was placed in Daniel's firm grip. *Dona* Dulce marveled as if Daniel had never performed similar feat before. "Eat everything" she commanded after each scoop.

When *Seu* Benedito and the girls returned from church and *Dona* Dulce yelled as loud as she could: "Dito, girls, come see!" And the three of them barged in afraid of the worst. But to their complete amazement they saw Daniel reclined on the hammock holding a bowl and a spoon, his feet dangling off the floor without a care in the world. Dalva and Delfina immediately jumped, clapped, and shouted ignoring *Dona* Dulce's demand for silence. *Seu* Benedito, on the other hand, had stalled, frozen in place, saying nothing.

With a transfixed gaze he paced backwards one foot at a time grabbing the walls for balance in total dismay as if a ghost sat in the room. Out in the yard he fetched his Bible from underneath the donkey's saddle. Back inside he signaled for the circle one more time. Still speechless *Seu* Benedito gently motioned for *Dona* Dulce and the girls to kneel beside him and in a hushed tone he bowed his head. "The Lord is my shepherd; I shall not want…" he read. But the words quickly faded under his heavy breath. Thick tears rolled down *Seu* Benedito's face and dropped on the flimsy pages of his Bible. The rest of the verses blurred out of sight.

EIGHT

Indifferent to the outburst of emotions around him, Daniel continued to swallow the *mingau* and did not make anything of *Seu* Benedito's abrupt exit. *Dona* Dulce on the other hand, took advantage of the opportunity and began talking like never before. She needed an outlet for the suppressed anxiety of the last days and saved the children no detail of what had just transpired. Stunned at the fact that he had been so close to death Daniel listened and tried to picture being out of touch for so long. The last think he remembered was the painful headache and dry cough after school but had no idea he had fallen victim of his invented villain. "Son" *Dona* Dulce concluded her long exposition "the Good Lord saved you for a reason" and she dropped her gaze to the spot where Daniel's nevus hid.

Out at the alley *Seu* Benedito ran. As fast as his trembling legs allowed he had left the yard, shoved the gate open and broke in a frantic gallop towards Lajedo's Evangelical church. If he kept at it he would arrive in time to catch Pastor Santos and the Elders before their weekly business meeting adjourned. "God help me. Lord!" *Seu* Benedito gasped in between throbs. Pastor Santos had to be the first to know about Daniel's marvelous recovery. He had to come back with him and anoint the boy with oil one more time, *Seu* Benedito repeated until he stumbled over the church's locked door. Before banging against it he took a few seconds to wipe the damp off his frown and catch his breath. It would be sacrilegious to stir commotion inside God's sanctuary, so he ought to regain composure.

From deep inside muffled voices reached *Seu* Benedito's ears and he let out a sigh of relief. He was not late after all. Fat drops dripped embarrassingly from his reddened face and armpits. The straw hat appeared a suitable tool to fan out his lack of self-control and a prayer, of course. Like never before he needed peace. The one which surpasses all understanding so the words inside his head came out credible.

All heads turned inquisitively to the door when *Seu* Benedito knocked. Pastor Santos was the first to get up and after a quick glance at the widened eyes staring back at him, his brows arched. "Had the worst come to pass?" Pastor Santos wondered. "*Seu* Benedito?" he flung the door open. "What's wrong, Brother?" he immediately grabbed *Seu* Benedito's arm and pulled him inside.

"No, Pastor, nothing wrong, Praise Jesus" *Seu* Benedito shook his head and tucked his hat under his arm. He was bouncing from one foot to the other searching for the right words.

"What is it, Brother?" one of the Elders called out from the front.

"Pastor Santos, Brothers" Benedito's eventually cleared his throat though his voice still came out warped. "I ran over here as fast as I could" his arms now spread out, "because my boy Daniel" and then *Seu* Benedito yelled: "he is cured!" He scurried to where the Elders sat. "Brothers" *Seu* Benedito screeched "my boy is at home right now eating and talking like nothing was never wrong with him, Praise Jesus" a nervous smile broke on his sweaty face. "The miracle we prayed for, Brothers, came to pass, Praise the Lord Almighty" he nearly broke in tears again. Chairs were knocked over as the men pumped to their feet and huddled around *Seu* Benedito.

Jaws dropped with grins, hands shot up: "Hallelujah" they yelled in unison. *Seu* Benedito took the cue and swiftly reported on Daniel's sudden awakening minutes ago. Pastor Santos called the meeting out even skipping over the Lord's Prayer. He dismissed the Elders with specific instructions: spread the good news to every church member in town. Meanwhile, he would accompany *Seu* Benedito back home to rub more oil on Daniel's forehead, just in case.

Jockeying through Lajedo's twisty alleys Pastor Santos elbowed *Seu* Benedito's ribcage, pressing for particulars. The scalding sun seemed to be impairing the pastor's judgment for he now insisted the story be told to as many people and as soon as possible. "An out-door revival *Seu* Benedito" he wiped his face while thinking out loud. "Later this evening in front of your home since the boy is obviously too weak to go anywhere else" Pastor Santos spurted. "Don't you see?" he pulled *Seu* Benedito under the crook of his arm. "This is the perfect opportunity to draw a crowd, to proclaim the Lord's gospel! Your son's healing is unequivocal proof of His power over death!" he tugged *Seu* Benedito closer. "I will arrange for music, an accordionist, drum players, and singers. You, *Seu* Benedito make sure the boy is ready for an appearance" the pastor squeezed Benedito again. "I hope this is, you know, agreeable to you?" he glared. "We can use your kitchen table as a makeshift pulpit" he went on without giving *Seu* Benedito a chance to interpose.

"What do you say?" the Pastor paused for a mere second but still did not wait for an answer. "Would Daniel be comfortable sitting on a chair while I preach?" Pastor Santos slowed down a little. Honestly, if *Seu* Benedito could have it his way, a lay of hands and anointing of oil was more than enough. That's why he had rushed back to the church in the first place but how could a fruit vendor challenge the man of God?

"Well, Pastor…" was all *Seu* Benedito could come up with until he pushed the crooked gate open. "This way, *faz favor*" he evaded the preacher's arm on the way to the children's alcove. The early afternoon sun sprawled lazily down the cracked roof tiles disclosing the needle-shaped crevices on the peeling mortar. From his hammock, Daniel had been studying the changing patterns against the light when Pastor Santos rambled in. "There he is" Pastor Santos exclaimed at Daniel who was reclined but not quite dozed off yet. He wore a pair of clean shorts, which he urgently demanded as soon as he noticed the rags draped around his waist. With similar decisiveness he had also rejected *Dona* Dulce's offer for a shirt. "Too warm" he shook his head and crossed his arms defiantly. Afraid of upsetting him anymore she agreed as long as his hair was properly parted and combed.

"God Almighty!" the pastor clasped both hands under his chin. "A miracle indeed, *Seu* Benedito" he dabbed the corner of his eyes. "Blessed be the name of the Lord" he shouted. "Like nothing has happened" Pastor Santos affectionately squeezed Daniel's blushed cheeks unable to contain his elation. "You are a gift my boy; a gift from the good Lord above to us here in this sinful village" he ruffled Daniel's hair. *Dona* Dulce sniffled in exasperation and Pastor Santos finally acknowledged her presence. "*Dona* Dulce, there you are" he offered his hand for a shake. "I was just telling your husband…" and Pastor Santos related the plan for an outdoor revival gathering.

Dona Dulce nodded in agreement although she added a few non-negotiable conditions. "He can't be too tired, Pastor" she fingered Daniel's hair back in place. "Steady on the chair" she demanded.

"Perfectly fine, *Dona* Dulce" the pastor conceded. "No need to exert him though I must repeat he looks as good as new, thanks be to God!" he reached for the brown bottle in his pocket. "Before I leave let me rub your forehead, Daniel?" and bent over the hammock he uttered a heartfelt prayer.

"*Amém*!" the family complied.

The preacher shook hands with *Seu* Benedito and Daniel and headed to the door declining *Dona* Dulce's offer of fresh coffee. "Much obliged, *Dona* Dulce, much work to be done" he hurried out. "I will come back at five with a steady chair for Daniel. Promise!" he shouted from the gate. "Don't you worry about a thing" he rushed in haste.

Later on, punctually at five o'clock, Pastor Santos returned to the house on his old pick-up truck. Out of the vehicle's flatbed there jumped an accordion player, a drummer and two young ladies who had volunteered as crooners for the improvised ensemble. An oversized chair and an embroidered tablecloth also materialized from inside the truck's cabin.

While waiting for the preacher's next instructions the musicians strapped their devices on and began to warm up. The ladies shuffled through a hymnal discussing which numbers would best fit the fire and brimstone sermon Pastor Santos was known for. Not too far off a few neighbors peered out the windows attracted by the unexpected bustle. *Seu* Benedito met Pastor Santos at the gate to assist with the tablecloth and chair. "A table", the pastor yelled, "bring it to the curb, would you?"

By the minute both the drum and the accordion strikes boosted louder, drawing more snoopers from the alley. The nosy children Daniel used to dread crept closer in, wondering what the fuss was about in such a lazy Sunday afternoon. Most of them already knew the way to the gate but had never seen a truck parked there before. When the musical keys and voices found their harmonizing sequence the children followed the noise. It did not take long for the grownups to join them and speculate on what kind of concert was in the works. At the end of August there should be nothing else left to party over. *Carnaval,* Saint Joseph's, Easter and the June Feasts had all long passed.

Aware of the buzz, Pastor Santos and *Seu* Benedito offered to explain. Though it might look like it, this was not a pagan party. Rather an evangelical revival. If they stayed put or returned a little later, with friends and relatives too, they would hear first-hand about the miraculous event taken place inside the house. Trying his best to sound as cordial as the preacher *Seu* Benedito addressed the neighbors with uncommon deference.

"T's true" he tried to sound friendly. "God cured my son Daniel from the fever. Be here at six o'clock" he offered his callous hand for a shake. "Pastor Santos here is leading the worship and will tell you all about it, how my boy came back to life through the power of our Lord Jesus Christ" *Seu* Benedito sounded uncharacteristically articulate. "Please stay—*por favor*" he urged. "Six o' clock? Hang around if you prefer" and some turned their backs laughing at his clumsiness whereas others agreed to loiter. This could turn out to be another amusing spectacle sponsored by the peculiar Evangelical family.

Foot traffic increased when the church folks arrived. "God bless" they hugged and kissed one another joining in the improvised sing-along. Pastor Santos and *Seu* Benedito continued to encourage the passers-by to form a circle. In his twenty years of preaching in the *sertão* Pastor Santos could not remember the onset of a revival gathering as promising as this. Not even during election season, he reckoned, when the local bosses lured voters with free entertainment and handouts had a group this size gathered in such short notice. The Good Lord never failed to provide.

To keep up momentum Pastor Santos flagged both hands at the accordion and drum players urging them to repeat the line up as he continued to draw more people closer. Many responded to his animated pats and tugs under the mild August sunset right when the Virgin's protective dome gently descended on Lajedo. The bell of Saint Joseph's also added to the solemn atmosphere, followed by its daily *Ave Maria* rendition. The six resounding bangs brought Pastor Santos to his senses and he checked his watch. Perfect timing, he sliced the air above his head, and the musicians quit playing.

The sudden silence created a suspenseful anticipation. The air froze still when a sea of eager eyes turned to the draped table. Pastor Santos had reverently positioned himself behind it and *Seu* Benedito escorted Daniel out of the house. Whispers immediately erupted as if a cloud of furious mosquitoes hovered the circle. With another ominous gesture Pastor Santos urged everyone to hush and draw closer to the table. His grave voice eventually drowned the humming.

"Beloved, brothers and sisters in Christ, welcome" the preacher roared like a bailiff in a courtroom. "We are here today to worship the precious name of our Lord and Savior Jesus Christ, to give Him thanks for the miracle of life" he clamored while rolling his sleeves up to elbow length, ready for action. "Jesus Christ not only saves sinners, beloved, but also cures the sick, rebukes evil spirits, and raises the dead." The opening line had its intended effect as the *crentes* rejoined with heartfelt concurrences. 'Amen! Hallelujah! Praise the Lord!' "Praise Him indeed, beloved. As many of you know young Daniel here" the pastor pointed to this left "fell sick to the deadly fever a few days ago. He was seriously ill, brothers and sisters, unable to eat or walk" he paused for effect. "Now as you can all see" he stepped next to Daniel "this morning as a matter of fact, the Lord awoke this boy from a deep sleep and restored him to perfect health." The pastor ambled to the back of Daniel's chair and continued. "Tonight" he moved forward to where the audience stood "we gather here to proclaim Daniel's cure as a miracle of God!" 'Hallelujah! Amen! Praise the Lord!" the *crentes* rejoiced.

"Brothers and Sisters in Christ" the pastor elevated the tone. "I am here to tell you how this happened. You will indeed marvel at the infinite power of the Lord Jesus when you hear Daniel's story" he stretched his arms as if trying to hug the entire group. "But first let us raise our voices in grateful praise, shall we?" Pastor Santos turned to the musicians with another emphatic gesture. At once they responded and engulfed the confining alley with a cheerful vibe.

> "*Salute the name of Jesus,*
> *Archangels worship! Archangels worship!*
> *The King who was humiliated on the cross*
> *Glory to Him, Glory to Him*
> *Glory, Glory, Glory!*"

The large drum pounded in concert with the shrilling accordion as passionate voices flared. "*Glory, Glory, Glory!*" the cheerful praise reached its peak. Such rapturing words mesmerized Lajedo's Catholics who had never attended a religious service so animated. Those who had stayed to watch were not disappointed and their curious eyes riveted from the enthused preacher, to the elated singers and musicians.

Daniel, too, felt the impact of the thundering surge. The ground beneath his bare feet shook and tickled him with delight. A sudden current of energy shot up his head like lightening on a rod. "GLORY, GLORY, GLORY" Daniel's heart pounded at the same tempo of the drums. "BOOM, BOOM, BOOM."

What a thrill to feel his legs and arms alive again. If he did not hold firmly to the chair he might soar to the skies again. It had been so long to have vigor return to his body. With each breath the congealed lethargy on Daniel's joints dissolved. He also noticed his arms waver. Was he growing feathers again? The urge to fly returned as he looked at the wall of people before him. He had seen them during many feverish visions. The same loud instruments had played to that same melody except that in his dreams he was the one who spoke, not Pastor Santos. The words returned now as brightly as the full moon crowning over Lajedo's sky. "Glory, Glory, Glory to God who speaks through me. I am His messenger."

Thc music was dying out under another of Pastor Santos's dramatic signs. The sermon was about to begin and the pastor had just pressed down on the tablecloth, closed his eyes to pray when an unscripted change followed. Daniel leapt from his chair, unassisted, and threw a glowing stare at the onlookers. To everyone's astonishment his voice resonated strong as he repeated the words out loud: "glory, glory, glory to God who speaks through me. I am His messenger."

Taken aback the crowd gasped and recoiled. It took people a few seconds to identify who had spoken. "The preacher or the boy?" all faces turned for confirmation. On the first row a handful of *crentes* dropped to their knees and began babbling in a tongue other than Portuguese. Amidst the confusion *Dona* Dulce understood what was at stake. Her eyes locked into Daniel's and she nodded encouragingly. It was safe to proceed, she implied, and Daniel continued with impressive eloquence.

"People of Lajedo: listen up" Daniel pushed his right palm forward. "God speaks to me in dreams. He cured me from the fever so I can speak to you also. Before getting sick I thought the drought and the fever were my enemies. God wants me to fight but not these villains. The real fight is against sin. It's time people of Lajedo, to repent! This is God's will for all of you" Daniel pointed at the circle. "Repent" he shouted. "Join the Evangelical church" Daniel added through a penetrating gaze. Not only were the participants awed but Pastor Santos, too, seemed speechless for once. Nobody dared to move until a grave voice speared from the back: "*Amém.*"

From the middle of the circle a young lady rejoined, "Glory to God!" Someone echoed "Hallelujah!" In an instant more exclamations popped up like corn kernels in hot oil. "God speaks through the boy." "The boy is a prophet." "Yes, let's hear more from the boy" the demands for Daniel to continue fused with more 'hallelujahs.' A frightening howl shook Pastor Santos out of vacillation and he walked away from the table demanding silence. In vain the pastor tried to regain control of the tumult. His booming voice could no longer compete with the widespread frenzy.

Stretching their hands like beggars the villagers pressed onto Daniel. They pleaded for another revelation and in the thick of the commotion *Seu* Benedito cut through the crowd and scooped Daniel out. In panic *Dona* Dulce ran for the girls who had been briefly swallowed by the closing ring and dragged them both inside. She slammed the kitchen door and immediately took a headcount. They had all made indoors and crammed together by the woodstove.

Seu Benedito sat Daniel on one of the wobbly stools and sunk his long nails on the boy's shoulders, praying. "God deliver us from the snare of the trapper" he murmured. Like everyone else he feared a break-in. Dalva and Delfina hugged each other while *Dona* Dulce went through the house shutting windows. After the house plunged into darkness she reappeared with a kerosene lamp and broke the frightening stillness by handing each one a half-cup of sugary water.

Undistinguishable protests against Pastor Santos' orders of dispersal could be heard outside. Angry shouts penetrated the cracked shutters as the villagers insisted Daniel returned. They threatened not to leave until the boy prophet spoke again although the pastor affirmed there was nothing else to be said. Eventually, he struck a deal. The boy would speak again but not tonight. Next Wednesday evening everyone should gather at Lajedo's Evangelical Church.

Partially satisfied, the circle of villagers broke up under Pastor Santos's stern watch. Not until the last one left did the preacher turn around and discretely knocked on the front door. It was past seven o'clock when *Seu* Benedito cautiously ushered Pastor Santos inside making sure he was alone. Still trapped in the kitchen the family watched the preacher walk in and quietly refuse *Dona* Dulce's offer of sugary water. It was already too late for a visit, he argued.

Taller than the average *sertanejo* the Evangelical preacher stood out even when crouching on the stool *Seu* Benedito vacated. Daniel studied Pastor Santos, expecting a spirited report of the confrontation outside but the exhausted preacher well known for his eloquence chose simplicity this time. He grabbed a handkerchief and slowly wiped his forehead. Daniel could tell he was buying time before making an important announcement.

Tonight marked his second encounter with the preacher although at present he did not seem as elated. The pastor sat with both hands wrapped around his knees as if afraid of tipping. He had lost the imposing countenance everyone in the church admired him for. A former Catholic and partner at his family reputable law firm, Pastor Santos had given it all up to preach the gospel to the poor. In Daniel's case, he was about to explain, it would be no different. When God called, one had to answer even if a life of affluence and power must go. As the pastor often said earthly losses must be counted as gain. Embracing the truth requires ultimate sacrifices.

"*Seu* Benedito" Pastor Santos began. "I will be brief and clear" he looked straight at *Seu* Benedito's wrinkled face. "What happened tonight was a sign from God. He has a plan for your son. "No denying it after what we heard," he turned to the boy. "Daniel's life has been saved for a purpose; the boy said it himself. It is now up to us, *Seu* Benedito, to help him fulfill God's plan for Lajedo at this time of despair" he lifted his broad chest up and gently patted his knees. "I would like Daniel to speak at church next Wednesday and I hope you will consent. His story is a powerful testimony of God's grace, *Seu* Benedito. We need to share it with the lost. I believe this is the Lord's will" Pastor Santos concluded in a solemn tone.

The Pastor's speech enveloped the room like smoke from the woodstove at lunch time. *Seu* Benedito remained silent scratching his unshaven chin as if a mosquito had bitten it. He jacked up his head at the unfinished ceiling then down at the dirt floor, pacing. Daniel's future had already been decided, he kept on scratching. Sell fruit at the *feira*.

"He will be there, Pastor" Dulce's husky voice broke the stalemate with unexpected boldness. "What you said about Daniel, Pastor" she slashed the thick silence in the room "t's all true" she stepped right in front of the preacher. "I've known it for a long, long time. Since when he was in my belly" she hugged her stomach. "The Lord speaks to him in dreams, Pastor" *Dona* Dulce went on. "When my Daniel first learned to talk he told me them things he saw in them dreams. The boy was born to preach the Word and that begins next Wednesday evening, God willing—*se Deus quiser*."

NINE

Seu Benedito and Pastor Santos examined *Dona* Dulce's contour against the kerosene flame. The crisp and articulate speech out of her mouth did not match the feeble silhouette of an overworked backland housewife. Its dense authority had adhered to the walls like grease in a frying pan and stuck evenly to the corners of the kitchen when her pronouncement ended. Daniel was going to make an appearance at the church on Wednesday, *God willing*, had been *Dona* Dulce's final statement. The question at hand now was whether *Seu* Bendito and Pastor Santos should ignore or reprimand the insubordination.

Always struggling with what to say next *Seu* Benedito settled for the first option and turned his back on *Dona* Dulce. His head twitched in the direction of the front room and Pastor Santos understood the cue. The two men moved silently away from the dim kitchen while the lamp continued to burn on top of the stove. Daniel and the girls watched the shadows of tension dance around the walls unaware of how much their lives would change as soon as the front door clanked shut.

Out in the alley the moon's milky light and the tall preacher's head hovered over *Seu* Benedito with similar authority. Scattered stars dotted the dark sky as far as the eye could reach while the two men took some time to breathe the evening's temperance. The awkwardness bridging them needed to disappear if they were to speak candidly. After a few minutes of stillness Pastor Santos spoke up, resorting to whispers rather than abrupt gestures in hopes that *Seu* Benedito's uneasiness would turn to trust. Face to face they stood when the pastor offered a reassuring clasp.

"There is nothing to fear, *Seu* Dito" the preacher assured. His long fingers landed on *Seu* Benedito's hunched shoulders as he proceeded with care. "God is using us. All of us" the pastor pressed on a little more. "This is not about you, me, or Daniel" he paused. "It is about God's will and how we must carry it out. Do you understand, *Seu* Dito?" he waited for a nod. "Remember that it is during hard times that God reveals His plans best and there has been no harder time for us in recent years than this drought, this epidemic…" the pastor slowly released the grip.

The argument made sense and *Seu* Benedito took a step back as the moon shaft fell squarely on him. "Pastor" he timidly ventured "you are right and I think my wife, she is right too" *Seu* Benedito aimed his glassy eyes at the preacher. "But what do you want me to do?" his lips quivered with impotence. "You need to tell me what you want *me* to do" the shaking spread to this whole body. Dramatic Biblical scenes paraded inside his head—from the waves of a stormy sea where Noah's ark sloshed onto the the crashing wall of Jericho. Images of Lajedo's dead orchards and the *barreiro* came next. Were the drought and the fever also part of God's mighty act? If what the pastor said was right, if Daniel had indeed survived the fever for a reason, God must be in charge of the outcome just as it had happened in all those ancient moments.

If what happened today was part of God's will he knew better not fight it. Still, this was not exactly what he had bargained for. Who was going to help him at the *feira* from now on? Or fetch water and run household errands? It took the preacher a few other Biblical references to convince *Seu* Benedito Daniel had received a prophetic calling.

"Remember Samuel, *Seu* Dito?" Pastor Santos returned to scripture. When called, he was young to understand the demands ahead but all he had to say was "here I am, Lord" the pastor smiled for the first time. *Seu* Benedito nodded reluctantly at Pastor Santos' reference.

Within a week Daniel was healthy enough to leave the house and walk a path quite different than the one to the *barreiro*. The water-fetching and *feira* duties had prepared him well for the intense training Pastor Santos introduced, which included daily readings of scripture at his church office. Before long Daniel's natural aptitude for recitation took him away from home for prolonged hours at a time, which *Seu* Benedito secretly disapproved of but found disrespectful to contest. In the following months Daniel was increasingly exempted from all household chores so he could also accommodate Ms. Cabral's renewed pressure. As soon as Daniel told her about the church training she jumped at the opportunity to schedule supplemental instruction at the school. *Seu* Benedito came very close to declining the offer but could not come up with a convincing excuse. To deny her petition after having granted the pastor the same license would not hold as an argument with Ms. Cabral.

By year's end Daniel found himself busier than ever though with tasks superbly unrelated to those of man of the house. It was not easy for *Seu* Benedito to relinquish the help in a time when the drought's appetite for destruction had left the town's groves sterile. Travelling farther away each week *Seu* Benedito bore the heavy brunt stoically and on the occasions Daniel caught him grinding his teeth while dismounting the donkey he immediately warned Pastor Santos. Again, the pastor approached *Seu* Benedito with a deal. Some unemployed church members were willing to work in exchange for unsold fruit. "I will send them straight to the *feira* or the house whenever you need help, *Seu* Dito. Just say a word" the pastor asserted. "God sure hears prayers" *Seu* Benedito praised Providence's faithful assistance and grinded no more of his rotted teeth. After each passing year, he delegated Daniel's upbringing over to both Ms. Cabral and Pastor Santos.

Basking in the unprecedented attention and generous provisions of jerky beef, *qualho* cheese, and goat milk, Daniel latched onto his benefactors' abundance without sparing a thought about his family's deprivation. His secret collection of flatteries also expanded almost as rapidly as his waistline. Folks now called him the boy prophet for the right reason. No other child in town looked as well taken care of nor could match his achievements. Atop of a thirteen feet mountain Daniel delighted in the impression that Lajedo and all of the *sertão* envied him.

In those formative years Daniel's physical appearance also matched his godly calling. A preacher, Pastor Santos argued, had to look presentable and almost from the beginning of his performances Daniel replaced his tattered clothes for slacks, collar shirts and leather shoes. For *Dona* Dulce, the pastor's imposed dress code took more of her time. As Daniel grew taller and heavier she had to measure more, cut more fabric, and charge more to *Seu* Benedito's various accounts at the *feira*.

In preparation for Daniel's first church appearance *Dona* Dulce had agreed with Pastor Santos that Daniel's church clothes should always match his carefully washed, oiled and combed hair so no one would doubt God's hand rested over Lajedo's boy prophet. "He reads like a grown man" folks remarked that Wednesday. "Born for the pulpit" had been everyone's conclusion after the service.

All those years not once did *Dona* Dulce or *Seu* Benedito regret the overdrawn charge accounts. Daniel, also, began to feel more entitled as time went on. Whenever *Dona* Dulce's proud dark eyes reflected his growth Daniel felt vindicated soaking up the attention he had craved for so long. As soon as *Dona* Dulce stepped back wavering the kerosene lamp over his scrubbed face, she nodded approvingly "it's time" and wheeled him out the door.

In the backyard *Seu* Benedito stood by the saddled donkey patiently waiting. He, too, got carried away about Daniel's appearance and even before Pastor Santos insisted on retiring the boy's sandals *Seu* Benedito had laid a pair of lace shoes away with one of the *feira* merchants. When Daniel turned thirteen *Seu* Benedito also gave up the donkey's saddle.

Atop the beast's back Daniel nearly exploded with pride. "This must have been how the Lord Jesus felt on Palm Sunday", he mused while the skinny *jegue* crossed the crooked gate under *Seu* Benedito's harsh whip. In such moments of sacrilegious reverie Daniel remained oblivious to the donkey's lazy gait as well as of his father's yelling to keep the animal on a straight line. To the side, back, and front of him, a large cortege of pious villagers saluted his triumphal entry in his imaginary Jerusalem. Waving leather caps and wrinkled handkerchiefs Lajedo's villagers cheered their boy prophet, the one raised from the dead to preach God's messages. For years to come Daniel's delicious illusion was impossible to wipe off his tricky mind. Whenever he rode the donkey Daniel turned discreetly from right to left nodding and smiling at the invisible, adoringly crowd.

TEN

For the next three years, on any given Sunday morning and Wednesday evening *Seu* Benedito led the family on its solemn church-bound convoy. Atop the donkey Daniel sat lost in his pretentious reverie whereas Dulce, Dalva and Delfina lagged behind. When approaching Saint Joseph's tower Daniel invariably interrupted his musing and yielded to the beast's gentle sway to the right. Impossible to ignore, the tall structure crowned with its prominent bells demanding immediate acknowledgment from those below.

Lajedo's Evangelical church, however, was located far away from Saint Joseph's commanding location, invisible from the edge of the plaza. Once an abandoned warehouse, the modest meeting hall was squeezed in between the town's slaughterhouse and junkyard, stripped of any sanctity. If the local Catholics ever passed by the flimsy plywood door they would not recognize the place as a sanctuary. On the contrary, deprived of relics, stained glass windows or life size sculptures, the cavernous room would be taken as an affront to God's majesty.

When Daniel considered the shocking disparity between the two buildings he inevitably snapped out of his lofty Palm Sunday fantasy. He headed to that hole in the wall where half a dozen kerosene lamps barely disclosed a gloomy, suffocating ambiance. Admittedly, the same lack of spark affected the impoverished semi-literate flock inside. Those toothless grins gave Daniel the creeps and the urge to fly away returned. It was with reluctance that he dismounted the donkey and walked through the rugged benches, nodding and smiling at the squalid faces of famished sharecroppers. Was Daniel's story the answer to their prayers? If God saved him from death there was still hope for the rest of them.

In the years during which Daniel's tale spread through the backlands scores of *sertanejos* found their way to Lajedo's Evangelical church. From miles away they walked to the dim room to see the boy who had outlived the fever. At times when sitting became limited, the hopeful either squatted on to the dirt floor or lined up against the cob walls. In no other town had a destitute boy been able to read and speak like that. Until then, literacy had been a privilege of landowners, priests, and political bosses. "Who is this?" they all pried. "How does he do it?" they wondered. "He is the boy prophet" was the unanimous conclusion.

Within a year's time so many came to the church that Saint Joseph's priest found it imperative to admonish all Catholics against heresy's mortal dangers. Local authorities also joined the chorus warning everyone to stay away from the Evangelical rebels. This was not the first time the devil had misled against Rome's authority. *Crentes* were apostates, wolves in sheep's clothing. Wherever they went dissension erupted like poisonous weeds—*ervas daninhas.* Only fools believed the Almighty spoke through a destitute unlearned boy. "Do not fall for such travesty" the powerful warned.

Still, folks came. After Daniel's first full year of training with Pastor Santos more villagers converted. Others followed suit on Easter Sunday and requested to be baptized by immersion. For the first time they learned to read the Bible under Daniel's assistance as a Sunday school teacher. In no less than three years Pastor Santos's initial prediction turned into reality. Daniel began to preach the gospel without a script. His natural eloquence radiated through a falsetto tone, and to those who had been following Daniel from the beginning it was a thrill to watch the boy prophet become a charismatic preacher.

By the age of fifteen he had exceeded all of his mentor's expectations and impressed listeners with an engaging style. Able to measure the tempo of his speech Daniel captured his audience's attention by incorporating some of Pastor Santos broad hand gestures. Proper inflection and dramatic expressions turned paramount when relating his near death experience.

He usually began in a hushed tone to describe the onset of the fever and the long days of unconsciousness during which he plunged into total darkness. Then, moving on to a dramatic crescendo his voice filled the room as he related the day of his awakening. The concluding, gripping remarks always referred to the dramatic statement first uttered in the outdoor revival gathering: "glory to God who speaks through me. I am His messenger."

No eyes shifted except to respond to the altar call. Moved to tears, one by one, the sinners of the *sertão* walked forward and received Jesus as their Lord and Savior.

Years of widespread misery had confirmed to those who heard Daniel that God had handed him what the drought had taken away: grace and purpose. For those who stayed in Lajedo and patiently waited for a rainfall every year after March 19th Daniel's story encouraged endurance. When the feast of Saint Joseph neared the only enthusiastic person in town was the Saint Joseph's priest who insisted on parading the large statue around the plaza after Mass in front of a dwindling crowd.

Daniel was among the many who refused to attend the festival anymore. Instead of wasting time with paper lanterns and folk music he stayed behind cuddled with his Bible preparing for his Sunday's obligations. When morning dawned and no rain came he became convinced of the Catholic charade. As for the rest of the family they too woke up at the rooster's crow to repeat their church-going routine. *Dona* Dulce knelt at the stove kindling the fire while *Seu* Benedito hurried to the *barreiro*. For breakfast there was always a serving of manioc pancakes—*bijús*—sizzled in the large fry pan with a little butter, which was getting more difficult to buy. The mug of black coffee was also being served with less sugar but as soon as the potent aroma of brewed coffee engulfed the kitchen *Dona* Dulce yelled.

"It's time" she slapped the bottoms of Dalva's and Defina's hammocks first. "You, you and you, get up" and stooping over Daniel she carefully checked the signs. He usually looked dazed and his sealed eyeballs shifted fast. What *Dona* Dulce suspected was true: Daniel was at the end of another baffling dream. A blurry image blocked his mother's face as he labored to figure its meaning. When he finally lost track of it *Dona* Dulce called out: "you done, son?" and she let go of his hand as soon as Daniel opened his eyes.

With a long yawning he left the alcove for the outhouse and no longer forgot to wash his hands at the cistern. Over his dry pancakes and bitter coffee, he struggled to recall the overnight dream but his mind quickly went blank as attention shifted to girding him up. *Seu* Benedito would prop the washing tub in the kitchen while the girls filled it up with clean water. In the front room Dulce starched the collar shirt and slacks while yelling orders for the comb, coconut oil, and a quick shine of Daniel's lace shoes.

Moments later Daniel passed *Dona* Dulce's scrutiny and followed everyone to the yard. *Seu* Benedito thrust Daniel up the saddle and pulled the bridle hard to stay ahead of *Dona* Dulce and the girls. No matter how bigger their feet grew Dalva and Delfina always managed to lag. Along the alley Daniel nodded and smiled at this his imaginary cortege of cheerful hats and handkerchiefs until he reached the plaza.

On one special Sunday morning it so happened that as he stared far ahead, past the bell tower, Daniel noticed something different. A body of water glittered in the direction of the warehouse. "A sliver of water?" he squinted under the blinding sun.

When the donkey left the plaza behind an unexpected screech broke the stillness. Annoyed by the disruption Daniel jolted and turned back at the girls. Dalva was known for teasing him about a *cascavel* crossing over the path but this time around it was both girls shouting. "Look up" they pointed at the sky. Daniel obeyed and shaded his eyes with his hands. Straight above clouds churned slowly, blocking the sun.

A thick shade formed overhead, propelled by a sudden gush. Out of nowhere grayer clouds gathered fast. The girls looked at each other stunned. When they were about to ask *Dona* Dulce what was happening another screech blasted out. Dalva and Delfina covered their ears without dropping their eyes from the sky while a flock of *Asa Brancas* zoomed through the misty haze.

"Why are they back?" Daniel wondered. These birds had left Lajedo years ago when the drought first hit. *Seu* Benedito threw an astonished glance back at Dulce. "It's time" she waved him on.

All over the plaza trash from Saint Joseph's feast had not yet been cleared and the donkey trampled over lumps of corncobs and cigarette butts. Daniel also observed the lack of ornaments hanging on the church's front door. No wild flowers or colorful paper flags this year. So ironic the *Asa Brancas* flew over spoils of devotion to a deaf Saint Joseph. He had done the right thing by staying home cramming the passage for today's service.

Pastor Santos had settled for a passage from chapter eighteen in First Kings, which Daniel had memorized the night before. The verses referred to Prophet Elijah's call for rain after a long, judgmental dry spell in ancient Israel. The pastor found it an appropriate reminder that rainfall is under the Lord's command, not Saint Joseph's:

> *"And it came to pass at the seventh time that he said, behold, there arises a little cloud out of the sea like a man's hand. And it came to pass in the meanwhile that the heavens were black with clouds and wind, and there was a great rain."*

Daniel looked up again and slapped his forehead. *"Claro!"* he gasped as the images from his last dream flashed back. He had seen those dark clouds, and heard the loud birds already. The dream warned him about what was about to happen today!

In front of the plywood door Daniel quickly dismounted. He no longer doubted the dark clouds, the wind, and the *Asa Brancas* meant rainfall was on the way. God had sent him the message to be delivered at once.

While Benedito stood by the door waiting for *Dona* Dulce and the girls, Daniel stormed into the dim room nearly stumbling over one of the rear benches. Blinking hard in all directions he searched for Pastor Santos who should be there, somewhere.

"*Ai!*" Daniel recognized the tall frame crouched up front and bustled straight over.

"Pastor, Pastor" Daniel called out and shook his mentor out of deep contemplation. No longer able to contain the excitement he shouted: "rain will fall on Lajedo today, Pastor. The drought is no more—*A seca acabou!*" he declared.

PART II

THE NOVICE

"And what you thought you came for
is only a shell, a husk of meaning
from which the purpose breaks only when it is fulfilled
if at all. Either you had no purpose
or the purpose is beyond the end you figured
and is altered in fulfillment. There are other places
which also are ***the world's end****, some at the sea jaws,*
or over a dark lake, in a desert or a city (...)"

(T.S. Eliot, *Little Gidding, I*)

ELEVEN

It must be Sunday morning. She is here in the alcove with my church outfit in hand. Buried inside the hammock I glimpse at her bare feet. They scurry over. A nudge on my left arm tells me she is beside me. Her voice quivers and the whole room trembles. "IT'S TIME."

I can't get up. A blow on my bottom is coming but when I crane over there is no one there. The alcove is ghostly empty.

Mãe?

No one is here. Not in this room or anywhere else in the eerie house. Have they all disappeared? I could swear she walked in here a minute ago. She has never been careless about my clothes. Why are they lumped up on the floor? They look like trash. Dirty rags like that stray dog.

LIXO.

Hop down. Alone to be dressed? Why am I shivering in this steaming heat? Shoe hanging off a foot. The other? Unlaced.

Pai? Mãe? Dalva? Delfina? Your silence fills my ears. My startled voice ripples off the crumbling walls. It bounces off in all directions. I gotta go. Did they leave me behind?

Glide.

Dim, deserted kitchen. Cold stove. Stupid donkey grazes around the dry well. What you looking at? Glazed eyes, gooey mouth. Pathetic. Foolish beast, only fur and bones. Where is everyone?

Look!

Under the scrawny graviola tree. The dry well is shut. Stupid old jegue is thirsty. For many of my questions there are no answers only assumptions. He nods and smiles.

It's time?

Clouds scatter across the light blue canopy. The sun beams so confidently. A breeze tickles the clouds, merging the puffy shapes. A pau-de-arara trolley arrives, packed with retirantes. It breaks through the vapor and turns into an Asa Branca. Large white-trimmed feathers flutter with purpose. They coo raucously behind my cupped ears. My neck stiffens. The rowdy Asa Brancas zoom by.

Keep looking!

Cheerful cries stir the hot air. Can't be. All birds abandoned Lajedo long ago. Why are they back today? Stupid jegue, why you grin? Long pink tongue disgusting with saliva and dirt.

Ai!

Mount, "it's time." Don't waste any. Don't be late for church. Where is father? Grab the rein. Move. Out of the yard, to the alley, straight to the plaza. Pay the Asa Brancas no attention. Enough fuss already.

Ai, I gotta scream!

The bells. Why is this stupid beast turning left? The birds too. Wrong way. I yank the bridle. To the right, you beast. To the church! Is this animal deaf?

No! Not to the barreiro. To the Church. Why is the plaza fading behind me? Lajedo is disappearing. Where is the graveyard? The bells?

The feira? Only dead shrubs ahead. This stupid donkey wants to chew on brown leaves? Come on!

Keep on, it's time. Over the clearing is the big desert—the sertão. Nothing but agony grows there. Now I'm thirsty. My head aches. So lonely. Where is this jegue going? Why is he after these crazy birds?

Look!

The mandacarú cactuses. We've gone too far.

Have I been here before? Look at the leafy trees, the budding flowers, the tall boughs! White and red petals fall like rain drops over the moist grass. Are the trees standing in attention, bidding me farewell?

Son, you dreaming?

I know this husky voice! Why is the sun talking to me?

Listen!

The Asa Brancas chirp at the clouds, playing a game of hide-and-seek. Why are they luring the donkey so far away?

'Follow us out,' they say.

Behind the green shoots a gang of peasants point at the talking birds. They look at the sky and smile. Farm tools on their backs they head for the orchards.

Why bother? There are no more seeds left.

Stupid donkey is going too fast. I wannna scream.

Back to Lajedo! The other way, I yell inside my head.

My tongue is flat dry. No sound comes out. I turn back for one last glance at the blooming forest.

It is a hazy mirage. The dim church hall is packed. People's eyes are shut and they sing: "Nearer, my God to Thee, nearer to Thee" My favorite hymn. I choke up trying to yell again.

Stop it. Let me off!

Mist gushes out of my lips. I gasp, I pant, and the donkey gallops. Its legs leap the dust. I see nothing ahead.

Lajedo is no more… Saint Joseph's Church, Ms. Cabral's schoolhouse, the feira, the church hall, dissolved in the dust. Where is this beast taking me?

The sun turned dark. How long have I been gone? A sheet of lead rises before me. Night is falling in the middle of the day. Fat drops fall. A clap echoes. Rain? Thunder? Where are my wings when I need them?

I jump off but my legs don't move. Tears puddle between my lips. Where did the donkey go? What now? Am I crying or is it the rain? My bones are drenched under my clothes. I run without moving. Stuck in the mud.

A silver truck is parked in the clearing. I am so lost, so confused, so far away from home. How do I go back? The driver calls my name and points at the block words on the windshield. "RIO DE JANEIRO, CAPITAL."

Climb on.

I obey. Hunchbacked and defeated I scan the lengthy corridor inside. Tall chairs align in pairs all the way to the end. I am the last one in. I take the window seat next to an old man. The driver pulls a long handle and bangs the metal door shut. He steps on the pedal attached to the floor and jerks a large stick at the same time. The smoky truck jolts back away from the curb. The smell of diesel burns my nostrils. I lean on the window. Queasy. I hold on for dear life.

My clothes are dry now. A white dress shirt under a black suit and matching bow tie just like Pastor Santos wants. My feet are trapped inside a pair of shinning shoes, anchored to the trembling surface. My wristwatch lets me know it is late in the afternoon of which day and month I have no clue. I touch my prickly face. A string of hair is lining my upper lip. I keep hearing the birds and thrust my head out the window. Pastor Santos is waving behind the smog and the Asa Brancas.

The truck is moving so fast, like a flying carpet. It cruises along a smooth road sandwiched between the lush forest and the blue ocean. The sun pours down without burning the dense foliage. Cities, large and small, flash by my window. Cars and buses hurry back and forth. Everyone is moving in some direction or another.

Which one is mine? I turn to my seat companion. Maybe he knows where the truck is going. He looks at me, perplexed as the donkey. Points at the block letters stenciled on the windshield. "Why son, we are on the way to Rio de Janeiro!"

This must be a mistake. I live in Lajedo. My tongue is dead and I hear a loud beep through the window. More birds? Beep, beep, beep. My eardrums will explode. Beep, beep, beep…

TWELVE

"Daniel?" the tone in no way resembles mother's bottled down agony.

"Brother?" the word carries an unfamiliar tenderness.

"Wake up!" the pitch is high and joyful. "Your alarm clock has been buzzing for ages" a gentle nudge follows. "If you don't get up now you will be late for Old Testament class" a round grin looms over my slumbered eyes. I slant lazily up and begin to piece the moment together.

"Brother, clock, class" I manage to string all into context. The face talking at me is Antônio's and with a sigh of relief I recognize my roommate. He is now jokingly slapping my chest with a pillow urging me to hurry, get up, and please turn that obnoxious alarm off. I remember having set it for six the night before and, what you know, the culprit has obeyed my command. It has been ringing for the past five minutes or five hours?

I slam the metal pin down to cut the nuisance and jump out of bed giddy, dodging Antônio's playful blows. Grumbling my way to the communal bathroom at the end of the hallway, I escape Antônio's strikes. I look forward to the cool water that will freely spray down the showerhead. I yearn for the gleaming drops of clarity that will unscramble my thoughts.

Crisp and cleansing the jest generously flows over my body without missing a spot. The sensation reminds of the spontaneity of rainfall restoring life to the parched *sertão* soil. For obvious reasons I have never taken the flow of water for granted before. This novelty—the indoor shower—continues to astound me with its promptness. At the same time, it triggers some uneasiness. What if the water breaks off before I rinse the lather off? I am still not used to the consistency of plumbing. It's hard to relax beneath the nozzle. One of these days I will stand under the bountiful gush without any fears of interruption.

Since I arrived in Seminary I must shower often. At least twice a day I slip into the tiled stall of the dorm bathroom. My roommate Antônio can't fathom my fascination with this contraption let alone can he validate my compulsion to use it whenever I get a chance. When I marvel about the gadget's function Antônio rolls his pale green eyes. He will never understand that where I come from fresh water is a rarity. Out of his thin rosy lips all I get is a sympathetic 'tsk-tsk' as if he were saying 'whatever…'

Come to think about it the shower is not my only source of wonder on this campus. Since I arrived at Rio de Janeiro's Evangelical Seminary there has not been a day without a stunning revelation. I am relearning to perform trivial tasks in the most unimaginable ways. An indoor toilet instead of the outhouse and soft pillows above a padded mattress are a few of the most remarkable extravagances around here. Little by little I ease into the new habits but must admit that the abundance of water is by far what captivates me the most.

No matter where I go on our spruced up oasis there it is: at my fingertips, spurting from faucets, spigots, jugs, and drinking fountains as if obeying a supernatural command.

If folks in Lajedo knew how inexhaustible water in the city of Rio de Janeiro is, they would probably swear the interstate bus I boarded in Recife dropped me off in paradise instead of Brazil's capital. That is why the slightest squirt of moisture on my skin carries my thoughts back home, to those who will never learn about the purpose of metal pipes, sprinklers or garden hoses. Sometimes I do feel awkward whenever a drop of moisture hits my charred hide. Do I deserve such privilege? Should I gulp the glasses of crystal clear water from the fountain next to my room without giving it much thought? Around here these are deeds taken for granted but when it is my turn to pretend I am used to them, embarrassing gestures give me away.

I usually look around to make sure no one can read my distorted face while remembering the devastating drought, the one that almost killed me. When I bend over the water fountain snippets of life in Lajedo pop up. There I am again shouldering my family's hope for survival feeling overwhelmed by the weight on my back and the despair framed on Lajedos villagers' faces. The unwashed, malnourished bodies fuse with the withered landscape, and the stench of the dead animals. When I watch my classmates stroll by these manicured lawns laughing and horsing around as if life were supposed to be this *pleasant.* I also feel the thorny texture of the *barreiro* tickling my soles.

"What am I doing here?" I wink at the enormous mango trees lining the hills behind our campus, knowing that those sensations are forever sealed in my body. Until I arrived here, it had never occurred to me that people could live any other way. I had never fully comprehended why the *retirantes* gave up and left Lajedo until I took my first cold shower in a tiled bathroom stall. An epiphany of sorts overcame me as I realized how cheated I had been all along.

So, whenever I stand here, foamed up and puzzled, I wrestle with these thoughts. My stomach tightens as I consider the contradictions between the two distant universes: Lajedo and Rio. One cursed with absence the other blessed with abundance. Why does God wait so long to pull His children out of the wilderness? When I watch my classmates carry on so leisurely with life I want to shout: "have you any idea of how lucky you are?"

They have no idea that thousands of miles away in a place called *sertão*, children, men and women are born doomed. When asked where I come from, heads shake quizzically, "Lajedo?" and I must elaborate on the geographic coordinates. No one seems to know where the state of Paraíba is on the map. "A couple of states north of Bahia on the border with Pernambuco," I catch myself explaining. "Ah…" they sigh indifferently as if I were referring to another planet in the solar system. It's not their fault though. I am the one who doesn't fit in their orbit. The fact that I actually got here is the real enigma.

A good cold shower in the morning usually helps washing my shame away.

Every time I scrub my face clean the two worlds split apart. Lajedo and Rio, north and south, desert and forest, hades and heaven. They can never be bridged. I don't want anyone here to know that not too long ago I read under a kerosene lamp and hauled stagnant water on my naked back. By the way, I could spend my whole day flipping wall switches just to watch glassy light bulbs sparkle. Inside our classrooms the wall-mounted fans also move at the command of our fingers and the same happens to the tall lampshade by my bedside.

As I doze off to sleep, I see Lajedo's alleys juxtapose with Rio's cobblestone avenues. The dusty pavements and the jammed roads form ghostly shades on the wall and I drift in between the two labyrinths, trying to find my way out. During the day I take it all in stride but at night I struggle to process this life in exile. Baffling dreams return as I try to relive the scenes of my departure and if it were not for the sound of my alarm clock early in the morning I would not be able to discern whether I sit dumbfounded inside the interstate bus or lie comfortably flat on a spring mattress.

Now here I am, staring at the mirror trying not to cut my face with the metal razor Antônio taught me to use. How does this thing work again? Not sure I have to twist the bottom so tightly. There. Got it. Another trick I ought to master. It's time! I must get dressed before the chapel bell. Cannot afford to be late for Old Testament and disappoint my instructor. Low marks and tardiness are out of the question and would also be perceived as ingratitude to Pastor Santos and the Northeastern Evangelical League Board. Thanks to their monthly support my Seminary training is fully covered.

Looking into this mirror now, I realize my life is indeed a miracle. Not only did I survive the fever but made out of Lajedo after all. I am now enrolled in the country's leading preacher's college, living in the big city of Rio de Janeiro never to return. That is if I play my cards correctly.

Moving so far away to attend Seminary did take me by surprise. I was given only a few months to warm up to the idea while Ms. Cabral launched a brutal preparation for the qualifying exams. As usual she told me not to worry because I had what it took to impress the League's Board. Goodness, all I did was study.

In the end Pastor Santos could not hide his pride telling me I had passed both the written and oral tests with flying colors. I had no idea then that I would have to travel alone for so many days. Two long thousand kilometers separate me from Lajedo but I wished this soap bar could scrub the frightening bus trip off my head. I also wished it would make me stop dreaming of those things I must forget. Pastor Santos's last eager wave at the station platform is one of them. Did it ever occur to him then that I might not want to return to take his spot behind that cheap church lectern? I suspect his parting gift was meant as a subtle reminder.

I need to wind it up so it doesn't trick me into believing I am late again. It is six forty and Old Testament begins punctually, top of the hour. I need to rush and get dressed. I hear no more chatter in the hallway. Am I the last one out? No hair pomade today then. Will flatten my hair with the wet comb instead. Wait, at least a splash of aftershave. There: not bad, Mr. Reverend. Not bad at all for a wild *cabra* who had not tasted mint-flavored toothpaste until a few months ago. Bow tie? Check. Belt? Check. Shoes? Check. It's time! Breakfast will have to wait until recess.

THIRTEEN

Fortunately the lecture hall is not far from my dorm. A few wide strides and I cross over the smooth green patch of grass in the middle of the courtyard. I adamantly overlook the sign "DO NOT STEP ON, PLEASE" and dash. It's time. I must run as fast as I can to beat *Senhor* Grant, the elderly American missionary, to the door. Unlike us Brazilians *Senhor* Grant can be unforgivingly punctual. At seven o' clock when the chapel bell announces the beginning of a new day, he locks the door. "A pastor is never late" he admonishes while twisting the key. That might be true back in America but here in Brazil, give me a break, *Senhor* Grant, and I glance at my wristwatch. Two minutes to climb the neatly painted steps and claim my seat.

I sincerely hope not to snooze while Mr. Grant lectures. Sometimes his foreign accent is impossible to understand and it sounds like he is chewing a mouthful of uncooked rice. Honest to God, I try my best to follow the obscure dictations with my own Bible but in the process of moving my index finger over the narrow lines I crouch so close to the pages that before I can help it, I am dozing off. *Ai!* Not sure whether I am cut out for seminary.

One…two…three. My watch is on time, thank you, Pastor Santos for the perfect go-away gift. Time is since strapped around my wrist, which is great for calculating the next move. See? *Senhor* Grant is now at the door and returns to his desk. Seven o' clock on the dot and he will call names that only exist in his fabricated diction. I do feel bad for the man when the whole class breaks out in chuckles as *Senhor* Grant gurgles the "Rs" and skips the "Hs." Our silent 'H' never fails to throw him off track. An eternity of ten minutes passes, according to my watch. Now *Senhor* Grant's voice transitions from one incongruent vibration to another. His sluggish yelps resonate as if from underneath a tight muzzle, rising and dropping with each deep sigh. From verse to verse he takes us through chapter two of Exodus—Moses's wicker box floating at the bank of the Nile. The simple mention of water is enough to highjack my thoughts to the *barreiro*. Before the old man gets going about Pharaoh's daughter providential rescue I find myself dunking my toes deep into the soggy mud. Rusty buckets dingle on my back and I lower them below the opaque surface.

Above the raised platform *Senhor* Grant's hypnotic recital fades into a murmur. He is moving through an endless string of mispronounced terms, which in the end assure me that Moses's good fortune is the least of my concerns. What I really want to know is why was baby Moses the one delivered, and not me? Away from the banks of the *barreiro* I trek under the roasting sun. Sweat is dripping down my forehead. I nearly faint, and fly away. Not even then did God send somebody to give me a hand.

My watch tells me to hang on for another twenty minutes. Painful twists in my gut protest against the suggestion but I am used to waiting. When the bell buries *Senhor* Grant's voice I will be free.

Seating beside the door is convenient for a quick exit and I will execute the maneuver with precision. Going to the dining hall for meals is as refreshing as my frequent showers. I must admit that not having to wait for someone else to sit down before I eat is a relief especially at breakfast when I am starving. Antônio has taught me to dunk the fresh buttered French bread into the steaming cup of sweet coffee and milk. He claims that soaked bread is easier to swallow and I agree that there is something special about how easily the soft pulpy texture travels down my throat.

The dining hall is one of the few spots on campus where we can break loose from the regimented prudish routine of the ministry and socialize. During mealtimes the kitchen aids turn our short cafeteria visits into rare moments of innocent frolicking. Most of the servers are eager to please us future Reverends and don't even wait for our coffee demitasses to go empty. They somehow predict the time of a refill and glide about the room with a thermos in hand as if they were pollinating butterflies.

Getting our cups refreshed is the perfect excuse for small talk with the young ladies, which I find no harm with. Antônio, on the other hand, is a bit shy and rarely returns the attention. He never risks a smile or a quick brush of hands whenever the coffee is poured. One of the aids in particular is very kind. Her name is Lúcia (or Lurdes?), and she speaks with a thick *Carioca* accent putting an "X" sound at the end of every *S. "MaiSS café?*—more coffee?" and I can't resist the hissing. Antônio, who has heard that all his life, sees absolutely nothing charming in it.

This Lúcia (or is it Lurdes?) wears her straight black hair down her hips. She tucks some behind her ears just like my mother used to and when she bends over our table her charcoal eyes twinkle with deference. I wonder whether she is Catholic or *crente*. She could also be *macumbeira* for all I know. She might even practice that disgusting voodoo and litter the crossroads with burned chicken, yellow *farofa* and candles. Those people actually believe spirits from beyond return to feast on the horrendous platters in exchange for miracles. Broken hearts or bones are supposedly mended as long as the menu is right. If Pastor Santos saw any of these pagan displays he would call for an emergency revival meeting. Exorcizing wickedness could turn into a full time job in this lost city.

The tiny pointer hand on my watch tells me I can begin the countdown to the bell strike. *Senhor* Grant's arched shoulders turn to us and my fingers tumble impatiently on the desk. Oh, no! He is adding more terms to the chalkboard. Should probably copy them down before closing my notebook out. "Covenant", "commandments", "monotheism." Will look them up more carefully later. Midterms are approaching and I am determined to ace each one of them, no exception. Ms. Cabral used to say I am a swift learner. So far my scores do confirm that. I am at the top of my game whereas Antônio, poor fellow, needs to go over and over every detail on his study sheets.

Three, two, one… It's time. "BANG." *Senhor* Grant's bony fingers halt and the white chalk falls on the board ledge. He paces to the door and unlocks it. "*Boa dia, todas*" he waves at us without realizing why the whole class cracks up. My stomach is tearing me. Oh, is that Antônio behind the column? Heads are bobbing everywhere. Of course it's him. Who else would smile like he just came out of a *carnaval* ball rather than a theology class?

"*Oi!*" I mouth back and raise my hand halfway not quite as jubilantly. "You made to class in time sleepy head?" he greets me with a soft slap on the shoulder. I nod, smile, and push us along the edge to avoid a stumble.

Fortunately Antônio is keeping up pace and we both step out the narrow hall in one piece. The late May sun greets us gently. I hear someone behind me rave about autumn though I am not sure what that means. Lajedo has only two seasons all year round: rain or no rain. I assume the fellow refers to one or the other.

"Good morning, gentlemen" a friendly hiss trails in our direction. "Coffee?" the girl beats us to the table. Her lustrous eyelids blink.

"Yes, please—*por favor"* I sound eager and pull the chair out. "That is enough, *obrigado*—thank you" I cover the demitasse. For a split second our eyes lock.

"*Irmão*—Brother" Antônio begins chattering. "You made it to class after all, huh?" he takes a long whiff at the breadbasket and takes a warm baguette out. The round butter dish is where he directs full attention now while I blow away the rising steam keeping track of our server.

"Barely" I say after a quick sip. "I keep having this awful dream and can't hear the buzz. Thanks for saving my skin again, Brother" I nod and smile.

Antônio smiles back approvingly at the sound of the word Brother. I am finally adapting to Seminary jargon and Antônio is pleased. When we first met he offered me a few basic survival tips and one of the first was to always call a fellow student *irmão*." Our instructors believe brotherly behavior is as key element of discipleship. We are part of Christ's family united in the sacred mission of the gospel, they often remind me. To be quite honest I feel somewhat awkward calling Antônio my brother since we have met only a few months ago, and definitely do not look alike.

At any rate, Antônio not only calls me brother but acts like one. A couple years older than I he is just a sophomore who never uses his seniority against me. I secretly envy his humility and blind devotion to the Evangelical cause. His sincerity and commitment are so obvious. Near him I feel like an impostor. He has a genuine zeal for the salvation of others and strives to be like the Lord. No one else has made the decision for him either and this is one of the reasons I envy Antônio. His honesty is intimidating.

I have never thought someone could be this tall, bulky and yet meek. His round, moon-shaped face radiates pure contentment and when he greets someone it is usually with a firm handshake followed by a tight *abraço*. What makes Antônio cheerful all the time is a mystery. Is it faith or purpose? From what he tells me his upbringing has been uneventful. His father owns a grocery store in the outskirts of Rio where he was born and raised. Neither as a child nor now as an adult has Antônio ever lacked provisions of any kind, I presume. Each of his hundred kilos can vouch for that though he is incapable of bragging about his family's affluence.

On the contrary, he is unassuming and kind to all regardless social standing, skin color or education. He even feeds the stray cats roaming the grounds from his own plate! To me this is a terrible waste but I have given up protesting it. This is Antônio: a true Christian no matter what.

On my first day he volunteered to escort me to our dorm room. Along the way he pointed at all the important landmarks on campus: "dining hall to the right, chapel ahead, and lecture building and the library on the left." Having been a resident for a year he knew the premises and the students quite well. Not once did he complain about the weight of my suitcase, which he insisted on carrying up the flights of stairs. At the room entrance he held the door open for me, and let me choose between the two twin beds even if that meant he had to give up his. "As long as you are comfortable, Brother" he said at the doorframe. I could not believe my ears and without giving the matter a second thought I took the bed by the window. "All yours" he immediately pulled off the sheets.

Since that first encounter Antônio has treated me as the brother he calls me. For the most part he gives and I? I take it. Greedily, hurriedly, shamelessly and we both seem quite *comfortable* with the arrangement.

"*Irmão*, would you like to come home again with me this weekend?" Antônio asks me as he scoops more butter over his second slice of French bread. He can eat a whole baguette loaded with *Minas* cheese and ham every morning.

"Oh yes, *obrigado*" I readily accept the invitation. "It is always nice to eat homemade food for a change… I mean" I quickly rephrase "it is such a pleasure to visit with your parents."

"*Ótimo,*" Antônio wipes his greasy lips and gives me two thumbs up. "Let's catch the four o'clock tram at the square and head over to the Central Station" he repeats the instructions every Friday. "If we board the six p.m. train there should be plenty of time to be home for dinner at eight o'clock" he continues as if I have no idea of the plan. "Bring your Bible along, will you?" Antônio chews fast. "We can discuss some of the passages Mr. Grant read in your class today" he dunks another slice of bread into the coffee and milk. "I find him so knowledgeable about the Old Testament, don't you Brother?" a poweful bite follows. "Pity" he says after swallowing "I did not pass his class with a better grade. There is so much I still need to grasp" Antônio looks into the breadbasket contemplatively, not minding that his blond bangs drop over his eyes.

Eventually he takes another piece out, butters it thick and dunks it into the cup. It amazes me how casually Antônio surrenders to mediocrity and empty chatter. Yet, his boring company is not a bad price to pay for a change of scenery in the weekends. When he invites me for sleepovers at his parents' I know my free time is compromised. Antônio never relaxes from his evangelist zeal and unfortunately finds great delight in shifting from one theological doctrine to the next during our train rides. While he talks I nod and smile, keeping my mouth busy with roasted peanuts I buy before we climb to the platform. Hot toasted peanuts are the best excuse to remain silent.

"More coffee, *senhores*?" the sweet hum returns to our table. Is it Lúcia or Lurdes? She offers us more coffee.

"No, not for me, *obrigado*!" Antônio pushes the chair far from the table so his stomach is released in one try. "Greek next" he lets out a loud burp. "Pardon me" he covers his mouth and tucks the chair back under the table. "How about you, Brother?" his blond hair flings back.

"Well" I glimpse at my watch. "I will have a little more coffee" and lift my cup in a salute. "Still have a few more minutes before Protestant Philosophy" I nod and smile.

Antônio's clomps fade behind my chair and I am left alone to muster all the courage gained from the coffee jolt to ask a question I rehearsed for the past few days.

"So, what is your name, *menina*?"

"Lurdes, *Senhor*"

“Lurdes?” I nod. “Please, Lurdes, don’t call me sir. It’s Daniel” my dimples show.

“Is the coffee hot enough, huh, Daniel?” her tone is smooth and servile.

“It’s delicious, Lurdes” I clack my tongue in appreciation.

“Well then… Daniel” she chuckles “let me know when you need more” she lifts the thermos.

“I will, *Obrigado*—thank you” I track her moves.

Since when has coffee tasted this sweet? Its warmth gently envelops my tongue and slides down my tickled throat. A timid voice inside me begs Lurdes to bring me more of what she has just dispensed but I gaze at my watch again. It’s time. The tiny pointer ticks on and compels me to move. Out in the courtyard I trip over the ‘DO NOT STEP, PLEASE” sign and keep going.

FOURTEEN

Antônio's home is tucked in the folds of Rio's northern hills. An hour's ride from downtown's *Central do Brasil* Rail Station it is part of a peripheral area of the city known as *Zona Norte* where I finally find much needed relief from the overwhelming rush of feet and wheels surrounding our Seminary. I look forward to these Friday escapades when I unplug from the urban jack and slow down from the weekly pressure. As soon as the train lurches off the platform my thoughts shift from our regimented routine to the bounce of prolonged leisure.

In route, I ease into the exquisite anticipation of untimed laziness and possible amusement. Two days without instructors, staff or my watch telling me what to do and where to go, *ai!* From Monday through Friday all I hear is the scripted demands: "read, write, pray." I rarely have a moment to sit down under the courtyard *Ipês*. Why put benches there, anyway? I feel like a soccer ball kicked in a match with no half-time. To the chapel (forward), to the lecture hall (dribble), backtrack to the library (pass), cafeteria break (score!). I compulsively wind up my wristwatch to avoid being late and before I know it, it's time to collapse in bed, feeling beaten and irritable.

Fridays are different though. When I board the northbound train I succumb to the gentle bounce and let the iron rails rock me through the suburbs of Rio de Janeiro. If it were not for Antônio's incessant rattle these trips could pleasant. To make it worth my time I seize the first available window seat in the car which is not an easy task at peak time on Fridays for sure, but I have no qualms turning my suitcase into a shield a soon as the car door slides open. I plow against the crowd and urge Antônio to follow until I successfully claim a two-seater. After we conquer our nook I do my best to act interested in whatever Antônio's yacks on. Honestly, I do; one eye on him and another out the window.

Thankfully, Antônio is too naive to notice my disinterest. He is too immersed in his own narrow eschatological world to notice anything real and as long as I nod and smile I can get away with day-dreaming. My persuasive choreography of pretense consists of tilting my head discreetly over Antônio broad shoulders. In case my move fails and I happen to miss a segment of his dull monologue I let out a polite "that's right", which Antônio interprets as approval and keeps on with a "let me tell you" of additional boredom. Every now and then the screeching rails drown his soft voice and that's when I lean an inch closer and point to my ear. Antônio relishes in repeating whatever he is talking about and like a zesty parrot he cries "sure!"

"That's right" I nod and smile.

Curt statements recharge Antônio's battery. He shifts topics with each breath and when he finally engages in a whole sentence it is safe for me to return to the pane and paste a fitted grin on my face until it is time to get off. Out the window the unfolding suburban landscape is enigmatic. Like the shuffling pages of a book the scenes change so fast. While I chew on the roasted peanuts my mind drifts.

Within a mile out of Central Station Rio's complexity gives way to a raw scketch of rustic overtones. Unkempt homes and idle shops built closely together crop up on the other side of the track patching up the bucolic *bairros* against a backdrop of wavy hills and sunken valleys. Rio's suburbs remind me of Lajedo somehow. Cut off from the city's famed sandy beaches most of the *Zona Norte* streets have never been asphalted or swept. This side of town is off-limits to tourists who are interested only in the cable-car rides up the Sugar Loaf to admire the famous Guanabara Bay. On this side of the tracks, apart from the newly built Maracanã Stadium there are no attractive landmarks able to match the impressive Christ monument atop Corcovado Mountain either. Funny that even the stony Christ gives its back to Rio's needy.

The *Zona Norte* people though gracefully coexist with negligence. Judging from my limited square-framed perspective they seem to be content with penury. Any time I glimpse out the window I see the lit up faces of ragged children chasing a makeshift ball through the littered streets. The grownups move about with remarkable indolence, disregarding the established boundaries between roads and sidewalks. Here there are no traffic jams and it is common to spot horse-pulled carts, bicycles and stray animals competing for space between the narrow hedges dug long before cars were invented. In this unruly, yet peaceful negotiation of place and time there is no need to hurry. "*Pra quê tanta pressa?*" I can hear the musical *Carioca* accent.

When the train finally stops at Antônio's *bairro* this nonchalant attitude becomes much more evident. When we step on Vila Nova's raised platform and stare at the cluster of concrete tenements below I realize the contrast between past and present. Antônio tells me that centuries ago, before the railroad cut Vila Nova in half, the *bairro* was a prosperous slave-operated sugar mill. Today, however, the only testimony from that thriving era is an overwhelming number of mulatto residents. Visible evidence of the old farmhouse—*casa grande*—and the slave quarters—*senzalas*—has long disappeared.

Once the sugar mills collapsed and slavery ended, says Antônio, Vila Nova's residents reclaimed the space in a disorderly manner. On the opposite side of the station, the unplanned grid leads us to the unpaved lanes where several multi-family tenements crowd up. The more decent houses stay at a distance from the track, and there is where my host family lives. Antônio assures me that if it were not for the railroad linking Vila Nova to downtown Rio the *bairro* would have been abandoned long ago. No large businesses exist here except for a few essential establishments including the grocery store his father owns. For the most part Vila Nova residents commute to Rio daily as part of the legion of *suburbanos* recruited as underpaid domestic and construction workers with whom we compete for a seat in the crammed train car every Friday.

Our walk from the platform to Antônio's house is effortless despite the dirt pavement and we blend with the throng of jaywalkers crossing the main road. A car or two brake so we can reach the other side where my hosts' grocery store, the largest business in sight, stands tall. Just like in the other suburban enclaves everyone in Vila Nova cleverly elude traffic and disregard usual norms of safety. Antônio and I pass by torn doors and broken windows all wide open to the scrutiny of snoopers like me. Through the corner of my eyes I can't help to recognize Lajedo's lack of privacy. People here also enjoy a spectacle at others'expense.

At this point of our journey I can't help to think about home. I close my eyes and picture the alley, the crooked gate and front parlor. At this hour the family should be getting ready for the evening devotional and I realize that nothing similar to that is bound to happen in Vila Nova. Weekends here are made exclusively for amusement, for playing shoeless soccer—*peladas*—flying kites, and cookouts. Beginning on Friday makeshift grills light up on the sidewalks, chairs are brought out and hours of barbequing extend to dawn. While the adults sizzle the meats and sip iced beer the youngsters listen to radio broadcasts of their favorite soccer squads. With each score everyone erupts into a howl of cheers—*"gooool!"* like a cannon ball went off. Then someone shows up with a guitar, another brings a tambourine, someone else a drum and it's time for the *Samba* circle. Waits twist, feet skip, and hands clap until the first rays of light pierce the clouds.

A secret part of me envies this unique *Carioca* outlook at life. One of these days I might give in to the *Samba* beat to find out how it feels but so far I have only given myself permission to glance over during our walk to Antônio's. When we stumble on acquaintances for the usual handshakes, smacking kisses and firm hugs I steal a glimpse at the nearby *rodas* where those who have known Antônio all his life now also call me *camarada*. I am pulled over with effusive embraces and invitations for a *pelada* Saturday afternoon and follow Antônio's lead saying, "all is well"—*tudo bem*—with my thumb up. By the time we reach his street my mouth is cast in a frozen grin, my shoulders feel alive again, weightless as if no yoke had ever bent them.

At the corner of the block we hear Marte, the friendly German Shepherd, barking with anticipation. Antônio swings the gate open and we both drop our bags to let Marte lick us all over. Behind him

Teresa comes in her loud clacking flip-flops. She ferries our luggage inside giving way to Antônio's parents who, arms wide open descend on us with kisses on both our cheeks as all *Cariocas* do. For a few seconds we stand in an awkward hurdle figuring a way forward without stepping on Marte's tail or on each other's toes.

Seu Orlando and *Dona* Sueli besiege us, asking questions without offering time for answers. "Did you have a safe ride? You hungry?" and pulling me up the veranda steps I am told how nice of me to come again, and what kind of drink I would like, iced water or lemonade? "Teresa?" *Seu* Orlando shouts from the doorway "something cold for the boys" and *Dona* Sueli moves aside waving Marte away with her manicured hands. "Never mind Marte now boys. You can pet him later" she leads us around the flowerpots, up to the airy veranda and finally into their comfortable living room. On the large coffee table I catch Teresa setting an ice bucket, tall glasses and a pitcher of lemonade.

Until coming to Vila Nova I assumed home to be a fabrication made up in the novels Ms. Cabral lent me. I sure lived in a house but never had a home where affection and food abounded. Goodness, there is so much of both at Antônio's. When I first came I suspected these folks were pulling some kind of an act to impress me just like *Seu* Benedito did in front of a costumer. But each weekend *Seu* Orlando and *Dona* Sueli dispense attention to both of us quite consistently. Ocassionaly I wonder that if they found out where I come from they might disapprove of me as their son's companion? I avoid talking too much about my life in Lajedo around them. God forbid they learn my father is not the fruit farmer I hint he is or that my mother does not order servants around, unless my sisters can be counted as such. When questions about droughts in that part of the country surface I hastily tell them not to worry because the well in the back of our property is always full.

To prevent these types of conversations I usually deflect their curiosity with questions of my own or just fill my mouth with Teresa's food. To me what really matters is that once we are here, Antônio and I just go with the household flow. Soon after washing up the trip's sweat and snacking in the living room Teresa calls us to the long *jacarandá* table where a variety of platters and bowls have already landed. An enticing smell of cheese rolls hover the linen-covered breadbasket and I instinctively seize my butter knife.

Teresa's feast is in full display for our delight—terriness of white rice and black beans flank a silver tray layered with grilled *picanha* steaks. I salivate in anticipation of my first serving while listening to Teresa's menu announcement. "*Picanha*, *farofa*, fries, toss salad."

Sheepishly I lift my glass so that she can refill it with more lemonade while whistling through a row of missing teeth. "Save room for dessert, Daniel" her thick black lips smack loudly. "Antônio?" she slides behind our chairs "*pudim de leite* is in the fridge" and she brings the jar near *Seu* Orlando. Pretending to be offended he covers the brim and asks Teresa for another cold bottle of *Antártica. Dona* Sueli winks at Antônio and he proceeds with a short prayer so we can start digging. Teresa waits for the "*Amém*" by the doorway and carries in *Seu* Orlando's chilled *Antártica* by the neck. *Seu* Orlando smiles broadly. I can tell he is ready to deliver one of his signature speeches, either about his store success or the state of his hunter green *Vemaguet*. After a few gulps of beer we will find out which one takes precedence tonight.

I am convinced Antônio takes after his father when it comes to idle talking. If *Dona* Sueli doesn't interrupt *Seu* Orlando with another *picanha* steak he may go on for hours about the importance of hard work and proper planning—two vital character traits he learned from his late father as we have been repeatedly told. Without them, he proclaims, the family's store would not have turned into what it is today.

I do appreciate Antônio's brevity in meeting our religious duty so I can fill my plate while nodding at *Seu* Orlando and smiling at *Dona* Sueli. He talks like Antônio, and the two look a lot alike. I get to eat and that is just fine with me. Now he is describing how his immigrant father prospered from store clerk to manager, eventual owner of 'Best Price.'

"The secret, Daniel?" he waves his steak knife at the ceiling "hard work and proper planning" he chomps on a thick bite of *picanha*. Pity Antônio doesn't want to take over the family business" he looks at the meat platter planning on another forking "but as long as he applies himself to his studies that is what matters, cheers" he lifts his beer glass.

"I am very proud of my son's religious calling, Daniel, even though I am an agnostic" he gulps up the whole thing. "One has to live in accordance to one's own consciousness that is for sure. Mine is about hard work and planning. These should also be the bedrock of a nation's growth, cheers!" he repeats loudly and refills the glass.

"If only Brazil had adopted these ideals long ago" he grinds on "our country would be a powerhouse today just like the United States" there goes another swig. "But we will get there eventually" *Seu* Orlando lands the empty glass on the table. "Modernization is on the way: just look at the inauguration of Brasília, boys. Highways will link the new capital to the rest of the country, mark my words.

Brazil is the country of the future, Teresa!" *Seu* Orlando points at the empty *Antártica* bottle.

"You might be right, *papai*" I hear Antônio's soft voice cut through the abrupt silence. He has just emptied his third glass of lemonade and looks around trying to decide what else to add to his full plate. "However, there is so much more beyond building roads and cities" he yanks a thick steak out. "We need more public schools and land for small farmers. I do hope President Quadros will be addressing those needs soon. All this talk of progress sounds great but not fair until the government supports land reform and keep the children out of the fields and inside school" he calmly cuts his *picanha* in large cubes.

I cannot believe my ears or my eyes for that matter. I am witnessing a civil exchange between father and son. Both *Seu* Orlando and Antônio disagree while still sitting at the same table. They are clearly enjoying each other's input, but out of habit I stop chewing in anticipation of a blow out from *Seu Orlando.* To my surprise what I see is even more remarkable. *Seu* Orlando taps Antônio's shoulder and pours more beer into his glass.

"Son, you are a young idealist and I admire that. What I say, however, is based on facts. The future of a country is in the hands of entrepreneurs, the leaders with capacity to invest. Think of the United States where industrialists have been lightning rods. Rockefeller, Carnegie, Vanderbilt and the like. Once our entrepreneurs begin investing on roads, oil, and metallurgy the foreign automakers and bankers will beg to join in. Proper planning, son, and everything else falls into place" *Seu* Orlando waves his knife in the air. "The poor?" they will always be with you, right?" he winks knowing we get the meaning. "In due time, son, they will benefit from progress, have jobs and schools, see?" he taps his temple with his index finger.

Antônio smiles, shakes his head and decides to drop the subject to answer *Dona* Sueli's timely questions about school. Now it is my turn to reach out for seconds whereas *Seu* Orlando asks Teresa for another bottle. By the end of Antônio's detailed recital on our uneventful week Teresa is on her final comeback from the kitchen. She holds a shiny silver tray where an ornate urn towers over a set of porcelain cups and sugar bowl. We all know this is a cue to move to the large living room for coffee and dessert.

There we spread over plush couches and armchairs to enjoy the breeze blowing through the draped windows. On our way over we agree with *Dona* Sueli that our chat must switch away from politics.

"Right you are, Su" *Seu* Orlando takes a seat on his armchair. "Let us change the subject" and the three of us take to the couch. "Perhaps the boys would like to take the Vemaguet for a ride along the rail track?" *Dona* Sueli smiles approvingly behind her porcelain cup.

I emulate her and smile at the family's momentary stillness, finding it conducive for another bite of Teresa's velvety *pudim*. Quietly sipping my sweet *cafézinho* I daydream again, of Lajedo, of the nostalgia of an hour ago. What used to be must go and what will be takes precedence. I no longer see myself roaming dusty alleys, barefoot, but walking into a bricked suburban house where my own Vemaguet is parked at the door.

FIFTEEN

Over two years have gone by and Antônio is ever so determined to convince me "patience is *more* than a virtue." Every time I whine about how much longer to graduation my brother peremptorily reminds me of the etymological meaning of this Greek word. "*Pathos*, brother, means to suffer, remember? What a profound spiritual concept behind it" he stretches his bulky arms across the dining hall table and grabs my clenched knuckles.

I avoid his riveting stare and roll my eyes down into the abyss of my morning coffee. "Suffering entails deliverance no matter how long it lasts" he begins the endless chatter. "*The long suffering of our Lord is salvation*' Second Peter, chapter 3 verse, 15" he dunks his buttered baguette. "After death there is life, after suffering there is redemption, and believe me after Seminary, a blessed future is in store for us who serve the Lord" Antônio chews pensively.

I finish my drink in silence and watch him get up as if all of a sudden he remembered something. Antônio walks out of the hall and I am relieved to be alone. Personally, I find patience to be no virtue. As far as I can tell there has been no redemption for my share of suffering up to now. Perspective, on the other hand, is a better principle to adopt while coping with the mounting demands of junior year. Perspective about the Vila Nova getaways, for instance, helps me endure the weekly grind. As long as I know that at the end of five days I leave this cloister I no longer feel like a caged bird but more like a tamed dog waiting to be unleashed at the park.

Surely I cannot evade my academic responsibilities but I also know that Fridays do come. With this in perspective I cross each day off the calendar with an "X" though on Fridays I switch the mark to a "!", anticipating the three o'clock bell. The vibrating chime can be heard anywhere on campus but it is inside my head that it triggers a shift from profound tedium to effusive elation. Time to leave and decompress, toss the week's stress out the train window and fake interest in Antônio's animated jabber while the bucolic scenery rushes by.

Perspective also helps me during the trying train rides. The more my companion talks the less I have to, and the less I have to, the more solitude I enjoy. With this perspective in mind I appreciate the fact that in less than a year's time these getaways might turn into foggy memories. This is Antônio's last semester and he is leaving in a matter of months. Once that happens I will be spending weekends alone.

Every predicament in life is temporary and presents its own duality. Depending on what perspective I adopt benefits manifest. For instance, my decision to secretly join the Vila Nova shoeless soccer—*pelada*—squad has presented me with a rare opportunity to enjoy myself despite crossing a dangerous line. Antônio's family has no idea I have been recruited as first goalie in the local team. Fantasizing about being a soccer star has been the best outlet I have found to endure the weekly rigors at Seminary. However, I must keep Antônio and his parents in the dark. As far as *Seu* Orlando and *Dona* Sueli know my Vila Nova weekends are for resting. No one in the house suspects that after our Saturday *feijoadas* I join those *bairro* dubious types to play ball. My mischief is executed with flawless discretion and in perfect synchrony with the instituted household rules.

By now I am well acquainted with my hosts' domesticity and their established meal times. Breakfast is served at seven, lunch at noontime, afternoon coffee at three thirty, and dinner precisely at eight in the evening. So when Teresa is done clearing the *feijoada* plates around one o'clock on Saturdays I find myself in the spacious living room surrounded only by framed family portraits and picturesque prints of colonial Rio.

Antônio and *Dona* Sueli predictably retreat to their *sestas* whereas *Seu* Orlando drives back to the grocery store. Marte heels Teresa to the detached shed in the backyard where they both hibernate for at least another two hours. It is then that the entire compound descends into blissful slumber. Sitting on the couch pretending to read the Bible I perk my ears. When the kitchen faucet stops dripping I know Teresa is done with the dishes and gone for a long nap. This is the moment I keep in perspective all week. I then slide into the bathroom and quickly change out of my pants and collar shirt for a pair of shorts. Slick as a cat I sneak out, barefooted of course, since shoes are expressly forbidden in an authentic *pelada* match.

My teammates are always eager to see me at our designated checkpoint in front of *Bar Brasa*, the borough's popular beer joint not too far from the train station. From there we walk together to the "field", which consists of an unpaved street. There we quickly discuss the line up and match tactics because for the sake of my circumstances I must return to Antônio's before the household resumes its regular pace. My teammates have also assigned me the goalie position to avoid getting me suspiciously drenched on my way home.

That is also why I keep my watch fastened during the matches. All I have is an hour to spare before I shower and reclaim my original position on the couch with my Bible in hand. Out in the field, however, I concentrate on the task ahead and cheer my mates as they furiously chase the ragged ball as if the World Cup were at stake. If we happen to win I stay a little longer to celebrate with a few *Antártica* bottles. I have only agreed to the invitation under the condition Antônio hears nothing of it. We Evangelicals abhor alcohol, tobacco or any form of exhilaration apart from praise and praying. Drinking cold beer is an indulgence I ought to keep secret and my mates assure me of their discretion whenever we head over to Bar Brasa.

Our laughter fuses with the thumps of the Vila Nova *Samba* School percussionists who gather on the bar's sidewalk every weekend to rehearse *Carnaval* songs. All sorts of people end up there—young and old, drummers and crooners, burble away the latest *Samba* hits in between swigs of sugarcane brandy—*cachaça* and cold beer. I have never done anything more sacrilegious in my entire life and cannot reason why I hang out with this mundane troupe but what I can tell is that something happens to my religious countenance whenever chilled beer touches my tongue. By the second glass I can do the unimaginable: I sing along with the group, laugh at their bad jokes, and throw my two cents into the most trivial of arguments they get into.

Lately everyone is obsessing over the next World Cup in Chile. It's a year away but Vila Nova folks talk of nothing else. "What about you Daniel, who do you think will make Brazil's next squad?" a drummer eyes me through his tumbler. "Me?" I look around to make sure he is actually pulling me into the discussion. "Well" I pause and take a deep breath "I have no doubts Pelé will make the team" I pronounce with feign authority. "He is our best player and is in excellent physical shape" I resort to my preacher's tone.

A teammate shouts louder behind my shoulder and cuts me off. "You gotta be kidding *camarada.* Have you seen Garrincha play yet?" he challenges. "Waaay better than Pelé. He is the one who will score our way to victory in Chile, you'll see, man" and I blush at the rising tide of approval.

"No way he won't!" I lash back defiantly. A heat wave surges behind my neck and I feel the urge to defend my point. "With those wobbly useless legs Garrincha may be a dribbler but can't score" and a raucous laughter ignites the circle. "Alright then, Daniel" a fellow wipes his foamy lips and offers his free hand. "It's a bet" he pours more beer in my glass. "Let's talk about this next year, *camarada*. This one is on me: *tim-tim*" he lifts the glass.

I feel the chill on my fingertips and I find no strength to refuse. "Sure…*obrigado*" and double-check my watch. I can finish another glass and gallop back in good time. "Well fellows, must fly now. Thanks again" and I raise a toast to everyone's health: "*saúde.*"

On Sunday evenings I bring these silly snaps back with me to Seminary. They stay alive during the train ride to *Central do Brasil* and as I prop my head against the window I no longer bother to look outside. I prefer to stretch my mind into a wide white screen like the one I saw at a *Cinelândia* theater once. I paste the moments together into a film I watch with my eyes shut. When I recoil into this daze Antônio thinks I am praying and mercifully takes his Bible. At some point Teresa's feasts invariably intrude in my imaginary script. Her fabulous dishes parade along the starched tablecloth and one by one her sweet cakes, cheese platters, and breads pile up around bowls of ripe fruits and flasks of lemonade. My mouth waters at the sight of sliced cheese and guava paste. This perspective lingers on for another week.

Soccer, beer, and food are definitely worth keeping in perspective. In times of stress when essays are due and exams dates are set, I find solace in those moments. Not that I am worried about my grades but my ultimate goal is to qualify for an internship in one of Rio's *Zona Sul* parishes. I must stay away from the suburbs though Antônio disagrees. He believes new graduates should serve the poor. Serve the poor? Give me a break. If that were the case I might just go back to Lajedo as Pastor Santos begs me to in his monthly letters.

No sir, not me. I am here to stay. Rio is the largest of all tokens I will ever collect. Where else will I stand a chance to live in a *Zona Sul* flat and drive a *Vemaguet*? I am told that the Copacabana congregation is growing in membership. Its parishioners can certainly afford to pay a good salary. For quite some time I have been assessing *Seu* Orlando's progress theory and its potential religious application. I am inclined to believe that religious leaders, like those in the government, must come from the ranks of the affluent. That is the best way to fund missionary work in the long run. Their resources will eventually benefit the poor. Evangelicals need to establish a strategy of growth within wealthy enclaves first, and then reach out to the suburbs.

Arguing this viewpoint with Antônio is risky though. He might get disappointed with me and quit the invitions to Vila Nova. Thank goodness today is Friday and he is leaving for Vila Nova in a little while. I am not sure I can handle Antônio when he is stressed. Our last exam results are out and his mediocre performance is probably to blame for his aloofness today. He didn't eat as much and is now back, twisting a newspaper as if it were a wet towel. Something is up.

"What' s going on?" I point to the wrinkled log in his hand. "You look like you've seen the devil" I try to lighten up.

Shrugging off my bad joke Antônio sits down and flattens the newspaper on the table saying nothing. He is tense and lost for words for the first time in two years. His forefinger flutters like a windsock over the bold headline: ***"JÂNIO QUADROS HAS RESIGNED FROM THE PRESIDENCY EFFECTIVE TODAY: AUGUST 26TH, 1961."***

"Where did you find this?" I inquire thinking it might be some sort of a prank. But again, Antônio is not the type to pull tricks. I am the one known for that around here.

"Where?" his eyes narrow at me quizzically "at the newspaper stand down at the square, where else?" the tone comes across unusually raspy.

Antônio pulls the chair closer and lowers the tone. "I had to get my own copy after what I heard on my way to liturgy class earlier" he cautiously leans over as if about to tell me a big secret. "I spotted some guys hovering over today's edition and I asked to take a peek, see?" he points at the strange caption. "I still can't believe my eyes, brother."

"Umm…" I ask to take another look at the block letters and skip through the article without understanding much. "Now what? We have no president?" I focus on the black-and-white picture of President Jânio Quadros.

Antônio blinks incredulously at my ignorance but offers an explanation nonetheless. "For now, brother, the Leader of the House of Representatives will be sworn in as President until Vice-President Goulart returns from China. When that happens he becomes President, which I hate to say, is the actual problem" Antônio is now whispering. "Many military officers and right-wingers in the Quadros government dislike Goulart. Say he is a radical, a Communist even. I suspect they are just waiting for a good excuse to sack him. We are in for some trouble ahead, brother" Antônio looks around the room.

"Umm…" I whisper again in an honest effort to empathize. "It says here Quadros wrote a three-liner message to Congress and left?" I point at the article unsure of what else to say.

"An unprecedented move" Antônio gruffly remarks. "See here where he claims 'obscure forces' have pushed him out?" he directs me to the middle of the page. "I wonder what that means, brother. We need to pray for him" he concludes in a disturbed tone.

"You want more bread?" I change the subject as Lurdes enters my camp of vision. She is moving straight over to our table with a coy smile. Her long black hair is a cascade of curls.

"No" Antônio answers still staring at the paper. "I will head over to the library and finish reading the paper. Also need to do more research for my graduation sermon" he slowly pushes the chair back. "Hard to believe I am leaving at the end of the year, isn't it brother?" he fakes a smile. "Anyway, see you at three thirty?" he rolls the newspaper back into a log.

"Well…" I stammer as Lurdes closes in. What I am about to disclose has been the result of serious consideration over the past few days. "I have lots to read this weekend" I look stone-faced. "Will stay back and barricade in our room with the books" and blatantly lie. "Please give your parents my best, will you?" I sternly nod and smile.

"That's perfectly fine, brother" Antônio nods back. "I thought you were all done studying but sure do whatever you need to do. *Tchau*" he playfully rattles the newspaper on my back and keeps moving.

I watch Antônio amble to the door and picture tonight's intense exchange with *Seu* Orlando over the recent news. Another reason to stay behind and execute my well-thought plan. I will accept Lurdes' invitation for a picnic at Urca beach tomorrow. A week of lengthy essays has burned me out and I deserve more than just a *pelada* match in Vila Nova.

"*Oi* Daniel, more coffee?" Lurdes has sneaked behind me. She lifts my empty cup up.

"A little more, *por favor*, Lurdes" I smile back. Her hair falls over her shoulder.

Thanks to Antônio's hospitality I have so far declined Lurdes' suggestion to explore Rio's tourist sites. The weekend trips to Vila Nova are coming to an end with Antônio's graduation though, and I need to find something else to do if I am to survive my senior year with any perspective left.

"Enough?" Lurdes hums.

"*Sim, obrigado*. That's plenty…" I nod, smile, and as usual my tongue betrays me.

"So, Daniel" Lurdes comes to the rescue. "Have you given any thought about Urca beach yet?" she leans over the table and I smell lavender in her hair. "How about a ride on the cable car up the Sugar Loaf Mountain?" the tip of her curls land on my arm.

"I have heard it is a gorgeous view from up there" I let my guard down a bit. "Tomorrow, maybe?" I offer.

"Sure thing" she quickly agrees. "Ten in the morning?" she adds before I change my mind. "I can pack a few boloney sandwiches for a picnic if you'd like?" her finely sculpted brows arch at me.

"Sounds great, thanks." I nod and smile again quite aware of another forbidden line crossed.

"Perfect" Lurdes hugs the thermos. "Meet you at the front gate, ten o'clock" she repeats.

Nearby a few heads turn at me disapprovingly and I deflect the incriminating glances by draining my cup with one long slurp. On my way out I return the fellows' scrutiny with an expressive bow making a mental note to leave campus unnoticed. If anyone catches me walking out the gate alongside the kitchen girl I might have some serious explaining to do.

SIXTEEN

A swish of air tickles my eyelids as I struggle to blink. This is the highest I have been above ground and I don't want to miss a thing. A breathtaking vista unfolds before me and despite the apprehension to look down I am transfixed. At the bottom of the majestic Sugarloaf Mountain a fleet of sailboats bob like toys in a giant tub. Guarding them from the rippling ocean beyond Guanabara Bay, brown hills roll towards the horizon fainting underneath a cluster of puffy clouds. How peaceful Rio de Janeiro appears from this height. Deceivingly helpless it nests in between the lush tropical hills and the blue vat of the Atlantic. To the right of the guardrail where Lurdes and I hold hands a stretch of pearl colored sand curls along Copacabana beach. Its famous Atlântica Avenue limestone tiles undulate in a black and white pattern that vividly mimics the crash of waves.

Up here the air feels remarkably crispier and the transient wind hurls Lurdes' untied black threads against my face. I follow every turn she makes pointing out sections of the city I don't recognize from this far up. "Over there?" I follow her index finger. "Botafogo Harbor next to Flamengo Beach" she sings to me. Enraptured by such natural beauty I can only nod and smile. “Over that way” Lurdes turns my chin to the left, “downtown.” I vaguely recognize the Glória Hotel and the high-risers along Rio Branco Avenue. “Now over on this side” my jaw is encased in her hand and with her fingers Lurdes traces a perfect arch in the air “Leme, Copacabana, and Ipanema” and I let her waltz me all around the observation deck.

At every corner tourists prop their cameras to frame the splendid scenery. Since I don’t have one myself I imprint Rio’s fabulous shoreline on my dilated pupils. Every so often I lean over the fence tempted to trail the people and vehicles below but my head retracts in fear of falling off the sloping cliff. Before taking the cable car up I had no idea how enormously solid the Sugar Loaf ascended above the sealine. The colossal rock resembles the sail of an indestructible galleon forever anchored in its original shipyard. The massive brown stone has been destined to stand guard over Rio’s duplicity.

From this vantage point the city appears defenseless against the mountain’s enormous weight. Its meandering enclaves below overlap in a complex grid of avenues, buildings and slums crisscrossing in so many directions that I seriously doubt my ability to ever chart a straight path once I return to the ground. I stand no chance decoding this intricate riddle but one thing is for certain: Rio’s magnitude frightens me. It reminds me of the dark pit spiraling below our Lajedo dry well.

When the drought struck and water disappeared I remember bending over the brink pleading for a gush back so I wouldn’t have to make another run to the *barreiro.* The dark pit seized me with angst and I felt being pulled deep down its bottom never to return. Stooping over this immense crater I again dread being sucked under.

If I am not careful Rio will swallow me whole. I ought to remain vigilant.

Choosing where and with whom I go is priority to prevent a fatal plunge. As *Seu* Orlando says, 'proper planning' is key. I am glad I planned accordingly this morning. When the time came to leave campus I stood behind the iron-cast bars and surveyed the entrance area before sneaking out. No one saw me leave and when Lurdes walked down the hill I was already on the other side of the street hiding behind the newsstand. As soon as she approached carrying a greasy paper bag and a scarlet smile on her lips, I rushed forward to meet her halfway.

I didn't bother to explain why I did not wait for her at our designated spot and immediately offered to help carry the sandwiches to avoid any questions. Mine had not been an act of chivalry. It was proper planning in case curious eyes lurked by. "*Oi*" was all I uttered while throwing furtive glances back just to be safe. Lurdes kept up with me as we set down the street and did not break the awkward silence separating us. I think she understood what I was doing and played the part compliantly.

At first it was difficult for us to strike a conversation. Apart from coffee-related sentences Lurders and I had never communicated before. In deep introspection we slanted towards the street corner and only then I felt compelled to thaw the ice. I casually brought up President Quadros' recent resignation trusting that our country's escalating political drama might ignite a lively discussion such as the one Antônio and I had the day before.

"So, Lurdes" I ventured tentatively "have you heard the latest news from Brasília?" But receiving only an evasive shrug in return I immediately regretted the miscalculation. She obviously had no idea what I was talking about and I had to think on my feet to find a more trivial subject. "How about your parents, how have they been?" I faked some interest.

"Oh, you must mean my mother" she reworded the question letting me know she had never met her father. "She's fine. Already at work at her Mam's house" and we veered towards the bus stop.

"On a Saturday?" I pried not out of curiosity but satisfaction for having settled on a promising topic on my second try.

"Yep" she nodded matter of fact. "Sometimes the whole weekend too." Her *Senhora* is very demanding and lazy if you ask me. When relatives visit from out of town Mother has to stay on call and spend nights at that windowless hole they call the maid's room until the guests pack away" Lurdes snorted.

"Ah…" was all I could come up with to conceal my lack of empathy. Fortunately at that precise moment our bus arrived and I hailed. Promptness is not to be expected from Rio's public transportation service on a Saturday morning so I took that as a promising omen. Off to a smooth start, I presumed, studying the vacant seats. After paying for our fares I motioned Lurdes to a bench. Holding on for our dear lives we staggered along the narrow corridor as the impatient driver stepped hard on the gas. Right through the red light he plowed in such a jolt that we both lost balance and clumsily fell in place unable to suppress a nervous laugh.

This time around I did not take the window seat as I would of if riding with Antônio but politely offered it to Lurdes. I also slid the window wide open so she could enjoy the nice breeze as the bus muddled over Tijuca's cobblestones. As we distanced from our constrained turf Lurdes and I slowly relaxed. We commented on the nice change of weather after the overnight storm that cleared this morning sky. The sunlight tinkled beautifully over wet boughs and roof tiles along our way out of *Saens Peña* Square.

I couldn't resist the temptation to show off my familiarity with some of the landmarks towards downtown. Before long I began to sound like Antônio during a Friday afternoon train ride. "Look!" I pointed left. "The *Capuchinho* Church. Did you know Rio's founder Estácio de Sá is buried there?" and Lurdes' eyes widened. "There: the Education Institute" I quickly summoned her to the left again. "An authentic sample of neocolonial architecture" and Lurdes chuckled at my phony tour guide impersonation.

Past Flag Square the bus beckoned onto President Vargas Avenue where the large clock tower loomed by the *Central do Brasil* Station. I bragged about my trips on the northbound train through the suburbs of Rio pleased to have awoken Lurdes's curiosity. She had never gone very far from Tijuca except to the *Zona Sul* beaches and I proceed to entertain her with selected Vila Nova anecdotes.

When the bus stopped at Cinelândia Square we got off and waited for the Urca Beach connection. We strolled leisurely about the unusually empty hub and to break another round of shyness I impulsively mentioned the movie theaters behind us. "Perhaps we can watch an American film one of these days?" and Lurdes clapped excitedly at the idea telling me she had been to the movies only once but a long time ago. She would love to see a color picture some time. "Next weekend, perhaps?" I offered as we both read the titles aloud: 'El Cid?' or 'Breakfast at Tiffany's'?

During the second leg of our trip we speculated on which picture might be best based on the colorful posters until the view of Guanabara Bay caught our eyes. As the bus skirted along *Beira-Mar* Avenue the stunning contours of Glória Marina and Flamengo Beach gripped us. By then we both snuggled closer to the window to admire the colossal Sugarloaf boulder. When we arrived at Urca Beach our suppressed apprehension had finally evaporated into the ocean's salty air. We were far from Seminary and no one here knew or cared about who we were or what we were doing.

At the bus last stop the driver killed the engine with a dramatic jostle letting us know it was time to get off. Lurdes and I eased out of timidity. Hand in hand we have skipped over the sandy beach splashing our bare feet over the shallow waves. Roving at the edge of Urca's serene waters sinking my feet into the sodden sand evoked conflicting sensations of joy and sorrow. There were times when wetting my toes caused me revulsion. Today is different. Listening to Lurdes' easy laughter at my attempt to run from the harmless foam I am flooded with joy.

Never have I felt this alive before. There is power in the deliciously tangy seaside air and it had not occurred to me that breathing it in could be so invigorating. Happiness is as tangible as the caress of a cresting wave.

Later on I steadied my feet inside the cable car gliding above the thick forest and recalled my childish yearn to fly away from Lajedo. Climbing over this marvelous city with Lurdes close to me I wonder whether I am finally living that dream. We have been up here all afternoon basking in the anonymity of a perky crowd not worrying about time. At the far end corner of the observation deck the late afternoon clouds gather behind the pointy Corcovado summit. Lurdes cheerfully drags me to a spot in front of momumental Christ the Redeemer statue. Behind its stretched arms and petrified face the faint winter sun gradually ebbs away.

Twilight is fast approaching and Lurdes wants me to observe the subtle shade over the gray surface. Instead, I stare at her. She looks prettier at sunset. I hope she won't hear my heart explode while I keep staring at her. Will Lurdes know this is my very first date? Yet she doesn't show any contempt for my ineptitude.

For what it seems like eternity we quietly ignore the visitors footsteps and their popping flashes. Reluctantly we both look into each other's eyes. The late afternoon mist lands on our skin as we continue to walk about the deck. My left arm rests beside Lurdes as we walk some more. The sun begins to set behind Corcovado's summit and we loop around one last time before I declare: "it's time."

"We better go, Lurdes" and she agrees to ride the cable car down the mountain. "Your mom must be worried" I caution as we step off the landing.

"Not really" the answer follows a smack on the cheek. "She told me this morning she has to work late tonight. I don't expect her to come home at all" she winks.

"Well, we better not chance it" I insist. "If she comes home and you are not there she might be upset" I forewarn.

"Over what?" Lurdes laughs and throws her head backwards. "She will be thrilled to know I am out with a Seminarian instead of those slum bums. No, Daniel, don't you worry any. I am not a family girl with a reputation to protect" she tickles my ribcage. "You, Mr. Reverend, on the other hand, should be more careful. If one of your mates catches us together *they* will be upset" Lurdes casually leads us to the bus stop.

After a long wait we decide to hop on a downtown tram instead. At Central Station we wait some more until a northbound bus finally arrives. By now the Marvelous City has plunged into darkness. When

Lurdes and I gaily take to the rear of the bus we admire the flickering electric bulbs ignite over the slum hills. During the long ride back we again loose track of time. My mind is focused solely on suppositions regarding Lurdes' past. Judging from her height I assume she is slightly older than I am. Twenty, or twenty-one? No more than that for sure. What about other guys? With whom has she gone out on a date before? Lurdes acts like a teacher handling a student who has been called to the chalkboard for the first time.

With each bounce of the bus we jerk off our seats until a passenger up front pulls the stop-off cord. The sudden buzz echoes through the dim cabin and we both bend forward with the sudden brake. Curious, I look outside the window to find out we have gone past our intended stop and in between renewed titters we yell at the driver to hold up. I waive the collector's change and push Lurdes through the metal buffer. We both run up front just in time to jump off and once on the sidewalk we break in a belly laugh welcoming the long walk to campus. Back on our familiar territory, however, we must comply with imposed social rules and let go of each other's hands.

Dodging a group of night revelers we make way through the busy sidewalk of *Conde de Bonfim* Street. It is a typical Saturday night and Rio vibrates with partygoers heading to and from restaurants, clubs and *Samba* circles. We break through a throng of loiterers in front of a live *Bossa Nova* trio, and stop to watch. Those already seated inside the bar compete loudly for the servers' attention franticly demanding more *chope* and *salgadinhos*. In a cool winter evening such as this *Cariocas* do what they like best, barhop until dawn and sleep through the morning.

We obviously don't expect to bump into anyone from Seminary but remain cautious along the steep climb to the gate. Lurdes drags behind a little realizing how close we are to the end of our outing. Under a weak lamppost stream she stops and I reach for her hand. "I think it is very late for you to climb up the hill alone Lurdes. Let me escort you home?" I venture. The faint light prevents me from seeing her reaction but after a brief pause Lurdes' voice rings out affirmatively.

"Sure, Daniel" she squeezes my hand and we proceed uphill. "It's a bit of a hike" she warns as we march silently up.

In front of the pointy gate I intuitively slow down. The elevated arch rises accusatorily over us and I peer through the metal bars. I check my watch barely visible under the penumbra and learn it is quarter past eight. My view of potential lookouts is compromised but I assure myself that the brickway to the courtyard is clear. I take a deep breath and yield to Lurdes' draw up the graveled slant.

I am about to cross another forbidden line. Many of my fellow seminarians refer to the *favelas*—slums—as Rio's dumps where the destitute and depraved coexist in open disregard for morality. Of course Antônio has conjured a much less degrading depiction of these hilltop squats. According to him Rio's shantytowns are illegal settlements not because the residents are outlaws. His mild voice follows me upwards. "*They live there out of necessity brother. Not spite or defiance. Rent in Rio is prohibitive so they build homes in places no one else will. Sure these are disorderly and filthy camps but the problem rests mostly with the authorities. Sewage hook ups, garbage collection, and electricity lines should be accessible up there. By the way, this is exactly where we pastors must minister, brother. There is so much need for God up there.*"

Antônio's voice comforts me like a prayer as I skip over muddy potholes and trash. During our ascent I begin to notice what my classmates have described as shacks—*barracos.* It is dark tonight but even through my peripheral vision I can tell our house in Lajedo is not as run-down. Instead of brick and mortar, *favela* dwellings are made with scrap wood, tin, and cardboard in the most disorderly fashion. Each shack is propped next to the other for support and together they conjure rows of frail sheds. Lurdes interprets my silence as sudden aversion, and looks over her shoulder.

"Are you alright, Daniel? We're still far. I live all the way at the top" she pauses and points at the stretch. I nod and smile barely able to utter an answer while bustling forth to catch up with Lurdes. Both my shoes are caked with dirt and whatever else I smell but cannot see. In a few yards I halt again. A deafening sound escapes the only lit *barraco* on the left row.

"What is that noise?" I cup my ears at the pounding drums and stomps. A strong whiff of cheap incense and wax trickles closer. "And this nasty smell?" I wrinkle my nose in disgust.

"Oh that?" Lurdes points left. "It's the *Umbanda* Temple" she says casually. "I know you don't believe in this type of religion Daniel but here in the *favela* most of us do. This is the house of *Exú* and every Friday night folks come here to ask for the *Orixá's*—protection and blessing" she proceeds in the same nonchalant tone. "Come see" she pulls my hand. "Don't be afraid, silly" I nearly stumble over her.

Before I am able to protest Lurdes drags me to the shack clasping my hand tightly and mocking at my sullen face. The soft moonlight reveals the frame of a spooky façade in desperate need of painting and when we hit the door both the noise and the acrid smell thicken. A curtain of smoke envelops the small interior and in the middle of the room a presence draws my attention. An elderly man, whose shiny black head is cropped with tuffs of white kinky hair, is comfortably cross-legged on the ground. The smooth of his ebony hands stand out in shocking contrast to the white of his wrinkled linen suit. He is muttering undistinguishable words to no one specifically though around him, two bulky mulatto women fling their long skirts and turbans, drawing a perfect circle on the dirt. They are in an obvious trance and whatever they chant sounds as foreign to me as the old man's mumble.

Lurdes and I stand a few feet behind the crouched devotees all dressed in white apparently intoxicated by the stinky smoke. Ours are the only eyes open as the rhythmical jumbling escalates into a chain of convulsions and shouts. Nervous, I consider darting out when an intense brightness bounces off the back wall where candles are ablaze at the foot of a full-size statue. The realistic features draw me back to the image of Saint Joseph and I can't take my eyes off the handsome brown face. He is dressed in a fancy dark suit, black tie and neatly hemmed red cloak. On his right hand an oversized silver trident towers over the fancy top-hat covering his perfectly combed hair.

Nearby, the drummers bang on enthusiastically, their eyes closed as everybody else's until the spectacle reaches a bizarre frenzy of sounds. With our backs to the entrance Lurdes and I watch for a while longer until I finally muster enough courage to step back. Before I leave though, the old man raises his right hand and the room plummets to a dead silence. Sheepishly the leader opens his bloodshot eyes. I can barely see the yellow around his onyx pupils as he conjures a wide smile. A set of brown gums becomes visible and I can tell he is closely scrutinizing me. I feel self-conscious to stare back and drop my gaze. He slowly turns to Lurdes and whispers: "*Exú* walks behind him, girl. *Exú* has marked him, *menina*."

All eyes in the room open before my alarmed face. I turn to Lurdes even more terrified than when I first walked in demanding my legs to obey me. They stubbornly buckled while Lurdes takes hold of my damp hand and glows proudly at me. It seems that I am the only one here in a state of fright. I gather whatever courage is still left in me to wheel back when the old man flutters his right hand again and the strange moves resume.

"What a profane place" I yell at Lurdes out in the dark alley. "What is that demonic-looking statue?" I cough my fear out. "Who is Exú?" my mouth dries faster than I can keep on coughing. Lurdes stands by me suspiciously undisturbed. If the pale moon is not tricking me she is actually grinning.

I pull away from her but she is fast in swinging my shoulders to her and holding my chin with both hands. She looks cheerfully into my glaring eyes. "Daniel we have just visited the house of *Exú*—the *Umbanda* god that links our world to the next. He is a very powerful *Orixá* and the statue you just saw inside is him" she explains without letting go of my face. "And the priest says that you and him walk together."

"Nonsense" I push her aside. "Quit this absurd chatter right this minute" I yell.

Lurdes moves closer."Calm down, Daniel" her arms stretch closer. "Look, let's forget about all this and get out of here. Pretend this did not happen" she holds my shoulder and hugs me to a stop. "How about a bite and a drink at the bar up the road before you walk me home?" she suggests. "It's been a while since we ate. I am very hungry, how about you?" she brings me back to my senses.

"Fine" I grumble. "Actually, I'm famished" I confess. "Sorry for yelling at you. I didn't mean to…" but she takes my hand we and slowly proceed towards the corner where a couple of empty tables and chairs are scattered in front of a scabby shack. On the wall a cheaply framed clock hangs with both pointers on the number nine. I realize why I am crabby. "It's way passed dinner time" the clock screams at me.

Lurdes draws the chairs from under a metal table and throws a scornful glance at the attendant. Leaning behind the counter the lonely keeper salutes Lurdes by name and points his chin at me inquisitively.

She ignores him and quickly directs my attention to the scarce menu written on a propped board. We play safe and order a platter of boiled eggs, salami cuts and a baguette before committing to the soup special.

"*Antártica*, Lu?" the young bar keeper yells behind us.

"Sure, Zé, and two glasses" she commands with her index and middle fingers up in the air.

"Do you come here a lot?" I study Zé's movements behind the counter while he does the same to me.

"I grew up here, Daniel. Everyone in this hill-*morro*—knows me and my mom" Lurdes nods at Zé as he lands the bottle on the table.

"*Tim-tim*" she proposes a toast and and we empty the first bottle before the food arrives. Zé returns with another bottle as if anticipating our intentions and before long the nearby tables and chairs sway out of focus. I try to make sense of the clutter on the table but my droopy eyes roam about. With some effort I identify an empty tray and an unfinished bowl of collard green and sausage soup—*Caldo Verde*—which I don't recall ordering.

Rumpled napkins are about to fall off the top covered with empty *Antártica* bottles. I straighten my back up to count them. Six, seven? Not sure at this point. I giggle myself silly at the touch of Lurdes's silky curls. Though the cool night advances into its dew hours my forehead grows strangely damp and my cheeks burn as if branded with hot iron.

PART III

THE INTERN

"If you came this way,
Taking any route, starting from anywhere,
At any time or at any season,
It would always be the same: you would have to put off sense and notion.
You are not here to verify,
Instruct yourself, or inform curiosity
Or carry report.
You are ***here to kneel****."*

(T.S. Elliot, *Little Gidding, I)*

SEVENTEEN

Ai! This tap-tap on the window! It's getting to me. It's so hot in here. Let the water topple already for goodness' sake. Let the clatter and the heat be gone. I' m desperate for rest, can't survive another steaming night besieged by these hungry pests. Do they even care? Evidently not. Why should they? Suck me dry is what they want. Good-for-nothing fan can't even keep'm off my ears. What wouldn't I give to be that piece of fabric hanging on the window—flapping and flowing at the rustle's will. No resistance, no purpose except to usher in the moans and smells of perversion from below.

I can tell Copacabana's drunks are on their way home. At least I am not the only one out of whack in this tropical Gomorrah. Off me! I'm loosing my mind. Can it get any worse? If I don't catch any snooze before dawn no way will I look presentable tomorrow.

Look at the curtains dance. Oh, lull me to a doze, will you? Rock me like a hammock, slow and steady. If I don't fuss these suckers might leave me alone. Should I refill the glass? Usually that helps. Nah. Can't get up anyhow. Enough for one night. Is that possible? There is never enough. Only when I' m down and out. Double shot on the rocks. On the rocks to rock me off. Where to, I wonder? To the rest of the bottle. Ai! Let…me…up…

Wait. Why are the floorboards quitting? How come my feet can't touch' m? And what is Antônio's bed doing here? Hidding under Dona Sueli's tablecloth? Brother, is that you? Grab my hand, talk to me. Help me up? It's hot! Ai! My head hurts. Easy… Breathe… The room is not sliding. It's the storm outside running wild. It will pass and then I'll get up. Look at the curtains dancing. Specks of light shearing through the fabric. It's the lightning breaking through. Where's the rumble? Thunder, oh, how I hate thunder. Why does it have to be so loud?

BAM! My head is spinning. Stupid bugs. There is light outside. BAM! Thunderstorms can sure shred my nerves. What's wrong with this room? BAM! Why the shadows on the walls? This furniture doesn't belong here. Why are they airborne? Ai, my head. The whole room is sloshing. BAM! Let…me…Arr…Not yet. My back is pinned down. Can't move. BAM!

Where am I? Is the whole room bouncing? The mattress is prickly. Like my parent's straw-filled sac. That can't be. Look at the curtains, Daniel. Still flapping. So indifferently. Stay still and focus. Why are they so dirty and threaded? Lurdes' barraco. Is this where I am? Why is Seu Orlando's armchair next the window though? Someone is sitting there. Antônio? Is that you, Brother? Say something. Talk to me Antônio. No. It's not you. Too slim and tall. What's behind the smoke? A tall hat. Can't be Antônio. He would never trick me.

BAM! The wind is picking up fast. I need to shut that window. Ai! Can't move. My hands, can't feel them at all. I'm trapped. The wind is rushing in. Off me, stop poking. Ai, it hurts. If only I could swat, I swear, I'm gonna kill you. Stay away from my nose you stupid…letter?

"My Dear Daniel: It has been quite a while since you last wrote. I pray for you everyday and know that the Good Lord is providing." Goodness. Pastor Santos' letter I have never bothered to answer. Many are still sealed up inside the bookcase. How did they escape? Oh, no, here comes another jab. "My Dear Daniel, since you left three years ago our church has been growing steadily and we are planning on moving to a larger hall. Do you still remember the day you dreamed of rainfall? The very day the drought ended? You must know Lajedo still boasts about you as our 'boy prophet', the one God rose up from the dead."

What now? Wait! Let me finish the Pastor's letter. How can a piece of paper float in the air by itself? Oh, my head. That atrocious calligraphy, the embarrassing strokes. "To our son Daniel: this is your father and mother writing. All is well here by the grace of God. We pray all is well there. Your sisters send regards—lembranças. We know you work hard, son, but drop us a line when you can. "Daniel: Your mother is asking me to ask you to send a photograph. How is your health? (this is my question not hers.) Signed: Benedito, your absent father—seu pai ausente."

BAM! What an obnoxious noise. Papers flying everywhere. BAM! Duck. Here they come like bullets from a rifle. Under the covers quick. This one hovers like a sheet on a clothesline. "Dear Brother: May the Peace of our Lord Jesus Christ be with you. It has been over two years since we last saw each other..." That long? "I still believe patience is more than a virtue, brother." I hear the jolly voice. "Married life couldn't be better, it is a divine reward after years of solitude in Seminary. Vera is such a dedicated partner in ministry. Together we run an after school program offering slum children daily snacks and tutoring."

Antônio, are you there? "Daniel, let us plan a reunion so you and Vera can meet? I talk about you all the time and she would love to have you over. I realize the distance between us is forbidding. Caxias is worlds away from Copacabana but one of these dasy, brother, God willing, we will reunite. I treasure the memories of our weekends at Vila Nova. By the way, everyone sends big hugs—abraços."

The strong air whips the papers to a dance. The noise is aggravating though. Out the window the storm escalates. I can tell. Better wait for the end. I need to sleep. Why is the mattress jolting? Wait, what is this? My knees are jerking. Can I use my hands now? I need to block this clatter from my ears. My stomach is twisted to a knot. I'm gonna puke. Ai! My head.

Should I get up or close my eyes until the queasiness settles? These papers must return to where they came from. Better yet disappear altogether. I must reply those letters but for now I just want this whole nightmare to end. I want to scream but my voice is trapped. My ears clogged, my teeth locked. I want it all gone.

Ah, no more thunder. The noise is over. The mattress is steady. Has the room stopped bouncing? Is it safe to open my eyes and get up? This can't be my bedroom. What is the Seminary's library bookcase doing opposite my bed? My wardrobe should be there not these lofty shelves. The shelves are about to crack under the clutter. Novels or theology books? I just hope they don't fall and crush me. The storm is passing. I can tell. The wind is dying out. No more thunder, thank goodness. The letters are landing on the ground. No noise, no bouncing. All is quiet. No one here to witness my agony. Wait. The foggy silhouette in the corner. Pitched on Seu Orlando's armchair. Right there by the window where the curtains dance.

Look at the curtains, Daniel. Cheap strips of fabric swaying back and forth. Stay focused. You, don't come any closer. Off my shoulders. I don't like being tied up. What is lacing my bare chest? No, not again. Stop! Who are you? Off me. I can't move. These ropes are lengthy but soft. Lurdes' hair. That's it. I need to untangle the loops but my wrists are frozen. Ai! The soothing scent of malt, I want more. I know the face behind the dark braids. My arms are folded across my chest. I feel like an embalmed corpse. I breathe in the perfumed air. I relax in the snug swaddle and give up. Lurdes is here. It's her hair that is wrapping me.

It's her face I see, the wide black eyes like those of the actress in the first movie we saw together. "Breakfast at Tiffany's." The small bridge of her nose, the prominence of her cheekbones, her glistening lips. I give up. I surrender. Her hands land by my side. She glows at the sight of the round birthmark stamped by my navel. She finds it special, a token of fortune. She is smiling, repeating the words from the Umbanda priest. 'Exú has marked you."

Blasphemy, I want to shout but I long for her embrace. I am so lonely. Her hair wriggles around my neck. The thick threads tighten and turn scaly and heavy. My neck! The scales are choking the air out of my lungs. "Lurdes, why are you angry? Did you believe I was going back?"

See? The downpour is over. The tapping is fainting. The drops trickle down the wet glass. Ai! How I hate the sound of silence. Lurdes, why are you smothering me? Please, let me out. What do you want from me? I need to breathe. Ai! Is this how it ends, Lurdes? Is that you? You are strangling me. Let go, please.

"Behold, Daniel"

Antônio? Is that you, then?

"The hope of a man is false;"

Antônio, if that's you show your face!

"He is laid low even at the sight of me. No one is so fierce that he dares to stir me up."

What do you mean, Antônio?

"Who then is he who can stand before me? I see everything that is high; I am king over all the sons of pride."

Antônio, am I dead?

EIGHTEEN

Daniel's heart pumped so fast he could barely open his eyes. Blinking with suspicion at the window he noticed the lingering fabric frozen in place partially hiding a streak of raindrops sliding down the glass. The tiny bubbles burst like fireflies in a summer evening reflecting the glow of Copacabana's streetlights. On the nigthstand Daniel's lamp had not been turned off and traced hazy contours on the opposite wall. Ever so slowly, the familiar landscape of his new dwelling emerged.

Before Daniel's wary gaze a reflection of his own frown appeared on the mirror-lined wardrobe door. Along Rio's shoreline darkness lifted under the summer's mighty light as it advanced inside the cramped studio. The ugly armchair and its wasted upholstery caught Daniel's attention first. Beside it, the glass-paned bookcase bought to store his growing collection of novels stood locked up. Above it a small fan span furiously, and the loud hum finally restored Daniel's earthly senses.

Nothing in the room escaped the fan's futile battle against Rio's humidity not even Daniel's Bible, which had somehow fallen open on the parquet floor. The paper-thin pages shuffled at the mercy of the rhythmic blows producing a melodic crackling. "Had he accidently knocked the book off?" Daniel craned over the bed's edge. At this point he remembered absolutely nothing except for the obnoxious buzzing of mosquitoes.

Rubbing his reddened eyes out of numbness Daniel stooped a litte closer to the ground curious about the Bible's bookmarked page. The long silky ribbon rested undisturbed over chapter forty-one of the Book of Job suggesting that he had been studying the passage when the pests launched a fierce attack. He had most likely used the Bible to ward the pests off, loosing his grip in the process. His head weighed a ton and it was hard to lower it back on the pillow. The alarm clock ticked relentlessly declaring he had five minutes until the unpleasant beep rattled his brain out. Unless he slammed the metal pin down at once he was bound to lose the race against time.

"Sunday" Daniel painfully faced the flood of light through the window. "I'm preaching today" he hit the buzzer and stared at the fallen Bible again. The bookmarked page on the Book of Job pointed at the passage he had been reading on the monstrous sea creature called Leviathan. "The dream" he sat up and dropped his feet on the ground. "The nasty creature had nearly killed him with fear" and Daniel felt the crushing weight on his chest.

"How dreadful" he took a deep breath knowing exactly what he needed next. A cold shower would wash off the overnight jitters and restore his sobriety. He had a busy schedule ahead and in a few hours he needed to look sharp in front of his mentor and congregants. Cold water always reconnected him to reality. There was nothing to worry about, except for the ten o'clock performance, which was a reason to celebrate not to fret.

Delivering a sermon at the prestigious Copacabana Evangelical Church was confirmation of his proper planning all along. Not long ago he had been appointed an intern at the large *Zona Sul* congregation exactly as he expected. The coveted assignment came with many perks, including free lodging in Copacabana, credit at the local bakery, chauffer rides when needed, and a generous stipend.

Daniel looked around the room one more time, contemplating his favorable circumstances. The studio apartment offered to him for the year was snug and cozy. He did not mind the second-hand furnishings because more important to him was solitude. Out of the campus dormitory he no longer shared his inadequacy with a roommate but most importantly a milestone approached. Ordination at the end of the year would surely grant him a position at the prestigious *Zona Sul* church. Hardly out of Seminary he was about to launch a brilliant career as a Reverend. It took him four arduous years to place himself here. Each step was carefully calculated, and today, Daniel yawned, he woke up particularly mindful of the fact.

"All is well—*tudo bem*—as the *Cariocas* say" Daniel nodded at the subdued clock. In no time a nice cold shower, followed by breakfast at the corner bakery, would completely erase the frightening Leviathan ambush out of his mind.

Ambling confidently out of bed Daniel trusted both feet to the ground and stooped over to collect his Bible. On the way to the water closet he felt his head throb a little but not as bad as when he began fighting the vicious mosquitoes a few hours back. Still tipsy, he was grateful the water closet stood only a few steps away. If he put one foot in front of the other while keeping his head up he should manage just fine.

Sliding the plastic curtain aside Daniel eagerly stepped into the shower stall. His shaking hands impatiently twisted the metal knob to let out the profuse coolness. Soaking in the drench he bowed down as if receiving a sacrament of atonement. Since the early days of Seminary when similar dreams plagued him Daniel had resorted to the redeeming power of running water in the morning. A few seconds under the gush made involuntary tremors disappear and the knitted lumps beneath his skin disentangle.

Indulging in this daily habit had also fueled Daniel's reveries about a plentiful future. Fortitude would soon flow precise and functional as indoor plumbing. "It's time" his mother's axiom encouraged him. "Don't give up, stay the course, until you see the finish line" he often cajoled remembering the old crooked gate at entrance of his Lajedo home.

Having journeyed this far from that dire path Daniel had not forgotten the importance of moving on. He would never return to Lajedo. Never. Except in dreams he could not avoid but when those came flowing water worked miracles. It grounded him on the present moment and ushered pleasant thoughts of his weekends at Vila Nova. Antônio's moonlit face usually flashed back front and center when Daniel's eyes closed and his hands began scrubbing his hair.

His friend's perfectly aligned teeth barged in like a lighthouse beacon in the middle of a dark sea. If it were not for Antônio's timely rescues Daniel's graduation might not have happened. "Where would I be instead?" Daniel winced and pressed the coconut soap bar on his head. While his scalp frothed Antônio smiled down at him. His departure from campus two years ago proved to be a difficult adjustment. Waking up without clumsy teases and pillow fights turned into a daunting task.

On those trying days Daniel's alarm had gone off expectedly while the new roommate remained absolutely oblivious. A few times Daniel had overslept and just the thought of it now sent a shiver up his spine. 'How insensitive' he still blamed the aloof freshman for threatening his report card with a tardy mark. As a result he had turned into a fussy sleeper unable to block the unbearable tick of the alarm clock. Most nights he spent monitoring the tiny pointers on the glass trying to beat the six o'clock blare.

"How did I ever survive on so little sleep?" he scrubbed his arms next acknowledging that he had somehow managed. 'So, who needs you now, Antônio?' he sneered and walked out of the stall. He now lived alone and at the end of the year was going to be ordained Reverend. Daniel had gone far without Antônio despite the morning willies.

After shower and breakfast the needles usually quit poking. "Coffee" Daniel mentally traced the short walk to the bakery. As soon as he was done shaving and dressing he would numb the pain with several black and sweet *cafézinhos,* which he learned to gulp soon after Antônio's departure. "Without those merciful sips" he salivated at the urgent crave "I would not have lasted long either."

In hindsight those years without Antônio were not so bad. It was then that Daniel accepted Lurdes' invitations to go out whenever her mother was working. Snapshots of those illicit encounters invariably made Daniel blush. Lurdes had envisioned a crafty scheme to slip him out of campus unnoticed. On those Fridays she dragged her feet in the kitchen washing dishes until Daniel was out of the library. When the entire staff left, she turned the lights out (the agreed code) and waited for him at the servants' entrance. From there they walked, single-file along the rear wall, all the way to the foot of the *favela.*

Daniel now shrugged in front of the sink mirror trying to place the sequence of events in straight order. On those risky evenings he was double conscious of time because of the eleven o'clock curfew. "We only had a few hours at Zé's bar before the gates locked up" the scenes returned as he squeezed the tube of shaving cream.

"One evening though" he smirked at the face on the other side. "Senior year, I guess" he stared at the mirror. "The air had turned milder and the moon shone full and glossy" Daniel rubbed the foamy cream over his cheeks. "Zé kept pouring bottle after bottle of *Antártica*" he grabbed the steel razor. "And I lost track of time" he propped the blade inside. "Lurdes' mom was away at work" Daniel squinted at his frothed face. That night he crossed a seriously forbidden line. "Why did I not tell Zé to cut back on the beer?" Daniel gently slid the razor. "Oh well" the powerful flying sensation crept back. "Something special happened that night" he nodded at his shameless reflection. "It was surreal" he blinked mesmerized. "How else would an insomniac like me stay asleep for hours?"

Daniel lowered his guilty eyes at the sink thinking of the many times afterwards he broke the curfew rule. "It was then I found the cure for my nightmares" he splashed cool water on his face. "Incredible" Daniel tapped the aluminum razor under the running faucet "the solution had been right before my very eyes" and shook his dizzy head.

Those mischievous nights at Zé's bar reset the course of his life. "Things were never the same again" Daniel patted his soft face with a towel. Lurde's erudition on bohemian matters had initiated him to the power of liquor.

"Lu, is there anything other than *Antártica* that might keep me asleep until morning?" he had innocently probed.

"Of course there is silly" Lurdes answered with a soft slap on his forehead. "You never heard of sugarcane brandy—*cachaça*—before? " she chuckled at his empty stare. "No, of course not, Mr. Reverend" she smiled. "How could you, huh? They don't serve *cachaça* at Communion do they?" she cracked up. "Let me tell you one thing: you have not enjoyed a true black out unless you had a shot or two of *cachaça.* Come home with me and I'll show you" Lurdes urged him.

After leaving Zé's bar that fateful night Daniel vaguely recalled leaning on Lurdes while his feet missed a step or two on the way to her *barraco.* "Here" Lurdes handed him a tumbler the moment he sunk down on her mattress. "An artisanal kind from a farm south of Rio, a place called Paraty. If you want more let me know" she kneeled down and pulled his shoes off.

Daniel still remembered lifting the dismal glass against the candle flame intrigued by its size. Back then he assumed Lurdes was pranking him because the liquid inside looked exactly like water. He now smiled at the misunderstanding remembering the moment the rim touched his lips. An overpowering smell of fermented sugar itched his nose and threw his neck back. Lurdes's witty expression was precious. Like a nurse she closely watched Daniel hold his breath and swallow the whole content a few times in a row. With every sip his throat burned like a Saint Joseph's paper lantern up the Lajedo sky. He had almost choked in the process of spitting out what felt like lumps of blazing coal and did not know whether to cry or laugh. Then Lurdes let out a amusing shrill. "Oh my!-*'Ai!'*—I'm so sorry—*desculpa*— " she said dabbing her fingers around the corner of her eyes unable to stop laughing. "This might not be a good idea, Daniel. Look at you: all red in the face" and Daniel heard her loud yelp all over again.

Standing in front of the mirror Daniel could not keep a straight face. "How about we ask Zé for something else next time?" Lurdes' silky voice returned. The comical *cachaça* incident left such an impression on Daniel that he had thoughts for nothing else afterwards. He was determined to find something as bold as sugarcane brandy to make him fall and stay asleep. Lurdes suggested he asked Zé for advice and despite Daniel's gratuitous dislike for the bartender there had been no better action plan to follow.

"Zé knows everything about drinks" Daniel heard her say again. Zé's movements at the bar came to life in front of the mirror as he held a slim light green bottle on one hand and a shot glass on the other. After wiping the glass clean Zé proceeded to fill it up with a translucent amber dose of *Passport* whisky. "Yes" Daniel reenacted the first smile he ever aimed at Zé. That was exactly what he had been looking for. "A smooth yet strong substance that does not make me gag" he winked at the mirror and grabbed the Aqua Velva aftershave. A few long gargles every night does help with insomnia.

Daniel grabbed a comb, thinking of the opaque shade of his precious green bottle, its sleek black and red label neatly glued to the front. He craved the velvety odor of malt tickling up his nostrils while his tongue stretched out to suckle mouthfuls of cheap sedation. The 'solution' has of course called for strict discretion. "Just like in the Vila Nova days", Daniel reached for the perfumed pommade. "This is my secret" he winked at the respectable image on the other side of the glass.

At the Copacabana studio Daniel's bookcase served as the bottles safe and on his way down to the bakery he always inspected the lock and threw the key in his pocket. Out on Paula Freitas Street he usually took to the shade under the towering apartment buildings and paced anxiously to the corner. More than three months had passed since he last saw Lurdes. Over two years since he spoke to Antônio, and nearly five since he departed Lajedo. "I should forget about these people" Daniel watched the flow of traffic. "Nostalgia serves no purpose" he ran to the other side.

"Perspective" he reminded himself. "These people are of no value to my current plans" Daniel had arrived at Copacabana Avenue. "Everything is well" he scurried to the bakery. "I'm out of that campus" his eyes hungrily shifted to the plates of fresh pastries. "Almost at the finish line" he inhaled the warm scent of fresh baguettes. "No more students pestering me, no more professors to woo, and no more exams to ace", Daniel claimed his seat at the counter. His fingers drummed cheerfully on the glass as he waited for the server.

"This is what I must think about" he smiled absentmindedly without noticing he was being addressed.

"*Bom dia*, Pastor. The usual?" the voice was welcoming.

"*Bom dia*, Mário" Daniel snapped back to reality. "Sure. A *cafézinho* first, and then a *média*" he ordered mechanically. "Here is to the bright future ahead" he gulped the first *cafézinho* of the day and felt the needles on his temples dissolve. Mário returned with the buttered French bread and a tall glass of coffee and milk.

"*Ô* Mário!" Daniel yelled as soon as he dunked the first slice inside the glass. When Mário turned Daniel pointed to his plate. A refill was in order.

NINETEEN

Sunday mornings in Copacabana are deceiving. On his way out of the bakery Daniel observed how unnaturally peaceful the street seemed. At the mercy of the gentle breeze blowing from *Atlântica* Avenue Daniel walked, mindful that the bustling overnight storm had cleared the clouds. "It is going to be another stuffy one" he predicted pulling the cotton handkerchief out of his chest pocket. Along the deserted sidewalk he found himself virtually alone. Stripped of its regular bustle Paula Freitas Street stretched lazily like a dormant serpent waiting to be tackled. At this early hour only bakeries, newsstands and churches opened, and that was precisely what Daniel enjoyed most about Sunday mornings in the *bairro*—the illusion of tranquility.

Most Copacabana residents were still recovering from a night of *farra* at the local nightclubs allowing Daniel to stroll from block to block virtually unhindered. Tenting his eyes from the blinding sun he peered at the modern apartment buildings cropping up in the concrete jungle. The structures were lined so close together that there was virtually no space in between them. Not a soul peeked down from the broad windows. No darts of blame could puncture the thick bubble of hypocrisy enveloping Copacabana on a typical Sunday morning.

At least once a week this perverted part of Rio presented itself blameless. Daniel enviously pictured hundreds of the local wretches sleeping their wickedness off since unlike him, they did not have to report to work. "Seven thirty in the morning for crying out loud" he flipped his wrist for a quick glimpse. "Better get a move on" and picking up the pace he pictured Reverend Firmino sitting at his office. Their private conference would begin in about half an hour, launching a day packed with preaching, praying and ingratiating. More nodding and smiling as far as Daniel was concerned. "Maybe I should show up a little early just in case" he broke into a contained trot. Sweat drops already budded across his hairline and threatened to melt the perfumed pomade.

Ideally, Daniel mused, no surprise hospital calls or administrative meetings in the afternoon. At five o'clock his beloved *Vasco* would face off its archrival *Fluminense* and he was planning on listening in to the live radio broadcast. "Shouldn't get too wound up about it though" he paused at the corner of Copacabana Avenue. Last week's engagements had suffered a last minute adjustment and he ended up at an Elders' meeting instead. At the humming sound of an engine Daniel stopped and waited before crossing. He consulted his watch again and waved off the puffy discharge on his way to the other side.

Sticking to the shady marquees again Daniel made it back to the church annex with some time to spare. The lock gave in easily to his key and he knew the reason. "*Dona* Carmen" the pleasant thought floated in. Reverend Firmino's young secretary had indeed arrived. Daniel could sniff the luring scent of brewing coffee at the end of the hall. If he climbed to the loft two steps at a time he stood a chance of freshening up before joining *Dona* Carmen for a *cafézinho*.

"Bom dia *Dona* Carmen! *Tudo bem*—Everything well?" Daniel rolled buoyantly into the airy kitchen parroting Rio's popular greeting as if he were an authentic *Carioca*. *Dona* Carmen's taut posture beside the stove, however, suggested the task at hand was her priority. Anchoring the thermos on the counter she carefully lifted the fuming kettle and slowly poured the boiling water down the cloth drainer, cautiously estimating the speed with which the dark grind leached down.

To avoid breaking her concentration Daniel slunk behind her back and reached for a demitasse in the overhead cupboard. *Dona* Carmen's impeccably coiffed hair and clinging earrings did not budge while Daniel tiptoed backwards awkwardly juggling the cup as if it were a toy pistol. He aimed furtive glimpses at *Dona* Carmen every time she bent over the thermos, and though aware of Daniel's peering, she punished his impertinence with a cruel indifference. The hot sieve received her undivided attention and only after completing her chore did *Dona* Carmen greet Daniel.

"Oh, hello there" the salute came across cold as she screwed the thermos lid shut. After a long pause she dryly added "*bem, obrigada.*"

"Glad to hear" Daniel turned the cup up.

"I must go" *Dona* Carmen announced haughtily to her long red nails openly ignoring Daniel's expectation. "Help yourself" she pointed at the thermos on the counter and shifted her stern gaze past his staged smile. *Dona* Carmen knew Daniel had been watching her evenly powdered face and perfectly applied mascara all along but pretended the opposite.

Still trying to prolong the encounter Daniel probed: "Is Reverend Firmino in?" and began to fill up his cup.

"Yes, but he can wait until you are done here I suppose" *Dona* Carmen declared in her usual bossy tone. "I must fold the bulletins" she continued to study her long polished nails.

"It's delicious, *Dona Carmen*" Daniel sipped and nodded. "Exactly what I needed this morning" he lifted his cup from the saucer as if offering a toast but *Dona* Carmen had already moved away from the counter. Daniel poured out another *cafézinho* and watched *Dona* Carmen walk out of the kitchen atop a pair of fancy stilettos without missing a beat.

Daniel dreamingly listened as the soft pattering faded and after licking the sugar-smeared cup he placed it in the sink. *Dona* Carmen's husband, Bento, the muscular yet slightly cockeyed janitor would clean it up later. Daniel felt good about leaving extra work for him. "What in the world has she seen in that fellow?" he shook his head on the way to Reverend Firmino's office. A strong scent of Pine Sol permeated the air alerting Daniel to be careful. Bento was never too far away and he better be discrete. At the end of the dim corridor he consulted his watch before knocking. Afraid to come across either too eager or too slack he paused and rapped softly.

"Come on in" a hoarse voice traveled from the depths of the windowless den where a floor fan droned fiercely.

"Good morning, Reverend, *Tudo bem?*" Daniel sounded less intrepid then he had in the kitchen. With his head cocked he waited for further confirmation to approach the Reverend's desk. Invariably, the prospect itself turned his pace to a stealth glide. When his feet sunk in the soft rug leading to the mahogany piece Daniel felt as if trespassing into forbidden territory. The loaded bookcases were also intimidating. Reverend Firmino's smooth and hairless skull crowned above his clasped hands and Daniel regreted the miscalculated interruption. In haste to apologize he nearly stalled and came close to a retreat but the Reverend's soft voice detained him.

"*Senta, filho*—sit down, son" Reverend Firmino motioned at the armchair. "You are three minutes early" he smiled.

"So sorry, sir, *desculpa*. Should I wait outside, Reverend?" Daniel took a clumsy step back.

"No need, Daniel. This is good timing" Reverend Firmino affirmed.

"Is everything well, Reverend?" Daniel asked while cautiously crouching on the seat.

"Oh yes it is, son" the elderly preacher placed his eyeglasses back on. "When you get to be an old goat like me" he chuckled and crossed his languid arms over his tailored suit jacket "the worries are so many that you can't let them take too much space up here" Reverend Firmino tapped his oval skull. Daniel nodded and smiled. He did not dare interposing and assessed the situation.

After a brief pause Reverend Firmino continued in a contemplative mode. "The way things are going" he looked at Daniel inquiringly noticing the young man's nervous blinks. "Nothing to do with you, Daniel" he flagged both hands.

"What things then, Reverend?" Daniel eased the grip on the strap of his satchel and sunk down the chair. "Is it your health?" and he immediately bit his lower lip for the slip.

"No, no…" Reverend Firmino cleared his throat. "That should be a good reason to worry though" he chuckled. "No, Daniel, it's about our country if you really must know. I worry about how the recent events are shaping up. I fear we might be heading for a long and heated quarrel over who controls the federal government" Reverend Firmino sighed. "Since President Quadros' resignation nearly two years ago everything seems to be falling in disarray" he pulled his spectacles out and wiped them up.

Daniel leaned his head forward and clenched his hands. Should he say anything? He tried to read his mentor's move, the arching brows over the languid blue eyes, the trembling doubled-chin quivering with each of the old man's breath. Reverend Firmino's customary self-confidence was missing.

"I am not sure I understand, Reverend" Daniel timidly nipped the extended silence. "I mean, I do understand that President Goulart has been under severe criticism given his recent proposals" Daniel wanted to come across well informed. "His land distribution idea and minimum wage hike are raising eyebrows according to the papers but why is the country in trouble?" Daniel convincingly masked his blunt indifference over the mounting political tension in Brasília. Honestly, he had barely been tracking the news since the day Antônio showed him the inflamed headline back at the Seminary dining hall. *Dona* Carmen collected daily editions on top of her desk but Daniel had purposefully skipped the front-page articles and editorials to check the soccer scores instead. There was a lot he did not fully grasp though he didn't want others to assume, especially Reverend Firmino, that he was not up to date with the latest.

The military opposition against President Goulart was puzzling but Daniel could not picture the danger Reverend Firmino suggested. On the contrary he sincerely trusted the new democratic order would prevail. While Daniel studied him, the elderly preacher took his time adjusting his spectacles to his owl-like nose. Then he carefully rose from the leather chair. Daniel then watched the short man drift away and pace along the tall bookcases with his clasped hands behind his back.

"Daniel" the Reverend's voice shifted to an inquisitorial vibe. "Do you recall your history lessons?" he paused behind Daniel's seat.

"Of course Reverend, I…" but Daniel stopped in obedience to his mentor's gentle tap on his shoulder.

"I know you do. Your high marks speak for themselves, son. Mine is a rhetorical question" the Reverend commented in a suspenseful tone. "I want you to think about those crucial moments in our history when there were profound changes in the national government" and he let Daniel mentally string the episodes together. "I mean profound as in transformative" he had now leaned in front of the mahogany desk. "Now, tell me" he pressed both palms against the edge "how many times have profound changes happened in Brazilian history?" Reverend Firmino's used two fingers from each hand to draw a quotation mark sign in the air after mentioning the word 'changes.'

"Not many to be exact, Reverend" Daniel got the meaning. "Essentially, we are talking about three distinctive moments: Independence from Portugal in 1822, the Republican Proclamation of 1889, and most recently the 1930 Revolution" Daniel related while lifting three of his fingers.

"Very good, Daniel" Reverend Firmino slapped his thumb and forefinger together and straightened his silk necktie before resuming. "Those were moments of rupture or at least that is what historians claim" he sounded a bit skeptical. "What I am getting at is: after each of those ruptures our country immersed in years of adaptation" and again he flexed his fingers up in the air. "I believe that President Goulart's presidency might not stand the test of adaptation and we run the risk of another rupture. That is what worries me" and he returned to his chair looking even more aghast. "How long will democracy survive in Brazil?" he mused.

"Well, Reverend" Daniel interjected wishing to sound as concerned "let us wait and see. So far President Goulart is holding up…"

"True, Daniel, and I do hope my concern is based on mere historical speculation" Reverend Firmino clapped his hands as if swatting a bug. His kind smiled returned as he tried to remain optimist. "Enough of doom's talk, son. Let me take a look at your sermon notes. Book of Job, correct?" he sat down.

"Yes, sir" Daniel flapped the satchel open. "Book of Job, Chapter Forty-One as you recommended last week" he went on while handing over the sheets. "I am interested in some feedback particularly on the insights regarding the figurative meaning of the Leviathan" Daniel began to tap his feet on the soft rug waiting for his mentor to scan over his neatly typewritten notes.

"Well done, Daniel" the Reverend nodded approvingly as his eyes roamed the pages. "The analogy between the indestructible beast and human pride is perceptive and visually rich. I can already picture you describing the Leviathan's thick scales, its smoky snorts and sharp claws" the Reverend's hands went up in the air his long thin fingers curved down like an eagle's talon.

"I'm not sure it will be as good as yours, Reverend" Daniel grinned at the old man's clumsy humor "but I will do my best."

"I have no doubts" the Reverend returned the folder. "See, Daniel, what is important at this time is to steer the flock from politics. This topic right here is just fine, son" the Reverend approved.

"I'm not sure I could preach on politics if I tried, sir" Daniel carefully stored the folder back in the satchel. "I personally think it is irrelevant to the mission of the Church" Daniel fastened it.

"Wise approach and will save you a lot of grief if you stick to it" the Reverend stood once again. "How about some coffee or iced water before we continue?" he rang *Dona* Carmen's phone. "Please excuse me for a minute, Daniel. Will be right back" he stood up and plodded calmly to the man's room.

Daniel knew the Reverend's geriatric needs could keep him a while and decided to kill time by examining more closely the old man's bookshelves. He was especially curious about the pieces by the acclaimed colonial Portuguese Jesuit Vieira. He counted fifteen volumes worth of sermons alone and became so absorbed by the table of contents in the first volume that he did not notice *Dona* Carmen's hills over the rug.

"Careful with those, mister" she set the tray roughly down the mahogany desk. "You could get in trouble if caught messing with the Reverend's treasures without permission" she warned.

"Ah… *Dona* Carmen! Here we meet again" Daniel walked closer clutching the book to his chest. "Thanks for the warning but I can think of so many other troubles I wished to get caught with" and he pressed the book against his lips and let a grin escape out of his gleaming eyes.

"You are getting way too fresh young man" she tried to sound offended. "Wait until I tell my husband about your ridiculous remarks" her superior head flung without letting any of its perfectly sprayed strands out of place.

"Why would you tell him, *Dona* Carmen?" Daniel swayed his feet side to side subtly blocking her way. "I am so sorry my compliments sound ridiculous to you but it is probably because I become so…so agitated, yes, that is the word. I become so agitated when you are present. Your beauty begs to be admired even if from a distance. I cannot help…" Daniel took another step forward but *Dona* Carmen curtly interrupted him.

"Excuse me" she pushed him aside. "I am not done folding the bulletins" her pointy nails stabbed Daniel's chest. On her hurry towards the door *Dona* Carmen nearly tripped over Reverend Firmino. At once recovering her regal stance she dabbed at her hairdo and gravely announced that there was an hour left to service.

"Thanks, *Dona* Carmen" the Reverend acknowledged "we are almost done here. Oh, could you please ask Bento to turn the fans upstairs? It is so muggy today" he continued without paying attention to her nervous departure.

"Certainly. He is going to the sanctuary next" she dutifully retorted before shutting the door.

"Thanks, dear…" the Reverend said to himself and turned to Daniel. "Ready for a *cafézinho,* Daniel?"

"No need to ask, sir" Daniel put the book back on the desk and offered to help.

"You are welcome to take that with you" Reverend Firmino pointed to the small leather-bound volume. "In fact, you should study all of Father Vieira's sermons, Daniel. If you really wish to improve your rhetoric he is an excellent choice."

"Thank you so much, Reverend. I will take you up on the offer" Daniel said while stirring a teaspoon full of sugar into his mentor's cup.

"Anytime, son. You are free to take whatever else you fancy from these shelves" the Reverend fanned his hands about the room.

"Really?" Daniel nearly shrilled. "You don't mind me snatching your treasures?" Daniel repeated *Dona* Carmen's words.

"As long as you return them when you are done, no, I do not mind. It is crucial for a preacher to read as much and as diversely as possible. If you can do so in other languages even better" he advised. "You are still young and have plenty of time but speaking of which" and Reverend Firmino glimpsed at the antique box placed to the right of the desk "let us go over this week's schedule."

"Any hospital calls today, sir?" Daniel tried to sound relaxed while watching the Reverend reach for the sheet *Dona* Carmen typed.

"No" the Reverend surveyed the list. "Not that I can see. Wait a minute" and scrolled down the memo. "No requests for hospital visits today but the Elders' meeting at four I want you to attend" the Reverend said gravely. "You must keep tabs of *church* politics young man" he winked.

Daniel managed to nod and smile although inside his head a string of expletives erupted. "*Ai!*" he sighed "going to miss the broadcast again. Oh well. Will wait for tomorrow's paper highlights" he sipped his coffee trying to suppress the frustration.

"Before I forget, Daniel" the Reverend landed his empty cup on the tray and picked up a linen napkin "you have been invited to lunch after church today. This engagement is not listed on the schedule" he put the sheet aside. "But I thought you would not mind a last minute inclusion?" Reverend Firmino's cocked his head inquisitively.

"No, sir, not at all" and Daniel's irritation lifted a bit at the mention of free food. "May I ask where, Reverend?"

"*Claro*—of course—you may" Reverend Firmino said. "At the Kruel's. You have met Coronel Edgar Kruel at your internship interview last December" the Reverend reminded Daniel.

“Yes, sir, I have. His questions on religious vocation were tough” Daniel shifted on his chair.

“Indeed” Reverend Firmino laughed. “But don’t take him too seriously, Daniel. Coronel Kruel is a very dutiful officer of the Military Police and does not always know when to leave his cap at the barracks. He has also been a loyal member of this church, serving as an Elder for many years. Once you get to talk to him you’ll like him just fine, I promise” the Reverend assured in a friendly tone.

“I trust your counsel, Reverend” Daniel helped himself to some cool water from the crystal pitcher. “I am flattered to be included in the guest list” he said politely.

“Very well then. Bento will drive us right after service. Did I mention my wife Isabel is also coming?” asked Reverend Firmino.

“Not until now, but I presumed so, sir. Who else will be there, if you don’t mind me asking? Daniel probed.

“Quite a few of us, I assume.” Reverend Firmino resorted to his fingers “Coronel Kruel and his wife Sílvia have four children—Manuel, Maurício, Alba and Ida; the boys are both married with little ones of their own. Alba has recently married Francisco and they are expecting anytime soon” the Reverend looked concentrated trying to count all the names. “Oh, you do the math, Daniel” he threw his hands up.

“Sounds like a large party to me” Daniel smiled. “Isn’t Ida the church organist, Reverend?” Daniel casually asked.

“Indeed” the Reverend smiled from ear to ear. “The whole family is very active in service here. A fine group of people you will get to meet today” the Reverend pointed upwards. “Hear the organ upstairs? Ida is fabulous, Daniel. We are so blessed to have her” and they both stopped talking. The drizzling melody seeped through the ceiling and like dew on fertile soil, it tilled Daniel’s oneiric mind.

TWENTY

Up in the sanctuary Ida's spirited notes made the air dance. It stirred the specks of dust in merry pirouettes as they seeped through the altar's windows. The translucent particles adhered to her pitched back and slipped down her pearly hands as they moved diligently on the organ's tiered keyboards. Ida's small bare soles also glided over the bass pedals below as the enrapturing melody flowed. Resembling a heron in flight her body regally flexed across the hymnbook releasing the soulful melody Daniel heard underneath.

Clinging to each note he tracked Ida's accords closely though his face appeared attentive to whatever Reverend Firmino said. Soon, Daniel found himself drifting away to a distant shore like a shipwrecked sailor seduced by a Siren. His mind succumbed to the organ's eloquence while the sentences catapulting out of Reverend Firmino's lips tuned to burbles. The spellbinding vibrations quickly billowed and pulled Daniel under.

A pit of darkness surrounded him. All traces of reality disappeared and Daniel no longer sat on a chair facing the imposing mahogany desk. The whirlpool of notes had sucked away the other fixtures in the room leaving Daniel afloat in a churning black hole. He had ears for the organ only and latched to its comforting tune while the dark vacuum expanded. At a distance a glowing flame pierced the darkness. The mild beam burned steadily and at its very top smoky traces of a human torso emerged. Daniel squinted at the evanescent contour and adjusted his mental lenses to capture its ghostly details. The strange meandering reminded him of the Leviathan of a few hours back only less intimidating. "Why is this creature chasing me?" he winced.

This time at least he did not fear for his life. On the contrary the smoky specter evoked in Daniel a soothing stillness and made him think of the casual encounters he had with Ida in the past months. Either at the altar during services or at coffee hour afterwards he had come across her flattering figure but never paused to contemplate its nuances. No doubt the sinewy milky arms and the poised marble neck forming behind the beam belonged to her. The lines of her alabaster skull garnished with a lush of black hair neatly braided were becoming more distinctive as the vapor thickened.

To Daniel's delight the image briefly congealed revealing subtleties he avidly anticipated. It was possible now for him to distinguish the shallow cavity chiseled around Ida's eyes and the bending edges of her delicate nose. Though he could not yet see anything below that range he yearned for a better angle of her raised cheekbones. But the surreal image skipped to a beat of its own. Back and forth it floated as if teasing him to a game of hide-and-seek. He took on the challenge and tried not to blink when at some point an extraordinary disturbance caught the corner of his eyes. From the fringe of Ida's long braid a single thread of hair reeled and coiled lifting the long braid up towards her shoulder line. The windy threads paused and in perfect synchrony strung together to spell the words of the hymn she executed upstairs.

Perplexed at the mystical spectacle Daniel observed the slithering lines encase Ida's head in a frame of words. The enchanted portrait was now fully visible and alive. For a moment Daniel considered the vision to be the product of a new machine he had heard about that could simultaneously display image and sound from behind a luminous screen. He had not seen one yet to find out how it worked but what appeared in front of him fit the description. Overtaken by the vision he wondered whether he was in fact watching Ida's organ performance as it went on upstairs.

He could see Ida's body wavering, all the way from her chest as she leaned over the organ, to her resolute head as she pensively read the notations on the hymnal. Convinced the picture was real Daniel was tempted to stretch his hands and touch it. Were her hands really that graceful? Daniel could not take his eyes off Ida as she continued to rap the keys unaware of their effect. At some point, however, her neck rotated and cast a languorous gaze at Daniel. She blinked and stretched her lips. Daniel grew encouraged. Had she finally noticed him? Eagerly searching for another hint Daniel stared at the dimples denting Ida's cheeks when with no forewarning a burst of light flared forward. Like a burning star Ida's smile dispelled the surrounding darkness and nearly blinded Daniel.

The organ's unfaltering crescendo magnified into a deafening clamor, and out of Ida's braid the words continued to ascend. Those were the words of Daniel's beloved hymn stringing vividly above the glare. "*Nearer, my God, to Thee.*" How many times had he parroted them without any conviction or reverence? But determined to believe them now Daniel fidgeted on the cushion looking for something to do with his sweaty hands. When would he touch the radiant face and tender fingers that plucked at the strings of his heart? Knuckles clasped under his chin he looked transfixed at the last strophe rising up from Ida's braid. The pungent scene, the same one that since childhood had fueled his desire to reach the clouds, deeply moved him.

> "*Or if, in joyful wing, cleaving the sky,*
> *Sun, moon and stars forgot,*
> *Upward I fly,*
> *Still all my song shall be*
> *Nearer, my God, to Thee*
> *Nearer, my God, to Thee,*
> *Nearer to Theeeee…*"

Under Ida's arched hands the powerful accord faded and Daniel's vision puffed away at once. A shallow sigh escaped from his dry lips as he caught himself leaping out of the dark pit. How long had he been gone? Daniel glimpsed at his watch and then at the Reverend. Fortunately, the animated chatter rang on reassuringly. The old man spurted out like a locomotive in full speed; something or other about next Wednesday's Bible study.

Daniel sheepishly nodded. His moist eyes landed on the pitcher *Dona* Carmen had brought and he lifted his shaking hand. Pretending to be thirsty was a perfect excuse to remain silent and a drink of water seemed appropriate to cool off. The office had suddenly turned into a furnace despite the fan's speedy blades. As they spun right to left Daniel pleaded for a direct blow. "I'm burning in here" he wanted to scream into the empty glass.

An imminent encounter with Ida upstairs overwhelmed him. In a matter of minutes he would be sitting across the organ and she would be listening to his sermon most likely staring at him like everyone else in the sanctuary. No longer a figment of his imagination Ida's existence loomed frighteningly real. Without much warning his insides turned tingly and he caught himself returning the empty glass to the silver tray. He had to step out or else, and stammering badly he interrupted Reverend Firmino.

"Sir, if, if you please?" he mumbled. "I need to be excused" and before he could regain control over his numb feet they were already stumbling out of the office in the direction of the men's room.

Meanwhile, up at the altar Ida progressed with her practice still lost in its poignancy. As far as she was concerned nothing beyond the sound of her instrument mattered. She still had to go over a few other pieces in the bulletin *Dona* Carmen had handed her and paid no attention to what was happening inside the nave. Bento had just hurried throught the altar's trapdoor knowing that within twenty minutes the whole space would fill to capacity and the fans had not yet been turned on.

Overly conscientious about Reverend Firmino's orders he banged the ladder against the walls flipping the switches. Next, he set the window sashes in proper position to usher the fresh air in. Satisfied with the flow, he took to the central aisle to inspect the burgundy runner bridging the front door and the altar. Everything looked good under the fluorescent bulbs and there were still five minutes to spare before folks flocked in, fashionably late, *Carioca* style.

Not much longer after Bento retired, footsteps could be heard from the sidewalk outside. Ready to greet the flock *Dona* Carmen had finally succeeded in unhinging the double front door and dutifully guarded the display table where all of her folded bulletins had been stacked. Precisely at the top of the hour a large crowd swarmed the block from all corners. Kissing, hugging, and clutching hands as if a long time had elapsed since their last encounter the Copacabana faithful clogged the narrow foyer. Inside the nave a torrent of merry murmurs eventually drowned Ida's accords. Ladies paused to squeeze children's cheeks and distribute compliments on each other's outfits, hairdos and fragrances before taking to their favorite pews.

Plugging right along Coronel Edgar Kruel and his wife Sílvia had reached the top of the stairway when they caught up with two of their grandchildren. Before they could scoop them up their eldest son Manuel yelled, "No, not yet, *papai*. I will take these two to Sunday school and come join you in a minute

"Don't worry Edgar" *Dona* Sílvia smiled at her husband "we will squeeze them all we want later… Oh, hello Marisa *querida*, how come I didn't see you there?" the Kruels chatted on patiently negotiating a path behind the climbers.

Back in the sanctuary Ida had briefly stopped to flex her stiff fingers. Landing both her hands across her lap she searched for her relatives three rows up from the organ. She smiled cheerfully and did not return *Dona* Sílvia's wave knowing that it was not meant as a salute. To her left, Reverend Firmino's bald head could be seen ducking under the trapdoor. Ida nodded obediently and summoned the rowdy audience to a hush. Sunday service was about to begin under her mastery and as soon as organ's deep notes whirled, faces turned straight ahead to the altar.

Downcast and solemn the altar party paraded in. Daniel was the last one trailing behind his superiors—Reverend Firmino, the Assistant Pastor and one of the Church Elders in that exact order.

Still a bit shaken by the surreal vision, he held his Bible and sermon folder tightly pretending Ida was not there. It was difficult for him to sing along through the first hymn after what had just happened downstairs. As the liturgy sequence unfolded he barely followed. At some point he had to climb up the pulpit but in the meantime he simply remarked the obvious cues.

"Good morning and welcome my beloved Brothers and Sisters" Daniel heard the Elder's welcome. "Let us give thanks to the Lord for another glorious sunny day. Please open your hymnbooks in praise" commanded the assistant pastor and Daniel obeyed. "Let us bow our heads in prayer" and he did that also. "Bring your offerings forward for God loves cheerful givers" he heard Reverend Firmino's husky voice. "Holy, Holy, Holy, Lord God Almighty…" he sang along with the congregation.

"Greetings in Christ beloved brethren" the proclamation rippled forcefully down the pulpit. "Please open your Bibles on the Book of Job, Chapter 41" Daniel heard his thunderous command. Whenever edgy Daniel's tenor sounded more potent than usual, his forefinger pointed more accusingly than ever, and his sense of inadequacy peaked. Nonetheless, it was then that he outdid himself and pulled off a compelling performance. No one in the audience would ever suspect his apprehensions because what they saw and heard was of exceptional quality.

His sentences flowed with remarkable logic and the punch lines were delivered timely. Daniel's arms rose so assertively that nobody would have noticed them quiver or imagine his hands perspired. Out of the depths of his throat the signature pitches flung far like a fish line across a rushing river.

Fresh out of Seminary, Daniel carried an affected stance whenever ascending to the pulpit. From the dignified summit he studied the audience carefully, seizing control of the moment, and steering all whichever way he saw fit. Years of practice with Pastor Santos had also prepared him to read faces and subtle moves. Fluent in anticipating reactions he knew quite well the reasons why people sat on a hard bench for over an hour every week. A balanced dose of guilt and reassurance was what believers craved.

"*Behold the hope of man is false*" he quoted verse nine reminding all of mankind's weaknesses before God's judgment. "Let us live a life of righteousness and sanctification, Brothers and Sisters. Our Lord is fair and forgiving" Daniel sounded convincing. "He sees everything that is high, says verse three, and he is king over all the sons of pride" he roared while brandishing his Bible. "God expects us to behave like Job: faithfully enduring our present circumstances for there is much to rejoice and hope for, Beloved. Let us relinquish pride and turn to the Lord's merciful guidance and far from the Leviathan hiding within our own arrogant hearts" Daniel finally pleaded.

In the course of the sermon not once did Daniel glance at Ida's corner. Each word, however, he crafted for her ears. Poised to impress only one person in the sanctuary he remained austere but charming. When it was time to climb down the pulpit stairwell Daniel felt quite satisfied. Ida's keys responded with enthusiasm while a sea of entranced eyes followed Daniel's theatrical exit. Under the final accords of *"Nearer, My God, To Thee"* he touched the carpet nodding and smiling at Reverend Firmino. "An exhilarating delivery, son" the Reverend seemed to say.

TWENTY-ONE

Nothing had prepared Daniel for what he witnessed at the Kruel's. When he left church, memories of the Vila Nova visits where he grew so used to the gorging as much as to the dullness, resurfaced. Back then, during those uneventful occasions Daniel seldom spoke unless propped to and out of resignation for the established domesticity among his hosts he easily accepted the role of "needy guest." With an ear leaning toward *Seu* Orlando's gibberish and and an eye on Teresa's platters he was thankful for the predicament of a sideliner.

At the Kruels, on the other hand, Daniel was thrown off track. Originally he blamed the initial shock on his warped state of mind following the reveries of the morning. The daze from which he had not fully recovered had affected his sense of perspective and instigated the feverish tone with which he delivered the Leviathan sermon. Afterwards, it was with inordinate effort that he stood at the exit queue enduring ardorous embraces and handshakes the parishioners poured.

With each tackle and pat his bones quivered. By the minute energy leaked out of his rubbery arms and his cramped feet. The mid-day sun raided the crowded vestibule trigerring in Daniel an unpleasant queasiness. When the time finally came for one more 'God bless you'—*Deus abençôe*—he could not figure out where to go. Eventually, he headed to the sidewalk and saw Reverend Firmino's *Aero Willys* idling by the curb. Bento' thick arms arched over the steering wheel from where a loud honk came. Failing to conjure the logical connection between sound and place Daniel stared dumb-struck at Bento.

"We are running late" the janitor grunted when Daniel eventually plopped down on the passenger seat.

"*Desculpem*—forgive me" Daniel turned to his mentor and *Dona* Isabel instead. "I completely forgot we were leaving right away" he apologized.

"Oh Daniel, never mind Bento" *Dona* Isabel exclaimed. "You were terrific this morning, my dear" she fanned a wrinkled bulletin across her damp face. "No wonder everyone wanted to hug you at the end. I will save my compliment for later" she tapped the wasted sheet on Daniel's shoulder. "Now take this jacket off and roll that window down" she commanded. "You will melt in that suit otherwise" *Dona* Isabel shouted as Bento screeched the tires off.

Like a marionette Daniel lifted his arms and clumsily removed the jacket. What felt like a jagged stone went down his numb throat as the sedan peeled off the hot asphalt and steered in the salty air from *Atlântica* Avenue.

Fortunately the Kruel's apartment was not far, *Dona* Isabel warned. "Almost there, dear. Enjoy the ride and the view" she pointed out the window. "Isn't this the most beautiful beach you've ever seen, Daniel?" she sighed. "I will never get tired of this Brazilian Eden. No gentlemen, not as long as God grants me another day in this marvelous city, I will not get tired of staring at this ocean."

Daniel couldn't agree more and nodded contemplatively at the vast blue sea. There was nothing comparable to its scent and nothing more hypnotic than its breaking waves. He angled his face farther out the window to listen to the crashing sound and watched the foam disappear on the sand. Under the lazuli canopy the Atlantic spread confidently oozing an intermittent hiss. It sang on to Daniel, 'You…are…being…taken. To…an…unimagined…place. You…are…being…pushed…farther…out. Follow…my…currents. Far…far…from…the…*sertão*. The past…is…buried. Deep under…my…soggy…ground."

Ida's ghostly radiance leapt off the surf and stood again before Daniel's face. He gulped the mist conscious of the wide gap separating them. He had come out of the desert whereas all she knew was water. Could the chasm ever narrow?

"Here we are, dear. Not too bad, was it?" *Dona* Isabel's lull pierced through Daniel's listless ears. Bento killed the engine and jumped out of the car to open the rear doors before Daniel had time to nod and smile.

Tucked a few yards from the famed oceanfront boulevard the Kruel's apartment building claimed a provisional shade at the edge of a charming tree-lined street. A pair of towering *Tipuanas* mercifully preserved during Rio's shoreline remodeling flanked a couple of flowerpots in front of the building and trapped the veering sea breeze. Within a couple of steps from the curb the doorman rose from his desk and ushered them in.

Out of curiosity Daniel studied his round bronze face wondering whether he had seen him before. A mosaic of Lajedo faces appeared. A *retirante*, perhaps? One who escaped the drought aboard a *pau-de arara*? Daniel carried the thought all the way up to the fourth floor. This was his first ride inside an elevator and he had to lean against the paneled wall for support. Eyes fixed on the receded fluorescent bulbs Daniel tried to hide his dismay. How could it be that at the touch of a button one ascended without moving out of place? Moreover, shortly after, the metal shutter mysteriously slid sideways and there she was.

"*Bem-vindos*" Ida's glowing smile appeared behind the door. "Follow me, please" and Daniel treaded after her not knowing where to. At the end of the hall Ida pushed a door into a torrent of giggles. Two toddlers recklessly raced around the furniture whereas a crawling baby appeared from nowhere ignoring a chorus of voices hoping to prevent a clash.

"*Mãe*" Daniel heard a male voice in the back. "They're here."

"*Já vai* Manuel" a shout travelled by. "Get your father, please" *Dona* Sílvia scurried into the living room.

"*Entrem, por favor*—Come on in please, everyone, sit down and never mind the kids" Marisa, Manuel's wife hunched up behind holding a pair of tiny hands.

"Something to drink Reverend, *Dona* Isabel, Daniel?" someone else spoke. "Lemonade, water, *guaraná* or iced *mate?*" the eager voice offered.

Daniel's head span as he tried to identify who was saying what but before he had any time to match a sentence to a face Ida reentered the room balancing up a heavy tray.

"Let me go grab the jars from the fridge while you are at it" sister-in-law Eunice volunteered.

"Here" a tall gentleman joined the group. "I've got the *tira-gostos*. Appetizers anyone?" This time Daniel recognized Coronel Kruel as he tried to outdo his vociferous children.

"I'll get that, *Papai*" Maurício shouted back taking the platter from the Coronel and passing an assortment of pickled olives, cold cuts, fried sausage, and warm rolls around.

More conversations erupted in the meantime and Daniel could not track any since each one was quickly disrupted and restarted. It was amusing to watch the Kruels talk and hop around the furniture as if engaged in a game of musical chairs.

"How gorgeous your plants look" Daniel tracked *Dona* Isabel's index point to a luscious display of ferns by the window. She had seized a pause in the commotion to address *Dona* Sílvia who had finally approached the animated circle with a dish of cod fritters. Taking a corner seat on the couch he had decided to eavesdrop.

"Ah, Bel, *obrigada*" *Dona* Sílvia said. "I must say though Ida is the one responsible for that. You know me, I'll rather be in the kitchen."

"Nonsense, *Mãe*" Daniel shifted to Ida's singing voice as she poured the drinks. "You were the one who taught me how to prune the *Samambaias*" she handed him a glass of lemonade.

Pleased with the deference Daniel gulped it down without losing sight of Ida's moves. She wheeled past him thumping noisily after her little nephew Carlos and his sister Marina who had both snuck under her legs to reach the appetizers. Ida let out an impetuous growl at the toddlers as they stole the prizes in shrieking laughter. Daniel noticed how gracefully she disguised her height with high heels and pretended to look slimmer under a corset. The pair of golden rings rattling on her ears was also magnetic. Wherever Ida went in the room there he turned, his neck wiggling left and right while the chatter exploded around him.

At some point his name came unexpectedly up. “Right, Daniel?” the call came from Coronel Kruel who was now looking straight at him. Taken by surprise Daniel bought some time by grabbing a cod fritter. As a guest in Vila Nova he had gotten away with just a nod and a smile but the same strategy might not work here.

“Pardon me, Coronel?” he wiped his lips with a napkin. The Coronel’s stare was intimidating. His intent eyes had landed on Daniel like a pair of magnifying lenses but Daniel detected none of *Seu* Benedito’s bitterness or *Seu* Orlando’s patronizing in them.

“I am talking about the role of our Church at this political crossroad, Daniel” the Coronel’s blue eyes collided with Daniel’s burning coals. “Wouldn’t you agree we ought to remain apolitical at this juncture?” his long crossed legs dangled by the table’s marble slab. “Give Caesar what is Caesar’s as the Lord mandated, right Daniel?” he repeated the question and clasped his bony knees. “Patriotic Christians must act with decency and order, right?” he pressed on.

Daniel nodded and smiled before commenting. “Huh…” he cleared his throat. “Yes, Coronel, I do believe you are right” his voice shook a little. In truth Daniel had not yet formed an opinion on the developing political crisis and felt the same way now as he did when Antônio first warned him about the possibility of one. Not even after the exchange with Reverend Firmino earlier in the morning had made him reconsider. “Why is everyone so worried about politics?” he thought to himself while grabbing another fritter.

“That is exactly what I told him today, Edgar” Reverend Firmino cut in. “We as Church leaders ought to reassure the flock that regardless of what happens in the world there is no need to fear.

Our home is elsewhere, praise God for that" and he took a long swig of sweet *mate*.

"*Amém*, Reverend" Ida's playful voice trailed in as she offered a refill.

"No more my dear, thanks" the Reverend waved. "By the way Ida, fine job this morning" and the old man's eyes sparkled with flattery.

"Well, Reverend, the line up you chose for today was inspiring" she deflected the compliment with a wink.

"*Pai?*" Manuel cried out. "Shall we eat? The kids have had too many of those cheese rolls" he pleaded.

"Sílvia?" the Coronel cocked his long neck.

"In the kitchen with Alba, Marisa and Eunice" Maurício yelled from the window.

"Then, you go tell them we are ready, son" the Coronel commanded. "Ida, *filha*, your mother needs you in there too" he added and rose to his feet.

From the corner of his eye Daniel detected Francisco, Maurício and Manuel clear off all platters and glasses. Extra chairs quickly materialized and were taken to the extended dining table. Coronel Kruel remained standing in observance as his children executed a well-rehearsed drill and when he deemed it appropriate, stretched his long arms inviting *Dona* Isabel, Reverend Firmino and Daniel to join him.

"Daniel" he looked at him in the eye while pacing forward "it is our pleasure to have you here for the first time and I do hope you will come often" his tone was formal but friendly. "Come to dinner during the week whenever your schedule allows" he stood at the head of the table. "I already told Reverend Firmino that you ought to be eating homemade meals. That kitchenette of yours is unfit for proper cooking" he helped *Dona* Isabel to her seat and pointed at two others.

"Coronel, I could not agree more" *Dona* Isabel spread the pressed napkin on her lap. "Daniel should be eating a decent dinner every night. "In fact, I meant to tell you Firmino" she turned to her husband "I passed a sign-up list at our last Women's Auxiliary meeting asking for volunteers to host Daniel one night a week."

"We begin today, Bel" *Dona* Sílvia retorted reassuringly as she and her daughters arrived carrying the heavy tureens. "Daniel will join us every Sunday after the *culto*" she smiled at him with the same easiness Daniel had seen on Ida's face.

"Watch out, ladies! This way you will spoil him" Manuel joked as he took the chair next to his father. "I already feel sorry for his bride-to-be. She will have to labor hard to match such high expectations" he chuckled.

"Not if the bride-to-be has been well trained" Alba pronounced while pulling out the chair next to her husband Francisco. "I know of many candidates in our church who can rise to the occasion, don't you agree Ida?" and she looked straight across the table at her blushing sister.

"Are we ready to pray?" Coronel Kruel's grave voice rose again trying to break the burst of laughter around the table. "Daniel, kindly lead us" the Coronel ordered.

Taken by surprise again Daniel thought he had misunderstood the request and looked at Reverend Firmino for confirmation. Alba's ludicrous remark made his stomach churn and now all eyes descended on him. "Were Ida's also?" Daniel's tongue flattened. "Fast, Daniel. Think" he faked a smile at the Coronel and bowed his head.

What came out was *Seu* Benedito's old mumble, the same humdrum he had memorized years ago. "Lord, accept our gratitude for this food we are going to eat. Bless our bodies in need of nourishment. Bless the hands that prepared it. In the name of our savior Jesus Christ, Amen."

"Short and sweet, Daniel" Francisco slapped the table effusively. "That is how I like it" and he turned to Alba right away: "*querida*, pass the bread basket this way. No one likes cold *feijoada,*" he quickly snatched two round slices.

"Not me, *Tio*" little Carlos shot both his hands up in the air triggering another round of loud laughter while the women in the family began taking plates from around the table.

"Sundays at the Kruels are known for two mandatory events Daniel: church and *feijoada* in that order" Maurício announced as he waited for his wife Eunice to fill up his plate.

"Hopefully, this will not scare you away next week, Daniel?" Manuel added while forking a juicy orange chunk.

Daniel's neck tensed up. "At my friend Antônio's home over in Vila Nova" he slurred a little, "Teresa served *feijoada* on Saturdays."

"Well, in many households that is how it is done, Daniel" the Coronel followed up. "But at the Kruel's, as far as I can remember…"

"Forever, that's how far" Ida interrupted.

"I still remember my first trip to the butcher don't you Maurício?" Manuel chimed in.

"The one on the corner of Copacabana Avenue and Bolívar Street? *Dona* Isabel asked curiously.

"The very same, my dear" nodded *Dona* Sívia. "He is still in business after all these years."

"What you know" exclaimed Reverend Firmino who had just began to knife his smoked sausage.

"Indeed, Reverend" the Coronel regained control of the conversation. "I would not buy anywhere else either. There is no other place in Copacabana where you'll find good dry beef straight from the northeast" the Coronel brandished his fork.

"And how about his *paio,* the bacon, the sausages?" Maurício dangled a link.

"The tastiest and most tender for sure, don't you think Daniel?" Alba jabbed.

"Oh, yes…" he muttered without lifting his eyes from the plate.

"These collard greens, Sílvia!" *Dona* Isabel leaned forward to the right searching for her friend at the opposite edge of the table."

"Those, Bel, are fresh picks from the *feira" Dona* Sílvia looked to her left. "All the ingredients for our *feijoada*—the *lima* oranges, the onions, the garlic, you know, even the bay leaves I…

"And the black beans, white rice and the…" Ida interrupted her mother this time.

"Ida, let me finish. Everything is freshly picked and…" *Dona* Sílvia tried again.

"Always has been" Ida insisted.

"*Ai, ai, ai,* Ida. Let *mãe* talk!" Alba reproached her younger sister.

"Fiiiine!" Ida sassily retorted.

"Girls, please?" Coronel Kruel pleaded gently.

"Anyway, Bel," *Dona* Sílvia went on "I have also been buying my produce from the same *feira* merchant for years. Since the children were old enough to walk they have joined Edgar and I to our Saturday *feijoada* shopping."

"Now the grandchildren go too…" and Eunice offered a spoonful of black bean broth—*caldinho*—to her little girl while glancing tenderly at Carlos and Marina seating by their Grandmother's side.

"Look at the outcome of my first *feijoada*" Francisco proudly rubbed Alba's round stomach breaking down in a hearty laughter.

Daniel listened puzzlingly to the bits and pieces of family candor. He eventually learned how the Kruel's children began to court their spouses by inviting them to Sunday *feijoadas*. Was he reading too much into it or was he also being subtly ensnared? It had been a demanding day so far; the restless Saturday night was beginning to catch up with him. There had been so much to process. After two servings of *feijoada* nobody is fully functional no matter how many cups of black coffee follow in the end.

"That is why people have to nap afterwards" Francisco reminded everyone. Like in Vila Nova, Daniel recalled waiting for his hosts to disappear on Saturday afternoons. "More coffee, Daniel?" Ida approached but it no longer mattered. Reverend Firmino and *Dona* Isabel were both saying their good-byes and cueing him to follow.

"Thanks for coming" Ida offered him a friendly handshake. He held her hand for a second longer than necessary. No ring to be found, he noticed.

"I thank you kindly, Ida" he solemnly bowed before tagging behind Reverend Firmino and *Dona* Isabel.

PART IV

THE REVEREND

"There are flood and drought
Over the eyes and in the mouth,
Dead water and dead sand
Contending for the upper hand.
The parched eviscerate soil
Gapes at the vanity of toil,
Laughs without mirth.
This is the death of earth.
Water and fire succeed
The town, the pasture and the weed.
Water and fire deride
The sacrifice that we denied.
Water and fire shall rot
The marred foundations we forgot,
Of sanctuary and choir.
This is ***the death of water and fire****."*

(T.S. Elliot, *Little Giding, II)*

TWENTY-TWO

Senhoras e senhores a very good afternoooonnn!!! If you hear me crisp and clear it's because you are tuned to Rio's most popular dial, Global Station 98.1 AM. Broadcasting live, in real time, from the world's largest soccer field, the temple of Brazilian futebol, the majestic Maracanã Stadium, I am your host Coronel Edgar Kruel.

Ladies and Gentleman, do not move too far from your receiver, do not switch your frequency. Raise your antennas and stay put to the one and only source you need to keep up with this fantastic 1963 Carioca Tournament. Global Station 98.1 AM delivers accurate and timely information straight from the field. Grab a seat and don't forget to enjoy an icy bottle of Antártica, the official sponsor of the tournament. Share this treat with your family and friends while you listen to this live transmission.

As your host I, Coronel Edgar Kruel, and my faithful assistant Francisco pledge to bring you inside the stadium. Whether you are at home, at the beach or driving around Rio, you will miss nothing. Whether you root for the brave Vasco da Gama squad or you are a fan of the untouched Fluminense player, be prepared to witness the most exhila-

rating combat of this week's soccer series. All athletes are currently on the grass, warming up and dribbling the ball near the halfway line, right Francisco?

Copy that, Coronel. A very good afternoon to you and to all our loyal listeners during this special coverage. I am your eyes and ears standing a few yards behind the sideline located directly below your box, Coronel. From this vantage point I can see all, and I mean all of it! You will miss none of the moves exactly as they happen on the field. No pass, dribble and most importantly none of the goals will be left uncovered as long as you stay put on Global 98.1 AM, ladies and gentlemen. With only another five minutes to kick off the men are getting ready for the referee's whistle. Some players can be seen casually kicking the ball on their side of the arena whereas others sprint and stretch near the center field mark. Both team captains stand by watching the referee toss the fatal coin up in the air and let me tell you they do look prepared for battle.

The coin has spoken and the captains shake hands on the call claiming their respective sides. On your right-hand side, Coronel, the valiant men of Vasco take position wearing their trademark white jerseys slanted with the single black stripe where the famous four-edged red Maltese cross hangs atop its left corner. The left side of the field will be defended by the vigorous Fluminense Football Club players who by the way are keeping with tradition as well, ladies and gentlemen. They look very smart on the celebrated tricolored red, green and white striped jerseys. For the record both teams wear white shorts and black cleats.

One more comment, Coronel, before you take over. I spoke with Fluminense's coach a few minutes ago after he conferred with his cast by the bench. In case of another victory today his men are sticking to the same exact outfit until the end of this championship. Coach Fleitas claims wearing the same uniform every match is bringing Fluminense great luck. When you are winning, ladies and gentlemen, why change, asks the coach. What is not changing today is the weather forecast, my friends. We could not have asked for a more perfect day. The sun is spraying the entire stadium with a shower of yellow rays this afternoon; only a few puffy clouds hang over, none threatening to pour. Coronel, we are in for warm temperatures all into the evening.

Thank you, Francisco, and stay in touch, please. Superstition or not, loyal listeners, this might be the match to seal Fluminense's fate in the 1963 tournament. We will find out whether Coach Fleitas is right at the end of the regular ninety minutes. A clash of Titans. Two of the most traditional soccer squads in the city of Rio, if not the whole country will face off, and you my friend, will miss nothing, pledge renewed, courtesy of Antártica Beer and Gillette blades, right Francisco?

You can count on that, Coronel. Am as ready as you to relate the action as soon as it begins. We still have another minute to kick off but the crowd is growing impatient. The stadium has been cut off in the middle. On the right side the organized Vasco enthusiasts hurl huge banners all the way from the bleachers down the blue chairs section. The same can be said for all Fluminense fans who have powdered their faces white and now wave tricolor flags franticly on the left side of the Maracanã. The rising roar is contagious. No one can remain seated as long as the drummers beat this whole place into madness.

Obrigado, Francisco, for the updates. Ladies and gentlemen it looks like both goalies are also warming up. Daniel is the lined-up defender for Vasco this afternoon and Bento for the Tricolor. They have taken their respective places on both rear ends of the field and are stretching before kick off. All players are currently taking positions, ladies and gentlemen. We, too, want to see the ball rolling on this smooth green carpet. Don't forget gentlemen, your skin can be as smooth as the Maracanã grass if you shave with Gillette blades; the guaranteed sharp cut.

Who is going to win today? Where is your money on? Stay with us at the one and only Global Station, 98.1 AM, your reliable dial; don't miss a second of the rush officially on. Senhor Firmino, a most experienced referee in this league has blown the whistle in favor of Vasco. Assisting him in this match are also two reputed flaggers, Maurício and Manuel. The crowd is already going insane, Francisco, howling the team's names from all nooks of the stadium. I hear firecrackers from up here, too. Am I right, Francisco?

Most certainly, Coronel. A curtain of smoke has descended on the bleachers, growing thicker by the second. I am having trouble seeing across the field at the moment. The drums are booming, the shouts are deafening. Are we living a dream ladies and gentlemen? Placards, flags and jerseys ripple the bleachers, the lower stands as well as in the moat, the popular 'geral.' The stadium mantled in white, black, red, and green. Thousands prance and wave their jerseys off under a shower of confetti. Beautiful display of support on both Vasco and Fluminense sections, Coronel.

No doubt about it, Francisco. A beautiful spectacle as we get to the ten-minute mark. Now let me draw your attention to Fluminense's Carlos Alberto Torres, ladies and gentlemen. He drills like a torpedo. He is a one-man show and no one from Vasco is able to keep up with him. On the right flank of the field Vasco's right-fielder Telê pants after him. In full possession of the ball Torres gives Telê and Célio no room to run. For the last few minutes, in fact, Torres has been fencing the ball inside the adversary's right corner camp with faithful Escurinho. They are putting a lot of pressure on the Vasco defenders as I speak.

I have my binoculars on, Francisco, and must affirm that it has been a while since I've seen a player control the ball like Carlos Alberto Torres is doing today. He now flies through the middle, ladies and gentlemen. Beside him there come Altair and Evaldo once again for support but nobody from Vasco is fast enough to challenge the advance. Torres receives the ball from Altair and cuts Telê off at the goal line. Célio tries a steal but is too slow. He must do a better job covering his zone if he is to assist Telê. Good luck Daniel is what I have to say, Francisco.

Right you are, Coronel. There is no one else nearby at the moment to offer Daniel coverage, especially along the small goal line.

That is a dangerous spot for the defense line and here he comes again my friends! Carlos Alberto sees the breach between Telê and Onofre. It is a wide gap and he knows he can easily shoot straight on. Like a gazelle he runs, ladies and gentlemen, he yanks on the right leaving all Vasco midfielders sucking their thumbs. I see it coming, Francisco?

Copy that, Coronel.

Ladies and Gentlemen: are you with me? Carlos Alberto Torres is approaching the small goal area and prepares to kick. He sees Daniel too far out from the left pole and he is gonna waste no time. He is calling it on the left corner, there. It is in: gooooolll. Ladies and Gentlemen, goooooooool! The ball drops deep inside the left corner—no filó, Francisco! A bomb from Carlos Alberto, an unbelievable cap over Daniel's head, it clipped the top of the unlucky goalie's hairline and landed on the far left corner of the net. Fluminense scores, ladies and gentlemen. No defense against it, was there, Francisco?

No, Coronel. Senhor Firmino nearly missed the play it unraveled so fast. Fortunately, both flaggers were close on watch to sanction Altair's pass to Carlos Alberto Torres. Vasco's players are crying out fault on Onofre. They are ganging the old man pointing to their fallen mate who is cur-

rently down rubbing his left shin and rolling on his sides. From up close it does look like a fake act. Carlos Alberto Torres was in perfectly legal condition to infiltrate and take the Vasco defenders by surprise. Fluminense: 1; Vasco: 0 at the seventeenth minute mark of the first half. The Tricolor crowd goes into total delirium, ladies and gentlemen. Can you hear the shouting, Coronel? M-E-E-E-N-S-E! M-E-E-E-N-S-E.

Indeed, Francisco. Don't go away friends because Senhor Firmino is in a hurry to resume the game. The ball is at mid-field and he whistles with twenty-eight minutes left in this first half. Poor Daniel, he didn't see this coming, ladies and gentlemen. Had no time to diffuse the bomb. Where were Joel and Caxias, I ask you, Francisco? They both left Daniel all open, didn't they? No one came to rescue Daniel. Will Vasco recover, friends? Stay tuned La-a-a-d-d-dies and G-e-e-e-n-t-l-e-m-en, Global Station, 98.1. AM, for more action courtesy of Antártica Beer and Gillette Blades.

Right again, Coronel. Vasco's defense is disjointed to put it mildly. Instead of playing safe in the back they are pushing too far ahead. When it is time to run back into position it is impossible to catch up with Torres. See now? Same mistake. All players up front and running apart. Nobody in the rearguard to assist Daniel, I'm telling you. This is exactly what Carlos Alberto Torres wants. As we approach the thirty-fifth mark on this first half Fluminense's defense blocks another advance from Vasco as the ball bounces out of bounds. Over.

Copy that, Francisco. Evaldo takes command for Fluminense. He fires at Maurinho on the other side, he receives and quickly carries it to mid-field. He rolls the ball to Altair who catches it in the first try and dribbles it perfectly to Escurinho on the left, leaving Caxias kneeled on the ground. Escurinho spots Evaldo on his right. A few yards ahead Carlos Alberto Torres, ladies and gentlemen, in perfect position to fire another torpedo. Meantime, Telê and Célio are still trying to keep up with Fluminense's offense. Daniel is sliding in front of the goal like an electric saw. He looks nervous trying to figure out where Carlos Alberto Torres is going. The Tricolor player is possessed today and the ball falls on his feet again. I see Brito, Fontana and Paulinho fencing Carlos Alberto in as he approaches the large defense zone. Three of them trying to steer him out of the left sideline. They plan to send the ball out of bounds but Carlos Alberto Torres tells them: 'not so fast, I got this', ladies and gentlemen.

And he is right. He zooms between Brito's legs and carries it over another few yards. He has the option of handing it over to Maurinho on the left or Altair on the right. Both men are in legal position to hand it back to him when the time is right. Altair gets the ball and wastes no time moving passed Paulinho. Carlos Alberto yanks on and raises his hand to Altair who obeys the call and crosses the ball over, right back to Carlos Alberto. A perfect pass and Daniel is in real trouble now, ladies and gentlemen. He is desperately trying to predict where the ball is coming from because it is coming, no doubts about it. Carlos Alberto Torres again in possession of the chubby, takes a second aim with his right foot and launches another powerful rocket.

Daniel guesses the right corner and stretches thin in that direction. He manages to knuckle it up on the pole but it cocks back. It lands inside again! Gooooooolllllll! Goooooollllll! Ladies and gentlemen, gooooollll! Fluminense: 2, Vasco: 0 is the official score on the Maracanã scoreboard updated by Antártica Beer and Gillette Blades. Forty-third minute of the first half, Francisco. Tell us what you see on the ground, pleeease!

Hang on Coronel! I can barely see what is happening. A barrage of smoke and sparkles are blocking my view. The dense plume comes from the Fluminense side of the stadium. The Tricolor crowd is known for its firecrackers, my friends, but today they are going overboard. Don't get me wrong they should be excited about the score. With it they secure the number one spot in the tournament. Let me draw closer to the sideline, Coronel. Give me another second. I am cutting through the fumes. Ai, ai, ai: what you know, ladies and gentlemen? Something is very wrong here. Senhor Firmino is waving for the assistants, calling for a pause in the match. I don't get the reason yet but listen up. Senhor Firmino now calls for first responders to bring a stretcher. I think there is an emergency in the field, Coronel. There could be a man down. Let's see…

A party of four is rushing to the center field and it looks like a young lady is joining them as well. She is carrying a notepad and takes dictation from the referee. Believe it or not, my friends, there is a frozen silence all around. People are not moving or talking. You better come down here too, Coronel, for this is the most unusual turn of events, sir.

Silence, please, everyone. I call this emergency meeting to order. Dona Carmen, please take note of today's date, time and attendance. There are five of us city league members present around this stretcher myself included. Daniel, is in need of medical assistance as you can testify. According to the bylaws of Rio's Soccer League this is the proper quorum to approve an intervention. Do I have a motion to proceed with this gathering? So moved, Senhor Firmino. Thank you, Maurício. Is anyone able to second Maurício's motion? Second, Senhor Firmino.

Much obliged, Manuell. All in favor? Very well, hearing no opposition, I urge you to assist me with a most important decision before this match goes on. Vasco's goalie, Daniel, is injured. Under the authority invested in me I need to address Daniel's present performance and rank as Vasco's goalie. I'm afraid we have to remove him from this position since he is unable to play. However, I do not want to make this arbitrary decision without the counsel of other league members. Who would like to start? Manuel: go on, please, what is on your mind?

Senhor Firmino, it seems obvious that at this point in the game Daniel is not going to hold the Vasco gate shut. Not only is he injured but also his performance lately is a concern. One glance at this stretcher seals the argument. He must withdraw from the team. We are about ready to resume the second half, gentlemen, and Vasco could benefit from the switch. I also believe that with further training Daniel will improve to be Vasco's chief goalkeeper someday. He is young and willing but has to conquer his own worst enemy: his nerves. I propose we transfer him to a smaller club after his contract expires at the end of the year. He can be a great asset at the Encantado second division. The minor league is a less stressful environment for Daniel. In the meantime he will acquire maturity to someday play in the majors.

Dona Carmen: are you recording Manuel's statement?

Yes, sir, every word.

Excellent, thank you. Now, do we have a motion on Manuel's proposal for Daniel?

Yes, Senhor Firmino. For the record, sir, I so move that Daniel be transferred to the second division club located at the suburb of Encantado at the end of the year.

Obrigado, everyone. All in favor say "I"?

"I"

Any nays? Hearing none, I declare the motion unanimously approved. At the end of this year Daniel will be transferred to Encantado Futebol Club. For today he will be replaced and removed from the match. Thank you all. The meeting is adjourned. Let us proceed with the second-half.

Is the half-time break over, Francisco? What has just happened?

What a strange turn of events, Coronel. In an unprecedented decision from the league referee Daniel has been ousted from the match and the city's first division roster. I cannot imagine his disappointment after trying so hard but he will certainly mature while playing in a smaller club.

Who is then defending Vasco's goal, Francisco, can you confirm?

Miltão is coach Otto's choice, Coronel. He has returned from the locker room with the rest of the squad and is warming up under the poles. Daniel's wrist is patched up and he is benched next to the other Vasco backups. I hear the whistle blowing, ladies and gentlemen. Senhor Firmino has authorized the beginning of the second half. Grab a bottle opener and let Antártica quench your thirst because this game is about to get hotter. Another forty-five minutes of combat is on the way brought to you as a courtesy of our generous sponsors—Antártica Beer and Gillette Blades.

Great coverage from the sidelines Francisco, obrigado. Let me also add that there are no changes to report on the Tricolor squad. Coach Fleitas is sticking to his mantra: when winning why change, ladies and gentlemen? Bento kicks the ball far from the goal line to Altair on the right side of the field. Next to him and ready to receive is Escurinho who manages to take it further despite Telê's attempt to block. Escurinho runs with it whereas Vasco's midfielder Paulinho cuts in. He chooses Célio on the left and the ball is back on the Fluminense's turf. Vasco is pushing on, ladies and gentlemen, they have nothing to loose as we approach the fifteenth minute of the second-half. It is all or nothing now, Célio!

He darts through the middle now only to be stopped by the efficient Altair who quickly sends it off to Escurinho. Two options here: either a pass back to Bento or over to Denílson who is waving and asking for it in the middle of the field. Escurinho goes with Denílson but throws it a little too far and it is in Telê's feet that the chubby lands. Telê's swerves towards the extreme right where there is no one from Fluminense at the moment to stop him. Right on his heels, however, there come both Carlos Alberto Torres and Altair. Let's see what Telê does. This could be Vasco's best chance, ladies and gentlemen, as we advance into the last fifteen minutes of the match, Francisco?

This is it, Coronel, Vasco's best chance to score yet. Lets follow this closely, my friends. Telê is forcing a rift between Altair and Bento but Carlos Alberto Torres is on the pursuit.

I see Telê in good condition on the left but if Carlos Alberto Torres succeeds on his chase Telê will miss a fantastic opportunity. Telê holds on and finally spots Célio zooming on the left. He crosses over and Célio swings to the center where two Fluminense's defenders obstruct. Telê tries again running parallel Célio who manages a pass in that direction. The ball meets Carlos Alberto Torres right foot and slows down in time for Telê to arrive at the threshold of the small goal zone.

Bento anticipates Telê's move. He sprints forward and confronts the adversary with arms wide stretched. Escurinho and Altair approach Telê who swings to the right but hesitates, ladies and gentlemen. Bento sees the adversary's vacillation and dives under Telê's feet knocking him on the ground with a ferocious, clever, unexpected safe. He completely disarms Telê a yard off the small goal line. What in the world, Telê? No wonder Célio is angry, Francisco?

Another opportunity like this will not come around today, Coronel. Bento was prompt and agile this time while Telê like the rest of Vasco flicked again. The Tricolor crowd is unforgiving and waves Vasco good-bye with their banners. It does not look good for Vasco at the fortieth minute of the second half. They are going home defeated unless a miracle happens, Coronel.

Yes, Francisco. The noise from the Fluminense fans is now deafening. Ladies and Gentlemen, we are very close to the end of this match as Senhor Firmino urges Bento to resume the play. Bento is in no hurry as to be expected. Fluminense is winning 2 to 0 and when you are winning, don't change! Bento bounces the ball and looks for a mate to kick. Altair is nearby. And slowly rolls the chubby to Carlos Alberto Torres. Everyone is taking time and the Vasco players are in the ring like a wounded bull. 'Olé!, Olé!' the Fluminense crowd yells.

Coronel, Senhor Firmino has blown the whistle one last time. Fluminense defeats Vasco two to zero after ninety minutes of a nail-biting match brought to you live, my friends, thanks to Antártica Beer and Gillette Blades.

Thanks to you too, Francisco, and all who joined our broadcast today. Stay a little longer so you can hear from the players themselves, Francisco, who do you have on the microphone for our loyal listeners?

Let's begin with the Vasco men, sir, since they are obviously the first ones leaving. Daniel is at the dugout, looking a bit shaken but willing to talk.

Daniel, please, can you give us a minute? This is Global Station, 98.1 AM, what can you tell us about today?

Bad luck no doubt. When you least expect things change and luck abandons you to favor another. Today it favored Carlos Alberto Torres. He was unstoppable. He was the lucky one. There was nothing I, or my mates could do to restrain him.

Any comments on the transfer decision, Daniel? Do you find it unfair?

Look, I'd rather not say anything about it right now. This is a decision from the higher-ups. My job here is to comply not to complain.

Not all is lost, am I right Francisco? And who is the young lady with a pretty smile standing next to Daniel?

The rumor is her name is Ida, Coronel. Judging by the band on her right hand one may assume the couple is engaged to be married. More to follow on that I am sure. Stay tuned!

TWENTY-THREE

'Stay tuned, Stay tuned' Daniel's head flapped over the pillow. The cheerful command echoed from behind the walls leading him to believe someone had broken in. Briefly considering the possibility he peeked at the pre-dawn veil outside the window but his head ached so badly that his neck refused to move. As far as he could remember the front door had been double-locked. Could the jolly shout be coming from a wasted hobo down Paula Freitas Street? Anything was possible at this hour in Copacabana and Daniel slowly steadied his pounding head. The room span dizzily out of control and he desperately clung to the mattress. If there were an intruder he better hide under the covers.

Over the ruffled sheet Daniel groped for the comforter but the bed felt bare and damp. No matter how eagerly he fumbled there was nothing to hold on to and trying to come up with an explanation for the missing spread Daniel quit fussing. His eyelids lacked resolve and needed another minute or two to be reassured. Was he still dreaming? A sharp pinch over his stomach redirected attention to the area where his nevus itched wildly.

An electrified current suddenly hit his dormant body and his nails went to work.

"Stupid mosquitoes" he cursed under his fermented breath. With a drowsy swat he searched the elusive targets but his sluggish hands kept flopping about. As the urge to scrape eventually subsided the familiar pulsating nip crept underneath his temples reminding him of the vengeful needles ready to poke his brain flat unless he ran for the shower.

"Where in the world is the cover?" he tapped the foot of the bed. He must wrap his head or else the pelting would drive him madder. After a restless night of tosses and turns he was grateful to be above ground. One painful breath at a time and he managed to recover his earthly senses. The skin over his lips felt dry and chapped. A sour goo covered his lifeless tongue and he felt awfully thirsty. "Water" he whispered and reached under the pillow. A nagging noise rattled his cheek out of dormancy with a pleasant tickle that reminded him of yet another mishap. In the struggle to stay asleep he had not only shoved the bedcover off but also forgot to turn off the radio. For how long was the static carrying on? Right now his pricking mind was in no condition to figure the time but he still risked a squint at the shady window.

"Stay tuned!" the call echoed again as if from under the pillow. "*Tudo bem, tudo bem*" he focused on the window and watched night gradually surrender to the advance of dawn. Within the hour a new day was about to break and usher the impudent sunbeams. The alarm clock ticked confidently away and it soon jolted him up. With a shaky hand Daniel seized the clock and beat the race against the buzzer, a frivolous achievement that had afforded a momentary illusion of control.

Reality proved to be quite different and Daniel knew it. From the minute he got up others dictated his moves. Just as Pastor Santos and Miss Cabral had done in Lajedo, the Copacabana staff made that fact crystal clear. The alarm clock though was the only object under his direct command and when he crushed it silent, Daniel felt vindicated.

A foolish quirk no doubt but it built up self-confidence and inspired him to take charge of other unsettling aspects of his scripted routine since Antônio's departure from campus. It was then that his insomnia intensified and he heeded to Lurdes's suggestion. A swig or two of *cachaça* at bedtime kept him asleep except that the powerful sugarcane brandy left a nasty aftertaste. It was Zé's trick that made all the difference, thank goodness. Cheap whisky worked much better than *cachaça* and by the time Daniel left Seminary his evening routine was well established. Reclined in bed playing *sertanejo* tunes on the radio he sipped *Passaport* whisky until passing out. If he were to survive the demanding internship he had to get a few hours of sleep anyway. A nightly black out worked just fine so long he looked presentable in the morning.

Alone in the dark Daniel escaped to another dimension serenaded by *sertanejo* tunes and the lukewarm texture of whisky. After a few swigs his mattress began to sway just like his ugly Lajedo hammock. His frazzled body then spiraled into a deep hole and like a light feather it floated to total stillness. Taken to an imaginary Elysium he heard nothing, saw nothing, and more importantly, felt nothing for hours in a row.

Ironically as it seemed the evening blackouts were worth the queasiness and aches of the mornings. Discomfort had never been a stranger to Daniel and when the pinching needles returned at dawn he resorted to the cold showers and sweetened *cafézinhos* until bedtime. The only grievance was the occasional tangle in the head when waking up. In that foggy state between dozing and rousing when he couldn't discern reality from illusion Daniel could swear someone was nearby. That spooked him out and led to thoughts of the Umbanda priest of few years back. Since that impressionable encounter Daniel could not shake the feeling the grotesque *Exú* statute followed him around.

Lurdes had been so impressed with the old priest's revelation that Daniel forbade her from bringing the subject up again. However, every time she looked down at his stomach where the misshapen dark patch stretched like a flattened cockroach, she smiled. He, too, could not help looking at it in the same way anymore. Whenever it itched for no reason like a moment ago his heart thumped. Lurdes and that demonic old man had not been the first ones to notice Daniel's uncanny trait. As a little boy his mother made ludicrous references to the birthmark as God's branding. '*God has chosen you, son*' *Dona* Dulce's husky drone sounded almost the same as the black man's slur, "*Exú walks with you.*"

Daniel swallowed the dry goo with disgust. "How preposterous" he licked his numb lips thinking of water again. Through half-shut eyes he surveyed the room that no longer spun when the first sunrays seeped in. He sluggishly tracked the dancing beams. "I'm finally living my mother's dream" he shifted from the old armoire to the precious glass-paneled bookcase where his whisky bottles and novels remained carefully locked up. Turning to the front door he saw no sign of forced entry. He had been dreaming again and it was now safe to get up.

Both clock pointers warned Daniel of time's unstoppable mission when he finally slammed the metal pin. At six o'clock his favorite soccer show would begin on Global Station 98.1 AM but until then there were a few minutes left to track a *sertanejo* tune. From under the pillow he retrieved the hand-size transistor radio and squeezed it closer to his ear. The soothing static lingered quietly while his thumb turned the knob ushering a stream of raucous sounds. The dull voice of a Catholic priest recited a Hail Mary and skipping over it, Daniel picked up Elizete Cardoso's sorrowful cry—"*Vai minha tristeza*"—*Go my sadness, tell her, without her I cannot live."*

Compelled to a moan Daniel blurted, "oh for goodness' sake" and braced for another prolonged *swishswishswish*. "Is anyone up yet?" he turned to the flashing window. "*These are the headlines from your Radio Clock Station. Attention listeners: President João Goulart is in Teresina today to connect a new water line to the Paulo Afonso system."* Daniel blinked slowly and kept on turning the knob. "Does anyone in this country still care about what the President does?" he shrugged.

There. Luís Gonzaga's booming voice burst like a brass horn. His unmistakable accordion quaked like a pipe organ and jolted Daniel's achy head.

"*Quando olhei a terra ardendo,*
qual fogueira de São João,
eu perguntei, ai, meu Deus do céu
ai, por que tamanha judiação?

When I saw the land burning
like a Saint John's Day bonfire,

I asked God of Heaven
why so much cruelty?"

"How could anyone sing so cheerfully about tragedy?" Daniel wondered. "If Luís Gonzaga knew what droughts entailed how could he glorify it? Had he seen the land wither or had he smelled the stench of dead cattle?" Daniel's tongue curled at the thought of a time gone by. "Why so much cruelty?" he had asked God that same question but now, living away from Lajedo, Daniel let Luís Gonzaga's thundering voice disarm his frown. "And then I said, so long Rosinha, keep my heart with you, la, la, la, la, la, la…"

Daniel squeezed the radio harder and let out a yawn. His glassy eyes turned to the nightstand where a *Passport* bottle sat nearly empty. The pale green glass trapped the day's first brightness and lit like a torch revealing the amber colored content at the bottom. Brows arched in disbelief Daniel let go of the radio and grabbed it. "How did this happen?" he measured a finger's worth of whisky left at the bottom. "Did I drink this much in one night?" he could not remember.

"Ladies and Gentlemen: let me be the first one to whish you a very good morning" the buoyant radio announcer came mercifully on. Daniel tracked the muffled Samba drums in the background and listened carefully to the host of Ball Planet deliver updates on the *Carioca* tournament. Not until the drums fainted and the report ended did Daniel consider getting up. Today, however, he had not much going on. Within twenty-four hours he was scheduled to move out of the Copacabana studio and literally shut the door on his lofty career plan. He was not being considered as Reverend Firmino's suc-

cessor after all, and to his absolute dismay had been transferred out of the *Zona Sul* congregation.

At week's end he would be ordained Reverend at Encantado Evangelical Church, a place he had never seen before except from the window of the northbound train. During the recent and fatal decision-making process the Copacabana Elders in collusion with the city synod did not bother to consult Daniel. The blow had triggered a binge of whisky and music for the past few days, which explained the nearly empty *Passaport* bottle on the nightstand.

On his way up Daniel grabbed it. He would have to buy another one later, he decided, and hid the bottle inside the glass-paneled bookcase. "A shower is what I need" Daniel fumbled to the stall hoping to settle the nasty hangover. A foggy picture of Encantado formed in his mind as he turned the water on and threw his head against the wall to gargle and spit the first gush that poured out.

A dull dump was how he remembered the place where the northbound train no longer stopped. During their final conference Reverend Firminio had casually mentioned that from Central Station he would need to get off in Piedade and then backtrack to Encantado on a tram. On moving day though, Bento would drive him there, not to worry.

"Not to worry, Reverend Firmino?" Daniel soaped up his thick hair. "Had he or any of the Copacabana Elders considered how much effort he had put into the internship?" he scrubbed hard. "How hard had he tried to impress everyone with his mild manners, poignant sermons, and meekness?" the foam thickened under his angry hands. "God's will Daniel" the Reverend had affirmed. "Always" the rest of them had chimed in. "Droughts, fevers, and death too?" Daniel wanted to slam the wall. "Yes, son, of course" he pictured Reverend Firmino's lips widen from behind the imposing desk.

"I asked, Ai, my God in Heaven, Ai, why so much cruelty? La-la-la-la-la-la…" Luís Gonzaga's voice joined the chorus of bad news. Two weeks ago, at the end of one of those Sunday afternoon meetings Daniel had been diligently attending, Coronel Kruel announced the decision. Daniel felt so betrayed. He had accepted the Kruels' weekly invitations as a welcoming gesture into the Copacabana inner circle. Trying his best to appear professional, prudent even, Daniel had hanged to every word the Coronel said and avoided opinions on polemical matters regarding the country's political crisis.

Some Elders had questioned the legitimacy of Goulart's government whereas others suggested caution. Either way Daniel had no ideological backbone and found it safer to stand by those who possessed the greatest influence. "What would Antônio say?" the moon face lit up large and bright. It had been a while since Daniel had received a letter from him and reaching out for a towel he waved Antônio's boyish grin out of his mind. There were more pressing issues to consider among which was his relationship with Ida. Since that first Sunday dinner at the Kruel's the family had insisted on his weekly return and soon afterwards the Coronel gave Daniel permission to nap at the boy's old bedroom after lunch, so he could escort Ida to the evening youth service. The family quickly warmed up to him and he knew that Ida's subtle attentiveness was the reason.

With each passing encounter Ida had grown more interested in Daniel's Lajedo past, asking questions about family, friends and dishes he enjoyed eating so she could try them out next time he came. He remained as evasive as possible and did not reveal too many details except for his instruction under Ms. Cabral and Pastor Santos.

Ida found his gilded descriptions of the backlands fascinating and his peculiar northeastern accent unusually dulcet. Your "ts" and "os" carry a musical ring, she remarked one evening while they rode the bus back to church.

A week ago she had broken with the family protocol and prepared a stew of dry beef and pumpkin from a recipe clipped out of a housekeeping magazine. "Does *Jerimum* mean *abóbora*?" she had asked at the dinner table to show off her new vocabulary. "And *Carne de sol* means dry beef" she announced to the clan with a spirited laugh while filling his plate. "So curious to have different words for such common foods, don't you all think?" Ida invited the rest of the group to share in her exotic curiosity. "Or could it be we *Cariocas* are the ones who say it differently?' she switched the focus noticing Daniel's reluctance to take center stage.

He would always be the outsider among them no matter how hard he masked his northeastern accent. Still, Ida's candor nurtured Daniel's appetite. Their friendship was ingratiating and could well be the key through the Copacabana door. Ida's family was well regarded in the southern zone Evangelical circle and her father was an influential Elder. The Coronel could put a good word on his behalf in time for the end of year ordination, or so he thought.

Keeping that in perspective Daniel tactfully responded to Ida's inquiries, smiled and nodded in a way Coronel Kruel and *Dona* Sílivia surely approved. In the end, however, his calculations failed miserably. His future was again being decided without his input. If they didn't want him around in the first place why lure him in? Daniel stepped out of the shower.

Yet, Ida's charm had been irresistible. Other than Ms. Cabral she had been the most cultivated woman he ever met. A trained musician and Normal School graduate Ida also possessed a reputable family name to fall back on. "What had she seen in him, though?" Daniel studied the puzzled reflection on the mirror with uncommon rigor.

He was not even that good looking. This was a puzzle he still had to solve. Would it be appropriate to pursuit the courtship from a distance? If he could not open the Copacabana door quite yet, should he still pocket the key? Today was his last full day in the borough and he had to pack and clean up. At eight o' clock the Kruels expected him for a farewell dinner when Ida promised to serve broiled goat chunks with buttered yucca. "So rich and spicy you will soon be back for more" her comment struck him as an ultimatum rather than a hint. In less than a year Daniel would fully understand why.

TWENTY-FOUR

"*Seu* Daniel?" An impatient call thundered behind the studio door. Two loud pounds nearly shook its hinges off.

"Whooo isss ittt?" Daniel hissed incoherently through his gooey lips. "Wall jeering again?" he tried to lift his heavy head. At the room's intrusive brightness his eyelashes blinked tiredly and froze open when faced the clock. "What?" he could not believe his eyes. Last thing he remembered was squashing the pin before six.

"Had he blacked out again?" Daniel tried to reason it out. "Why was he still in bed?" the murmur from under the pillow sounded crispier than usual. "No static" he scooped the hand-size radio with a puzzled look and turned the volume up to an incoming message: "Your Radio Clock Station inform. Today's high is 36 Celsius, humidity levels mount with no chance of rain."

A flash of late December radiance nearly blinded Daniel as he craned his neck at the windowsill. "What?" he rolled panicky onto his elbow. A harsher blow rattled the wood as the voice returned.

"It's Bento, *Seu* Daniel" the aversion was thick. "It's Saturday and you're leaving, remember?" the tone rang grimmer. "You ready?" Bento insisted.

"No, I'm not, you beast—*sua besta*" Daniel said under an overheated whiff. He had overslept for the first time ever and scowled silently at the ticking clock contemplating his next move. Should he open the door and admit to the mistake or pretend to be busy getting dressed? To be on the safe side Daniel chose the latter and clutched the clock, tempted to toss it out the window.

"*Já vai*—coming, Bento" he wobbled out of bed enunciating each word cautiously. "Just about finished tying my shoes" he lied.

"*Tudo bem, Seu* Daniel*"* Bento replied gruffly. "Be right back—*Já volto*" he slapped his flip-flops noisily down the stairs.

"Stupid clock" Daniel gritted his slimy teeth blaming the device for the oversight. In the first attempt to stand upright he landed falteringly on one heel and tripped over the comforter rumpled by the nightstand. In a fit of fury he nearly lost his balance trying to yank it off the floor. Hurriedly, he smothered it over the sheet predicting Bento's suspicious browsing if he entered the room. At least, he had the sense of leaving a dress shirt and pair of pants ready before blacking out. If he winged it accurately there would be enough time to look presentable.

Like a grasshopper Daniel staggered about the parquet trying to button the shirt, clip his bowtie, and lace his shoes at the same time. "No time to shower and shave" he lamented on his way to the water closet. Desperate for a cool splash he turned the faucet on. "Everything is already packed" he surveyed the empty cabinet shelves. "No pomade, no *Aqua Velva*, no problem" he nodded confidently at the mirror and kept a straight face. There was a spare plastic comb inside his rear pocket and after a few sprinkles of water he should be able to tame his ruffled hair. Extra sprays of deodorant would give the impression of tidiness.

"That shaggy werewolf—*Lobisomen*—is coming back in no time" Daniel flew out of the water closet to fumble the suitcase for the pine-scented *Rexona* flask. "I bet he is down there right now telling Reverend Firmino I'm late" he sprayed away. "Won't let him have the last laugh though" and the deodorant landed back in the suitcase. Wasting no time he fastened the belt up and turned to his wristwatch quickly. "Eight o'clock in the morning" he shook his head. "I've never slept this late" he zipped the skimpy suitcase. "Good that I own more books than clothes" and with one pluck placed it against the bedstead. There was nothing else left to do as far as he could see.

"Ah!" he snatched the green bottle from the nightstand and stowed it carefully inside the bookcase. The small key used to lock it he safely pocketed. "All set" Daniel tapped his loins for reassurance. Key, comb, and wallet were all evenly distributed. As a precaution he counted a dozen neatly wrapped book bundles piled on top of the bookcase.

"*Tudo bem*" Daniel smiled and nodded realizing why Bento had knocked on his door so persistently. Reverend Firmino had assigned the custodian to assist with the move to Encantado. Bento knew the route well and would help load the *Aero Willys*. "The books fit on the floor behind the front seats" Daniel dreaded spending the rest of the morning near Bento. "The suitcase goes in the trunk, the bookcase on the back seat." He was pleased with the trifle loot of five years when comparing it with what he carried out of Lajedo.

"*Seu* Daniel?" Bento's rough knuckles on the door interrupted again.

"*Entra* Bento, come in" Daniel retorted in the same curt tone. No farther than an inch from the door he dug his heels and passively refused Bento the courtesy of opening it.

"You ready now, *Seu* Daniel?" Bento thrust under the threshold, his deep and set-apart eyes flashing and his broad shoulders arched up like a stalking Jaguar cornering a prey. Up close Bento appeared so much taller that Daniel instinctively stepped back. No doubts the janitor was also cross about the delay.

"Take these first" Daniel pointed at the bundles atop the bookcase.

"Fine" Bento moved closer. "It will take us two to haul this thing down, *Seu* Daniel" he chinned up at the bookcase and then glanced at Daniel as if saying "you just got up, didn't you? Who you trying to fool?" and stomped down the stairway.

"When are you going to start calling me Reverend, Bento?" Daniel yelled haughtily from the top of the stairs.

"When *Seu* Daniel? Well, whenever you become one" Bento answered not bothering to look up.

"Soon, then" Daniel's squealed but Bento had already stepped out of range and did not catch the impudent proclamation. "This is going to be a long day" Daniel sighed checking his watch and plodding the narrow perimeter separating the door from the window. "Actually, a long week" he mumbled and reopened drawers and cabinets compulsively. Had he forgotten to discard any incriminating evidence? He took one last look out the window only to painfully catch Bento hurling the neatly wrapped bundles all over the car floor. Disgusted, he smacked the windowsill and withdrew to the water closet.

His thoughts shifted to Reverend Firmino's commendable descriptions of the Encantado's parsonage, a newly built addition in the rear of the premises "much roomier than the rabbit hole you are stuffed in" he assured Daniel. It comprised of a three-bedroom residence equipped with a telephone line and modern kitchen appliances "just waiting for the perfect mistress to preside over" the old man had winked.

"Am I imagining things or the pressure to pop up the question mounted this past week?" Daniel consulted his watch at the sound of Bento's loaded feet up the steps. During the farewell dinner at the Kruel's the Coronel had also spoken effusively about the expanding membership in Encantado. "An enthusiastic congregation, Daniel, in much need of vigorous leadership" had been the Coronel's assessment. *Dona* Sílvia, less discretely added about the need for a "*permanent*" organist as well.

"*Seu* Daniel, the bookcase here" Bento drummed on the varnished piece.

"Huh?" Daniel looked away pretending not to have noticed the janitor's arrival.

"This one thing here" Bento smacked the wood again. "Grab the other end and follow me down" he barked.

"Is the Reverend in yet?" Daniel clumsily lifted the assigned portion and panted down the steps trying to keep up with Bento's trot.

"Yep. Waiting for you at the office I reckon" Bento grumbled. "Is something broken inside this thing? I hear a cling" he paused suspiciously midway.

"Could be a loose glass on the panel. Careful not to trip over and wreck it" Daniel scolded. "It should fit easily along the back seat" he immediately changed the subject.

"Don't see why not" Bento wobbled out of the building's entryway while Daniel puffed behind.

"Daniel, wait!" a raspy shout crept up from the end of the hallway. "How about breakfast?" Reverend Firmino waved and shut his office door. He skipped towards the entrance as fast as his short legs allowed but Bento and Daniel had already crossed into the blazing sun.

On the sidewalk where Bento had parked the car a potted almond tree struggled to stay erect. Its skinny limbs possessed barely any leaves to offer relief from the sizzling sun and it was underneath it that the Reverend found the two men catching their breath. By now Daniel was transpiring uncomfortably not just on account of the humidity but Bento's roughness with his cherished possession. "Easy, *calma*, Bento" he repeated after each bang the janitor produced to squeeze the piece through the rear door.

"*Seu* Daniel shut that one door there on your side" Bento shouted while slamming the other end. Daniel's heart skipped a beat as he heard the blow and immediately bent inside the car to check on the outcome. After gently pressing his hip against the door Daniel turned around dying to scream at Bento but Reverend Firmino's reddened face jumped in front of him. Daniel quickly replaced his frown with a meek smile and nodded.

"So very kind of you to come, Reverend" he pulled a cotton handkerchief to wipe his hand before stretching it.

"I would not have it any other way, son" the Reverend took Daniel's hand. "A year ago I escorted you in and it is my duty to bless you out. Shall we go to Mário's for breakfast?" he let go of Daniel's grip and beckoned broadly towards the ocean. To Bento, who was dutifully standing by, he softly instructed "please, Bento, bring everything else down in time for a nine o'clock departure. *Obrigado*."

"You don't need to bother…" Daniel fanned both hands in a gesture of pretense humility. "Really, taking time away from your free day, Reverend" he nudged the old man away from the custodian.

"Oh, Daniel, in ministry there is never a free day. You should know that by now" Reverend Firmino walked pleasantly beside Daniel. "I do find it important to send you off with a friendly memory of your stay with us and what better than reminisce on a stroll towards the beach in this fine morning? One last breakfast at Mário's is a must" the old man spread his hands theatrically. "However, this is not good-bye, Daniel" he grabbed Daniel's forearm. "We will see each other less but I want you to know that you can call on the phone and visit anytime you want" he let go of his grip shifting to a solemn tone. "What you are going to face from now on is both exciting and stressful, you know? It takes me back to when I started. No one took the time to warn me about the joys and grieves of being a clergyman. So, I am here to let you know that you have my prayers and support as you walk the peaks and valleys of your calling. Trust me, Daniel, there will be difficult times; temptation prowls like a leashed lion. Learn to walk away. Prayer and Scripture reading specially Proverbs' "Thirty Sayings of the Wise" is sound counsel. Read it as often as you can, memorize all thirty verses and make sure to listen to your Elders before making a decision. I think you are a good listener, Daniel. Based on what I observed this year I can tell you are paying attention. It's a good start, son" the Reverend pinched Daniel's elbow.

At the corner of Copacabana Avenue they paused and waited for traffic to clear. Daniel absorbed his mentor's speech hesitantly. Had he been really a good listener or rather a good cheat? Frankly, he couldn't wait for the moment to speak his own mind especially now that he was a free agent. The fresh air grazed Daniel's hair and for an instant he pictured himself out there in middle of the broad blue water sailing. It was about time he issued orders instead of following them. He was ready. "Yes, sir" he remarked compliantly to the Reverend's comment and stopped short of blurting out "I am ready to lead and shine."

The moment he had been waiting for was at hand, his own pulpit, a furnished office, a decent house of brick and mortar. He was getting so close. And Daniel took a deep breath watching the beach goers ramble by with their colorful towels and umbrellas. It was a seasonably scorching Saturday morning and very few people in Copacabana could be seen wearing anything but bathing suits and flip-flops at this hour except, or course, for him and Reverend Firmino.

Daniel was going to miss the indolence of the seaside. Encantado was so far from the shore, he moaned discretely to avoid Reverend Firmino's attention. Supposedly its only source of water was a tainted embanked creek for which the borough was named. Bento had grown up in those parts and wasted no time poking fun of him as soon as he heard of the transfer. "Don't lean over the banks when it rains, *Seu* Daniel" he had giggled too friendly at the end of last week's service. "Legend says no one escapes the muddy bottom of the Encantado creek during a March thunderstorm. The water pulls you in. That's why it's Enchanted" he laughed in Daniel's face.

"Here we are" Reverend Firmino's pointlessly announced. The words floated inside Daniel's heedless ears while his legs climbed the bakery's dirty steps one last time. He breathed in the smell of warm bread and salivated at the sight of the pastries. Looking around Daniel noticed that most stools in front of Mário's counter were still vacant. Only the beach goers get up this early on a Saturday morning.

"*Reverendo*! What's the occasion?" Mário's plump lips broke in a friendly grin. "Tell me, when was the last time I fixed you a *média?*"

"*Bom dia,* Mário. I know, I know… I have been meaning to pay you a visit and today is the day" the Reverend shook hands with the server. "It is Pastor Daniel's last breakfast here in Copacabana and I would not miss it for anything. How have you been, Mário?" Reverend Firmino wobbled over the round stool throwing his small hands across the counter. His chubby legs dangled playfully above the greasy tiles.

"*Beleza,* beautiful! Last day, huh Pastor?" Mário expediently set two small cups on the counter and poured down Daniel's first fix of sweetened black coffee. For the Reverend he brought a tall glass of coffee and milk. "But why?" Mário asked without taking his eyes off the counter. "Don't like my coffee no more?" and then he drooped the corners of his round unshaved cheeks faking a mourning grimace.

"What Mário, you make the best coffee in this whole *Zona Sul*" the Reverend interjected. "The reason he is leaving is to take a church in the suburb of Encantado" he proudly reported. "Next time you see him, Mário, make sure to call him Reverend Daniel, *viu*? The ordination is a week from today" Reverend Firmino winked at Mário and blew the steam out of his coffee and milk.

"*Meus Parabéns,* Pastor. I mean congratulations, Reverend Daniel" Mário clapped his bear hands as soon as he hanged his work towel on his shoulders. “Don’t you forget the old friends when you leave, huh?”

“No, I will be back, Mário” Daniel smiled downcast and Lurdes’s despondent face flared from the bottom of his cup reminding him of the same promise he made a year ago. “Cheat” was the word coiling out of her pursed lips. He gulped the last drop urgently and grabbed a slice of buttered French bread to dunk it down the glass of coffee and milk Mário had just landed on the counter.

Daniel and Reverend Firmino took their time sipping and savoring their *Média* in silence, enjoying the energizing effect of Mário’s fresh brew as the server entertained them with a string of complaints about his soccer team’s disappointing performance at the end of the *Carioca* tournament. Reverend Firmino laughed along visibly amused by Mário’s sarcastic puns and when it was time to go he paid the bill and left a generous tip promising Mário to return. “Soon?” the baker widened his smile and stuck both of his thumbs up. “Deal” said the Reverend and they all shook hands pledging to stay in touch.

Back on Paula Freitas Street Bento leaned idly against the driver’s door chewing on a toothpick hoping to catch a sliver of shade under the barren almond tree. “*Pronto*, *Reverendo*?” he eventually noticed the old man. An affirming nod was enough for Bento to pull the driver’s door open and jump inside. He hummed the engine into action intentionally ignoring Daniel’s presence.

“Bento, take your time this morning” the Reverend spoke through the passenger’s window. “No need to hurry back. I have no place to go today but my study” he smiled kindly. “And Daniel: God bless you” the old man tapped his thick wedding band on the metal frame to authorize the departure.

"As you wish, Reverend. Carmen is already in if you need any help" Bento informed hunching over the steering wheel. "I will wax the sanctuary floor as soon as I get back, not to worry" and he clunked the first gear in place, stepping deep on the gas pedal. The heavy car jolted forward and Daniel instinctively looked at the back seat grudgingly whispering: "*Calma,* Bento."

"Do you know how to drive, *Seu* Daniel?" the janitor asked sarcastically stepping on the gas.

"That's not the point. I mean be careful not to break things" Daniel grabbed the dashboard.

Bento dismissed the rebuke by fiddling with the radio dial. He settled for a *bossa nova* tune and cranked up the volume to drown any potential remarks Daniel might stab at him. By the same token Daniel slid closer to the window widening the distance between them. Bento was an accomplished driver by *Carioca* standards and faithfully disregarded all rules of the road. He also relished in honking loudly at the equally reckless pedestrians who darted off the sidewalks expecting to be noticed. Fortunately, on a Saturday morning foot traffic slowed down to a minimum and Bento managed to swerve competently around the jaywalkers without too much noise or nauseous maneuvering.

At the last corner of Copacabana Avenue Bento pushed down on the gas to avoid a red light. He steered sharply to the left and skidded onto the far side of Princesa Isabel Avenue tugging Daniel's head off the window frame where he had leaned for a last look at Leme's blue sea before his pupils contracted inside tunnel Novo. Copacabana was now officially behind him. Bento plowed hastily through the borough of Botafogo and keeping up with such speed,

Daniel calculated reaching downtown in less than twenty minutes. From there, another half hour to the land of Encantado.

Would anyone be there to greet him? Daniel wiped beads off his forehead. Anyone to show him around? And Antônio's friendly face intruded taking him back to that first day at Seminary when he was so overwhelmed and tired. He made a mental note to write him a letter soon with the new address on Clarimundo de Melo Street, number 50. It was the least he could do after the past year without much communication.

"And how about Ida?" Daniel still wrestled over the proposal issue. Would she be happy uprooted from family, church, and of course the ocean? The only way to find out was to ask, Daniel speculated noticing the idleness hanging over both sides of a deserted President Vargas Avenue. From a close distance the clock tower emerged exuberantly. Its metal pointers stretched perfectly across the hanging circumference to mark twenty minutes past nine. Daniel secretly praised his own forecast when the *Aero Willys* zoomed under the landmark. He cocked his head up to admire the neatly placed spikes linking the twelve iron bars around a huge circle. The hovering loop struck Daniel as an urgent reminder. "A ring" he gasped. An engagement proposal does require a ring and for the last part of the ride Daniel delved into the logistics of selecting one. They now approached the decrepit landscape beyond Flag Square. Bento had finally crossed into the Northern Zone as the potholes painfully testified. The one-lane road parallel to the rail track had not been properly paved in years and despite Bento's agility the bumps were too many to dodge. Further into the impoverished neighborhoods the desolate stations of Engenho Novo, Méier, Engenho de Dentro marked their progress along the urine reeked pedestrian underpasses.

From this angle everything appeared more miserable than the snippets Daniel had archived during the rides with Antônio.

"Where will I find a jeweler around this dump?" Daniel shifted uneasily over the simmering car seat. He nervously appraised the tarnished façades on the establishments along *Vinte Quatro de Maio* Avenue. With no exception they all displayed a tacky inventory of items he found not use for. Plastic toys, used car parts, Catholic and Umbanda statuary, and sewing implements crammed up the narrow sidewalks to lure the stingy clientele. Daniel's sweaty thighs stuck closer to the burning cushion as if they too were about to dilute. From one train station to the next there was no variation in the scenery and Daniel checked his watch compulsively realizing how close he was to Encantado.

TWENTY-FIVE

Years later Daniel would remember that Saturday morning more intently than the day he left Lajedo. In the course of his adult life he equated both moves as momentous though conflicting reactions appeared whenever there was a comparison. The lonely and scary departure from the *sertão* at such tender age jolted a convoluted sequence in his mind that it was nearly impossible to judge whether the exodus had been a blessing or a curse. Sometimes he interpreted it as a miraculous escape from fate, an unexpected brush with fortune that offered him a new lease in life. Upon boarding the bus, he understood for the first time how other *retirantes* felt. Entire families had fled the deadly drought hopping on a *pau-de-arara* truck and like him refused to gaze back at the wasted fields of beans and corn leveled by the wayside.

He, too, held on to a one-way ticket with trembling hands unsure of what to expect from the uncharted route to bounty until dropped on the other end. Everything changed so completely in an instant. "Blessing or curse?" And Daniel found himself back at the window seat, throwing nervous glimpses at anguished faces searching for their own bus to catch. Indifferent to Daniel's blank stare they had no idea about becoming his last imprints of a place once called home. The scene had nearly paralyzed him with fear. Further along the bumpy road countless twists and turns stunned him as he watched the barren wilderness turn into a bright mix of vibrant green and blue. Five days later he found himself still perplexed though surprisingly stoic to comply with the rigidity of Seminary right away.

It was impractical to grieve a lifetime of sorrows in just five days and that was why Daniel was determined to cut off connections with the past and repress any false hopes of a return. Within months of his arrival on campus he deliberately stopped answering letters from home, a survival strategy that saved him from remorse in the long run. There was no alternative, no way back. Instead, he worked diligently to adhere to the intricate web of regulations doing his best to deflect attention from his northeastern accent and shabby attire. Alone in front of mirrors he spent many furtive hours hissing out the spirited 'Ss' and 'Ts' of the *Cariocas*. More difficult was to lower the high-pitch tone of his 'Os' but he got that down in the first few months. If he stood a chance to survive he had to camouflage fast.

Each year away from Lajedo Daniel's meticulous metamorphosis from backland migrant to consecrated preacher progressed. Through keen observation and emulation he retained the staged half-smile that had helped him mask suffering before. Later on, the *Passport* bottle made solitude so much easier. During the long restless nights when he felt like a fraud he drowned his inadequacy down the hollow pit inside his numb heart. Most memories of who he used to be were buried under thick layers of disdain and if it were not for those intrusive relentless dreams important scraps of Daniel's early existence would have vanished completely.

Some fragments stubbornly remained, however. One in particular resisted the longest and aroused in Daniel a fleeting queasiness best identified with the moment he boarded the diesel-reeked bus. When the memory returned he could still see the confused passengers on the station platform, their canvas sacks on one arm and a skinny child on the other. Strangely, an urgent need for water always besieged him and that was when he reached for his loyal green bottle. When the driver rattled the engine at the curbside he saw Pastor Santos's clumsy bounce one last time. A blast of combustion ripped the caustic air into a plume and finally blocked his flailing hands from view. A cloud of gray was all that was left of the past.

Why Daniel clung to that particular instant he never questioned. Years propelled in haste afterwards when professional obligations cluttered his ambitious mind. Ultimately under the spell of aging and inebriation the exodus memory faded. Flashes turned to evanescent puffs until one day he woke up from another blackout thirsty and dizzy racking his mind to chisel Pastor Santos's silhouette at the bus station. Which day was that?

The departure from Copacabana, on the other hand, Daniel revisited with less ambiguity.

At first he had taken the transfer hard and for a few weeks sulked in silence cursing the Elders under his intoxicated breath. But as soon as adulation from the Encantado congregants poured in and the comforts of an established suburban household expanded, Daniel was able to temper the sour taste of indignation with the sweetness of dependable bounty. Apart from Bento's eerie proximity that day, his arrival at the suburban church remained an elating memory. A well deserved award for many years of abnegation. A blessing, not a curse, had been his final verdict on the matter.

That day had also preceded Daniel's much anticipated ordination ceremony—the triumphal entry into his kingdom. That evening he crossed over into his promised land and in the minutes before walking out of his office to receive the blessings of his colleagues and flock he pressed the tip of a fountain pen down the blank page of his old Bible and scribbled: Encantado Evangelical Church, December 29st, 1963. At arms length he admired the inscription and directly bellow he added the flowery signature, which declared the title he now possessed—*Reverend Daniel Passos, Head Pastor.*

Whether a mark of vanity or just a plain reminder of ownership the fact was that whenever Daniel opened his Bible it was the self-proclaimed manifesto he read first. The inscription stood out as a statement of victory after a hard-fought battle. In between the lines one could read the unsuppressed pride of the starved boy from nowhere who carried *barreiro* water on his bare shoulders during Lajedo's treacherous drought. The same boy who was forced to sell fruit at the *feira* for a living, who survived the deadly typhoid outbreak only to be ordained a Reverend in one of Brazil's largest cities, was a hero. The impossible had happened, Daniel concluded whenever reviewing the signature. Would the folks in Lajedo continue to call him their prophet? If they could see him now, he often brooded, would they be envious? The imaginary prospect of showing them around the Encantado premises, its newly built annex, the Pastor's residence featuring indoor plumbing, a fridge, a gas stove in the kitchen, not to mention electric switches in every single room, enraptured him.

It never got too old for Daniel to ponder the feat. While preparing a sermon or pecking the Sunday bulletin on his *Olivetti* Daniel spent many afternoons staring out the window lost in thought, reliving his incredible saga from Lajedo to Encantado precisely when

Bento's drive through the city had come to a merciful end. Finally at Encantado, *Seu* Aloísio, one of the church Elders had been waiting on the other side of the gate ready to unfasten the metal chain and clear the way for the sedan to roll onto the driveway. Right then, Daniel had determined, his real life began.

"Reverend Daniel, welcome—*bem-vindo*!" *Seu* Aloísio had introduced himself with a broad smile and obsequious pull at the car door. "We are so grateful you answered the Lord's call" he declared even before Daniel had time to climb out. When he did, *Seu* Aloísio's hands had flown upon his with a shake that lasted several rounds. Caught by surprise Daniel stood there letting his fingers be crushed while staring at the tacky wool suit and felt hat *Seu* Aloísio sported. "Exaggerated formality" he had observed then but later on he would understand why. For two years the congregation's search for a full-time Pastor had led to frustrated dead-ends. The members had been thrilled with Reverend Firmino's stellar recommendation of Daniel's name which was signed off by the Synod.

"Please, Reverend, follow me, sir" the humble gentleman led the way. The profusion of dandruff dangling from *Seu* Aloísio's kinky hair had stalled him. "It is an honor being the first one to walk you around" he suddenly turned back to meet Daniel's eschewed gaze. "I do hope everything will suit your taste, Reverend" the Elder stated politelty. "We are a modest but hospitable congregation, sir" he turned towards the church's main entrance.

At the flat front steps Daniel paused to look up at the façade. A discreet choice of pastel yellow and white colors coated the building to the very top. Perched up on the scarlet roof an iron cross could be seen from any direction in the borough and such unpretentious yet tasteful details had immediately pleased him. Making way inside the hall he had observed that it was not large by Copacabana standards but it could comfortably sit a good number of members in its nicely varnished pews. There were ten rows on each side of the nave, symmetrically angled to meet the receded glass windows along the bare walls. The mild scent of wax permeating the spotless sanctuary had also been an encouraging sign of traditional Protestant tidiness.

Ambling towards the altar Daniel had leaned on the carved rail cordoning the auditorium from the raised platform. The pulpit at its center was a sturdy polished pillar guarding three tall chairs behind. Daniel sprinted up swiftly drawn by the prospect view from above. His chief concern was to eyeball the dimension of the room and in his curious haste he had paid no attention to the large words engraved on the wall, "GOD IS LOVE (1 John 4:8)."

Pausing at his imaginary summit, Daniel let a rush of approval flutter through him. For a split second he saw himself soaring over the sky of Lajedo again. But when he looked down at the vacant benches the feeling disappeared as fast as it had come and on the way down he remembered holding tightly to the wooded balustrade keeping his head high in case of being watched. It was then that his eyes landed on the small pedal organ tucked at the corner of the altar. "Ida will like this" he had thought.

A few feet in front, two tall pedestals flanked the altar. Each of them bore a white porcelain vase decked with red dahlias and baby's-breaths. The flowers added a festive touch to the otherwise dark furnishing. "*Seu* Joel, Reverend" *Seu* Aloísio seemed to be reading his mind. "He loves to beautify the sanctuary" the Elder tracked Daniel's furtive glance at the porcelain vases. "He brings the flowers himself and fusses over them every Saturday morning."

"Ah…they sure are pretty. God bless him" Daniel interjected before inquiring about his office location. "Through here, Reverend, straight this way" and the cordial host pointed at a passage behind the altar. It led directly down a set of narrow steps and continued onto a short corridor with doors on both sides. His office was the first small alcove to the right with a window opening over the driveway. It was furnished with a modest square desk and a tall chair neatly pushed in. Beside it a stand cradled a heavy black telephone for his personal use and on the corner a pair of empty bookcases completed the decor. "How do you like it, sir?" *Seu* Aloísio probed.

"Just fine *Seu* Aloísio, *obrigado*" Daniel replied with another staged smile.

"Snug I know" *Seu* Aloísio quickly beckoned out. "Now, let me show you the new addition" he hurried to the end of the hallway. "Finally" Daniel nodded and smiled instead. He had been growing impatient to check it out but kept a neutral gaze as well as a safe distance from *Seu* Aloísio. If the parsonage turned out to be as spruced up as the grounds it looked promising. Overall the Encantado church had not fallen short from Reverend Firmino's original appraisal and at the end of the visit Daniel had been particularly pleased with the place's upkeep.

No further than fifty yards out of the office wing a detached two-story structure marked the end of the driveway. On the first story, *Seu* Aloísio pointed out, a kitchen and social hall had been outfitted for holiday gatherings and communal dinners. On Sundays it functioned as a school for the children and young adults. "Here" he pulled a key chain out of his suit pocket. "This is for the door upstairs" he handed it over to Daniel. "I left it ajar for now so Bento and Levi, our sexton, could get in" he took time to wipe his forehead before leading the way upstairs.

That moment in the excursion Daniel relished the most. When he stopped at the top of the first landing and watched *Seu* Aloísio push open the wood door to the second story something inside him shifted. Crossing through the threshold of what would be his castle was exhilarating. A clump of blood escaped his heart and halted half way up his throat as he watched the gray concrete steps turn into slabs of marble on the other side. Before his wide eyes there spread a polished path of red tiles neatly cut into in hexagon patterns. The high noon sun layered the breezeway with a dancing yellow light and Daniel remembered thinking: "the finish line." That was it. He had crossed out of the wilderness.

In his sudden agitation his eyes swayed from the raised wall on the left side to the varnished doors on the right. He outpaced *Seu Aloísio* and flung the first one open striding into a spacious parlor trimmed at the opposite end with a set of French doors. Outside, a spacious and sunny balcony overlooked the back of the church. Beyond the living room a long corridor separated two sizable bedrooms at either end of the plant whereas in the middle it gave way to a tiled bathroom with a shower stall, tub, and a new piece of equipment he later learned to call a bidet.

From one end to the other he straddled trying to figure out how he would fill so much space with furniture. *Seu* Aloísio kept apologizing for the strong smell of fresh paint but Daniel did not mind that in the least. He finally reached the airy kitchen, well equipped with the modern appliances Reverend Firmino had mentioned. A roofless courtyard was attached to it and it was out there that Daniel resumed breathing. Not too far in the distance a northbound train screeched over the tracks. This was almost as nice as Antônio's house, he could hardly disguise his perplexity.

"It is somewhat void in here at the moment, Reverend, but in due time we will assist you with all your furniture needs" *Seu* Aloísio repeated assuming that Daniel's roaming hinted disappointment.

"If he only knew" Daniel had sneered. Since then year after year the generous Encantado congregation not only met his furnishing needs but nearly everything else. Beginning on that same day *Seu* Aloísio returned to the residence with his wife *Dona* Catarina to invite him for dinner at their home. "This is for tomorrow, Reverend" *Dona* Catarina retrieved a small package from her purse. "A simple keepsake—*um agrado*—for you to wear at the ordination" and she softly placed the wrinkled tissue-paper wrap into his reluctant hands. "Hope you will like the color" she gently tapped his tense wrist.

Many other thoughtful gifts followed—tailored suits, dress shirts, handkerchiefs, and golden cuff links, which he received regularly on birthdays and high holidays. It had taken him sometime to associate Christmas and Easter with the unwrapping of ribbon-laced boxes and egg-shaped chocolates brilliantly swaddle in foil. Daniel had no idea how much these courtesies would affect him until he came to expect them. The men and women of Encantado admired his credentials and never once doubted of his godly qualification. Though in time the excitement over his arrival wore out the church members remained consistently appreciative of his services. God had answered their prayers for a dynamic, talented preacher and finding a well-trained minister willing to shepherd a working-class borough had not been easy.

"We are so thankful the Lord God sent you, Reverend Daniel" they warmly hugged him after services. "We are living through so many changes lately, Reverend" and Daniel began to catch on the flock's increased apprehension. A few months after his ordination the country embarked in a tense political rupture just as Reverend Firmino had feared. On March 31, 1964 the Armed Forces ousted President Goulart and formed a new government to guarantee the future of democracy in Brazil. It was with growing confusion that Daniel listened to the radio updates right at the top of the hour before his favorite soccer show aired.

Marshal Castello Branco did not call for presidential elections after the take over and from what Daniel understood the high-ranked officer began to expand his executive authority. The military intervention should have been a momentary interruption of President Goulart's socialist policies but in the long run it turned into a unique regime. Occasionally Daniel connected the recent event with Antônio's flushed face as he pointed at the newspaper headline stating President Jânio Quadros's resignation in 1961. Three years later things changed profoundly just as Antônio prophetically warned. Vice-President Goulart stood no chance of keeping office and his ousting marked the beginning of a serious political rupture to put it in Reverend Firmino's words. It would take Daniel much longer to measure the actual consequences of those unstable years on his life.

As an ordained minister he focused exclusively on his increasingly anxious flock. "What do I tell them?" he agonized over his own apathy. The Encantado parishioners were as lost as he at the direction the country turned. A veil of secrecy surrounded the decisions out of Brasília. Radio stations and newspapers had fallen under severe censorship and for their abounding questions Daniel had no answers.

"What is a Christian to do now, Reverend?" they kept asking. "Turn the other cheek while the military takes over?" the body of

Elders pressed on after the coup. National politics was his last concern and Daniel could not yet see how the military intervention might affect his career. Whether the Generals stayed in power or called for new elections there were other problems Daniel wrestled with. The upcoming wedding to Ida and the administrative duties of Encantado took precedence. There were bills to pay, grounds to maintain, sermons to write, hospitals and homes to visit, office hours to keep, and of course a house to furnish.

"*Senhores*" Daniel urged the Elders "do not worry about what happens in this world" he leafed through his autographed Bible. "In First John, Chapter 4, verse 5 we read: *they are from the world and therefore speak from the viewpoint of the world*" he nodded and smiled. "We are not of the world and must not take stands on issues of the world" Daniel tried to calm everyone down. As the military coup soon turned into an authoritarian regime he continued to dismiss the flock's fears with several other holy verses throwing teacups of water on a fire that apparently raged far away from Encantado.

TWENTY-SIX

"Oh, Daniel, darling, this is absolutely gorgeous" Ida gasped with abandon. Her chest heaved between each deep breath as she stared at the ring.

It had been another sticky Sunday afternoon at the Kruel's when the autumn sun strained from the shore, barging luminously into the living room on its way to the foothills behind. "You did not forget pearls are forever my favorite" Ida winked at each tiny stone encrusted in the golden band. She spread her slender fingers against the fern leaves filtering the shaft of light, dazed with wonder. The rest of the Kruels gathered around burbling in their usual rowdy manner, one shouting over the other in a dissonant chorus.

"*Ai*, Ida, stop flaring and let me see it" cried her sister Alba clutching Ida's suspended right arm and holding it still.

"Rather elegant *filha*" *Dona* Sílvia, stood behind Ida and gently played with her daughter's braid.

"Nice work, Daniel Reverend, or should I start calling you brother Reverend?" Francisco sneaked beside Daniel and slapped his shoulder buoyantly.

"Come on, Alba, my turn now. Let go for a second" Eunice steered Ida's trembling wrist towards her.

"I'm next, Eunice" Marisa warned.

"How about a toast of *guaraná* everyone?" Manuel's voice could be heard from the kitchen where he ran looking for soda bottles in the fridge.

"I'll fetch the goblets from the buffet, *mano*" Maurício yelled over the group stepping out of the skittish cordon formed around the hypnotized bride-to-be.

"Why is everybody screaming, Grandpa?" little Carlos pushed himself through the barrier of legs and tugged at the Coronel's slacks.

"*Tia* Ida is getting married, Caco, and you get to carry the rings" Coronel Kruel scooped his grandson up to tickle his tummy.

"And how about me, *Vô*? Why can't *me* carry rings?" Marina whined loudly ready to cry.

"You, Mari, will carry the flowers, right *Vovó*?" the Coronel turned to *Dona* Sílvia. He bent down to lift his granddaughter with his free arm and kissed her knitted brow soothingly.

"Yes, and in a pretty basket too" *Dona* Sívia cupped her rosy cheeks. "Plus you get to wear a fancy laced dress, Mari. Here, let *Vovó* hold you" *Dona* Sílvia winked at the Coronel and reached out to their granddaughter.

Daniel had archived the day's commotion with reserved satisfaction. His eyes roamed eagerly across the bustling room as he observed the spirited reactions. No doubt Ida was impressed with the band design whereas the rest of the family clearly shared her enthusiasm. The cloak of ineptness Daniel had worn around the extroverted bunch came off once and for all that day after two months of savings and scouting up and down Rio Branco's Avenue for jewelers. It took him several tries until he finally spotted a pattern closest to what Ida had depicted during a Sunday bus ride to youth group.

The topic had come up by chance (or had it?) when Daniel casually poked her about the absence of rings on her fingers. Ida's answer had been categorically candid as he quickly learned to be her style. "Only the right one will do" she giggled charmingly studying her glossy fingernails. Her hands wiggled with emphasis as she proceeded. "To be frank any trinket clasping me when I am playing is a bother. It gets in the way, you know?" her voice rose with determination as she shot back at Daniel. "Why do you care?" she beamed with curiosity.

Not quite well versed on Ida's boldness at that time Daniel had immediately dodged the piercing of her pupils and hailed the bus to a stop. While climbing aboard he scrambled for words to rebound in the same tone. "I don't really care" he retorted once they had found their seats. The bus tossed with a vengeance whirling the heavy afternoon breeze all over the vehicle. A few of Ida's loose strands had fallen across her forehead and she impatiently coiled them behind her ears. "But suppose you were to wear the right one what would it look like?" he charily touched her left hand.

The exchange had stayed vividly with him since. Within a month of settling down in the Encantado residence he mustered enough confidence to hunt for the right one. On Saturday mornings he ventured in and out of downtown shops consulting attendants about what a young lady might find irresistible until he located something similar to what Ida had described that day.

"I know this is going to sound silly" she had cocked her slender neck up while taming the damp tufts behind her ears. "Most girls prefer diamonds, right? But to me pearls are the most precious of all gems" she had lowered her gaze to study the bareness of her hands. "A pearl-encrusted band" she whispered ponderingly "would be the right one, I imagine."

Daniel had found Ida's reply surprisingly thoughtful. It struck him as the result of deep consideration about the resilience random specks of sand possessed to form a perfectly lacquered sphere. As his confidence increased after that conversation he chose Easter Sunday, 1964 as the day to ambush the entire Kruel coterie by asking the Coronel for Ida's hand in marriage. Following a sumptuous codfish and potatoes entreé they had jubilantly dispersed from the dining table into the living room to enjoy coffee and coconut pudding. The children ran around recklessly as usual hunting for chocolate eggs around the apartment. Up to that point Daniel had felt inordinately disengaged from the family's domesticity and guarded his aloofness with care. Similar to his past experience at Antônio's he had stuck to the role of guest and cautiously evaded any bait for intimacy.

He had often suspected retribution was on the line especially at the end of those animated dinners when the conviviality grew disorienting and left him wondering how he would ever be able to fit in. Meanwhile he studied them closely, paid attention to how they talked and moved around the room hoping to decipher clues. Within a month he managed to put a finger on what the Kruels' expectations might be regarding him. Something was in need of fixing in their merry household and Daniel discovered it was Ida who needed attention.

The Kruel's youngest child had been a source of distress for a while and once Daniel earned the family's trust to escort Ida to Sunday youth meetings she began to disclose a few of the family's concerns. To begin with, Ida was five years his senior and had not shown much interest in romance. Previous courtiers were either 'boring' or 'shallow' according to her standards. The family's anxiety over Ida's prolonged spinsterhood seemed warranted since her siblings had married young and were already delivering a new generation of little Kruels.

Ida on the other hand had remained unresponsive to the godly call of matrimony. Only the right suitor would do she had finally confided in Daniel, and she had not met him yet. Outside the family circle Ida's unresolved fate had also been the target of speculation. Church acquaintances regarded her as a '*Tia*'—Auntie. At least once Daniel heard a few wisecrackers in the youth group chiming a popular children's rhyme that followed Mendelssohn's wedding march tune. "*Com quem será, com quem sera que a Ida vai casar?*"—"Who will it be, who will it be, the one to marry Ida?" and they rolled with laughter at the joke.

Ida's detachment also puzzled Daniel since she had warmed up to him quite naturally. From the beginning he felt attracted to her simple beauty. Compared to other women Daniel had come across in Rio, Ida's facial features required no artificial props to be noticed. Her fair skin shone with the golden lure of an assiduous swimmer and her dark brown eyes were magnetic. Daniel had watched Ida through that first Copacabana summer and could tell she spent a great deal of time at the beach. Sun and salt had left bleached patches on her long black hair creating a gleaming chestnut contrast that perfectly blended with the tan on her face. On the rare occasions she wore cosmetics Ida actually glowed. When she smiled, which was almost all the time, the deep crimson on her lips perfectly balanced the mild dab of glittery silver she wore over her eyelids.

It was impossible for Daniel to believe he had been the only admirer of Ida's radiance. How to explain her loneliness then? When he considered her many talents, the spirited almost childlike aura she exuded, Daniel became even more baffled as to why she was still single. Trained to be an industrious housewife she had prepared mouth-watering samples of northeastern cuisine, trying out his favorite recipes every now and then. The dry beef and pumpkin stew she surprised him with one time was as succulent as *Dona* Dulce's, Daniel had to admit.

More often than not when the family lounged in the crowded living room after Sunday dinners, offhanded chats persistently pointed to Ida's many other knacks. Whether as seamstress, housekeeper or schoolteacher the allusions to her dowers flew at Daniel like Cupid's sharp arrows. "Did you know Ida makes her own dresses, Daniel?" *Dona* Sílvia volunteered once when he complimented Ida's outfit. "Ida always so neat and tidy, she can't stand the sight of dust anywhere" sister Alba had pitched in out loud as if to no one in particular while Ida wiped the coffee table in front of Daniel preparing it for the appetizer platters. "Ida, dear, play a Chopin Nocturne, would you?" Coronel Kruel pleaded during their dessert and coffee sitting when the family finally quieted down for a brief interlude before retiring to their afternoon naps. "Ida, come here, please?" sister-in-law Marisa would call from one of the bedrooms looking exhausted. "Mari says she will sleep only if you sing her a lullaby…" And Ida would have to quit the improvised recital amidst everyone's laughter. "She is so good with kids" brother Manuel remarked out loud.

Eager to please, Ida multi-tasked the roles of dutiful daughter, sister, and auntie without protesting. Daniel was impressed with her apparent docility and although gradually aware of the obvious staging the family put out for him he did not resist the invitation to partake in the scheme. Shortly prior to his transfer to Encantado he finally conceded to the Kruel's crafty encouragement of their courtship and relaxed into the presumed role of future in-law. Rules of propriety gradually disappeared and the couple was allowed to be alone in the livin room from time to time. After lunch on Sundays they had the long couch to themselves while everyone flew to the kitchen to clean up. Daniel and Ida enjoyed being together and during those brief flirtatious moments their innocent romance blossomed. When no one was looking they stole quick kisses and held hands hurriedly staring into each other eyes afraid of getting caught.

On the day Daniel presented the ring their engagement became official. A wedding date was immediately discussed and agreed to, yielding to frenzied preparations for the ceremony. It was during that interlude of courtship that Ida and Daniel began to confront each other's assets and flaws. Against his wishes Daniel had to engage in lengthened dialogues with someone he barely knew. This proved a challenge because until then he had deliberately hid his thoughts and feelings from everyone.

From the onset of their engagement Ida challenged his reticence and in turn concealed nothing from him. Very soon she bravely tore her heart open to the *right one* and pushed Daniel to respond. The pearl band had transformed Ida from an apparently subdued creature into an impetuous Pandora ready to suck all she could out of Daniel's secret vault. After all she was going to be a Reverend's wife, she imperiously reminded him. Such glorious occupation should be met with zeal and devotion. She would not shy away from the combined missions of holy matrimony and church ministry. There was so much to do. A music program for the Encantado church was her first priority.

"We will need a choir for the adults, darling, and musical lessons for the children as soon as possible" she announced.

On the subject of children itself Ida's eyes lit up like a torch and she would get lost in another tangent speculating on their ideal family size. "At least four children, darling" she would repeat during their post-engagement exchanges. "A Reverend's family must be large, for children are God's inheritance" And without waiting for his response she would add "two boys and two girls to start with" and she pressed four stretched fingers against his parted lips refusing to hear a rebuttal.

How to say no to charming, beautiful, vivacious Ida became Daniel's impossible conundrum from the onset. All her demands disguised as suggestions spurted out through comical grimaces, winks and furtive kisses. When the time came to settle down at the Encantado parsonage how could he argue against her fine taste for furniture, fresh cut flowers, curtain fabrics, matching pillows, mats and tiny knick-knacks to be displayed in every corner? As the wedding date grew closer she also focused on Daniel's appearance. "This pencil mustache, darling, does not suit you" she declared with a broad grin. Though he tried to argue about the many years it had taken him to grow it Ida affirmed that a clean silky look perfectly matched the glossy texture of his clerical collar.

Daniel ventured to win other battles including the use of bow ties and hair pomade but gave up on the grounds of his own ignorance. Other than the basic philosophical principles presented in Seminary classes what did he know about aesthetics? Raised in an impoverished northeastern hamlet where most people walked barefoot and lived without indoor plumbing, electricity or furniture what did he have to offer? For his entire childhood the same spoon and aluminum cups were the only tableware available. He knew nothing about matching ties and handkerchiefs let alone home decor.

He also avoided arguing with Ida in fear of revealing too much of the past. He would wait a little longer (would forever be long enough?) to disclose his true identity. Later on perhaps, when it might be too late for Ida to change her mind about the right one. There was nothing to lose, he determined, except for the truth. Off limits to Ida and anyone else, Daniel had buried the past deep down a dark hole in his chest.

When questioned about his family and whether they would attend the ceremony, Daniel immediately made up excuses. His parents could not leave the family 'property' unattended whereas in reality he had not even sent them an invitation. Just the thought of planting Benedito and Dulce in the same room with Coronel Kruel and *Dona* Sílvia, or God forbid, watch Dalva and Delfina flump their elbows over their clothed table with no idea of how to hold the cutlery, daunted him. Like fire and water, Lajedo and Rio should never mix.

Almost imperceptibly the wedding day rushed near. For different reasons bride and groom succumbed to increasing agitation trying to control their emotions. Daniel did his best to cooperate with the family meticulous plans for Ida's sake and objected only to the suggestion of having his own pair of witness—*padrinhos*—during the ceremony. On everything else he conceded—the Copacabana venue, the number of guests, the choir repertoire, the flowers, the photographer, the reception menu, and the honeymoon destination, all of it was Ida's idea. He only nodded and smiled. When consulted about how many invitations he would like to send he said three would do.

One for Antônio, one for Reverend Firmino and the other generally addressed to the Encantado congregation.

Nearly a month prior to the date he retrieved one of Antônio's letters from the glass-paneled bookcase and peevishly copied down his postal address in Caxias. A cold, guilt-ridden note was all he could produce apologizing for the broken communication over the years. Recognizing the long distance between Copacabana and Caxias Daniel added: "do not feel obligated to come, brother. I am sure there will be another opportunity for a visit."

On the night before the ceremony Daniel battled insomnia as never before. He took long swigs of Passport whisky and managed to nap for two hours at at ime while keeping watching for the alarm clock. By cranking the volume on the radio he hoped to distract his anguish. Francisco had given him a small bottle of *Maracujina* the Sunday prior. "If you get a tinge of cold feet take half a cup before heading to the church Saturday night" he had discretely tucked the passion fruit tonic in his suit pocket while pretending to hug him goodbye. "All natural; nothing to make you dizzy, just more relaxed" Francisco had whispered.

By four in the morning Daniel took the first shot of *Maracujina* with a splash of whisky and slept until five minutes before the alarm blared at six. He then banged the pin down and bolted to the bed's edge, exhausted. Hands wrapped around his warped head he stared at his feet thinking of another sip. "No! I'll manage with extra-strong coffee and cold showers" he talked himself out of a blackout. His life as a bachelor was soon to end. Ida's arrival at the parsonage would happen at the end of their weeklong honeymoon at her beloved beach retreat, Paraty. However, Daniel already saw Ida everywhere. She had recruited *Dona* Sílvia and the Encantado women to nest all quarters of the house and together they filled the place with furniture, linens and God knew what else.

By mid-day on Saturday Daniel had already finished the entire *Maracujina* tonic and decided to buy another bottle at the local pharmacy just in case. Determined to stay away from his Passport bottle until after the honeymoon he kept busy packing his suitcase in between slurps of steaming black coffee. With an eye on his watch and another on the thermos he timed each of his last hours of solitude.

TWENTY-SEVEN

"*Good evening dear spectators, I am your Esso Reporter, eyewitness to history on this Saturday December 10th, 1966. Beginning your evening news briefing with exclusive updates directly from Brasília where President Castelo Branco has issued Institutional Act number four. The Act extraordinarily summons Congress to meet between December 12, 1966 and January 24, 1967 to draft a new Constitution. When approved, the 1967 Constitution will, and I quote, "institutionalize the revolutionary principles and ideals." The President will also retain additional powers to issue supplementary legislation concerning matters of national security until March 15th, 1967...*"

"*Oi* Ida, I..." Daniel's unfinished sentenced trailed off under the creaking sound of the living room door. He toddled cautiously inside guided by the bright television glare, the chief source of light in the space. The flickering rays bounced before Daniel's slanted eyes as they adjusted to the darkness draping Ida's rigid silhouette. She sat at the corner of the couch staring mindlessly at the monotone evening news indifferent to Daniel's trepid advance until he came close enough for direct contact. Ida then bolted from the couch in the direction of the television set and with her firm fingers seized the volume button. She turned it resolutely up and the roaring noise enveloped the room.

Purposefully ignoring Daniel's presence she didn't even bother to glance at him on her way back to the couch. Her slippers slid resentfully across the waxed wood while Daniel meandered a little closer. "So sorry I missed dinner, Ida. It was another of those Council meetings in Copacabana. You know how they like to talk" he mumbled hesitantly reaching out for her inflexible shoulders.

Sensing the closeness of his fingertips Ida winced and pulled the cord from under the lampshade nearby. Daniel caught a glimpse of her arms promptly squared across her heaving chest, her colorless pursed lips as if they were about to burst. He retrieved his hand and hovered for a moment gambling on a reply and when no sound emerged from below he tried again. "Is Beca asleep?" he muttered.

"Uh-huh…" Ida replied without taking her eyes off the bright screen from where the handsome *Esso* Reporter in his starched suit continued to parrot the newscast. Aside from the living room the rest of the house was plunged in darkness and Daniel proceeded quietly to the hallway. A mixed odor of floor wax and roasted chicken greeted him. It was Saturday and Ida had undoubtedly asked their live-in maid Nina to treat the floors to a shine in preparation for lunch the next day. Every Sunday after the service Ida had fallen into the habit of inviting a different church family to a meal, a practice she instituted shortly after returning from their relaxing honeymoon in Paraty. "It does forge bonds of affection in the congregation, darling" she tenderly squeezed his hand after noticing the initial hesitation.

Down on the hallway the door to Beca's room appeared shut and Daniel decided against a peek. Beca and Nina were certainly down for the night and to avoid any disturbances he simply leaned over the panel. Nina's deep breathing confirmed his suspicion and Daniel stepped away with the thought of returning to the living room. Ida should be going to bed also and try to rest. She was nearly nine months pregnant and complaining of uncomfortable cramps below her swollen stomach. The baby's drooping weight was also causing occasional stabs on her lower back making it difficult for her to lie flat for more than a couple of hours at a time.

"This one is bigger than Rebeca, darling. It must be a boy" she would stroke her stretched skin with anticipation. When doctor Oscar confirmed the advanced stage of her second gestation Ida spoke of nothing else. "He is going to be named Daniel, after you, *pai*" and she would reach for his hand and spread it across the tip of her flagging navel hardly containing the excitement. "Maybe not tonight" Daniel flipped the light switch on the kitchen wall. Yawning tiredly he surveyed the countertops for a bite to eat. "She is in a bad mood. Silence treatment mode" he concluded while scratching his brow. "If I say another word she will pounce" Daniel sighed at the sight of a covered dinner plate over a burner.

This had not been the first time he had arrived home past dinnertime without phoning Ida. Tonight, however, his excuse was legitimate. The regional council of Evangelical Churches had been called to an extraordinary session to deliberate on the latest political developments leaked in the press. Daniel's phone had rung early in the morning and when he answered it was Coronel Kruel's voice that sounded strangely pursy on the other end of the line.

"*Alô*, Daniel? Good morning, it's me, Edgar, how are you? Listen…" he gave Daniel no time to respond. "I just received a call from Reverend Firmino about an extraordinary meeting this afternoon in Copacabana. It's urgent, last minute but you ought to come at four in the afternoon" he ordered in one breath. A heavy silence had ensued before the Coronel broke it. "*Alô?* Daniel? Still there?" the Coronel breathed heavily over the receiver.

"Yes, sir, still here" Daniel confirmed dully. "Just wondering about the rush" he wanted to sound polite and disguise his genuine disinterest.

"Have you not tuned to any of the broadcasts yet, Daniel?" Coronel Kruel sounded surprised.

"A little bit. Earlier this morning after the soccer updates" Daniel had then consulted his watch wondering how long the call might last.

"Well then, either turn on the radio again or find a newspaper stand. Read the reports regarding this new Constitution business before you come to the meeting, will you?" the Coronel urged. "We need to stay informed about what is happening so that our congregations receive a unified position tomorrow morning, understand?" he came across strong.

"Yes, sir, I do. Huh-huh…yes… Sure… Understood. Will see you there, thanks. *Tchau*" Daniel had re-cradled the receiver the moment Ida strode into the study.

"Who could that be so early on a Saturday morning, darling?" she carried Daniel's second cup of steamy black coffee.

"Your father" he held the saucer and blew the rising smoke away.

"Why? What's possibly going on early Saturday morning?" she began rubbing her large stomach. "Please don't tell me you are leaving?" she did not hide the disappointment. "You had promised to help me shopping at the *feira* today and take Beca to the playground after her nap, remember?" she intently studied Daniel's face. "No" her head shook. "I can't believe this, Daniel" and Ida's long repertoire of grievances followed. Like an erupting volcano she could not stop once the spewing began and Daniel turned to his coffee waiting for the burst to pass. "You are going to let us down again? Nina is off after lunch and you know it. I'll be here all afternoon alone with Beca. So unfair and unkind of you to…"

"Ida, please stop" Daniel cut her off. "This is not time for arguing" he said after a slurp.

"Who is arguing?" she was now tapping her foot. "Tell me who? Me? No, I am not arguing at all. I am simply making a point. You must keep your promises, darling. That's all there is to it. When was the last time we spent time as a family? Honestly, I don't recall when it was the last time…"

"Enough, Ida" Daniel roughly pushed his chair back from the desk and stood up. "More than anyone else you ought to know how busy I am; too many demands and no time" he waved in a helpless gesture. "I do not need to hear when was the last time I did this or that. I have to get going on tomorrow's sermon before I leave for Copacabana anyway" he flung his Bible open on the desk.

"Well then, never mind" she shrilled irritably and grabbed the empty demitasse. "I'm off to the *feira* by myself" and out of the study she stormed.

In the kitchen she found both Nina and Beca just about finished with their breakfast. Beca's lips were crusted with sweet porridge and Nina was whisking the bowl away from the high chair when Ida barged towards the sink. "Nina, could you get the shopping cart, please?" she twisted the faucet knob so harshly that a torrential flow gushed down splashing water all over her housedress.

"Why *Dona* Ida? You are not going to the *feira* by yourself are you?" Nina pried disapprovingly while wiping the Beca's face with a damp cloth. "You shouldn't, you know that. You can't be pulling any heavy weight in this baking heat, *Dona* Ida" Nina protested while lifting Beca out of the high chair. "Where is the Reverend?" she pressed while Ida smothered a soapy sponge over the cup and saucer.

"Working at the study and then off somewhere again, Nina. A meeting I presume, after lunch. He has no time for us as usual and that is why he can't come with me" Ida reached for a dishtowel while frowning at Nina.

"I'm coming with you then, *Dona* Ida" Nina announced from behind the patio door where the shopping cart was stowed.

"Nonsense, Nina. Who stays with Beca? The Reverend will be locked in that study all morning you know that" Ida contended.

"Then I'll go and you stay. Just make me a list" Nina hasted to one of the cupboard drawers scavenging for pen and scrap paper.

"Hold it Nina" one of Ida's palms went up. "You've been with me long enough to know that I like to squeeze and sample all the fruits and vegetables myself before buying them. Besides, I want to butcher a chicken or two for tomorrow's lunch and need to find the fattest ones before the whole neighborhood descends on the aviary and beats me to it. That will take some extra time…" Ida went on wrestling the cart's handle away from Nina's grip.

"*Dona* Ida, are you out of your mind? Butchering chickens after coming back from the *feira?* In this kind of heat and in your condition?" Nina folded both hands on her skinny hips letting the cart stumble down the floor. Beca broke down into an amused 'oh-oh' and Nina's hazel eyes beckoned alarmingly at Ida after she lifted the cart from the floor.

"Don't give me that look Nina dear" Ida pinched young Nina's puffed up cheeks. "I am pregnant not sick and you know fully well the Reverend prefers fresh butchered chickens, don't you? They are tender and juicier or at least that is what he says anyway, and who is in charge here Nina?" Ida pretended to be cross. "It is up to me not you to make the decisions around here, end of conversation" Ida affectionately patted Nina's hair. The young helper lowered her gaze paralyzed with dread for her mistress' physical state but said nothing else.

Nina knew better. There was no use fighting Ida when a course of action began to unravel inside her zesty mind. It had not taken long for Nina to learn that whereas Daniel still struggled with Ida's strong temperament. He was not prepared to surrender his inherited man of the house dominance so easily and in the day-to-day domestic strife he resorted to a host of strategies to subdue Ida's will. In the first few months of marriage he had launched a persuasion-and-reward tactic to put an end to their frequent impasses. Depending on the severity of the issue—whether he should stop dunking his French bread in the coffee cup or yield to her hymn selections each Sunday—Daniel first appealed to Ida's romantic side to get his way.

At times a laced bouquet of red roses worked wonders on Ida's stubbornness for about a week or two. In other more contentious matters such as his increasingly heavy work load a more creative resolution was needed. A trip to the fabric and sewing shop for a few yards of silk or an increase on the weekly shopping allowance became common offerings upon the altar of marital compromise. But as soon as the hormones of pregnancy began to flare inside Ida's rounding body, Daniel found himself running out of options.

Shortly before Beca's birth the ground rules of engagement between Daniel and Ida definitely changed. Weary of the persuasion tricks that led only to fragile truces husband and wife often switched to resistance and defiance. Sarcasm and shaming seemed more effective weapons whenever they competed for dominance. When Ida's delivery date loomed closer the mounting apprehensions of labor and parenthood added to their insecurities and each coped differently with the unexpressed fear. Ida demanded more of Daniel's presence whereas Daniel sank deeper into isolation.

"Why can't you come home earlier and keep me company?" she pleaded. "You read far too much and far too late down at that study" was the sulking complaint against his secretive nighttime sessions at the church office where his bookcase remained safely locked and stocked. It was only after he recognized the numbing effects of the Passport shots that Daniel felt ready to climb up to the parsonage.

By then Ida would have retired heavy, tired and much less likely to initiate another duel. At that late hour Daniel had no disposition for confrontations either. If any erupted, he had a rehearsed defense. "I worked all day and need a few hours of rest before it starts all over again" he would flash the alarm clock at her.

During the week preceding Beca's delivery Daniel was convinced there was no use reasoning with Ida anymore. She had become irritable and unreasonable. He quickly reverted to old mannerisms and as a polite guest, nodded and half-smiled at anything she said. When she and Beca returned from the maternity ward the church office turned into a safe haven except when he had to pay home and hospital visits or answer the occasional funeral calls. Beca's endless wailing and Ida's resolute technique to tame them had nearly driven Daniel to madness.

"The nurses at the hospital told me to feed her anytime she cries, darling. That is the only way she feels secure, you know?" and she would latch the baby to her bosom so frequently that Daniel began to see the two of them as a twisted version of the mythological Medusa. Beca's tiny hands and legs flagged through Ida's chest just like the snakes allegedly did out of the hydra's head.

Ida proved to be a dedicated mother to Beca and spent most of her time holding the baby wherever she went. Against *Dona* Sílvia's counsel she refused to let Beca cry for more than five minutes or to encourage her to soothe herself alone in the crib. "That is plain cruel, *mãe.* How could you suggest such a thing?" Ida protested and ran when a peep escaped the baby's room. "Well, Ida, that was how I did with you, your brothers and sister" *Dona* Sílvia unsuccessfully dodged Ida's passage. "You will never get anything done around the house" she calmly patted Ida's arm. "That is why we got Nina, *mãe.* Now, if you excuse me" and Ida ducked under her mother's stretched arm to avoid hearing another of *Dona* Sílvia warnings regarding Nina's overload. "She is going to drop dead of fatigue one of these days, Ida" *Dona* Sílvia exclaimed.

Fortunately Beca soon showed her mild nature and with Nina's help she learned to stay in the crib all night. Within a matter of four months, in spite of Ida's resistance, Nina's crafty inklings to soothe the baby triumphed. "Leave Beca's last feeding to me *Dona* Ida. Between seven thirty and eight I'll warm up a bottle of *Ninho* powder, shut the door to the bedroom and rock her until she passes out" Nina explained. "I'll let her burp all she needs, promise" Nina went on before Ida interposed. "Some fluffy pillows around her in the crib and you'll see, *Dona* Ida, she will fall for it" Nina sounded so confident that Ida conceded.

On the first night, however, Ida stood behind the shut door eavesdropping on Nina's scheme as she tracked each of Beca's loud suckling. The predicted sequence of burps followed, and finally Nina's lulling hums. Not only did Beca fall for it but she miraculously stayed quiet all night until past five the next morning offering everyone in the house a much needed respite. "I swear to God, *Dona* Ida, and may the Good Lord forgive my taking his Blessed name in vain" Nina greeted Ida in the morning after the experiment. "This *Ninho* works like a potion."

That night Daniel arrived shortly after nine and met a radiant Ida, the one he had fallen for, waiting for him exuding the fragrance of a fresh shower along with the beaming smile he could not resist. "Beca has fallen asleep after the *Ninho* bottle, darling, and Nina is there on watch by the crib just in case" she threw her arms around his neck. In the months that followed Daniel felt they were back at their Paraty hotel. The following quiet and restful nights restored Ida's vivacity and to Daniel it was as if she could look even prettier and more charming than ever. Except for Wednesday nights when he had to lead a Bible study at the church the young couple spent many of their evenings together eating dinner after Beca went to bed with Nina, talking about future plans and reading the Bible together.

At other times they enjoyed watching television and during those months of renewed bliss Daniel skipped many of the late solitary sessions down at his church office. It was with a hint of nostalgia that he now replayed those scenes sitting alone in the kitchen eating a cool serving of spaghetti and sausage sauce topped with a smashed hardboiled egg. He wondered whether those times would ever return once the second baby learned to take to the *Ninho* bottle.

Out in the living room the TV hissing disappeared under Ida's muffled steps to the bathroom. The showerhead ran loosely for a few minutes followed by the sink faucet. Ida was certainly cleaning her teeth and dabbing her face, neck and hands with *Nivea* cream. Daniel heard the door of the sink cabinet cringe and pictured her pulling the blow drier out.

Ida's evening grooming unfolded predicatably. Her long braids were gone in anticipation of another round of nursing and she now sported a fashionable bob cut above her ears and kept it up in full volume with some kind of spray. It fell more in tune with the young actresses starring in the popular soap operas she liked to watch and plus it was easy to dry it out with the new machine. Daniel heard the buzzing in the bathroom knowing that in the morning Ida's hair would look impeccably coiffed. He wished a similar product existed to spray over the happiness they shared when first married.

"Wouldn't it be marvelous to freeze up those moments before the babies came along?" and holding on to that thought Daniel dropped his empty plate into the sink and headed for the kitchen door. Out on the breezeway a warm December blow brushed over his face. Memories of happier days carried him through the marble steps all the way down to the office. A picture of him and Ida swimming in the calm waters of Paraty after walking hand in hand along the sandy beach returned. He looked at his watch and calculated another three hours until midnight when he would make his way back upstairs to find Ida sound asleep and hopefully appeased.

TWENTY-EIGHT

At the dawn of a humid new year's day Ida's water broke. Hanging low over the Encantado sky a dome of teary clouds veiled the moonlight and saturated the summer air with hazy dew droplets. The unpleasant pressure over the borough closely resembled the final hours of Ida's second pregnancy when her placenta burst a week before the doctor's estimate. Initially, the surprise set Ida off track. Up to that moment the sizzling night had progressed in predictable misery interrupted now and then by the mounting urges of a late gestation. At the approach of dawn Ida found herself heading for the bathroom once again, drowsy and out of her wits, she was unable to discern reality from illusion. Her swollen feet dragged over the cool tiles and in slumbered prostration she plopped down the toilet seat crestfallen and yearning for rest. The sharp contrast between her dry lips and sweaty skin was exasperating.

She battled the overwhelming desire to plunge into a sweet sleep that lasted until morning but the anticipation of relief took precedence. Barely holding her head up, Ida waited. Patience was not one her virtues especially in the middle of the night. When she thought safe to hoist up a wet trickle rolled down her tights and the warm feeling annoyed her. “How come?” and for a moment she questioned her sanity. There should be nothing else left unless she had finally lost control of her basic functions. Stiff and puzzled Ida leaned against the brim of the sink blaming the sensation on the extreme fatigue gripping her body and mind. Perspiration oozed from all pores and most certainly her brain because it had now resorted to playing silly tricks.

That was it. She was just imagining things and priority dictated immediate rest. She ought to settle down instead of giving into faint impressions. Determined to proceed with her goal Ida flushed the toilet and twisted the faucet for a quick rinse. The cool jest ran loosely through her soapy hands. At last a hint of relief and to prolong the indulgence Ida splashed her muggy face a few more times letting the drips roll down her neck dissolving the irritable layers of sweat on her plastered skin. The fleeting deliverance tickled her skin and tempted her to an encore. If it were not for the fixating promise of sleep she would let the faucet run over her head forever but the need to lie down finally prevailed. She reached for a towel when again a flow of warmth reached her inner thighs. What she had a minute ago dismissed as pure illusion now felt dismally real. The steady drip of water travelled straight past her knees and she wondered whether a squirt had escaped the running faucet. More mystified than irritated Ida stretched her arm in the direction of the light switch to get a better look below her large stomach when a sudden gush reached her feet. Still in the dark Ida stalled soaked and perplexed.

It took her a gasping second to finally realize the original misperception and as much as she had yearned otherwise it was beyond her will to regulate nature’s course. Instead of objecting her predicament she had to resign to acceptance of what was clearly unfolding. Poise and restrain would serve her best in carrying out the next right moves presumably to the hospital. Beginning with what seemed the most logical task she spooled off a handful of tissue from the dispenser to wipe her legs dry. A change of clothes should follow since her nightgown felt uncomfortably drenched. She motioned to bypass the smear on the floor and return to the bedroom but before her legs obeyed her, a painful cramp made her halt. Ida cringed stoically reaching back for the sink to endure the brunt that finally confirmed her suspicion.

Going into early labor had been the last thought in her inflexible mind especially after the consultation with her physician three days ago. He had positively confirmed the delivery date for next week assuring all was in order with her and the baby. The anticipation of danger jolted her heart out of place and a million scary scenarios jammed her head. What if something had gone terribly wrong since? What if the baby had just stopped moving? And she groped her belly searching for evidence. No. Ida took a deep breath. Remember: poise and restrain, Ida. Stay alert and leveled. No need to panic, she repeated quietly and heeled on the ground until her mind unwound. A minute or two to sit down and gather her thoughts would keep dread at bay and as soon as her jellied legs allowed Ida ebbed out of the bathroom hugging her belly as if it were an distended balloon about to pop.

Clearly the time had come to execute the departure plan she had carefully conceived and rehearsed on and off with both Daniel and Nina. Except the original scenario had not included this uncommon twist. Now she had to rethink the logistics of leaving the house in the middle of the night with Beca still asleep. At this point, however, there was no use fretting. She had to keep focused on the approaching conclusion of her long awaited desire. Not for a second should hysterics or remorse steal the thrill of bringing baby Daniel safely home.

In between shallow breaths Ida kept on talking herself out of panic while scuffing across the unlit hallway. Wake Daniel up first was a must and still latching on to her precious bundle she sat by the edge of the bed and gently reclined on the mattress to better skid closer to the center. Mustering the softest intonation she could under the circumstances Ida cleared her throat and playfully drummed on Daniel's arm. The compelling call rang surprisingly cheery and inflective. "Wake up, darling. Baby Daniel is on the way" she chirped like a spunky *bem-te-vi*.

Once recovered from the spasm Ida's limbs recharged with purpose. Despite its encumbering shape her entire body complied with the instructions discharged from her hyper-vigilant mind. After rolling away she carefully returned to the bed's edge and set in motion the exit drill sketched weeks in advance. It all came flushing back to her, move by move, each task lined up in perfect order before her blazing eyes. If carried out as predicted it should take them less than ten minutes between getting dressed and walking out the door. She had timed it before which meant that the unforeseen darkness in the room posed no difficulties to the operation. All accessories required for a hasty leave had already been gathered at one easy spot to where she now charged.

Assuming Daniel had heard her melodic convocation Ida sprang up and advanced towards her designated launching station. Clinging on to the vanity's surface she shoved off her wet slippers and fumbled her puffy feet into a pair of flats stowed there after her last doctor's appointment. Flawlessly concluding the plan's first round Ida turned to the next phase with similar accuracy. Close at hand exactly on the right corner she had placed the diaper bag decked with an array of items. From booties to caps, wipes and diapers, receiving blankets, layettes and undershirts of mixing tones of light and lavender blue, Baby Daniel lacked nothing. Over the past six months Ida and *Dona* Sílvia had fun sewing, embroidering and crocheting each outfit and now Ida patted down the laden piece with renewed satisfaction. Just the other day when the time finally came to decide what to leave behind or take along to the maternity ward she had impetuously packed the entire loot as absolutely indispensable. There it stood, she touched the bulging bag, stuffed up and ready to go.

Folded neatly beside it Ida found the gown she had especially patterned for the occasion. Favoring comfort over style the plain malleable rayon frock had no lace or cleavage to speak of. The only non-negotiable detail was its color—powder blue to match Baby Daniel's layettes, and as she expected, the switch took place smoothly despite the shrouding darkness and the stickiness on her legs. Off with it in a wink Ida ducked her head through the top hole letting it hurl down her round hips in a smooth descent that made her proud of her measurements. Offhandedly she straightened the dress over her waist and declared herself ready. With her fingertips she pushed a few strands of loose hair away from her brows knowing it looked as fit as the night before after the blow-dry session. No time for more spray or makeup at this point. Her exuberance stemmed from unsuppressed maternal joy and when Ida peered triumphantly over her shoulder she was sure Daniel was tagging right along.

"Ready darling?" her second pitch reached a new height. By now they should be on target to leave the house unless something really wrong had happened to her projections. Ida squinted past the tenuous gloom separating her from her husband and in utter disappointment realized Daniel had not even gotten up yet. His curled legs had not budged an inch since she last time touched them and there was no sign of life out of his mouth except for hoarse grunts. "Good Lord, are you still snoring?" Ida shouted in frustration.

Given the lack of proper light she could hardly tell whether Daniel was about to uncoil or God forbid sink deeper into sleep. That was enough agony to trigger her notoriously untamed temper and go into attack mode. She could care less whether it was going to hurt when her nails clawed hard down on Daniel's ankles. "Up, Daniel!" she snapped. "We need to get going to the hospital" she commanded. Each wasted minute greatly compromised her established timetable and as Ida stood by the nightstand she grew more determined to pull Daniel up by herself if needed. She also glimpsed at the clock. "Four ten" she rambled in a low tone while snatching it off the side table.

If all went according to her estimates their potential arrival at the hospital could be calculated within half an hour. Granted no other contractions happened in the meantime she could spare five or ten minutes at the most, in which case, Daniel had to get up this instant, and Ida's mind raced at the speed of light. She mentally reviewed each step. A phone call to the obstetrician was in order—a task she had regrettably delegated to Daniel. Next on the list, Nina had to get up, check on Beca and then phone her parents around six o'clock. Ida stared at the clock again. Nina will haul the bag, she decided. No way Daniel will remember to bring it. Lastly, a goodbye kiss on Beca.

"*A-a-i-i*!" Ida shuddered bending over her enormous belly in sheer pain. "Heavens" she covered her mouth "another cramp" and her thoughts derailed. The jab cut up her insides like a blade sending her protective hands around her stomach again. Beneath her swollen feet the ground mysteriously turned to quicksand and her legs flickered. What she had dreaded the most came to pass. She lost balance and crumpled straight down on Daniel's head accidently letting go of the clock.

"What's the matter?" Daniel shouted on impact. "What's wrong with you?" he scolded about to push her off but at the sight of her raised hand, Daniel halted.

"A second cramp in just a few minutes" Ida informed brazenly. "My water broke; get up. We must go" she demanded impatiently and wobbled off the mattress. Visibly disoriented Daniel leapt off and raced to the armoire. Whatever clothes, socks, and shoes he could find in the dark would do. No need to question Ida's command. The vicious knit on her brow was enough to know she was in serious distress and they had to hurry.

"Call Dr. Oscar" Ida regained composure once the pain subsided. She hoisted up slowly both hands pressed hard against her waist. "Let him know we are leaving in a few minutes; five to ten I should think" she picked the clock up from the floor returning it to its place. Grabbing onto the bedrail she scuffed along just in case her legs faltered again.

"His number is on top of your desk, at least there was where I last left it, if you didn't move it. I'm all set to go, just need to get Nina and head down to the car with the bag" and at that instant Ida's lips ripped open leaving behind a trail of interrupted sentences. Daniel captured some of the flares while she disappeared down the hallway. "Don't forget the baby's bag, oh wait, no, Nina will do it. Don't expect to have any coffee ready at this time, hear me? I am just about to get Nina so we can leave right away. I should drink some water don't you think? My throat is sticky, oh my, this weather, when is it going to rain?" on she went until her voice faded down the hallway.

Off balance for reasons only he knew Daniel measured his unsteady steps paddling along the dark. He was barely dressed and combed let alone in full function of his faculties having gone to bed just a short while back and still felling drowsy. If he remembered correctly he had to dial the doctor's number? Thankfully, Ida had left the exact information in large letters under the phone box. As soon as he flipped the switch it came into full view. For the first time in years Daniel came to appreciate his wife's perfectionism and exhaled in relief when a voice reached his muddled ears on the third long ring.

At the other end of the hallway Nina pounced over the parquet. She sounded fully alert and prepared to carry out Ida's special plan and did not waver at the outpour of incoherence reaching her ears. Though spooked out of her peaceful sleep Nina quickly assessed the situation and knew not to add any more fuel to Ida's burning fire. Instead she swerved past her mistress downcast and silent remembering all the parts rehearsed countless times in the past week. In the eventuality Daniel was on the phone she had to fetch the bag from the master bedroom and there was where Nina darted.

"Nina?" Ida hoarsely whispered from Beca's doorway "throw my toothbrush in the bag, please? Ah, a tube of paste and a hairbrush? I don't know what I was thinking when I repacked it last night Nina, should I also bring makeup? You know, for when I leave the hospital? Why not? A lipstick at least Nina, forget about the rouge, only lipstick. Red!" and then she tiptoed towards Beca's crib while Nina swept through the bathroom like a twister tossing all the toiletries she could still fit in the loaded diaper bag.

"Everything is all set not to worry, Nina dear" Ida cajoled as she watched the girl hurry back barely keeping the bag strap steady across her skinny shoulder. "I'm doing just fine although it's a little too warm today, don't you think, Nina? We are overdue for a good shower, a thunderstorm actually, that's what we need, a good heavy summer downpour, Nina" Ida resumed her senseless litany letting out her mouth whatever popped in her mind. From the kitchen Ida and Nina stepped out onto the breezeway and gingerly crossed it towards the marble descent. One at time they climbed the steps down in each other's arms.

"Almost there *Dona* Ida, good, easy now, easy…" Nina spoke for the first time. "I'm not sick, Nina, just pregnant, you know?" Ida teased but did not dare disobey Nina's instructions. "Look at this clouds Nina, do you think it's going to pour?" Ida leaned on Nina and lifted her head up at the heavy sky. She had switched the focus to the weather as they progressed to the driveway but Nina dodged all of Ida's darts. Whenever they began zipping she had to duck until the volley ended.

Pausing in front of the old *Beetle* Nina pulled forcefully on the handle and flung the canvas bag on the back seat ignoring Ida's remarks. "Careful, Nina. You don't want to squash the outfits and get them all wrinkled, do you?" and making way for Ida to settle down the front seat as comfortably as possible Nina softly hummed, "huh-huh". "Nina? I forgot to get a drink of water when we went through the kitchen, can you believe it?" Ida murmured mindlessly. "Huh-huh" Nina hummed on, rolling the window down and secretly praying a nice blow of air might keep her mistress refreshed and quiet during the ride.

Still lagging behind Daniel finally sprinted to the bottom steps fumbling his pockets in search of keys when Nina locked the passenger's door. He then picked up pace and set to the gate to undo the padlock and chain while nervously sizing up the gap separating the pillars. Once in the car Daniel hustled behind the wheel still searching his pockets and nearly forgot to close the door. If it were not for Ida's unrelenting gabbing he would not have noticed the oversight. "*Calma Pai*—easy dad—shut the door first, we are doing just fine, right Nina?" Ida winked at her handmaid and stroked her puffed stomach at the same time. "Ah, Nina" she added. "I almost forgot! Please, call my parents at six, not a minute before not a minute after, hear Nina? They always wake up at six" she waved cheerfully through the window. Daniel turned the ignition and geared the stick to reverse. The *Beetle's* rear tires skidded noisily out as Daniel barreled down the deserted street.

By no standards was Daniel a graceful driver and although he would never admit it Ida had a point when she poked fun of him about having spent way too much time with Bento in the *Aero Willys.* However, on that oppressive and anxious night she secretly praised Bento for his bad influence on her husband's driving. She could tell the baby was in a hurry to leave her, jabbing down her pelvis impatiently charting its way out. It was also getting harder for her to breathe in that cooped up position pressed between the dashboard and the backrest. She felt like a crate stacked up in a cargo truck at the mercy of the Daniel's brusque shifts from gas to brake.

Along the way each red light and stop sign Daniel warranted an obstacle on his race against time. Wherever there was no visible surveillance he cut on through after a jerky pause that increasingly aggravated Ida's nausea. He had not expected to see police vehicles at this wee hour. Usually at daybreak there were no officers at all so why today of all days they seemed to be everywhere lurking in the dark? Every now and then Daniel peered at the officers strolling in pairs along empty sidewalks. It made no sense to have policemen on duty unless something was up. Things were taking a strange turn lately.

He had heard on recent radio briefs to expect increasing presence of armed troops in the streets. The government was in hot pursuit of underground groups, supposedly Communists who had infiltrated respectable civic circles. According to Coronel Kruel who had witnessed the arrest of suspects taken into custody at his headquarters there had been clear evidence of subversive cells acting inside universities, churches and labor unions. Not long ago, during a trip downtown Daniel had also noticed a tank stationed in front of Central Station. When relating that to Coronel Kruel he learned about the Army's decision to display a heavy presence in certain parts of the city. It was critical to scale down anti-government resistance, to keep the rebels in check, his father-in-law had confided. Hideouts were being raided, Marxist literature confiscated and ultimately destroyed to protect the Military Revolution.

"As long as they don't stop me tonight" Daniel grunted, "they can do whatever" he stepped heavily on the gas pedal barely stopping at a red light. Trying to find a tolerable angle for her queasy head Ida crooked her right elbow against the window frame and leaned her chin against it. Eyes transfixed on one single spot she continued to gaze up above. "When is it going to rain?" she quizzed the overcast sky. Speedily as Daniel's *Beetle*, Rio's tropical sun broke through. Intermittent shafts of orange smeared the dark horizon with a colorful spectacle of contrasts that bewitched Ida for a few minutes. Her urge to talk vanished as she reflected on the stunning, fleeting coexistence between night and day when they drifted apart.

Whether or not aware of the hypnotic scenery, Daniel also kept quiet. Considering the haste with which Ida's labor progressed it looked like baby Daniel had a mind of his own. What if he heard them talk and decided to join the conversation? At this frightening thought Daniel wiped his brows with the back of his hand while idling carefully at another intersection. He had to stay the course, ignore any distractions and look both ways in case a police car jumped him. From brake to gas he continued to switch so abruptly that Ida bent forward never letting of her gaze off the sky. There was nothing else she could do to persuade Daniel from loosing his grip over the steering wheel. He looked like a sea captain hunched over the helm of a ship caught in a blinding tornado. Ida refused to partake in his agony.

Oddly enough, tense moments such as this united Daniel and Ida. Complicity seldom happened in their complex marriage but when it did peace stood a chance. There was nothing to say, no one to blame or attack for the surprising twists of life. As long as they remained silent they could cross the bridge of truce to the end. Side by side they breathed the dampness of dread in a deep hush. Not even the eerie presence of lurking troops justified a remark that could escalate into contention. Ida's thoughts, like her hands, hovered over what was inside her as she anticipated the pressing course of events.

In a matter of hours the creature kicking inside her would look like a real person. How different this labor unfolded. Beca's had been a lengthy but predictable delivery after nearly a whole day of contractions. Dr. Oscar had even considered a C-section while watching her push bravely for more than ten hours but when he thought she had no more strength left Beca's head mercifully crowned. The baby girl had taken her sweet time before finally deciding to cooperate and do her share of the job.

"So tender" Ida's thoughts wistfully returned to that moment when she first kissed Beca's bald skull. She had not done much better in that department after a year either, and Ida pictured her hairless toddler peacefully asleep in the crib. "Would she love both her babies the same?" The question had not occurred to Ida until then. "Caring for a baby boy must be different" she brooded over the demands of disciplining boys. This one especially would require a firm fist if the present restlessness was just a sample of what was coming.

She whimpered at yet another cramp but Daniel did not notice. Having had little sleep as usual he resented the sharp needles stinging beneath his temples and couldn't remember what he had done last. A cold shower had been out of question under Ida's exit guidelines. He had no other option but to comply. Had he looked in the rearview mirror the sight of his unshaven face would have repulsed him. Beads of sweat clung on his wrinkled forehead and dark fat circles dangled below his bloodshot eyes as he tried to stay alert. A cup of black coffee would have dismounted his scowl but Ida had also eliminated that prospect. Maybe near the hospital there was a bakery. No telling how long the waiting game might last this time. His throat was dry and raspy. The imagined touch of whiskey appeased him for a short moment.

Soon he would return to the office and be left alone for a while depending on what the doctor had to say. At least Ida had quieted down, probably out of pain. If only we had a good downpour today to break this heat up. Not looking too promising. Here we are up the hill. We made it.

"It looks like the three of you are about ready?" doctor Oscar greeted them from behind the reception desk. He had stepped into the lobby to consult with the attendant when Daniel slowly ushered Ida through the front door. The doctor welcomed them both with the detached complacency of an experienced professional. "Right this way, *Dona* Ida" he instructed "sit up on the stretcher when you can and the nurse will roll you straight into the operation room." Turning to Daniel he pointed his chin down the hall "Reverend, you will find a seat at the lounge like last time and let the nurse take the bag" he nodded. "I will deliver the good news as soon as possible" Doctor Oscar let out a clumsy chuckle at the bad joke and gingerly strolled behind the stretcher.

Daniel consulted his watch after a nod and a smile. Quarter to five. They had made it in very good time indeed. Outside the lobby a brighter tone of orange dispelled the last of the darkness and on the sidewalk a small group of laborers gathered around a utility pole waiting for the bus downtown. "At least I drive my own my own car" Daniel examined the doomed faces and turned his back on them. He made past the reception desk without greeting the clerk and paced down the corridor.

Two other men occupied the lounge when Daniel arrived. They both stood apart from guarding their own corners of the room looking as flushed and frazzled as Daniel. One of them dragged hungrily at an unfiltered cigarette puffing out nasty rings of smoke. Daniel also kept his distance and paused beneath a wall-mounted fan. He was too fidgety to sit down and could not stand the stink of cheap tobacco. To and fro he paced impatiently and after a few rounds paused in the middle of the room. There he stood studying the patterns on the dirty tiles feeling the urge to drink. It now overwhelmed him and from the corner of his eyes he watched the smoker crush the butt of a cigarette on a metal ashtray and immediately light up another. Downcast and anxious Daniel resumed the caged pacing.

On and off he checked his watch and walked fighting the temptation to rush back to his office and twist the cork of his green bottle. "Last time I was here a while" he reasoned. "In less than an hour I can go home and come back. No one will notice I'm gone. No traffic this early in the morning either and one of these two fellows can say I stepped out to find some coffee." A chain of excuses set Daniel's own exit plan in motion. The non-smoker father-to-be gurgled and spat noisily out the window. That was the cue Daniel needed to justify leaving. Out the door he stormed clucking his tongue in absolute disgust.

TWENTY-NINE

TRIM. TRIMMM. TRIIIIIIIIIIIIIIMMM…

"Nina?" Ida's potent alto ricocheted across the hallway. "Can you get that, please?" she pleaded from her chair in the kitchen where Beca engaged her in a comical contest of wills. Between giggles and squeals Ida tugged a spoonful of *mingau* away from Beca's frisky hands, swaying it like a rattle. Smears of oatmeal covered the high-chair's tray as well as Beca's face.

TRIMMMMMM. TRIMMMMM. TRIIIIIIM…

"No, *Dona* Ida, changing Rose's clothes" Nina yelled back. "Let it ring. If it's any important they'll call back" her words jumbled as she also wrestled a pair of restless arms.

"Where is your dad when we need him?" Ida asked Beca who had successfully snatched the sticky spoon.

"Pricking, *mamãe*" she giggled and scooped another serving of *mingau.*

"You mean preaching, Beca, pre-a-chin-g, not pricking. Can you say it again?" Ida rolled her eyes amusingly.

"Pri-c-k-in-g, *mamãe*" Beca repeated spreading oatmeal over her cheeks.

"Ai, Beca…" Ida reached for a damp cloth "never mind" she faked disapproval. "Look at this mess, would you?" Ida changed the subject. "Do you think that's nice? Give me back that spoon and let's finish up here or we will be late for church." Ida stole a glance at the clock perched up the blue Formica buffet. Seven thirty it warned her. "Who could be calling this early on a Sunday?" she wondered once the ringing resumed.

TRIM. TRIMIMM. TRIIIIIIM…

Daniel had already left for his office downstairs and could not be asked to assist. Not that he ever did Ida sighed and pleaded once more time. "How about now, Nina?" she craned forward and lifted Beca from the seat. Pregnant again Ida's eight-month belly was impossibly in the way of things.

TRIIIMM. TRIIIIIMMM. TRIIIIMMM…

"*Já vai*" Nina's flip-flops slashed the parquet towards the study. "*Aah-lô?*" she panted over the speaker. "Yes, it is" she prompted. "No he isn't; yes, he is. No, he isn't. Huh-huh, yes, after church. One o'clock? Huh-huh…" Nina answered all questions curtly for her mind was back at the crib. Hopefully, Rose had not jumped off the guardrail yet.

"Nina: who is it?" Ida yelled from the girls' doorway carrying Beca on her hips. "If it is for me, I'll call back" she added. "It never fails." Ida mumbled thinking of her mom who often called at the most inconvenient times like on Sunday mornings when she was in the middle of her getting ready for church routine.

"Yes, Mam. Welcome. *Tchau"* Ida heard Nina's last words gratefully as the receiver fell noisily on the black vinyl box. She was literally off the hook for now.

"Who was it, Nina?" Ida shuffled through a collection of dresses inside the girls' armoire.

"Someone called Vera asking for the Reverend" Nina caught one of Rose's leg as it dangled halfway out of the crib. "Out, Nina, out!" Rose shrieked.

"Vera? Careful Rose!" Ida snapped. "Never heard the name before. Have you?" she sounded puzzled both about the phone call and which outfit to pick. The newest identical burgundy jumpers would do.

"Stay down Rose" Nina gently swung Rose's leg off the rail. "No *Dona* Ida, not from our church that's for sure" and Nina planted Rose upright on the mattress. "Your turn to get dressed little girl" Nina sang out.

"No, Nina, no dress-ehss. Shorts, please" Rose complained and clutched her chubby arms around Nina's neck. "Out now" she bounced off Nina's appeasing embrace.

"Yes, Rose, you are putting on a dress" Ida interjected. "Stop fussing and don't start with your silly fits, hear me? Today is Sunday; you and Beca will wear the new pretty jumpers *mamãe* sewed you this week" Ida frowned at Rose and then turned to Nina.

"Did she leave a message, I mean the lady? A number to call back or anything like that?" she pried unable to hide the curiosity.

"No, *Dona* Ida" Nina took Rose's white blouse and red jumper from Ida's hand. "Only the name and said would call back later" Nina wanted to drop the subject. "Here Rose, you gonna look so very pretty on this new outfit. Guess what? It matches your red shoes too" Nina sat Rose down to put on a pair of polyester socks and fasten the glossy Mary-Janes on Rose's tiny feet.

"I don't like it, Nina. Don't like this dress *Dona* Ida" Rose shook her head and pouted.

"Nonsense, Rose, of course you like it" Ida rebuked irritably. "Look at your sister. It's the same color and all" Ida straightened out Beca's outfit sending Rose another warning: "And quit calling me *Dona* Ida: it's *mamãe,* Rose. Why can't you behave more like Beca?" Ida scolded.

"Ugly Beca" Rose fired back and stuck her tongue out at her sister who started bawling at the hurtful remark.

"I'm telling you Rose: cut it out" Ida's temper heated. "Nina: what am I going to do with this girl? She is only two years old but has a mouth bigger than a pipe organ" she seethed. "Something has been wrong since the day she was born, remember Nina? All that hassle in the middle of the night on the way to the hospital when I was so sure she was a boy. Might as well. She acts like one, Nina. Rose is as strong-willed, stubborn, and mouthy like her father" Ida spewed angrily. "It's that weird birthmark on her tummy. Looks like a cockroach. How many times have I told you, Nina? Just like her father's. She has nothing of me, I swear. Not even close" Ida fastened Beca's shoe buckles.

"*Dona* Ida: Rose has a mind of her own. She little but mighty smart" Nina chortled trying to diffuse the rising tension. "She speak better than me it blows my mind."

"That's not called smart, Nina. Stubborn it is what that is called. I have to keep her in line all the time it drives me insane. Teach her to not talk back, not to call me *Dona* Ida, not to point at people and say the first thing that pops in her head, you know?" Ida lashed. "Can you imagine Rose a teenager? She is going to run this house if I don't stop her. Just as well, I ought to start now, hear me Rose?" Ida roared.

"Come here Rosy, come with Nina. Let me go brush your hair?" Nina dodged Ida's volley.

"No ribbons, right Nina? I don't like ribbons. They squeeze my hair like this" and Rose buried her tiny fingers down her black mane and squinted hard highlighting a pair of deep dimples on her cheeks.

"No Rosy, no ribbons today. Promise" Nina smiled adoringly. "C'mon now" and grabbed Rose's chubby hand. "Let's walk to the bathroom together and look in the mirror?" Nina could always find a way to bridge the rifts between mother and daughter.

Ida let Nina and Rose escape her wrath for the time being as her thoughts returned to the mysterious caller. This had been a first in all the years they had lived in Encantado. Except for wrong numbers or rare pranks phone calls invariably came from people they knew either personally or through the church membership, in which case there was always a specific reference or message left. Why would a stranger call and not leave at least a call back number? Why not ask for her either? Didn't this Vera know there was a lady of the house to speak to? That part of the incident bothered her most she had to admit. It oozed secrecy as if this Vera didn't want to be found out. If so, why not? She had to ask Nina about the voice on the wire. Whether there was anything suspicious about the timbre. Did this Vera sound young or old? Could she perhaps have come across frantic or composed? Sincere or sinister? It had to be one or the other Ida was convinced.

"Nina?" she yelled again. "Can you come here, please?"

"Coming. Almost done with Rose, *Dona* Ida" Nina shouted this time with the hairbrush handle between her lips.

"This lady, Vera, right?" Ida met Nina in the bathroom instead.

"Huh-huh" Nina ducked bracing for what could be a second volley.

"How did she sound?" Ida pretended to be casual and enunciated her words carefully.

"Sound, *Dona* Ida? Why, how would it be? Like the voice of a woman that's how" Nina shrugged and straightened Rose's thick bangs with her fingertips.

"No, Nina, I mean like the type of voice, you know? Young, old, happy, sad?" Ida clarified.

"*Dona* Ida, I don't know what you mean by type but she kinda sounded a little nervous now that you say it" Nina held Rose up in front of the cabinet mirror and pointed "who is this pretty girl, Rosy?

"It's Rose, Nina! Who else?" Rose looked at Nina wide-eyed as if in total disbelief.

"Nervous…" Ida interposed again. "You mean like worried nervous or afraid nervous, Nina?" she prowled behind them and looked pensively at the mirror.

"*Ai Dona* Ida, now you got me. Nervous is just nervous, ain't it?" Nina pecked Rose's forehead and put her down. In no time Rose pushed free through the four legs corralling her calling out to her sister. "Beca: downstairs. I'm ready!"

"Wait Rose" Ida bent down to stop her a little too late. "Not until Nina or *Mamãe* can come too" she tried.

"I can hold Beca's hand, *Dona* Ida*"* Rose shrilled back and kept on running.

"Nina, can you please stop her before they both tumble headlong down those steps?" Ida rubbed her stomach. She was in no condition to chase after Rose. At the end of her third pregnancy Ida had grown more indisposed on the account of the rapid weight gain paired with the increasing demands around the house. Nina was a reliable and solicitous helper but the girls required constant attention all day long. There was so much to fret over that she at times felt like an empty sack barely able to stand in one spot let alone run.

To make matters worse she refused to give up her church obligations and had remained committed as the organist and choir's accompanist. Rehearsals took place twice a week in addition to organ practices. On Sundays she still played during both morning and evening services despite Daniel's opposition. They had argued bitterly over a permanent alternate until the girls grew a little older but that was out of question. Ida could not fathom life without music. Never. It was only when she sat down to play that she actually relaxed and as infrequent as those hours had become lately they were the only satisfying slots available in her chaotic schedule.

"Got them *Dona* Ida!" Nina screamed from the breezeway. "Will take them down to the nursery."

"Oh-oh!" Ida stopped on her heavy tracks. "Am I on nursery duty today?" she wondered out loud before answering Nina. She would have to double-check the calendar on Daniel's desk.

"Fine! Go on down, Nina" she shouted and headed towards the study. Either way once the girls were gone she would be able to get dressed quicker and more importantly in peace. She would change right away and gamble on a few extra minutes alone practicing the morning line up just as she used to in Copacabana.

"Perfect! Off nursery" Ida breathed relieved at the empty spot on the calendar. At the corner of the desk the black phone box took the shape of a safety vault. Eyes transfixed on it Ida secretly fantasized it would ring again under her telepathic command and then she would be the one to answer it. "Vera," she weighed the name in. It sounded foreboding for some reason. Certainly uncommon, Ida stood there staring at the gleaming device. She could not quite put a finger on why the name abhorred her. Why couldn't she stop thinking about it? "Well, Nina said she is calling back. How about now, Vera?" and under Ida's grip the receiver immediately vibrated. TRIMM, TRIMM.

Taking a step back Ida cleared her throat. "Reverend Daniel's residence. His wife speaking" she firmly stated.

"Oh good morning dear! Am I interrupting? Just wanted to say hello to the girls before church" *Dona* Sílvia greeted.

"Oh, hello mother, it's you" Ida gruffly replied.

"Who else at this hour my dear?" she burbled. "Where are my girls? Can I talk to them now or this is not a good time?"

"You just missed them, *mãe*. Nina has taken them down to the nursery to play a little before Sunday school and I am late for practice as we speak" Ida cut to the chase unapologetically.

"Never mind then, dear. Go get dressed. Will call back later" *Dona* Sílvia promised.

"Sure you will mother, *tchau!*" Ida hung up annoyed both at herself for the unduly alarm and at her mother for exposing it. One more wasted minute and she would not have enough time to review the complete repertoire. "Let go Ida" she breathed heavily. "Focus on what is important" she began to hum a favorite hymn. Singing helped banish negative thoughts from her hyperactive mind.

"*Nearer my God to Thee, nearer to Thee!*" she set out on her way to the bedroom. *"E'en though it be a cross, that raised me"* and pausing at the armoire she pulled out one of her many maternity dresses. *"Still all my song shall be."* Goodness, I have not worn anything else for over three years" Ida rubbed her round stomach. Could this be the baby boy she had been praying for? "*Nearer my God to Thee, nearer to Thee.*"

"*Dona* Ida?" Nina's soft voice echoed from the kitchen interrupting Ida's reverie. "I'm back. Need anything?" she dutifully asked.

"No, thanks, dear. And the girls?" Ida hurled the large dress down and set out to the bathroom.

"With *Tia* Jujú. She is on duty today and said I could come up get ready myself" Nina shouted from the girls' room where she kept her belongings inside a closet.

"Good. Let them play a while. Were they behaving Nina?" Ida applied a perfect layer of red lipstick standing in front of the mirror.

"Of course, *Dona* Ida, what a question?" Nina chided. As far as she was concerned the girls could do no wrong.

"Nina, you know who I mean. Rose, of course. Was she good for *Tia* Jujú?" and with her pinky Ida dabbed a touch of silvery shadow over her eyelids as the long distance exchange continued.

"Well, now that you bring it up... You ain't gonna believe what Rosy just did" and Nina began laughing out loud. "Oh, well, I guess you will. It's Rosy" Nina could barely speak while recalling the incident.

"What Nina?" Ida yelled. "Please, don't tell me she came up with another one of her tirades?" she clasped her gold ear hoops in place.

"Listen to this, *Dona* Ida. You know *Tia* Juju now wears her hair up in the new beehive style, right? So, Rose looks at her the minute she steps in the nursery, and today *Dona* Ida, not making this up Juju's hair is done over the top, you'll see when you get down there" Nina cracked up again.

"No, Nina, please… Don't tell me Rose said something about it?" Ida peered out into the hallway holding her hairbrush in midair.

"Course she did, *Dona* Ida, you kidding me?" Nina shrilled.

"Oh my, Nina, what was it?" Ida waded closer to the doorway to better hear it.

"So, we are all in there" Nina tried to sound coherent "sitting on the floor with some blocks and puzzle pieces." Ida stopped breathing in expectation. "*Tia* Jujú walks in saying hello stooping down with kisses when Rose" and Nina paused while yelping "takes a serious look at her, points straight up to her hair and say: *Tia* Jujú is that a big wig you wear now?" and Nina bent over with a belly laugh.

"Oh my Nina" Ida gasped "Rose is something else" and quickly recovered her parental tone. "How many times have I told her it is rude to point at people, Nina? She never listens to me. She does that all the time it is aggravating. What did *Tia* Jujú say? I hope she was not offended…" Ida worried about her girls' behavior and others' judgment of her mothering skills.

"She burst out laughing too, *Dona* Ida" Nina wiped the corner of her eyes. "We all ended up laughing and Rosy rolled on the floor in pure hysterics. Beca too. Not sure she knew why but she does the same as her sister all the time, right? You should've seen them. Adorable…" and Nina returned to the bedroom shaking her head.

"What is so funny, ladies?" Daniel had sneaked in unnoticed behind Ida. "Did I miss the joke?" he grinned in an exceptionally friendly way.

"Oh, hello there" Ida glared back. "Why are you back up?" she stared at Daniel's eyes. They sparkled strangely. His cheeks glowed with a fiery tone.

"I need another cup of coffee" he deflected the stare and turned away. "Is there any left?" he walked to the kitchen.

"Yes, Reverend" Nina followed behind. "In the thermos. Still fresh, right *Dona* Ida?" Nina ran to the cupboard to fetch a demitasse.

"Thanks, Nina" Daniel sat down and waited to be served. "So, tell me, what were two laughing about?" Daniel uncovered the sugar bowl and began scooping.

"Rose came up with another of her keen remarks and it's not even mid-day yet" Ida sat down by her husband and related the story.

"She is her mother's daughter, isn't she?" he also broke down with laughter.

"What is that supposed to mean?" Ida pushed her chair over and stood up.

"*Dona* Ida" Nina tryed to appease "you better go down to practice, right?" she pointed to the door.

"Right Nina, but let me first make it perfectly clear that Rose's manners are nothing like mine. For the record I am not rude to people" Ida growled.

"Oh, Ida, Rose is not rude, she is just a baby" Daniel grinned again and sipped from his black coffee and declined Ida's invitation to quarrel.

"More, Reverend?" Nina closed in with the thermos just in case.

"One more, Nina, thanks" he pushed the saucer forward "I need to get going soon" he checked his watch.

"Before I leave though" Ida approached, her belly nearly touching his hairline. "A lady named Vera called you this morning. Who is she?" Ida fired.

"Vera?" he shook his puzzled head. "Did she leave a last name or a message?" Daniel looked up.

"No, nothing but the name" Ida searched his eyes again. "Who could it be?" she blinked.

"Haven't the faintest idea. It sounds familiar though" he held her gaze. "Not that I recall meeting a lady with the name but the name itself, you know what I mean?" he spoke slowly.

"No, I don't but at any rate she will call back after church, right Nina?" Ida stepped aside when Daniel suddenly snapped his fingers.

"Wait" he shouted "of course I have heard the name before. "Vera is the name of Antônio's wife. I knew I had heard it somewhere" he jumped to his feet.

"Antônio who?" Ida wheeled back to the table.

"My Seminary roommate, remember?" Daniel's pushed the chair back under the table. "I must have told you about him. I used to spend weekends at his house in Vila Nova during my first two years of school" Daniel began to pace the kitchen allowing the memories to flood in. The train rides, the lavish meals, the furtive soccer matches, and the occasional forbidden beers afterwards.

"I do, I mean, vaguely" Ida clung curiously to Daniel's every word. "Didn't you send him an invitation to our wedding?" she impelled him to continue.

"Sure did but they couldn't make it" Daniel uttered lowly, deeply entangled in the web of time. "He said it was too far for them. They live out in Caxias" he clawed the small of his neck as if pulling a thread out of a hank. "At any rate, he did send us a card. If we find it we will be able to confirm whether that is his wife's name" Daniel suggested.

"Perfect. I know exactly where it is" Ida marched out of the kitchen directly to the study. "I have put all our wedding cards and telegrams inside a box. It's on the top shelf of the bookcase in the study" she spoke as fast as she moved.

"*Dona* Ida" Nina heeled close behind. "Let me get that for you" and in a flash managed to beat Ida to the task before an accident happened.

"Well done Nina, thanks" Ida received the dusty box and removed the lid at once. "It's been a while since I looked at these but I have no doubts it's all in here" Ida sorted through a bundle of envelopes.

"Right there. That's Antônio's handwriting, Ida" Daniel gripped her hand.

"You sure?" she handed a large white envelope to him.

"Positive" Daniel' s hands shook with anticipation and guilt.

*"Dear Brother: greetings in Christ. What a joy to receive your wedding invitation. You must be ecstatic this week as the big day approaches. Unfortunately, I cannot promise Vera and I can attend the ceremony in Copacabana. We live too far and do not dispose of private transportation at the moment. Relying on the train and the bus would be complicated on a Saturday night as you well know but rest assured we will be in prayer for both you and Ida. When time allows we would like to deliver a gift in person. Thanks for including us on your guest list and for forwarding your new address and phone number. May the Good Lord richly bless your union… "*Daniel read out loud before tucking the card back in the envelope.

"Well, well, well, mystery solved" Ida handed the box to Nina.

"Not quite" Daniel took the envelope back.

"Why not?" Ida grew impatient at Daniel's interference.

“I would expect to receive a call from Antônio not his wife” he replied. “Why would Vera call and not him?” he murmured and flapped the envelope on the palm of his hand still in deep thought.

“Hah! That is easy, darling” Ida let out a sassy snort. “He is a Pastor, isn’t he?” she blurted out. “Therefore, he is way too busy for phone calls. You, should know the answer to that question, right Nina?” Ida winked opening the door of the study out to the breezeway without waiting for a reply. Her heavy feet plopped loudly down one marble step at a time.

PART V

THE NEMESIS

"And heard another's voice cry: 'what! ***Are you here?****'*
Although we were not. I was still the same,
Knowing myself yet being someone other—
And he a face still forming; yet the words sufficed
To compel the recognition they preceded.
And so, compliant to the common wind,
Too strange to each other for misunderstanding,
In concord at this intersection time
Of meeting nowhere, no before and after,
We trod the pavement in a dead patrol.
I said: the wonder that I feel is easy,
Yet ease is cause of wonder. Therefore speak:
I may not comprehend, may not remember.'
And he: 'I am not eager to rehearse
My thoughts and theory which you have forgotten.
These things have served their purpose: let them be."

(T.S. Elliot, *Little Giding, II)*

THIRTY

Punctually at one o'clock in the afternoon the Encantado telephone wailed its clamoring jingle. From Daniel's study the sound conspicuously meandered the hallway towards the kitchen where the family partook of Ida's sumptuous Sunday meal. At the center of the neatly draped table a large tray of roasted chicken pieces took over most of the space flanked with large bowls of a creamy potato salad, buttery *farofa*, and white rice mixed with diced carrots and peas. Nina had pulled out the built-in extension and added extra chairs so Ida's guests could skirt comfortably around the blue Formica table. *Seu* Aloísio, *Dona* Catarina and their daughters Jurema and Amália each took a turn passing Beca and Rose around as if playing musical laps. The girls basked in the adulation whereas Daniel, Ida and Nina enjoyed the break.

"Is that your phone, Reverend?" *Seu* Aloísio had just emptied a small bottle of Coca-Cola into his iced-packed glass. He cupped an ear inquisitively while the carousel of unfinished sentences span under a fizzle of giggles.

"*Dona* Ida?" Jurema wiggled a spoon of rice through Beca's lips oblivious to her father's inquiry. "This meat is so tender, so juicy, how do you?" she raved while Nina quickly jumped in to explain. "Ah, it's her special secret *Tia* Jujú" and before Nina could praise Ida's butchering skills Rose piped in peremptorily. "She kills the chickens inside the laundry tub out there in the patio *Tia,* like this" Rose balled her chubby hands side by side and arched them apart in a graphic demonstration of the odious slaughter. "And, then *Tia,* then, she, she" Beca stammered through a mouthful of rice and yelled in case nobody was listening "*mamãe* burns the dead chickens inside that box there" she pointed at the gas oven. "*Ai* Beca, really?" Amália howled and joined the others in hearty laughter.

"Reverend?" *Seu* Aloísio tried again this time resorting to a hand signal from the other end of the table. Thumb and pinky stretched over his ear he mouthed out the words slowly trying not to choke in his own cackle: "phone."

"Ah" Daniel clucked his tongue loudly. "Thank you, *Seu* Aloísio I'll get it" Daniel hoisted up and crumpled his napkin on the table. "Excuse-me everyone: I will return shortly" he gallantly bowed and pushed his chair back.

"Where are you going?" Ida glared at him. Her eyes swayed accusingly to emphasize the presence of company.

"The phone, Ida" Daniel thumbed over his shoulder holding her cold stare.

"Oh, is it ringing already?" Ida consulted the clock on top of the blue Formica cabinet. "One o'clock" she announced to no one in particular.

"*Tudo bem,* Ida?" *Dona* Catarina gently tapped Ida's arm and kept her eyes on Daniel's hasty trail.

"Yes, Catarina, all is well" Ida smiled disarmingly. "A pre-scheduled call; you know how it goes, right? It never stops around here" she sighed imperceptibly. "So sorry it had to interrupt our meal" Ida returned her guest's tender touch. "How about another serving of chicken?" she graciously enticed."It is exquisite dear, yes, I'll take another piece, please" *Dona* Catarina sheepishly lifted her plate up so Nina could assist from across the table. "Anyone else now that I'm at it?" Nina offered to an enthusiastic chorus of "yes, please!"

Ida was the only one to refuse Nina's favor preferring a refill of Coca-Cola instead. Her mind rekindled the unwarranted suspicion attached to the caller. As she had done throughout the organ practice and the entire duration of the service she conjectured why Vera and not Antônio had wanted to speak to Daniel. Why would Vera be the one calling *back*? The enigma ate at her so intensely that it ended up costing her a disgraceful slip at the postlude of *Holy, Holy, Holy.* Immersed in profound reflection her hands had frozen over the keyboard causing the hymn's final accord to linger beyond its scripted tempo. Daniel's furious stare reentered her mind.

A host of fabricated scenarios had been clogging her brain and none of them appeased Ida's apprehension over Vera's phone call in the first place. The incident bothered her to such an unprecedented and inexplicable level that she had not given it a rest. If anything, she ought to know whether something might have happened to Antônio. Had he fallen seriously ill and therefore was unable to come to the phone? Or had he gone on a trip and Vera needed some kind of assistance? If that was the case why not call her in-laws? No, that made no sense. Perhaps, a tragic accident. That could well be the reason. He had bumped his head and dropped unconscious on the floor but then again why would Vera call Daniel and not her in-laws or the

Caxias Elders? It had to be something else for sure. Hah! A sudden death in the family sounded more like it since Daniel knew Antônio's folks. Much more plausible. Vera had called to ask Daniel to officiate the funeral. No, wait, that sounded preposterous too. Antônio should be the one calling for the arrangement. So why hadn't he?

Cataloging the numerous possibilities and matching variables made Ida thirsty and she gulped the chilled soda down doing a fine job of concealing her distress. Deep down she understood Vera's conduct. Acting on her husband's behalf was a wife's primary responsibility. She had done the same many times when Daniel woke up with forbidding headaches, poor thing, and had to either postpone or cancel engagements. Not that she liked doing that, Ida secretly admitted, and wiped her lips not forgetting to beam at the ongoing tittering. It was a matter of marital duty for a wife to cover up for her husband, to make sure he always appeared professional, presentable, taken care of. He had an image to preserve and she was a Godly helper.

Same expectation applied to Vera, Ida justified. A decent Christian wife is above all a virtuous woman as Proverbs, chapter 31 stated. Vera had called because her husband had requested it and that should settle the matter, Ida poured some more Coca-Cola over the ice cubes switching her concerns to what was possibly being said over the wire.

"*A-a-lôu?*" Daniel answered the phone on its fifth ring.

"Is this Daniel, please?" a smooth questioner pried. Daniel interpreted the tone as assertive yet cautious. He began to imagine what kind of lips released such a blend of intentions.

"This is he" Daniel pressed the handset closer to his ear. "May I ask who is calling?" he feigned ignorance.

"Hello Daniel, my name is Vera. I am Antônio's wife" she pronounced solemnly.

"Yes" Daniel replied politely.

"Obviously you don't know me" she quickly added. "Earlier this morning I left a message with your maid. I hope you have a few minutes?" she enunciated each word crisply.

"Certainly Vera, I did receive your message this morning" Daniel confirmed. Vera's apparent coolness struck him as the opposite of Antônio's sparkly demeanor and at the intruding memory of his friend Daniel closed his eyes. Antônio's dazzling grin never failed to blind him. "How is he doing?" he promptly added. "It has been a few years since I, I mean, we" and for a split second Daniel's tongue curled. It refused to move as his brain wrestled with how to proceed.

Was this the right time for an open confession of remorse? For years he had dreamed of begging Antônio's pardon but ultimately had failed to act on it. Was this the proper moment to excuse his self-imposed isolation, the indifference with which he had nurtured their friendship? Or should he simply skip formalities and smother another layer of denial down his dark vault?

"This call is about him, Daniel" Vera ambushed Daniel's hesitation. "I must speak to you as soon as possible" she switched to a somber tone. "Not on the phone but in person" she hissed.

"Most certainly, Vera" Daniel immediately agreed presuming Vera was calling to set up the visit Antônio had alluded to on the wedding card. The initiative seemed providential, the perfect opportunity to orchestrate a meeting between their families. "Let me ask you one question first, if I may?" he cautiously prodded. "How is Antônio? Can you put him on, please? I would very much like to talk to him directly" he hinted Vera's wifely task accomplished.

According to Daniel's line of thought Vera had subjected to her husband's orders in placing the call but Antônio would soon take over the phone so they could catch up with the latest. With that in mind Daniel sat down and waited to hear the familiar cheerful voice but in the meantime a suspenseful silence pervaded. It appeared that Vera had somehow stopped breathing and assuming she had misheard his request Daniel rephrased it: "Hello, Vera? May I speak to Antônio now, please?"

Daniel had not planned on the words rushing out of his mouth with such fret but the prospect of hearing Antônio's voice after so many years suddenly stirred him up. His hands shook a little as he considered the possibility of having actually missed Antônio's antics. Up to then in the occasions Antônio's face crossed his mind it had been with a tinge of scorn. Unlike him, Antônio had intentionally pursued the stewardship of an impoverished parish away from Rio's circles of status and affluence. "What shall a man give in exchange for his soul?" Antônio's words chimed with innocence and humility. How often had Daniel berated him as an insipid preacher who preferred to stick to literal Scripture rather than an elaborate exegesis. "No prophecy of the scripture is of private interpretation, Brother" Antônio cited verse twenty of Peter's Second Epistle when Daniel confronted the plainness of his senior sermon.

"I am sorry, Daniel, but you can't speak to him right now" Vera's subdued voice reached Daniel's ears as if coming from another planet. "I can't speak to him either" her whisper carried a trace of anguish.

"Pardon me?" Daniel was conscious of the crudeness in the interrogation but could not suppress a burst of exasperation at Vera's ambiguity. "What do you mean you can't speak to him?" he elevated the tone.

"So sorry" Vera repeated sternly. "It's complicated. I don't even know where Antônio is right now" she conceded.

"What do you mean you don't know?" Daniel now roared. "He is your husband" he inadvertently condemned Vera's imprecision as negligence without considering his own deceitful omissions as a husband. How many times had he left Ida in the dark about his whereabouts? Another wave of stillness crested over the wire. Vera's gasp barely noticeable eventually crossed over while Daniel stood up twisting the telephone cord. He began pacing impatiently around the desk.

"Hello?" he shouted. "Still there, Vera? Can you hear me?" he disengaged the cord and proceeded to bang the hook.

"Yes" Vera's somber voice resurged brassily. "Still here" she confirmed.

"Oh, great. I mean good" Daniel shrilled embarrassedly. "Forgive me, Vera, I didn't mean to be rude."

"Daniel, listen" Vera cut him off sharply. "I am calling because I need your help. This is an unusual matter that requires time to explain in person. When can we meet?" she demanded. The impudence behind Vera's pitch clearly bothered Daniel but for Antônio's sake he was compelled to overlook it.

"I see" Daniel struggled to modulate his exasperation. "Give me a minute, please. Let me check this week's schedule" and Daniel rested the handset on the desk to pull a drawer open. A pile of outdated bulletins rose to the rim and he fumbled beneath it to locate his leather-bound planner. "Here it is" he murmured offhandedly.

"Daniel, I don't think you understand me" Vera accused as soon as Daniel returned to the mouthpiece. "I must speak to you in person sooner rather than later. Time is of essence and I cannot wait for you to find a convenient slot on your planner to clear, you see?" she pressed on.

"Alright then" Daniel conceded. The woman was testing his patience. He slid to the edge of the chair and studied the dates ahead. Before him two sheets of paper blotched with scribbles opened ominously side-by-side disclosing every move he ought to make in the upcoming week. It seemed he was booked solid and he felt terribly ambivalent about which event to cancel. Tomorrow was out of question since a burial was scheduled for mid-morning and most definitely a luncheon at the deceased's home would follow. That could last the whole afternoon his stomach churned dreadfully in anticipation. Of all the rituals he had been trained to conduct funerals were by far the most loathsome. The strange combination of tears and fresh flowers invariably made him lightheaded.

"How about first thing in the morning, Tuesday?" he proposed. It was the best he could do under the circumstances. He grabbed a pen and crossed over the morning bracket and then traced an arrow to the lines below. Both counseling appointments could be moved to the early afternoon while Nina would accompany Ida to Doctor Oscar's office at three-thirty. They would have to take a cab and most likely drag Beca and Rose along but the girls loved car rides anyway, Daniel acquiesced with a faint smile. Ida, on the other had, was going to throw a fit about another fall through.

He had missed the last appointment on the account of an emergency hospital visit. The muscles on Daniel's neck contracted as he replayed the shouting match. It was bound to happen again but this was the price of propriety. He bit his lips. Time had come to requite Antônio's friendship and, more importantly, find out what was really going on here. Why couldn't Vera speak to him? Where had Antônio gone? This was so unlike him to vanish without a warning.

"Fine" Vera readily agreed. "Tuesday, April first, where and when?" she asked for specifics.

"My church office at nine in the morning" Daniel suggested. "Unless that is too early…"

"No, no it works" Vera interrupted in case Daniel changed his mind. "Nine o'clock is just fine."

"Do you know how to get here?" Daniel wrote down Vera's name next to the number nine. "It just occurred to me you have never visited."

"Don't worry about that, Daniel" Vera assured him. "I'll manage."

"Sure you will" Daniel retorted cynically. He began to wonder how Antônio had met such an obnoxious woman. If he remembered correctly one of his first letters referred to Vera as a member of the Caxias parish. Perhaps she had grown up over in that area in one of those rough neighborhoods Antônio ministered at. For all he knew Vera could have been raised in a *favela*. Those were fearless people, Daniel stereotyped as snippets of his reckless encounters with Lurdes interloped quickly leading to an absurd hypothesis about Antônio's association with Vera. Had Antônio tried to save Vera from a shady past by proposing holy matrimony? Knowing Antônio's character that would not come as a surprise, Daniel shook his head.

"If transportation is a problem" Daniel derided at the speculation and shifted to another relevant piece of information received from Antônio. In the wedding message he had mentioned lacking private transportation. "Don't hesitate to take a cab. Caxias is a long ride but I will pay for your fare."

"That won't be necessary, Daniel, thank you" Vera didn't let him finish. "I will drive over" she announced casually.

"Drive?" Daniel fumed in silence. "Since when women drove cars?" he wanted to rant. Hadn't Antônio written about not having a vehicle in the first place? That had been the main reason for not attending the wedding. The situation was growing too surreal for Daniel to comprehend. Hopefully, the conversation on Tuesday would lead to a logical explanation.

"Oh, of course" Daniel replied smugly "and the street address, do you have it?" he volunteered out of formality.

"Clarimundo de Melo Street, number 50" Vera recited. "Found it in Antônio's address book."

"That's it. Encantado's main street" Daniel explained. "You won't miss the tall steeple as you turn either from the left or right. The church is in the middle of the road" he parroted the habitual directions to the building.

"Good" Vera uttered softly. "Daniel, I can't thank you enough" she sounded relieved.

"Please, don't" it was Daniel's turn to interrupt. "This is about Antônio" his voice quivered slightly. He was tempted to say more, to unburden the loads of remorse stacked under his pride and purge the nagging guilt out of his throat but his tongue had, once again, stalled.

"Yes, it is. Thanks again, *tchau"* she hang up.

"What in the world just happened?" Daniel asked the black receiver. He stared at it while the free line signal ebbed away and leaned back on his chair mesmerized. "Had he understood it all correctly?" he slowly re-cradled the receiver. "Antônio is gone, Vera doesn't know where and he is going to help her find him?" he stood up and rambled to the doorway aware of what waited for him in the kitchen. Ida would not relent until he delivered a detailed account of the conversation regardless of the guests' presence. Before dessert and coffee were over she would yank it all out of him.

"Oh, there you are darling" Ida spoke from inside the fridge. "Just in time for flan. Have a seat" she smiled invitingly.

"Coffee everyone?" Nina ferried the steel thermos to the table.

"Here Nina!" Rose clapped her chubby hands.

"Me too Nina" Beca tagged along making everyone laugh once more.

"A tiny bit with milk and sugar for Rosy and Beca, right *Dona* Ida? Leme get them mugs" and Nina placed the thermos down as soon as Ida assented.

"So, darling, was that Vera on the phone?" Ida fired straight. "You look a little worried, don't you all think so?" she recruited immediate assistance from *Dona* Catarina. Ida knew Daniel would not dare cross her in front of company.

"Well" Daniel said in a measured tone while reclaiming his seat at the head of the table. "It was her" he stopped once Nina poured the coffee.

"And?" Ida baited at him while the others also looked on expectantly.

"Is there a problem, Reverend?" *Seu* Aloísio broke in after sipping his *cafézinho*.

"Not sure, *Seu* Aloísio" Daniel turned to his Elder. "Let us wait until Tuesday morning" he divulged while lifting up his tiny cup.

"All that time talking and you are not sure?" Ida coaxed Daniel with a dish of caramel flan. "What is happening Tuesday morning?" she refilled her soda glass.

"Vera will be here at nine o'clock" Daniel took a large bite of the spongy flan.

"By herself?" Ida sounded confused. "How about Antônio? Isn't he coming along?" she poked.

"She wants me to help find him" Daniel shrugged indicating he had nothing else to say.

"Oh! Isn't that odd?" Ida smiled at *Seu* Aloísio and surprisingly dropped the matter. Daniel knew she was only gathering ammunition and would discharge as soon as the guests left. In the meantime he felt immensely grateful for softening his tongue with a second spoonful of caramel flan.

THIRTY-ONE

A very good morning listeners of 98.1 AM Global Station! On this first sultry day of April, 1969 we have one minute past six. A bit early I know but I will ask you anyway my friend: have you already picked a fool today? Your host Juca here from 'Ball Planet' reminding you that today all lies are sanctioned in the name of sport, no pun intended. Your latest soccer news is proudly brought by Antártica the official sponsor of Ball Planet. Are we here to drink or talk, ladies and gentlemen? Antártica is our beer!

Rio's temperature today is expected to soar to a scorching thirty-three degrees Celsius. How are you going to quench your thirst? This April's Fool is also expected to be sunny and humid. No rain on our forecast as we leave the month of March behind; nowhere to hide in this marvelous city where the overnight temperature might drop to 25 degrees Celsius along the shore.

"Lord help us" Daniel yawned on his way to the shower pressing the small radio close to his ear. It had been nearly impossible to unwind let alone sleep in such a scald despite the extra ice cubes on his *Passport*. For a while the fan's merciful blows fluttered the stagnant air in the bedroom but it eventually magnified Ida's thundering snores. As the baby's delivery date quickly approached her breathing grew forbiddingly labored and to Daniel's despair it startled him every time she fumbled trying to find a comfortable position.

In agony Daniel recoiled and watched her enlarged stomach heave against him like a tidal wave about to crash. He nudged further away towards the edge on the verge of tumbling off as night turned to dawn. Most certainly doctor Oscar would admit her at the end of today's consultation, in which case he might miss this baby's birth too. Overwhelmed with guilt and fatigue Daniel had clung to his pillow and vigilantly prepared to punch the alarm pin before six.

Ladies and Gentlemen: shall we begin with good news? Why not? This isn't a prank you have my word as I report on yesterday's relaxed press conference Brazil's new soccer coach João Saldanha conceded. There are twenty-two names on his recruit list, and the coach affirmed with great conviction and I quote: "I am optimistic", referring to the fine cast of players going to represent Brazil next year in Mexico. We do stand a very good chance to win the 1970 world cup, ladies and gentlemen. And how could Saldanha not be optimistic? Carlos Alberto Torres, Pelé, Gérson, Jairzinho and Tostão, all in one team, ladies and gentlemen, who will beat us? Isn't this the best ensemble of footballers alive in our Ball Planet?

"Nobody from Vasco, Saldanha?" Daniel closed the bathroom door flipped the light switch and blasted the volume to hear the rest of the report from under the showerhead. "Better buy the paper and read this whole interview" he released the cold stream.

This next piece of news is going to blow your minds ladies and gentlemen. The International Federation of Soccer, FIFA, is seriously considering the use of artificial grass in next year's World Cup stadiums. What do you have to say about that? Our phone line is open and you may cast a vote on this very controversial matter beginning now. At the end of the show we will tally the results and let you know how many are for or against this novelty. Call us with your opinion at 269-4653: 'yes' or 'no' to artificial grass in the Mexican stadiums nest year. At Global 98.1 AM your right to vote is still honored.

"For crying out loud" Daniel scrubbed his scalp with a coconut soap bar. "Artificial grass on a soccer field? Where in the world are we going with all these modern changes?" and the picture of Vera driving a car to Encantado trickled down Daniel's lathered head. "A woman behind a wheel?" he rinsed the foam off.

Moving on with this weekend's Carioca tournament roundup ladies and gentlemen. On Sunday afternoon Flamengo defeated Madureira with one goal at the fortieth minute of the second half, a tight victory that many didn't see coming. Also on Sunday, Botafogo mowed over Bangu at the great Maracanã stadium: three-nothing for the lone star players in an easy match. Fluminense tied in just one goal with Bonsucesso last Saturday and the same happened between Olaria and América. Attention Vasco fans for important news. After a few days of deadlocked negotiations forward Nei has signed a contract for the season and is expected to play the next match against Bonsucesso.

"Good for you, Nei. About time" Daniel turned the knob off, stepped out of the stall onto the cool tiled floor and waited for Juca to disclose details of Nei's purse otherwise he would have to buy today's paper for sure.

My esteemed listeners this is what you have been waiting for, the replay of all terrific scores in our weekend Carioca roundup. This next segment is brought to you exclusively by our preferred Shell Gas Stations. 'Shell Gasoline is life for your automobile.' Let's begin with Botafogo's easy ride against Bangu: Rogério grooms the ball for a long cross kick. From the deep corner of Bangu's right pole Rogério spots Jairzinho moving into position inside the small grid. Jairzinho is ready to receive Rogério's pass. The ball flies off like a rocket and Jairzinho takes advantage of Bangu's sleepy defense. With his left cleat he reaches the ball. In a flash he turns it over to Roberto who is legally, perfectly stationed inside Bangu's defense grid, ladies and gentlemen. Roberto is no more than two feet away from Bangu's right pole and up he jumps, higher than all Bangu's defenders, clipping the ball with the tip of his head. In it goes right where it belongs: gooooaaaaalll! The net is bouncing at the Maracanã already, ladies and gentlemen. The ball is in my friends. I saw it land with my own eyes. It is on the ground: Botafogo one, Bangu zero on the fourteenth minute mark of the match's first half.

Daniel smiled broadly at the scintillating mirror. "Wow" he squinted at his frosted face while cautiously scraping a batch of shaving cream up his neck. From bottom to top the sharp razor skidded lithely around Daniel's grin like an ice skater gracefully moving to the muffled drumbeats backing Juca's narration. Below his chin Daniel's tanned skin emerged soft and smooth in between patches of white puff. His juvenile imagination bounced off the luminous glass.

Wrapped in a soft towel he stood on his bare feet and fantasied about taking part in the moves Juca disclosed. Fully clad in professional gear—jersey, shorts, shin guards, stockings and cleats his magical reflection formed on the mirror. There he was pretending to graze the field ready to act. Depending on which squad Juca broadcasted those were the colors reflected on the mirror. Sideways he dribbled, forward he kicked and up high he stooped the ball straight in. Daniel's legs and arms flexed in perfect synchrony with Juca's words defying the laws of gravity, time and space encouraged by the chant of his name: "Daniel! Daniel! Daniel!"

For as long as the sound bites lasted Daniel's lungs swelled with pride as he breathed in the frivolous gusts of illusion. Those minutes of fantasy were a favorite part of his day, the perfect conclusion to his overnight *Passport* fix, a good reason to get him out of bed. Similar to the American astronauts who would soon land on the moon Daniel used the radio waves to skyrocket towards 'Ball Planet.' Behind the fiery blaze of imagination his earthly disappointments pulverized and he experienced a type of elation life had so unfairly denied him.

During those moments Daniel disregarded each unfulfilled aspiration of success, abundance and contentment with pure euphoria. What if the promotion to senior Pastor in Copacabana never materialized, or the brand new sedan he coveted was off budget, or the submissive wife he hoped for never existed? What if he had hit a pathetic rut at the prime age of thirty and there was no way out of it? Somewhere far away there was a place, Juca's Ball Planet, where he was forever hailed a soccer star.

How did you enjoy those fabulous plays ladies and gentlemen? If you want more of the same stay tuned for tomorrow's Ball Planet segment at six and I will bring you the great plays this time directly from São Paulo. Ball Planet is a courtesy of Shell Gas Stations and finally, as I bid all a fun April's Fool here is the result of today's polling. Only thirty per cent of our callers said 'yes' to the FIFA's artificial grass proposal in Mexico next year. Something to be said about tradition ladies and gentlemen. Real, fresh grass is what seventy percent of you want to see in the next World Cup stadiums.

Clean and fragrant Daniel's face stared at the mirror. After turning the radio off he splashed *Aqua Velva* over his soft skin, a crucial touch to the professional front *Dona* Dulce had first molded years ago. It was still early to expect Nina's fresh coffee but Chico's newsstand was already open. Daniel wagged his head for a final inspection and retired the shaving kit to the cabinet. The prospect of meeting Vera face to face still left him eerie not only because Ida's doomsday chatter about Antônio's fate but because his disappearance in itself rang so out of character. It was not like Antônio to cause distress in others. This disappearance could not possibly be of his making and the more Daniel ruminated over the matter the more bizarre Vera's tale sounded.

"Should I trust her?" he considered after walking out the bathroom. She did not strike him as reliable to begin with. A good wife should know the whereabouts of a husband. Vera's coolness through the wire had instilled in him a mix of repulsion and curiosity. The chilled inflection in her voice sounded suspicious. Within three hours there would be answers to his questions and until then he had to pass the time with today's paper.

As soon as he finished dressing up Daniel set out the kitchen door. A bright glare slapped him squarely on the face just as Juca's forecast had predicted. Daniel tented his dazzled eyes to inspect the unveiling brightness overhead where there was no evidence of accumulation. The dome of heat crushed down his head like a boulder and before crossing the church's front gate he had already reached for a handkerchief to wipe the sweat. A few steps further he began regretting the choice of attire. The bowtie clip rubbed irritably against the lump of his neck. Should he have settled for the clerical collar instead? No, an informal air might soften Vera's assertiveness and bring her guard down during the interrogation he had prepared in advance.

"*Jornal do Brasil* Reverend?" Chico greeted Daniel.

"*Oi* Chico, please" Daniel stretched his hand to collect the folded scroll.

"Charge to the account, Reverend?" Chico opened a notebook and scribbled.

"Sure. Will settle at month's end as usual" Daniel spoke without minding the young man behind the counter. His eyes had fallen on one the chief headline: "PRESIDENT PRAISES THE REVOLUTION'S IDEAL."

"That will be fifty cents, Reverend" Chico closed the notebook with the pencil still inside.

"*Ô* Chico? It was only thirty yesterday!" Daniel grunted.

"April's Fool, Reverend! You are the first one of the day" and Chico let out a delighted shrill.

"Not funny" Daniel smirked disapprovingly and bent over the day's other headings.

He walked away briskly while skimming the captions. "*President Eisenhower's casket headed for Kansas, Russians strafed protesting Czechs, U.S. troops corral Vietcong in Laos, Bank robbed nearby police station, Death declared to all slum goats, Easter eggs sold at $299.00.*" Some of the reports could pass as April's Fool jokes Daniel scrolled down looking for the updates on Vasco. To his utter frustration there was nothing printed upfront. "Why is the sports section confined to the last pages?" he tucked the paper under his armpit in protest.

Back at the office Daniel flopped down behind his desk and filled the tumbler halfway. He gulped and leafed through a list of milestones the military revolution had reached. Judging from the pictures and articles there had been nationwide celebrations to mark five years of success. In Brasília the government erected a special monument, in Rio a gigantic cake had been beautifully decorated and in São Paulo a thanksgiving Mass officiated. Through it all President Costa e Silva sounded as optimistic as Saldanha announcing his soccer squad. "All of the Revolution's objectives shall be accomplished" Daniel read the presidential statement wondering what those might actually be.

At least at the end of the Mexico World Cup Saldanha would bring home a gilded trophy whereas in the game of politics it was getting harder to pick winners from losers. If he were to take the president's interview to heart there was no question Costa e Silva deserved a trophy too. He was leading Brazil on an unprecedented era of peace and prosperity. Very soon the country would rank as the greatest in the world. "How about that?" Daniel refilled the tumble.

"What would be Antônio's take on this?" Daniel mused. Back in 1961 he had predicted the troublesome outcome of President Quadros' resignation but not this terrific upshot. That morning when Antônio arrived at the dining hall and warned Daniel about the military opposition against Vice-President Goulart he had no doubts he would never make it. For five years now a military officer still sat in the president's chair and showed no signs of giving it up. "The country is moving forward" Daniel finished the article and then turned to his watch. Vera's arrival approached fast. If as punctual as her husband she should be walking through that door in less than two hours. Daniel's stomach churned painfully. Nina and Ida should be busy in the kitchen by now, and he folded the paper to carry it upstairs. He would read the sports section while dunking some bread into his coffee and milk.

"There you are" Ida stood beside the table buttering a piece of French bread. "I was just asking Nina whether she had seen you at all today."

"Morning everyone" Daniel waved the paper in the air and walked downcast directly to the head of the table.

"*Bom dia,* Reverend" Rose skipped in from behind him.

"ROSE!" Ida yelled. "How many times do I have to tell you? It's *papai* and *mamãe,* not Reverend and *Dona* Ida."

"Fresh coffee, Reverend?" Nina began pouring it. "Bread?" she pointed at the basket.

"Me too, Nina" Rose climbed on the chair next to Daniel using her little bare feet.

"After you eat your bread, Rose" Ida warned. "If you finish it all up you may have a little coffee on your milk. You know that too, don't you?" Ida handed Rose a plate.

"Where is Beca?" Daniel tickled Rose's toes. "Still asleep?"

"Like a baby" Rose winked through a mouthful of bread.

"Let her be, Rose. Beca will be up soon and you Rose don't talk with food in your mouth, please" Ida instructed and added a spoonful of sugar to her coffee and milk. "So…today is Tuesday isn't it?" she finally sat down.

"Sure is" Daniel devoured his mushy bread from behind the paper.

"I was thinking, darling" Ida began rubbing her round stomach. "We must invite Vera to lunch after your meeting today, don't you think? We should not send her away without a proper, how would I put it, reception? After all this is her first time visiting."

"Sure is" Daniel repeated without lifting his gaze.

"Are you actually listening?" Ida tapped her wedding band over Daniel's watch glass making a dull sound.

"Sure am, and yes, I agree. We should invite Vera to lunch today" Daniel deflected Ida's touch and moved his hand out of range.

"Very well" Ida slowly jacked her cumbersome haunches off the chair aiming at the fridge. She geared up for action and yanked the door handle forth. "Nina? I'll marinate these *dourado* fillets with lime juice, salt and garlic; will bread and fry them in olive oil" she heralded. "Fresh rice and how about black beans? Do we have enough left?" she turned and smiled at Nina.

"How about you make a quick run to the grocer's, Nina? Charge a kilo of nice ripe tomatoes and a crisp lettuce head to the Reverend's account, please. A green salad will go well with the fish, right?" Ida now slid about the kitchen announcing the special menu to the four walls while Nina nodded cautiously, "huh-huh."

"Canned peaches, Nina?" she opened the cupboard. "Yes" she answered her own question "and plenty of table cream for topping" Ida continued out loud. "That will make up for an easy and tasty dessert, right Nina?"

"HUH-HUH" Rose yelped from her seat.

"Quit it Rose. Are you done with your bread? We need to clear the table, hear me?" Ida yelled.

"How about my coffee and milk?" Rose challenged.

"Fine" Ida conceded and mixed cold milk in a small cup adding two spoons of sugar. "Here" she handed it over crossly. "Be quick Rose. We need to clean the kitchen and get going with lunch."

"I am out of your way, ladies" Daniel took the cue gratefully and wiped his lips. "Heading downstairs to finish the paper" he checked his watch and bustled back to the office afraid Ida would find a way to sabotage his quiet time. During the unexpected idle hours that followed Daniel reread the entire sports section and sifted through several other articles until he came across a special report featuring the Apollo Nine lunar mission. He had been tracking its progress since the beginning and found it to be a fascinating endeavor. Fly to the moon and walk on it. "Who would have thought?" and deeply engrossed in the story Daniel zoned out totally ignoring the first light knock on the door.

He had left it purposefully ajar to detect any noise from the hallway but even after the intended precaution Vera's sneaky arrival startled him. A second knock followed by the sound of his name and Daniel bolted up.

"Daniel" Vera's torso leaned halfway through the threshold. "May I come in?" she peeked in unceremoniously. It had happened too fast, not the way Daniel envisioned. He should have been by the door before Vera even knocked and then gallantly invited her in. Then he would have pulled up the chair and initiated small talk. It turned out Vera caught Daniel off guard and he lost composure not to mention coherence as soon as he observed Vera's manners matched with great precision the curtness over the phone.

Before him stood a plain face covered with nothing but apprehension. There were no signs of rouge or lip-gloss on her pale skin. Vera hid nothing from onlookers and what you saw was what you got. Daniel discreetly surveyed her milky neck and arms. He searched for pieces of jewelry but the only visible article Vera wore was a thick gold band on her left hand. Frizzy hazel curls uncoiled recklessly above her bony shoulders falling a notch short of touching the collar of a peculiarly colored tunic. Blotches of red, orange and yellow reminded Daniel of those hippie garments he had seen on one of Ida's fashion magazines. Vera had driven with the car windows down, Daniel assumed. Her blunt bearing struck him as a bit out of focus as if he were looking at a photograph taken with a camera in motion. Overall, her appearance was not what Daniel would classify as alluring.

"Please, Vera" he staggered to the door. "Forgive my manners. I lost track of time reading today's paper and did not hear you knock" he reached closer to formally kiss both of her cheeks and caught a mild whiff of lemon scented soap.

"No need to excuse" she formally reciprocated the gesture. "It's nice to finally meet you, Daniel" she smiled dimly and moved brusquely ahead to take a seat in front of the desk.

"How was your drive over?" Daniel stepped back and noticed she was wearing trousers and a pair of flat leather sandals just like those same hippie types. "Was it easy to find the church?" he sprinted to his seat on the opposite side.

"I gave myself plenty of time to get lost" she snuggled a hemp bag against her chest. "It all worked out. My in-laws let me borrow their car" she added in a grave evasive tone.

"Excellent. Oh, before I forget. My wife Ida would love to have you over for lunch today" Daniel borrowed some time with the first of his rehearsed niceties. "I do hope you can spare the time."

"Thanks, I would love to meet her and the children. I mean, you do have children, right?" Vera hesitated.

"Two little girls and a third one due as we speak" Daniel answered perfunctorily.

"Nice…" Vera whispered while screening the surroundings.

"So tell me, how are things in Caxias? And how about *Seu* Orlando and *Dona* Sueli?" Daniel bent over the desk. "It has been such a long time since I…"

"Sorry if I sound rude, Daniel" Vera darted. "Let's cut to the chase, shall we?" she crossed her legs and hugged her knees. "Antônio has been missing for quite a few days now. Thursday morning was the last time I saw him. After breakfast he left on an errand and didn't come home. This is not like him. No phone call, no message" she spoke jus as clearly in person as she had over the wire.

"Well, let us begin there then. Where did he go on this errand?" Daniel frowned and reclined on the chair.

"Downtown" Vera continued promptly. "To pick up a literature order at the Bible Association—pamphlets, books, Bibles, and such to be distributed at our church. Nothing strange there because he has made the same trip at least once a month, always returning by late afternoon. Last Thursday, however, sunset came, but Antônio didn't. That's when I began to worry. He did not call the church office either. We don't have a phone line at home but like you we live right at the church. I sat by that office phone all evening waiting for it to ring. All night long and nothing."

"And on Friday?" Daniel impelled.

Vera shook her head and bit her lips. "On and off I remained at the office during the day Friday. Spent another night there also and at daybreak I finally reached out to our Elders. They came over and we began praying for guidance. Then I called *Seu* Orlando and *Dona* Sueli who advised me to wait still another day and when there was no news on Saturday they told me to go to their house. On Sunday morning they urged me to call you saying your father-in-law is a Coronel in the Military Police" Vera concluded.

"Huh…yes he is but why is this relevant?" Daniel shifted on the chair.

"Daniel" Vera exclaimed decisively "I'm not sure you know what is really going on out there. I mean, the current political situation" she squeezed the hemp bag closer to her chest. "There are people disappearing all over this country" Vera lowered the tone as if afraid of being overheard.

"Disappearing? Where to? That's nonsense!" Daniel flagged his hand disgruntledly.

"Let me finish" Vera raised her left hand at the same time and Daniel hushed visibly annoyed. "Newspapers don't say it, TV and radio either you see? But it's true. Based on Institutional Act Five people who resist the military or disagree with the government policies are subjected to persecution. Secret agents in uniform and undercover both are everywhere—watching, stocking, and accusing without evidence. No right to habeas corpus or due process, no court hearings, no justice at all for the suspects. Officers abduct, arrest, torture and *disappear* people who they claim to be anti-revolutionary, understand?" Vera paused to catch her breath.

"Institutional Act Five meant to get rid of Communists, those unpatriotic Castro-lovers. Those people have no sense of honor, no respect for God or country, and yes, I've heard rumors about them getting caught. They deserve it if you ask me" Daniel retorted angrily. "What I don't understand is where Antônio fits in this picture? He is not a Communist and you know it very well" he brandished his finger at Vera.

"Exactly" Vera exclaimed. "Antônio is not involved in any underground or so-called subversive group nor is he resisting or disobeying the military government, Daniel. All he does is help needy children in the Caxias slums, feed them one meal a day and teach them the gospel of Christ" Vera sounded emotional at last. "What I am afraid is that somebody sees our church mission otherwise. Maybe someone in Caxias thinks our ministry is to promote Communism rather than Christianity, you see? In that case Antônio could be in danger."

"Are you suggesting he has been abducted by the military police?" Daniel planted both elbows on the desk and clenched his hands.

"Yes, even if by mistake. I am not sure and that's why I'm here. I, we, need your help" Vera stretched her arms on the desk. "Help me find him, Daniel. You are the only person we know who has a connection with the military police" she pressed both palms on the surface.

"I see" Daniel looked down at Vera's bitten and unpolished fingernails. Her hands were thin and bony like the rest of her body. "I can give my father-in-law a call and ask him to investigate" he clasped her hands in his, reassuringly.

"When?" she demanded and pressed back pleadingly.

"At once" he promised.

"There is no time to waste" Vera scrunched back on the chair slowly untangling from Daniel's tight grip.

THIRTY-TWO

“You mean today?” Coronel Kruel blatant question crackled through the receiver. In the background a strident concert of typewriter clacks and phone rings competed unfairly with the Coronel’s bass pitch. “Not sure I can leave headquarters right now” he justified and paused to cover the phone’s mouthpiece. The short-lived silence innerved Daniel as he assumed the Coronel had hung up on him.

“Holy Week crunch, see?” Coronel Kruel eventually returned with a roaring shout.

“Certainly, Coronel” Daniel assented. “I do understand this is short notice and apologize for the inconvenience” he readily excused weaving his fingers tightly around the phone cord. “How about a lunch break?” he tactfully pressed. “You normally take some lunch time off, correct?” Daniel tugged hard on the tangled wire knowing his urgency to be out of bounds.

“What?” Coronel Kruel appeared surprised by Daniel’s insistence. “Well, at noon usually” he confirmed raspingly.

“Then, please, Coronel” Daniel resorted to begging. “Come over even if for a few minutes. You need to listen to Vera’s story. This could be a matter of life and death, for God's sake..." he cleverly appealed to the Coronel's Christian convictions.

"Well" the Coronel barked back. "Tell Ida not to wait for me. I might be late" and Coronel Kruel quickly disconnected.

Daniel whispered a timid "thank you "and took a few extra seconds before returning the phone theatrically to its cradle. To conceal the tremor on his hands he clasped them under the desk. The look on his face switched from apprehension to that of a magician. He blinked and smiled gleefully through stretched lips. He was now ready to pull the rabbit out of the hat while Vera, in turn, stared eager to hear the result of the phone exchange. From the depth of her seat she seemed to be asking, 'and?'

Daniel nodded and smiled some more suggesting the deal he had barely sealed transpired exceedingly easy. "All set" he announced. "Coronel Kruel has agreed to join us for lunch today" his fingers now drummed softly on the desktop.

"What time is it now?" Vera cocked her head. Daniel observed her every move. There was no watch on her thin wrist. Her flat chest heaved at ease for the first time and her shoulder sloped slightly.

"Ten minutes past ten" he flipped his wrist. "Would you fancy a tour of the grounds before we head upstairs?" he leapt off like a bird ready to hurl. "Ida serves lunch at twelve on the dot" he mentioned in passing.

"Oh, sure" Vera shrugged warily. "I could also use a glass of cold water if you don't mind" she slung the threaded strap across her shoulder.

"Not at all" Daniel was already at the door holding it open. "Let us begin at the communal kitchen then" he pointed to the right. "Straight out that door."

Once inside the social annex Vera outpaced Daniel screening the generous space and its tidy display of desks and chairs. She was particularly impressed with the sizable stage upfront. “This is a nice area you have here, Daniel” she wheeled around approvingly. “Big enough to fit a bunch of kids all at once” her voice echoed pleasantly about the empty auditorium as she strode to the kitchen in the back. Tracking a few steps behind Daniel inspected her legs extend in a graceful stride. It was not often he saw a woman move so limberly while wearing pants.

“This is a recent addition” Daniel informed pretentiously loud. “About five years old and quite roomy as you can attest but unfortunately we don’t have a large group of children like you do in Caxias” Daniel heeled a bit closer as they crossed into the unlit kitchen. “Ida wants to get a youth department going at some point but right now she is so busy with the girls, you know?” he grabbed a bottle of water from inside the fridge and quickly shut its door to cut out the blasting light.

“I cannot even imagine” Vera exclaimed. “Two toddlers and a newborn on the way, how does she manage?” and waited for Daniel to fill up the glass.

“She is constantly on the go that’s for sure” he poured water to the rim. “Here” Daniel solicitously handed the glass to Vera and guarded by the shadiness in the room watched her throat swell after each gulp.

“Thank you. Just what I needed” Vera wiped her discolored lips with the back of her hand.

“More?” Daniel lifted the bottle midair and smiled broadly. Their eyes locked momentarily.

“Why not?” Vera blinked intriguingly and let Daniel remove the glass from her hand. After refilling it he handed it back. Out of nowhere the urge to pounce the glass off Vera’s hand nearly whacked Daniel out of balance. It felt like eternity until he could finally exhale and speak again.

“We should get going soon” he leaned on the counter once Vera disposed of the glass. “Ida will skin me alive if she does not get to chat with you before lunch” Daniel turned restlessly towards the exit door.

At a distance Vera tagged along trying to catch up with Daniel’s sudden haste and in silence filed up the sun-bathed steps leading to the parsonage. Both refrained from commonplace grievances against the pelting heat aware that it was only expected to worsen as noon-time approached. Juca had already warned that in a day such as this there was nowhere to hide under the *Carioca* sun. It lashed punitively down on sinners and saints alike.

“IDA?” Daniel called irritably after twisting the door handle. “WE ARE HERE” he proclaimed from the threshold. “WHERE ARE YOU?” and pointed courteously to the couch. “Please, Vera, have a seat” he followed in a softer tone.

“COMING DARLING!” Ida shouted back from the other end of the hallway. “BE RIGHT THERE, DARLING” her flats pounded over the parquet floor.

“He-e-l-o-o-o-o!” a frisky chirp arose from somewhere below. Rose had beaten Ida to the living room and after parting Daniel’s legs in the middle had zoomed through it, straight up to the couch. “My name is Rose and yours?” she jumped ingeniously fast and offered her tiny hand for a shake.

“Oh, hello there Rose” Vera chuckled. “It’s so nice to meet you. My name is Vera but you can call me *Tia* if you prefer.”

"Just like *Tia* Jujú and *Tia* Amália?" Rose carefully screened Vera deciding whether to offer the honor.

"Ah, I imagine so, yes but who is auntie Ju...?" Vera jestingly pried the instant Ida marched into the room with Beca in tow.

"Never mind Rose, Vera, she is always like that you know?" Ida excused Rose's extroversion before introducing herself. "I'm Ida" the two women offered each other's cheeks for a kiss. "So nice to meet you, dear. I've heard so much about you and Antônio" Ida lied.

"Likewise, Ida" Vera held Ida's hands tenderly and smiled bashfully. "Antônio always had nice things to say about your husband and the good times they shared as roommates in Seminary" she added.

"Please" Ida captured Vera's affliction and motioned towards the couch. "Let us sit down and be comfortable" she crouched heavily on the overstuffed cushion. "Rose, scooch that way with Beca so we can all fit nicely" and sprawling her wide hips near the edge Ida assumed the role of benevolent hostess.

"Would you like a cool drink, Vera? *Mate*, *água* or *Guaraná?"* and while Vera pondered the option, Ida shifted to Daniel who was still standing by the doorway. "Darling, did you offer Vera a drink yet?" and then back at Vera without waiting for Daniel's answer, "isn't this heat overwhelming? We will all soon be evaporating."

Unsure whether she should address Ida or Daniel at this point Vera delayed a reply. Rose took advantage of the gap and waved her hand up: "I'm evaporating too, *Dona* Ida. I want *Guaraná*, please, Reverend."

"Rose!" Ida rebuked gritting her teeth. "Don't you start" and turning to Vera again she disarmed her brow "Ice tea, soda, water? It's no bother, really" she beamed.

"I just had some water downstairs, Ida, thank you very much" Vera declined. "Maybe later?" and lowering her gaze she politely inquired: "when is your baby due?"

"Oh" Ida studied her bulged stomach as if it had been there her entire life. "It could be today for all I know" she began to rub it. "I have a doctor's appointment this afternoon, you see, and depending on the circumstances might be advised to stay either at the clinic or be transferred to the maternity ward. My due date is in a few days, right darling?" she pulled Daniel into the conversation while he sat crossed-legged on one of the armchairs.

"I think so, yes" Daniel agreed dismissively. "I wouldn't be surprised if Dr. Oscar admits you today" and then abruptly slapped his forehead "*Ai*! Before I forget, Ida, your father is joining us for lunch."

"Today?" Ida sounded indignant as if Daniel had purposefully altered her arrangements. "How come?" she boldly contested "he didn't say anything to *me*."

"No, he didn't" Daniel ignored the scowling. "He did not know about it either. I called him at work about an hour ago; a last minute request" and Daniel went on to deliver a summary of his meeting with Vera.

"Oh my dear!" Ida squeezed Vera's hand. "You must be beside yourself, dear. This is absolutely awful. No, no, not just awful" she fidgeted for words. "It is beyond awful. Absurd. Unimaginable" Ida ranted while rubbing her stomach with both hands. "I have never heard anything this tragic before, dear, I mean, not in reference to someone we actually are acquainted with, right darling?" she had turned to Daniel as he proceeded with the account. So agitated was Ida that she could not stop gasping after each new detail regarding

Antônio's disappearance. "Oh Lord, help us" she rubbed her stomach and riveted at Vera at the same time.

Meanwhile, Vera's unassuming appearance caught Ida's attention. Such lack of grooming was unquestionably the result of despair. Only an anguished wife would leave the house in this state. Vera herself detected the unwelcoming scrutiny and cringed quite self-consciously of Ida's judgment of her disheveled hair, unpolished nails, and lack of make-up. Daniel proceeded to tell about the phone call to Coronel Kruel when Ida' gasps escalated. On and off Vera dodged the veiled censure by stealing sideway glances at both Rose and Beca who out of boredom had engaged in a ferocious tickling battle. The girls giggled uncontrollably while trying to trample each other off the couch.

"So" Ida bobbed her head from Vera to Daniel like a dummy in the hands of a ventriloquist "this is why Dad is coming over for lunch..." and eventually realizing what Beca and Rose were up to she screamed: "GIRLS! STOP IT RIGHT NOW, HEAR ME?"

"Rose started, *mamãe*" Beca accused terrified of Ida's wrath.

"WHY AM I NOT SURPRISED, ROSE?" Ida hoisted up but not in time to snag Rose's arm. She had already sprinted out of sight before the ambuscade. "BECA!" the shout flared despairingly. "GO TO YOUR ROOM AND STAY THERE UNTIL I CALL, UNDERSTAND?" Ida pointed her stiff arm in the direction of the hallway.

"Yes, *mamãe*" Beca tearfully limped away.

"Now, darling" Ida collapsed back on the couch as if nothing had happened and redirected her sharp glare at Daniel "what do you suppose Dad can do about this?" the rubbing of her stomach resumed. “He sure has connections at headquarters” Ida informed Vera.

“Well, I believe…” Daniel ventured.

“A couple of phone calls is what it will take” Ida cut him off. “I am sure this misunderstanding will be quickly resolved, don’t you worry anymore, dear” she announced and gently patted Vera’s flinched hand. “You’ll see. Antônio will be back soon, safe and sound. This is nothing but a horrible, horrible mistake, right darling?” she shifted to Daniel.

“Certainly” Daniel snarled at his impeccably waxed shoes.

“Then let us all cheer up a bit, shall we?” Ida anchored her elbow on the armrest and propelled her swollen legs. “Vera, come with me” she commanded. “Let me show you around the house before we sit down to lunch” and Ida’s plump hand stretched amiably out to Vera. “We will talk about other things, shall we not? Hope you are not starved yet?” she beamed her signature smile and took the lead to the corridor. “It will not take long before we eat. Step right this way.”

Daniel could hear Ida’s spirited shrills fade as the two women advanced down the hallway to the girls’ room. There, the rowdiness instantly increased as Beca and Rose engaged in earnest dispute for Vera’s attention. Scattered about the floor rows of dolls and kitchenware Beca had neatly aligned were being systematically dismantled by Rose’s windstorm of wood blocks and marbles. Daniel could hear Ida’s shouts at the danger of stumbling followed by final lunchtime instructions to Nina.

He checked his watch and calculated that in less than thirty minutes they would all gather around the blue Formica table for another round of Ida’s perfectly delivered entertainment. The intermission granted him enough time to run back to the office and quiet his nerves with a shot of Passport. To the front door Daniel tiptoed quiet as a mouse convinced no one would notice his absence until he had run right back to reclaim the same spot in the living room. Years ago he had perfected the same trick at Antônio's home and not once had been caught. What he did not count on now was that the return of such long-buried memories could rock his consciousness. Like a pendulum his thoughts began to swing from one prospect to another. Did he want Antônio found or did he want Antônio gone? By the time he reached the bottom of the bleached marble steps his head throbbed.

Coronel Kruel had alluded to torture practices used to extract intelligence from vile Communists. Electric shocks, sleep deprivation and beatings were common during interrogation sessions and visualizing Antônio in such humiliating circumstances tore Daniel apart. But when the lever swang the opposite way a macabre yearning lurked. What if Antônio *disappeared* forever, never, ever, to be found again? Neither dead nor alive he would turn into a ghost. Vanished somewhere far away beyond earth's orbit like the Americans inside their space ship. Then Vera would be free to…

"Daniel?" a grave voice stalled Daniel's wicked delusion. He tuned out the diabolical consequences of his chimera and lifted his head to the front gate. A police Jeep appeared on the other side and standing in front of it small dots danced in the air. Approaching its mid-day height the sun had sovereignly intervened with Daniel's visual perceptions and all he saw apart from the floating coins was a black cap. With a squint from beneath his cupped hands Daniel eventually recognized the tall frame of his father-in-law.

"Coronel?" he shouted unable to contain his relief. "So nice to see you" Daniel sprinted to the gate. "You made it earlier than expected" he pulled on the latch.

"Not a problem" the Coronel put his cap back on and told the driver to wait. "To be quite honest with you" he returned Daniel's firm handshake "I could not put the matter out of my mind. Minutes after we hung up I summoned a chauffeur and told him to hurry over" he pointed to the car. "Were you on your way out?" Coronel Kruel sounded puzzled. "I thought Antônio's wife was still here?" and he craned over Daniel's shoulder.

"No, no, I mean, yes, yes" Daniel's dry tongue tied up. "No, I am not going anywhere, and yes, Vera is still upstairs" he finally explained. "I just stepped out for some fresh air while Nina sets the table."

"Fresh air, son?" the Coronel chuckled and lifted his eyes overhead. "Actually, I am glad we have a minute before joining the ladies" he confided.

"Me too" Daniel concurred. "I would appreciate your professional input on this bizarre situation, Coronel" Daniel steered his father-in-law to the shady portico.

"I imagined so" Coronel Kruel's face contracted and he took his cap off. "Based on what you reported I have a few remarks to offer" he cradled the cap under his arm. "At this point my main question to you is how well do you know your friend Antônio?" the Coronel's lips wrinkled.

Noticing Daniel's hesitation he continued. "By that I mean I need to know how much information on his private life do you have before and after Seminary. How much of his general ideas, sympathies and associations do you know? For instance, how about his social and political, uh, leanings? I am not interested in his opinion on denominational doctrines or religious dogma but rather philosophical convictions. What type of social connections did he keep, his usual whereabouts other than church activities" and the Coronel briefly paused to seriously study Daniel's facial expression.

"Why is this important, Coronel?" Daniel looked confused.

"Let me be clear, son. Have you ever heard of the term '*watermelon*?" the Coronel smirked.

"No, not really. I mean not apart from its obvious reference" Daniel shook his head in earnest ignorance. "What does that have to do with Antônio's disappearance?"

"You see, amongst us military officers" Coronel Kruel touched the rim of his black cap etching a penetrating look at Daniel "the term '*melancia*' carries a specific connotation. It has been coined in obvious reference to the colors of the fruit, green outside red inside. However, we use the analogy to describe an individual's potential duality" he studied Daniel.

"I see" Daniel whispered. "In the political sense?" he pried.

"Precisely" Coronel Kruel nodded. "Since the onset of the Revolution we officers have noticed that a person, any person, who appears compliant with the law, loyal to the government, a model citizen to the outside world might be hiding something. His or her demeanor maybe a disguise, green on the outside for all intents and purposes. No one really suspects this same person nurtures Communist or Socialist ideals. Red in the inside. This same exemplary 'green' person has built a secret library somewhere full of Marxist, Leninist, Maoist and more recently Cuban literature. He or she not only reads the books but artfully circulates them underground. This same person recruits and trains operatives to carry out subversive acts against the revolutionary government. These are crafty and deceiving people by nature, Daniel. They organize secret cells and are well equipped with smuggled firearms, explosives, counterfeited cash and reliable vehicles used to execute terrorist attacks. These people rob banks, ambush and kill policemen, soldiers, and even kidnap foreign diplomats to demand ransom" Coronel Kruel paused to make sure Daniel was following.

"Forgive me, sir, but you are describing the Communists, the criminals and traitors who surely deserve to be incarcerated for their treachery. No habeas corpus needed, if you ask me, but Antônio, Coronel, he is not one of them. He is not a '*melancia*' I give you my word" Daniel pressed his hands defiantly on his hips.

"Fine" Coronel Kruel put his cap back on and took a step closer to Daniel. "I take your word for it. Still, for the sake of my consciousness I ought to repeat the question: are you sure?" and Coronel Kruel gripped Daniel's shoulders. "You must be open with me right here, right now in case we can find Antônio alive" Coronel Kruel pressed hard.

"Coronel" Daniel said emphatically "if there is one thing I know for sure is that Antônio is a good man inside and out. He has behaved honorably during all the years I have known him. I have no reason to doubt his integrity and you have my word on the excellence of his character for he was always a brother to me" and consulting his watch Daniel gestured it was time to end the conversation.

"One more thing" Coronel Kruel pulled on Daniel's elbow. "Let us not bring this issue up in front of the ladies. From what I gather his wife will strongly corroborate the statement you just made and there is no need to put her on the spot in front of Ida and the girls" the Coronel let go of Daniel.

"Wise counsel, sir" Daniel followed the Coronel down the portico steps. "As you can imagine Vera is extremely upset over this affair and needs all the support we can provide. To me personally this is a providential opportunity to reciprocate Antônio's kindness and generosity" Daniel confessed. "Did I ever tell you he used to invite me to his parent's home every weekend when I first arrived at Seminary?" Daniel engaged the Coronel in a lively recollection of his visits to Vila Nova, the train rides, and Teresa's fabulous meals. For obvious reasons the secret soccer games and beer tasting stayed out of the recital.

"Now you are reminding me of how famished I am, son" Coronel Kruel tittered. "Hope Ida has prepared enough" he winked.

"Excuse me, Coronel?" Daniel faked an offended glare "your daughter is ready to feed this entire borough anytime of the day should the need arise" and both men laughed in a rare moment of camaraderie at Ida's expense.

THIRTY-THREE

'Ninety million in action,
Forward Brazil of my heart
All of us together
Forward Brazil
Long live our team!'

"Rose: how does it go next?" Beca looked over her shoulder as Rose filed closely behind. Their imaginary *Carnaval* procession around the living room had just departed. Crayon-colored green and yellow paper flags in hand the two sisters launched a roudy parade trying their best not to bump into Ida's precious knick-knacks.

"You haven't memorized the song yet, Beca?" Rose nearly stumbled over Beca. "The big game is tomorrow. Are you going to remember then?" she stomped her bare feet in place.

'All of a sudden
An onward chain
Seems that Brazil goes all hand in hand

All linked by the same feeling,
We are all one heart beating...'

Rose sang flawlessly and urged Beca to keep up. "Come on now, keep going. You are blocking the people behind me" she poked Beca's ribcage with a popsicle stick.

"Ouch Rose, that hurts" Beca whimpered. "How can I go on if I forgot the words?" she grumbled while massaging the sore spot.

"Well then" Rose puffed her chest "if you can't remember anything I'll do the singing and you just the marching" and pushing Beca aside Rose thundered *'all of us together, forward Brazil, Brazil, long live our team!'* her flag fluttering on high like a weathervane in a gale.

"Hang on, Rose" Beca stopped again. She spread her palm up but kept on pounding her flip-flops in place. "I have an idea" she confidently announced.

"What now Beca?" Rose poked the popsicle stick again in protest. "We need to move on. Can't you see all this people behind me?" she pointed at the furniture. "They are getting annoyed with all this stop and go" and Rose turned around with her arm up. "Hold up everyone. New orders from the Marshal."

"Listen up people" Beca shouted at the back wall. "I just thought of something. Let's turn the TV on and wait for the World Cup song to play. When it does we will have real music for our parade" she beckoned at the couch and then at the coffee table.

"Beca" Rose shot a serious look at her older sister "you are trying to take over the game again" she accused.

"No, I'm not Rose" Beca held her ground. "I want real music for our parade that's all. If we are going to have a real parade we better have real music" Beca justified.

"You say that because you forgot the words" Rose sputtered. "You want the music to play along to remind you of the words. That's what it is" Rose cruelly charged.

"I'm going to tell *mamãe* you are being naughty, Rose" Beca threatened.

"Oh are you?" Rose kept tapping her barefeet on the waxed parquet "you know what's gonna happen then. She's gonna come in here screaming: GIRLS! STOP IT RIGHT NOW" Rose twisted her nose. "Then I'm gonna find a place to hide and that will be the end of our parade. Is that what you want, Beca?" Rose counterattacked.

"No, I don't want to end the parade, Rose" Beca retreated. "I want real music for the march, from the TV with all those nice people singing" she pointed at the large chest on the corner of the room.

"Alright" Rose thumped closer and twisted the round knob. "Which channel is the music on?"

"I don't know" Beca stood by and watched the flickering screen. "Keep turning until we hear it" she compelled out of renewed assertiveness. It was not an easy task persuading Rose to comply.

"What if it doesn't play?" Rose turned up the volume to its maximum as the black and white images shifted from cartoon characters to *Colgate* paste and *Doriana* spread commercials.

"It will" Beca sounded positive. "The big game is tomorrow and everyone wants to sing the song."

"True" Rose kept turning "almost *everyone* knows the song by heart" Rose stung.

"Move, Rose!" Beca elbowed Rose away and took over the knob. "I know where it is" she reclaimed the big sister status.

"Go on then" Rose instigated. "But if the song doesn't play what we gonna do, huh? The parade needs to move forward Beca. You are wasting everyone's time here" she waved her paper flag at the dormant furniture.

"How about you get two pots and two wooden spoons from the kitchen while I search?" Beca dismissed Rose's exhortation and kept fidgeting with the TV.

"What for?" Rose grinned at the splendid request.

"To drum to the parade music, silly" Beca squealed.

"Great idea Beca!" Rose dropped her paper flag and emulating her favorite cartoon character flexed her elbows and knees darting out: "*bip-bip, bip-bip…*"

'Ninety million in action,
Forward Brazil of my heart
All of us together,
Forward Brazil
Long live our team!'

"THERE!" Beca curled her forefinger calling Rose to the screen as soon as she reappeared dragging a stainless steel skillet and matching saucepan barely keeping them from scrapping the varnished floor. From her other tiny hand two burned wooden spoons dangled as she tried to keep balance.

"TOLD YOU!" Beca jumped up and down to the blasting tune.

'All of a sudden
An onward chain
Seems that Brazil goes all hand in hand
All linked by the same feeling,
We are all one heart beating

All of us together
Forward Brazil, Brazil
Long live our team!'

“Keep it there, Beca” Rose handed the saucepan and a spoon to her sister. “It's gonna play from the beginning soon. Now get in line” she commanded.

“Wait” Beca looked from her small saucepan to Rose's large skillet. “Why is your drum bigger than mine?”

“Because I was the one who sneaked into the kitchen to get them, ding-dong” Rose quickly proclaimed victory against Nina and Ida who had been too occupied with food preparations and did not notice the artful intrusion. With a loud bang she shushed Beca up and gripped both a paper flag and a wooden spoon.

“Not fair, Rose” Beca whined. “You always do that.”

“Do what?” Rose pretended innocence and turned her back to Beca. “Everyone ready?” she shouted at the armchairs. “March on one, two, three, go” Rose stuck her paper flag in her mouth simulating a whistle and ordered the rest of the invisible crowd forward.

Beca's flip-flops slapped angrily on the ground and she stuck her tongue out as far out as she could. Rose laughed out loud and moved her feet and buttocks in a swingy *Samba* step to deflect the confrontation. Slapping the wood spoon on her skillet she directed Beca to face forward and the *Carnaval* parade resumed in earnest. “*Um, dois, três*” Beca turned around and the procession moved from the TV chest, to the coffee table until it bent around the set of armchairs on its way to the balcony.

Out of sync the wood spoons struck the pans with deafening hits as the two little sisters sang along the blasting TV. In no time the living room boomed with a mix of shouts, off beat blows and foot thumping as the patriotic *Carnaval* parade progressed in honor of Brazil's final World Cup match against Italy.

"Long live our team! *Salve a Seleção!"* Beca repeated the song's last strophe as it approached conclusion.

"Three Times Champion of the World!" Rose waved her paper flag up high.

"Tri-Campeão, tri-campeão, tri-campeão!" Beca rejoined with bangs so loud that neither heard Ida's roar traverse the room.

"GIRLS: STOP IT RIGHT NOW!" she had already seized the volume knob when Beca and Rose froze in sudden silence. "WHAT DO YOU THINK YOU ARE DOING?" she towered menacingly in front of the TV screen. "DON'T YOU KNOW RACHEL IS NAPPING NEXT DOOR? ANSWER ME: DON'T YOU?"

"Yes, *mamãe"* Beca whispered.

"We are practicing for tomorrow's big game" Rose stepped forward courageously. "We are going to watch it on TV, remember?" she appeased Ida's fury knowing how excited she had been about the special event. For the past few days all Ida raved about was watching the final World Cup match live, directly from her couch for the first time, EVER.

"Right" Ida snapped out of hysterics and dreamingly contemplated the large chest. "Tomorrow at noon... "she murmured. Thousands of wheels turned inside her head at the same time and Rose knew it.

"I need to talk to Nina about that" she gazed at the girls pretending to still be mad. "Don't you two practice while Rachel is asleep, hear me? She still needs an afternoon nap otherwise..."

"She will drive you crazy at night?" Rose finished Ida's sentence. Beca cupped her mouth and chuckled.

"Now, Rose" Ida reset the cross tone. "That's enough. You and Beca, both, clean up this mess. Why did you have to throw the pots on the floor Nina waxed?" she surveyed the ground visibly displeased.

"Cause you came in here screaming and we got scared" Rose explained matter of fact and stooped down to pick her skillet up.

"I already said enough, Rose. Beca, clean up, right away. Go on" Ida walked away calling out "Nina? Nina, where are you?"

"Still in the kitchen, *Dona* Ida" Nina answered. "Need anything?"

"Yes, Nina" Ida reentered the kitchen where Nina had finally sat down for a coffee break after preparing the World Cup feast.

"I forgot to pass something by you Nina" Ida pulled out a chair beside her devoted helper. "Tomorrow" she sat down tucking her baggy housedress carefully under her thighs.

"Huh-huh" Nina opened a tin can and took a *maria* biscuit out. Both Beca and Rose had just tiptoed back to put their drums away and quickly disappeared from sight.

"Is the World Cup final" Ida reached forward and pushed the can lid tightly down.

"Yes" Nina placed the biscuit on the table and grabbed the coffee thermos. How could have she forgotten after spending the whole morning cooking?

"So, I was thinking, Nina, that maybe we should invite *Dona* Vera to lunch after church tomorrow to watch the game with us" Ida rubbed the tin lid.

"*Dona* Vera coming to church tomorrow?" Nina dunk half a biscuit in the coffee and took a bite.

"I forgot to tell you, sorry" Ida rubbed her flabby stomach. She had never let go of the habit even after her pregnant days came to an end.

"Why she coming tomorrow, *Dona* Ida?" Nina was curious since Vera had not returned after that tense lunch over a year ago. "Any more news on her husband?" Nina chewed on the biscuit.

"No, none at all but I did send her a card in the mail a few weeks back inviting her to church tomorrow" Ida revealed. "The lunch part, however, was not included in the message. That's why I am passing it by you now, Nina" Ida rested her chin on her hand waiting for Nina's reaction.

"Humm" Nina swallowed and dunk the rest of the biscuit in the coffee. "Why tomorrow?" she asked after mouthing it.

"Well, I thought by then she would be up for a visit. You know, after the baby grew bit older and all" Ida was not doing a good job concealing her real motives.

"Have you seen him?" Nina cut to the point.

"No, not yet. I just heard it is a boy and is called Antônio" Ida wanted to sound disinterested.

"She coming then?" Nina chewed some more.

"Yes, she did send a reply by telegram accepting the invitation" Ida nodded. "In the note I had sent I urged her to bring baby Antônio" Ida disclosed. "He must be good enough to travel now."

"Where from?" Nina washed the last of her biscuit down with a long sip.

"Vila Nova. Didn't I tell you she moved in with Antônio's parents?" Ida drew the buiscuit can closer and resumed rubbing her stomach.

"Maybe, *Dona* Ida. Don't remember..." Nina hesitated. "No, wait. You said something about her leaving the church house because the husband had not been found yet. Sad, ain't it?" she rested the cup on the saucer and grabbed the thermos for a refill.

"Oh Nina, don't even get me going on that" Ida lamented. "Pregnant and alone. Raising a child all by herself in the middle of this tragedy, Nina, can you imagine?" her voice faltered. "Thank God her parents-in-law came to the rescue and took her in. That was the right thing to do. Plus, they do have the means from what I gather. At any rate, Nina, I have not yet seen the baby or Vera, as a matter of fact, since that visit. Remember when she came over to tell the Reverend and the Coronel what was going on? Anyway, I have not seen her since but did hear about the baby's birth and the move to Vila Nova" Ida carried on pensively.

"Huh-huh" Nina slurped and braced for more to come.

"It all happened during that frantic search, Nina" Ida proceeded. "Right when both the Reverend and the Coronel started escorting her all over this city, going from one police station to the next, looking for Antônio. Do you remember that?" Ida turned to Nina.

"No much, *Dona* Ida" Nina reached for the tin can. "Rachel was a newborn then and we two were running round like headless chickens" she took another biscuit out of the can.

"So true, Nina" Ida pushed the tin can lid all the way down again. "So much to do. *Ai,* how did we manage?"

"Somehow we do" Nina smiled and patted Ida's hand.

"Anyway" Ida smiled back "it was back then that the three of them hopped from here to there almost every day searching for Antônio. For months it seemed they were gone, the Coronel making phone calls, writing letters, sending telegrams to Brasília. Goodness, and the Reverend, Nina, bless his heart, assisting in whatever way possible. Chauffer, witness, counselor you name it and he did it until Antônio's trail went dead cold sometime after Christmas." Ida brooded over the unsolved mystery.

"Huh-huh" Nina slurped.

"After the dust settled I felt in my heart a desire to invite Vera over for a visit. She must be feeling awfully lonely. The date I picked was tomorrow because that's when I assumed baby Antônio would be ready for an outing. Being almost three months old and less fussy. However, what I did not count on, Nina, was that tomorrow of all Sundays happened to be the World Cup's final. I had no idea our team would be disputing the trophy" and Ida digressed to relish on the unprecedented feat Brazil's squad was about to accomplish.

If victorious, Brazil would be the first nation in the world to permanently keep the coveted FIFA Cup. Only a third-time world champion qualified for such honor and tomorrow was Brazil's turn to shine all over the world. Ida could almost see the golden token in front of her.

"She confirmed, *Dona* Ida?" Nina steered Ida back to the conversation.

"Oh yes, Nina, didn't I tell she sent a telegram this past Thursday?" Ida asked.

"Huh-huh" Nina nodded.

"So, I am thinking, Nina, the polite thing to do is to have her eat with the rest of us after church since we are having a little watch-the-game party. What do you think? Isn't this a good idea?" Ida sounded remarkably unsure of herself.

"Maybe, *Dona* Ida" Nina stood up and took her demitasse to the sink. "But *Dona* Vera might not wanna watch a soccer game after church, have you thought about that?" she weighed in.

"Why not Nina?" Ida seemed shocked at the idea. "The whole entire country is going to watch it. Even President Médici is expected to be in front of the TV tomorrow. By the way, if we win the Cup he is going to declare a national holiday on Tuesday when our team returns from Mexico. Isn't that just fantastic?" Ida's brown eyes sparkled.

"Huh-huh" Nina began to rinse the demitasse. "But a mom with a suckling baby glued to her chest might not find that too fantastic, *Dona* Ida" Nina reasoned. "She might just wanna go home after church and rest" she stood up.

"Maybe" Ida mumbled. "Let me think about that some more. I have until tomorrow to decide" and she looked at the fridge. "We do have enough for tomorrow, right Nina? I mean, in case she comes?" Ida pushed her chair away from the table to double-check the covered stacks of trays and bowls sitting on the fridge shelves.

"Course we do, *Dona* Ida" Nina couldn't believe Ida's concern after hours of preparation. "Does the Reverend know *Dona* Vera is coming tomorrow?" she pried while washing her demitasse.

"Why should he care, Nina?" Ida spewed. "I barely see him anymore. That is the truth and you know it" she grunted. "Since Rachel's birth he has been out of this house more than he is in. Comes in late and leaves at the crack of dawn. If you ask me where he is right now, I won't not be able to tell you, Nina."

"Huh-huh" Nina repeated. "He gonna watch the game tomorrow though, right *Dona* Ida? Nina opened the cupboard door and put the demitasse away.

“I suppose” Ida shrugged. “Sundays after church he stays home to entertain our guests and take his nap. Besides, who in this country would pass on watching a live World Cup final in his own living room?” Ida’s eyes widened again. “Only someone gone mad” she rubbed her stomach.

“Not Beca and Rosy, uh?” Nina giggled. “They gonna put up a big parade on and make sure we all hear it pass” she shook her head amusingly.

“Tell me about it” Ida rolled her eyes and paired up with Nina out of the kitchen. Passing by the girl’s bedroom they both paused to watch Beca and Rose busy at work. Crayons in hand they were bent over a see of paper coloring more green and yellow flags. Ida and Nina exchanged an amused glance precisely when Rachel’s crying escalated into a distressed sob at the end of the hallway. At once their inner magnetic needle compelled them on the right direction and they hurried over to soothe Rachel knowing that pretty soon it was time to return to the kitchen and gather their precious trio for a mid-afternoon snack.

THIRTY-FOUR

"Good morning brethren. May the peace of our Lord Jesus Christ comfort and renew you as we gather to worship this Sunday morning. A hearty welcome to our first time visitors: we are delighted you joined us. It is indeed a privilege to behold the blessed assembly of Saints. Our Lord is generous and when I contemplate the sight of so many familiar faces, my brothers and sisters, I am reassured the Creator favors unity in our congregation. May you feel encouraged to return next Sunday to praise the Good Father for blessings given and forthcoming. Let us now worship Him with the first hymn printed on you bulletin, 'Great is Thy Faithfulness.' Ida, please?"

"What is the chaff to the wheat, Reverend?"

"Pardon? Whoever spoke, please, refrain from interruptions. Let us keep order during the service. On with the hymn, Ida."

"Ida is not here, Reverend."

"Excuse me but to whomever is out of line at this moment I repeat the warning. It is neither appropriate to interfere with the order of service nor to interrupt the officiator. If this is your first time with us kindly follow the service directions on your bulletin. If you have not received a copy

of today's bulletin please raise your hand and an usher will provide you with one. Now, let us raise our voices in praise 'Great is Thy Faithfulness', Ida.

"Ida is not here this morning, Reverend"

"Who is this, please? Show yourself."

"It is written on Jeremiah 23:28: 'let the prophet who has a dream let him tell a dream and let he who has my word let him speak my word truthfully. What is the chaff to the wheat? Says the Lord."

"Whoever you are remain quiet and do not temper with the sound system. You have been given no permission to amplify the volume. Either show yourself or leave at once. This is a sanctuary, a solemn place of worship, not an entertainment arena. I expect you to be silent and respectful. Also, reopen the blinds and reset the microphone to proper frequency."

"Very well, Reverend. Is this better or does the glare bother you?"

"Brethren, do not be afraid. Ignore this unexpected distraction and keep calm. Ushers, please survey the hall and locate the intruder."

"Brother: 'what is the chaff to the wheat'?"

"Antônio? Is it you behind the glare?"

"Can you still recognize my voice, Brother? Do I still sound the same?"

"How could I not? After all that time together."

"And how about now? How do I look?"

"Lord Almighty, what is this supposed to mean?"

"Still me, Brother, can't you see?"

"You have not changed a bit, Antônio. Same face and smile. What are you doing here? Wait. This is nonsense. It can't be you. No one knows where you are. No one has ever found you. This can't be real."

"I don't mean to upset you by showing up unannounced but yes, I have been found, Brother. Not exactly how some predicted but sure have been found."

"Your features have not changed at all, I mean, your face; radiant as usual."

"Is that good or bad?"

"Never mind. What are you doing here after all this time?"

"I have come to ask you a simple question: 'what is the chaff to the wheat?'"

"What for? This is not time for irrelevant questions. Come back another day."

"This is a good time as any, Brother. In fact, it is the appointed time. Go on and tell me what does that Scripture verse mean?"

"No, Antônio, you tell me. If this is about asking questions I have a few for you. Where have you been to begin with? We looked for you everywhere."

"I know. I saw all of it."

"How come? Why didn't you tell us where to search? You could have set us on the right track instead of watch us run from one police station to the next, not to mention the hospitals, prisons, and morgues. We carried your picture along hoping someone would recognize you. Every lead turned out a sham."

"I am so sorry, Brother."

"Are you really? A little too late to be sorry, don't you think, Antônio? Where have you been all this time?"

"Nearby. It is hard to explain with words but trust me I did try to connect."

"Connect? That is a lie, Antônio, and you know it. I received not one phone call, not one letter, not even a telegram, nothing from you since

your disappearance. Nothing! Weeks stretched into months as we chased dead-ends and cold trails. Don't you smile at me like that. This is not funny. Are you enjoying our misery?"

"Calm down, Brother. You are going to trip over that fine robe if you don't stop thumping."

"Don't you tell me what to do."

"Old habits die hard; sorry, no pun intended. Let's just say that where I have been there are no telephones, post offices or telegraph wires. Again, impossible to describe with human words."

"And do you expect me to believe that you tried to 'connect' from wherever this place is?"

"Yes, a few times."

"When? This is the first I have seen of you since I last…"

"Dreamed or thought of me? That was when I tried. Unfortunately, your thoughts shift too fast and before I could warn you, your mind was gone."

"Warn about what, Antônio?"

"Well, where should I begin?"

"Be brief. I don't have much time to spare."

"Give me only a moment and I will explain. However, I need to ask you the question first."

"You are disturbing the service, you realize that, don' you? I need to get back to the liturgy."

"Very well then, answer the question: 'what is the chaff to the wheat'?

"Now you are changing the subject. Typical of you to ramble isn't it? What does this question have to do with your alleged warning or with your mysterious disappearance for that matter? As usual, you make no sense."

"The question makes a lot of sense, Brother. Think about it. Go ahead, take your time."

"If there is someone who needs to answer questions it's you. You can't simply vanish without a trace and then come back as if nothing had happened."

"Agreed. One of these days my disappearance will be explained. Not today. It is too complicated."

"Complicated? Is that all you have to say for yourself: it is complicated. How convenient."

"Indeed. Certain things happen beyond our control, Brother. We try our best to control outcomes and end up miscalculating."

"Oh for goodness' sake, Antônio. Stop babbling for once, would you? What do you know about miscalculations? When have you ever had to worry about miscalculating any moment in your life?"

"A few times. Unintentionally, of course."

"You know nothing about miscalculations. Your entire life has been a series of lucky strikes."

"I am not here to talk about me, Brother."

"Good. Then go away. You are wasting my time. I have a duty to perform."

"I am here to ask you a question."

"Not interested in answering it. Get out."

"What is the chaff to the wheat, Daniel?"

"I already said this question makes no sense."

"Yes it does. Go on and answer it."

"No, I won't because it is absolutely ludicrous. However, if you want to give an explanation about where you have been all this time I am willing to listen. If not, go away."

"I was taken away by mistake along with many others. One day you will understand."

"So why come back? What do you want?"

"To ask you a question and give you a warning."

"Your question is preposterous and I don't need your help anymore."

"I can wait for a long time. Have nowhere else to go."

"Look Antônio, I have neither the time nor the desire to solve this silly riddle of yours. It is as absurd as it is pointless. Do I make myself clear?"

"No need to shout, Brother. If you don't answer the question someone else will."

"Excellent. Let him do it. I assume we are done with this conversation."

"Your choice to end this conversation might be a miscalculation, Brother."

"I don't think so. Find someone else to answer your question and leave me alone."

"It is not a 'he'."

"What isn't?"

"The person who will answer the question. It is not a he but a she."

"Whatever, Antônio. I don't care who it is. Now, please, go away. You are wasting my time."

"This is a good time as any, Brother. Answer the question and I will go away."

"Do you want to torture me, is that what you want?"

"Torture? Never. After what I have been through torturing would be the last thing I would wish on you or anyone else."

"What is that you wish?"

"That you tell the truth, Brother."

"The truth about what? Don't be foolish."

"I know it is frightening but all the same necessary."

"Oh, you know about what is necessary, do you? "Ah! That's a good one. What do you know about necessity?"

"Perhaps not as much as you do."

"You got that right Antônio. You know nothing about needing. Were you ever forced to haul your death sentence on your shoulders? When you know about that we can talk."

"I can only imagine."

"Right again. Picture a ten-year old boy, skin and bone, carrying buckets of dirty water everyday, no rest, no playtime, no food. Imagined it? It might help you feel even better about all those wretched children you rescued in Caxias."

"On Mathew 6:22 it is written: the light of the body is the eye…"

"Save your preaching for the folks in Caxias, Antônio. You are not good at it anyway."

"When we first met, remember? I carried your suitcase up the stairs and you looked at me with eyes that told me what words couldn't."

"Cut it out, will you? Go away and leave me alone. I need to get back to the liturgy and preach my sermon."

"Not before you answer the question. 'What is the chaff to the wheat?'"

"What if I refuse?"

"Then she will have to answer for you."

"Whatever, Antônio. Brethren: let us sing. Ida, please, 'Great Is Thy Faithfulness'."

"Ida is not at the organ today. I have come here to warn you, Brother."

"Why do you care? I told you to leave."

"Ida has nursery duty this morning."

"Stop interrupting and leave, Antônio."

"Fine. But before I go, let me at least warn you Brother?"

"I said G-0 A-W-A-Y, Antônio!"

"Ida is about to find out the answer to the question."

"There is nothing to find out. Get out."

"On Luke 12:2 it is also written: there is nothing concealed that will not be revealed, nor secret that will not be known."

"I said enough. Stop tormenting me!"

"Listen to me Daniel: Vera has just arrived at the sanctuary's front steps. You can't see her but she has handed the baby to an usher who is on his way to the nursery. Vera does not know Ida is on duty today."

"That's impossible. Vera is in Vila Nova."

"No, not today. She is here on Ida's invitation."

"Not true. Ida never mentioned this to me."

"That is why I am here."

"You are bluffing, Antônio."

"Listen carefully, Daniel: Vera does not know Ida is on duty at the nursery today either, otherwise she would not have come."

"GET OUT!"

"Look down from your pulpit, Brother. This pious congregation, these trusting faces gleaming at you will soon be weeping. When the secret is out their adulation will turn to judgment."

"Out of my way, I must stop Vera."

"Too late, Brother. Ida is now changing the baby's soiled clothes. She sees the birthmark on his tummy. Exactly where yours and Rose's are. Ida knows the answer to the question."

"Noooo!"

"Get up, Brother. Pull yourself together. It is time for me to move on. I have done what I came here for. You, I, all of us must move on now."

"Antônio, wait. Don't leave me. Come back, please."

"Get up Brother. My work here is done. I must go."

"No. Please, tell me, what is to become of this, this miscalculation?"

"It is written on Daniel 12:9, Go thy way, Daniel, for the words are closed up and sealed till the time of the end."

"When is the end, Antônio? Please, tell me when?"

"It is also written on Daniel 12:12: blessed is he who waits. You will answer the question I asked. I know you will. We all will."

Middletown PA, July 20th 2023 (Psalm 16:7)

ABOUT THE AUTHOR

Quelia Quaresma-McHugh was born and raised in Rio de Janeiro, Brazil.

After graduating from college, she immigrated to the United States to complete a Ph.D. in Latin American History, a subject she taught for many years at Colleges and Universities.

In response to the Lord's personal calling upon her life, Quelia left academia and has since been dedicated to ministering Jesus' gospel wherever He sends her.

At home in Pennsylvania, she is wife to Andy, mom to Patrick, and Mrs. Q to her church family.

Printed in the USA
CPSIA information can be obtained
at www.ICGtesting.com
LVHW090244240224
772639LV00001B/63